Out Of Nothing Something Comes

by

Paul Georgiou

Contents

Author's introduction

This is the fourth and final volume of the Truth series.

In the first book, *The Fourth Beginning*, the Smiths, together with their dog Luke, set out on an epic adventure to find answers to some of life's most challenging questions. Eve desperately wants to know why her daughter had to die; Adam is looking for reasons to live.

The questors' guide on the journey is the Storyteller. Their mode of transport is a campervan equipped with an exponential drive and a paradox device, the inventions of a couple of brilliant Irish engineers, the wizened Prune Leach and the long-legged Andrew Rimzil.

As soon as the journey begins, Adam and Eve are warned by the Breaker Nick Peters and his shapeshifter sidekick, Grimrose, that their quest is hopeless. Breakers argue that there is no truth out there to be found. If you want to understand anything, you have to take it apart. Undeterred, Adam and Eve persist, picking up an odd couple of hitch-hikers, the ever-curious Uncle Rambler and his willing pupil, Nephew Numpty, on the way.

The questors visit the God of the Old Testament in the Garden of Eden, near Hook, off the M3. The interview with God produces no answers to the questors' questions and, indeed, turns rather nasty when Eve gives God the sharp edge of her tongue. They escape a bloody end with the help of the enigmatic blind man Kit.

Next, employing the exponential drive and the paradox device, the questors travel back in time to the Caucasus, where they are greeted by Prometheus who has always looked favourably on man. The titan wishes to help but has no answers, other than to encourage the Smiths in their search for the truth and their hopes for the future.

The Storyteller then decides to give Adam and Eve a unique opportunity to witness the three great beginnings: the creation of the universe, the birth of life, and the emergence of human consciousness. None of these extraordinary events provides the Smiths with answers, but they do provide a feast for thought.

When the travellers return to the present, they find themselves in a mysland, a virtual replica of a part of the New Forest. The mysland is entirely under the control of the Breakers, who have a regional office at Cadnam. The questors are arrested. Adam is imprisoned. The Breakers fear that the questors will initiate a Fourth Beginning.

After a violent and vicissitudinal struggle with Nick Peters and the Breakers, the questors, aided by the military might of the Metaphorce, seem to be victorious, and the Fourth Beginning is set in motion.

At this point, *The Devil's Truth*, the second book in the Truth quartet, begins.

After the abrupt termination of the Fourth Beginning, Adam and Eve Smith reluctantly settle back into their old lives until, unexpectedly, Adam is approached by the business consultancy firm Slievins. David Minofel, a Slievins partner, makes an appointment to discuss Adam's future.

Adam's first Slievins' posting is in Geneva, as Marketing Director of ZeD, a major Swiss pharmaceutical company. Adam's mentor in Geneva is another Slievins' protégée, the beautiful and highly intelligent Miss Gorgeous Tomic, personal assistant to the MD of ZeD. Adam quickly learns the Slievins' philosophy: define your goals, devise the most efficient way of achieving them, regardless of moral considerations, and act, uninhibited by any scruples.

Meanwhile, at the Smith's house in Harrow the other questors, including Kit, the enigmatic blind man from the Fourth Beginning, have joined Eve. Kit is keen to reactivate the Fourth Beginning, but Eve and the other questors are less enthusiastic, fearful of swift retribution from whatever aborted it.

Kit, undeterred, visits Adam in Geneva to enlist his support but meets with a cool reception.

Adam feels challenged but fulfilled by the demands of his new job. He enjoys the power he has to get things done and the extraordinary financial incentives he is given to succeed, but he soon discovers that the application of Slievins' modus operandi involves him in bribery, blackmail and, finally, murder.

While Adam is in Geneva, Eve discovers she is pregnant. She misses Adam and becomes increasingly concerned that his work for ZeD is taking him over. As the weeks pass, their relationship deteriorates until she confides to Kit that she thinks she has lost Adam and that their marriage may be dying.

Although Adam does not fully understand Slievins' objectives, he enjoys tremendous success. Despite the collapse of ZeD in a maelstrom of corruption, his career, guided by Slievins, seems assured, and his financial future secure. Indeed, the prospect of real wealth beckons. Perhaps even more importantly, Adam feels he has found a kind of truth, not the abstract truth he had sought in the Fourth Beginning, but a practical, pragmatic truth about the nature of man – and his own true nature.

Adam has no idea that Slievins is preparing him for the Praesidium, a secret organisation that, for thousands of years, with the assistance of the Breakers, has been guiding man and directing history. The goal of the Praesidium is to enable man to be true to his own nature, and to reject at all costs any exhortations by what they call Emergents for man to aspire to be in any way better than he is. To this end, the Monitaurs, agents of the Praesidium, promote depravity, extremism, corruption, obfuscation and negativity in the affairs of men.

Minofel is grooming Adam. He knows that Adam and Eve had set out with the Storyteller to find the truth. Minofel is going to provide Adam with a different kind of truth, one which will satisfy him and ensure that he and Eve are never again tempted to set out on another quest.

At this point *The Praesidium*, the third book in the Truth quartet, begins.

Adam finds himself in a lavish apartment in London, located in a PCC (parallel coincident construct) anchored over Westminster. This PCC is the operational centre of the London Praesidium. Minofel informs Adam that he has done so well in Geneva that the Praesidium believes he has the potential to achieve even greater things. John Noble, the Chairman of the Praesidium, explains the *modus operandi* of the organisation and implies that, if Adam can successfully complete the Praesidium's training programme, he may be offered a seat on the Praesidium board.

Adam embarks on the training programme, guided by the Monitaurs, coloured glutinous essences of evil that are capable of assuming human form. In a series of excursions, the Monitaurs introduce Adam to key aspects of depravity, extremism, corruption, obfuscation and negativity. The goal of the training is to reveal to Adam that man is essentially a self-centred creature who is irredeemably selfish. What lesser men, especially Emergents, regard as sins are in truth virtues in that they are simply manifestations of man's true nature.

Meanwhile the other questors have gathered at the Smiths' house in Harrow where Kit is eager to reactivate the aborted Fourth Beginning. Rambler and Eve are less enthusiastic. Rambler is naturally more cautious; Eve is preoccupied with the baby she is carrying and the seemingly frail state of her marriage.

Kit is escorted by Jedwell Boon, Minofel's enforcer, to the Westminster PCC where he finds himself a prisoner at the mercy of the sadistic Deputy Chairman of the Westminster Praesidium, Simon Goodfellow. Kit is forced to witness Adam's progress through the Praesidium training course while his tormentor tries to determine whether or not the blind man is truly an Emergent. Adam applies himself to the training programme with enthusiasm, despite the warnings of his flat-sharing companion Miss Tomic that he is being irredeemably corrupted. For her temerity in warning Adam, Miss Tomic is cursed by Minofel.

Simon Goodfellow is ambitious as well as sadistic and has plans to become Chairman of the London Praesidium by ousting John Noble. When his attempted boardroom coup fails, largely as a result of the machinations of the voluptuous and promiscuous Kathrin Bloch, he decides, egged on by David Minofel, to kill the Chairman and blame the murder on Kit. A trial is speedily arranged and Minofel makes sure Adam, his protégée, is appointed as prosecutor. If Adam successfully prosecutes his friend Kit, whom he knows to be innocent, he will surely be worthy of a seat on the Praesidium board – and all the power, prestige and wealth that goes with it.

Goodfellow is confident the trial will proceed quickly to a satisfactory conclusion, but he has reckoned without the intervention of Aletheia, the goddess of truth, Prometheus' finest creation, whom the titan has sent to aid the questors.

In the end, Adam makes a stand. Following a traumatic but revelatory dream, he rejects the Praesidium's version of the truth and refuses to connive in the execution of Kit. With the aid of Andrew Rimzil's paradox device, the questors make their escape.

Aletheia exploits her cybernetic relationship with the paradox device and the Eternal Light, the Praesidium's power source, to destabilise and destroy the Westminster PCC. Then, before she returns to the Caucasus, she rescues Miss Tomic from David Minofel's clutches and removes the curse he has put on her.

Adam and Eve Smith find themselves back home in Harrow. At this point the fourth and final volume of the Truth quartet begins.

The Storyteller's preface

May I introduce myself. I am the Storyteller. You have, of course, met me before, in the first three volumes of the quartet, as an ever-present but generally passive character in the narrative. You may have wondered what I am doing inside the story when I should be outside, telling it. But, like most things, it's not as simple as that. This is no ordinary story. And my role in it is complicated, as I knew it would be. This is a tale that resists conventions and stereotypes. It has taken me outside my comfort zone. It has a mind of its own. Indeed, although I am the teller of this story I have never felt completely in control. That's why I thought I should be hands-on, in among the characters and plot, so that occasionally I could give things a nudge in what I hoped was the right direction.

I might add that the dual role I have fulfilled in this tale is not as odd as it might appear. After all, we are all storytellers of our own lives and involved in our own narrative. We live the tale our lives tell.

So why have I decided to speak to you directly now? The answer to that question, at least, is simple. As we embark on the fourth volume of the quest, I can see, ever more clearly, that the path is set. Of course I'm still needed – you can't have a story without a storyteller – but I think it's right for me now to withdraw into a more conventional role, outside the narrative looking in, so to speak. I may allow myself to make the odd personal comment, to express the odd opinion and fill in any necessary background information, but I'll keep any interference in the action to a minimum.

Before I adopt a more distanced and silent role, I think it fair to say that without me, both within and outside the narrative, this story would not have been possible. More on this at the end of this book.

Let's move on, because I can tell you that the next few weeks were full of incident for all those involved, especially Adam.

1. Debriefing Minofel

Roland Samiat was a presence so powerful and pervasive that he seemed to fill every nook and cranny of the Slievins building, even when he wasn't in it.

Most of the time, Roland was in a good mood. The Slievins Consultancy was highly successful and, as its CEO, he generally exuded a benign satisfaction with the way things were going. Governments might gain or lose power. Companies might rise and fall. Careers might blossom or collapse. But Slievins, perhaps the most highly regarded consultancy organisation in the world, always thrived. Even when a project failed, Slievins won. After all, the consultancy was paid anyway, and failure brought home to the client the gravity of the crisis they faced and just how much they needed help.

Yes, most of the time Roland Samiat was in an excellent mood. It was his practice every morning to tour the Slievins' city offices, floor by floor, spreading good cheer. But not so today. To be honest, today he was disappointed, even a little displeased, and the cause of his disappointment and the object of his displeasure was a partner in the consultancy: ex-SAS, ex-mercenary, accomplished practitioner, one David Minofel.

"A word," said Roland, poking his head round the door of Minofel's office. "Whenever you're ready ..."

David Minofel had been expecting the summons. There was no denying that his Praesidium assignment had been a monumental fiasco, a fiasco that stretched to its limit the arrogant complacency of the Slievins' official motto – "Succeed or fail, Slievins always wins". He closed the folder he had been reading (a highly critical profile of Mahatma Gandhi), stood up, buttoned the jacket of his suit and walked out of his office into the antechamber.

"A pity to spoil such a fine day," Minofel remarked to his new personal assistant, the replacement for the recently departed and now, courtesy of Prometheus, happily immortalised Miss Tomic.

Outside the sun was shining brightly on London. Inside the Slievins' office block the air was cool and pure. The building was fitted with laminated glass which eliminated almost all the sun's ultraviolet light. Minofel walked slowly along the top corridor.

"Come in, come in," said Roland affably when Minofel arrived. "Take a seat."

In common with many organisations in the twenty-first century, Slievins liked to present an egalitarian ethos, but in truth it was ruthlessly hierarchical. Minofel was a partner – a senior partner – in the company, but he knew well enough his fate was in the hands of his boss, the CEO, just as the lives of those who worked for Minofel were entirely at Minofel's mercy.

"Not your finest moment," observed Roland.

David Minofel had pondered how he would deal with the inevitably difficult debriefing with his boss. He knew that Roland Samiat responded poorly to excuses. It was best to find the positives and concentrate on them.

"We preserved the essences of the Monitaurs," he hazarded. "We can reconstitute them at any time. And we can re-establish the London Praesidium or its successor easily enough. Aletheia did less damage than she imagines. Most of the parallel coincident constructs around the world will survive. It's bad. Of course it's bad. But it's not a total disaster."

"Hmm," was Samiat's initial response.

Minofel waited.

"I suppose it could be fun debating with you your definition of a total disaster," Samiat eventually continued, the hint of a smile lurking at the corners of his mouth. "I have a feeling that had you been a steward on the Titanic after its encounter with the iceberg, you might have observed to an alarmed captain that the orchestra was in particularly good form that evening.

"Abandoning my maritime metaphor, allow me to summarise the situation. After months of preparation in Geneva, you took Adam to the Westminster PCC, one of our premier PCCs, and enrolled him in the Praesidium induction course. With the help of the Monitaurs you put him through a series of training modules covering depravity, extremism, corruption, obfuscation and negativity. On completion of his training programme, you recommended him for a seat on the Praesidium board. And yet when it came to the first serious test of his fitness to meet Slievins' exacting standards he failed. Or rather we failed. He succeeded in frustrating our plans and in escaping our clutches. Not only did we fail with Adam, we allowed a suspected Emergent, one Kit Turner, to get the better of us. You had Kit, the blind man, on a scaffold with the noose round his neck, and yet somehow he eluded his fate and escaped your custody. Finally, despite your best efforts, Aletheia, offspring of Prometheus, managed to rip the fabric of the Westminster PCC apart. When you have a spare moment, if it's not too much trouble, I'd be grateful if you could furnish me with an example of what, for you, constitutes a total disaster. I shall now have to deal with Adam and the Emergent myself, not to mention restoring the global network of PCCs to robust good health. Have I left anything out?"

"I'm not saying things went well," Minofel offered by way of a defence. "I'm just pointing out …"

"That it's not a total disaster. Quite," Samiat said, finishing Minofel's sentence. "Reverting to the maritime metaphor, let us not forget that not long after our putative steward commented on the fine playing of the orchestra, the captain and all eight musicians were dead. And as we sit here, in my mind at least, there has to be a poor prognosis for the fate of the putative, stupidly optimistic steward."

That sounded like both an insult and a threat. Minofel looked into Samiat's blue eyes, uncertain whether his superior was serious.

"Your summary is accurate but incomplete," said Minofel. Unlike the Titanic, he was not going down without a fight. "Adam performed beyond expectations in Geneva. We brought ZeD to its knees and earned Slievins a monumental fee. True, I sent Adam to the Praesidium, but I handed over his training and, indeed, the deconstruction of the suspected Emergent to the outstandingly perverted and sadistic Simon Goodfellow. You can scarcely blame me for putting my trust in a man with such an exemplary record. You also omitted the difficulties we faced in dealing with that bloody paradox device. I put Andrew Rimzil to work on constructing such a device for us in Geneva. And I then arranged for him to have all the facilities he needed in the Westminster PCC. He betrayed my trust which, I admit, scarcely came as a surprise, but I was astonished by the bungling incompetence of the Praesidium security in permitting such treachery. Again the fault lay with Simon Goodfellow and his Head of Security Silas Drahan."

Samiat laughed. "Good try, David. Happily, in our line of business there is always the chance of redemption, for you at least. Now, let me see. What's to be done? You did well to save the Monitaurs' essences, I grant you, but inexplicably you left the Crucible of Eternal

Light behind. I would like you to redeem yourself by returning to the Westminster PCC before it finally vaporises. Locate the Crucible and bring it to me here. Then it will be much easier for me to see the immense logistical and financial problems posed by the Westminster fiasco in a less apocalyptic light."

"The Westminster PCC is collapsing," said Minofel. "Aletheia and the paradox device rendered the whole construct unstable. If I go there now I may well be destroyed."

"If that happens," said Samiat, "I shall be truly sorry. Slievins will have lost a valued partner. Sadly I lack your talent for discerning the positives in disastrous situations, but rest assured I shall do my very best."

"Am I to have any help in what is obviously a perilous, life-threatening venture?" Minofel was determined to emphasise that he would be in mortal danger.

"In the circumstances," said Samiat after a pause, "my feeling is that you should undertake this mission alone. Despite your heroic efforts to disperse the blame, you, acting as a practitioner in the employ of the Praesidium, were and are solely responsible for the problem. It makes sense, therefore, that you should now solve it unaided. On the other hand, I'm rather keen to have an objective account of how you perform on this mission, so I'm going to send Art Shoat along with you, primarily as an observer. Art's a good man. I've no doubt he'll lend a hand if necessary."

The meeting was over.

David Minofel had always found it difficult to read Samiat's face. It was a pleasant, round, well-proportioned face, open and generally smiling. The dark-brown hair was combed back, neatly cut; the moustache and beard always meticulously trimmed. It was the face of a benign, affable, clubbable man. Only the piercing blue eyes gave some indication of the true nature of the Slievins' CEO, a hint of what went on inside the head. Samiat's eyes observed the world through horizontal slits, as though he was concealing something, or was about to burst into laughter, or was devising a huge practical joke, or plotting the most appalling crime. That was the problem. All of these were possible but you had no idea which it was.

Of more immediate concern was Samiat's choice of escort for Minofel. Art Shoat, one of three enforcers who served and protected Roland Samiat, was a brute of a man, powerfully built with porcine features. His parents were East Enders who moved to Essex when Art's father reached the end of his short but extraordinarily successful criminal career. Art was born one year after the move from London in his parents' new home, a large country house, southwest of Chelmsford, a house protected by an elaborate alarm system, with sensors every twenty paces, an armour-plated safe room and an electric fence around the perimeter of the extensive gardens, or killing ground as Art's father called it.

Despite a private education intended to tame and refine his violent inclinations, Art had soon shown himself to be his father's son. By the time he was sixteen, he had been invited to leave the public school that had reluctantly and, as it turned out, unwisely accepted him as a pupil. The headmaster had explained to Art's parents that as an unashamedly profit-oriented academic institution, the school had no objection to entrepreneurial zeal – indeed, it encouraged it – but an enterprise involving the distribution of both soft and hard drugs to fellow pupils and even to junior members of staff was a step too far. Art was making considerably more from his drugs business than the headmaster earned, so the wayward youth generously offered to put the headmaster on the payroll. To the ruthless but naïve young man's surprise, his offer had been rejected with some vitriol.

Freed from the shackles of academic discipline, Art went from strength to strength until by the time he was twenty, he had more or less replicated his father's business model but in rather more salubrious surroundings. As soon as he had the drug and prostitution business in Chelmsford under control, he set his sights on London. Each time he eliminated a rival gang, he commissioned a tattoo – as a mark of respect to those he had vanquished, he said. At twenty-one, he had an elaborate dragon depicted on one arm and an equally impressive serpent on the other, and was expressing concern that, despite being overweight, there might not be sufficient corporeal real estate to accommodate such pictorial tributes to all the other rivals he planned to eliminate.

Before he could complete his plans for conquests or tattoos, he was approached by Slievins as part of the company's outreach programme. At first Art was sceptical. What could they possibly offer him that could tempt him to abandon his burgeoning criminal empire, to sacrifice his autonomy, to become an employee? Then he met Roland Samiat who, in one brief meeting, expanded Art's horizons and persuaded him that his future lay with Slievins. For twenty years now, he had served Roland Samiat devotedly, using his strength when necessary and on other occasions employing his not inconsiderable gift for strategic thinking, always in his master's interests.

In a fight, there was no doubt Art Shoat was an asset, assuming he was on your side. But Minofel knew that the enforcer's loyalty was to Samiat. Any help Shoat gave to Minofel on this dangerous enterprise would be entirely conditional on Samiat's approval.

2.   Out of joint times

In the Smith's home in Harrow, there was an emotional maelstrom.

Eve was relieved that she and her unborn child had survived the questors' sortie into the Westminster PCC. She now wanted nothing more than to return to normality, whatever that meant. But it wasn't going to happen. Normality was a faraway land, a fading memory, a place of doubtful existential substance. After all, what was normal in a world largely controlled by a group of elite, profoundly evil human beings who manipulated the lives of men from within an invisible, parallel spatial construct with the help of glutinous, incorporeal entities?

And how, at the end of their sortie into the Praesidium's world, had she and her fellow questors extricated themselves from what had seemed an impossible situation? Kit was on the scaffold. The Praesidium staff were enjoying a carnival atmosphere at what was for them the entirely justifiable execution of the blind man who had murdered John Noble, the Praesidium's Chairman. Except that Kit, the condemned man, was innocent. Adam had eventually stood up and sided with Kit, which was a brave but seemingly pointless act. Then, somehow, they had all escaped, and she and Adam had found themselves back in Harrow. With a single bound they were free. For no obvious reason, Eve heard the tune 'The Devil's Galop' thundering in her ears.

Of course, Andrew Rimzil and his paradox device had played a part in their salvation and, for sure, they would not have survived without the intervention of Aletheia, the goddess of truth, the creation of Prometheus.

As Eve pondered her own account of events, she stood back and realised that any listener would conclude these were the ravings of a lunatic, a conclusion with which, at that moment, she felt inclined to concur.

If Eve was disturbed, Adam was lost in a world of profound emotional chaos. He felt immense relief that they had survived and that he, Eve and their unborn child were safe, at least for the present. But he feared for the future. The Praesidium was immensely powerful, and although the questors, with Aletheia's help, had bested it on this occasion, he was sure that was not the end of the matter.

The Praesidium would come after them. Even if they thought Adam wasn't worth the trouble, they would surely be determined to seek out and destroy Kit. And after all that Kit had done for them, he and Eve would be morally obliged to help Kit, wouldn't they?

Adam's only consolation was that he no longer had to worry about money. His remuneration for serving and destroying ZeD had been so generous that he was now a man of independent means. He could provide for his wife and his child whatever happened. Even if he died or was killed tomorrow, Eve and the child would be financially secure. That at least was a positive, some consolation for what he had been through.

And consolation was needed because hanging over Adam was a heavy black cloud, an overwhelming sense of guilt. He had done such things …

That was the problem. He found it difficult to articulate what he had done. But why? When he had been working at ZeD, he had thought carefully before each choice and felt justified in making it. Yet now he could scarcely admit to himself what he had done. Conspiracy to pervert the course of justice! Corruption! Bribery! Blackmail! Cruelty! Treachery! And murder! He had managed to compile a personal portfolio of seven deadly sins. He needed therapy; he needed resolution; he needed absolution. But there was no one he could talk to, no one to listen to him, no one to help him come to terms with what he had done and help him move on.

He desperately wanted to tell Eve, to talk to Eve, to explain his actions – but he couldn't. It was simple. He knew Eve. Eve would not be able to live with a man who had done what he had done. She would ask him how he could bribe an official to ignore the death of a patient in the Basel clinical trial. How could he put at risk the lives of other innocent patients? How could he corrupt the honest Guy McFall, ordering him to conspire in suppressing the Basel trial? How could he blackmail the medical director, Dr Reed, to the point where, his career ruined and his marriage destroyed, he killed himself. Worst of all, how could he murder Giovanni Spinetti and then let someone else take the blame? He had taken one life and irreparably damaged many others.

Eve wouldn't listen to his explanation; she would focus on the dreadful harm he had done to other people's lives. That was the way she would see it.

And, of course, all Adam's justifications for his actions were based on the false premise that it was in everyone's interest that ZeD should thrive and prosper, whereas the real purpose of his brief employment with ZeD had been to bring the company to its knees. That was an irony that David Minofel, his Slievins' mentor, had seemed to find particularly satisfying.

So there was no answer, no relief. Adam simply didn't want to be the man he was. In the past, he had wondered if he had a self at the core of his being. He had speculated that he was just a vessel for the accumulation of memories, most of them painful. But now, through guilt, he knew he had a self, a self that was responsible for decisions he had taken and what he had done.

He had told Eve how much he loved her. She had replied that she loved him. But she really didn't know the man she said she loved. And if she found out what he was, if he told her what he had done, he knew her love would wither like William Blake's rose.

3. Death throes

When David Minofel and Art Shoat reached the Praesidium, it was obvious the entire spatial construct was unstable. The Crucible of Eternal Light was still generating power, unperturbed by the chaos all around, but the building's electrical circuits were burning out. There was a smell of smouldering cables. Basic services, including garbage disposal, had broken down, so there was also a pervasive aroma of rotting waste. And every few minutes the entire construct shivered as though aware of its impending dissolution.

Most Praesidium employees had abandoned the PCC and, despite the obvious difficulties they would face fitting back into society, had returned to the cities from which they had been recruited. A few had decided to stay. The Praesidium had been their home and their life for decades; some had been born there. For them, it was the only real world and they had decided to stay with it to the end. Among these remainers was Manfred Bloch, formerly technical director, now enjoying what was doomed to be a very short tenure as Chairman.

"I hadn't expected to see you again," said Manfred when David Minofel entered his office.

"Nor I you," Minofel replied. "Are you staying here? At any moment, the entire Westminster PCC will evaporate."

"This has been my life's work. If it is to end, so be it. I will not leave."

"What about Kathrin?" Minofel was genuinely curious. Manfred loved his promiscuous wife. Was he going to force her to stay with him to the end?

"Kathrin has gone," Manfred replied. "I insisted. She is full of life. I know she loved John Noble in a way I cannot understand. But I also know she loved me in her own way. And I loved her. I still love her. I want her to live. But I now have to die."

"You're into futile gestures?" queried Art Shoat, who was lurking in the doorway of Bloch's office.

"And you are?" asked Manfred.

"You don't need to know who I am," said Art, "but I'll tell you what I'm here to do. I'm here to collect the Crucible of Eternal Light. And while you two ladies natter on about domestic affairs,

I'm going to fetch the Crucible and bugger off asap. If you haven't noticed, this place is coming apart at the seams."

Manfred Bloch was momentarily stunned by Art Shoat's ill manners. No one spoke to a Praesidium board member, much less its Chairman, in such rude and crude terms. And, of course, he could not allow anyone to take the Crucible. The Praesidium had been the custodian of the Crucible of Eternal Light for centuries. The Light had been the source of its power and the heart of the organisation. No one was going to rip the heart out of Manfred's life's work. Manfred stood up.

"You will not be taking the Crucible anywhere," he said flatly.

"Come on, Dave. Tell him," said Art. "We can't fanny about. We need to do the business and get out before we end up in the same pickle as Mr Futile Gesture here."

"You will not take the Crucible anywhere," Manfred repeated.

Manfred was a powerful man, broad-shouldered, bull-necked and muscular. As chief engineer he had taken pride in the fact that he was as strong as any of the men under his command. It was clear to Minofel that Bloch meant what he said.

"You're a bit old to be telling me what I can and can't do," said Art, moving towards Bloch.

In fact, there was no more than ten years difference in age – Manfred Bloch was in his early fifties and Art in his early forties – but Art liked to think of himself as still a bit of a lad.

To the casual observer, Manfred Bloch might have seemed to have the edge. Although a little older, he was in better physical shape. Also, he was driven by a conviction that while he lived he must protect and retain the Crucible at all costs.

In comparison, Art showed signs of the dissolute life he had led. He was a tall, big-boned man but he had a fat belly, a consequence of the large volumes of beer that a man in his position was obliged to consume, and his unusually ruddy complexion suggested his lifestyle had taken its toll on other vital organs. Yes, Art Shoat might have seemed to be at a disadvantage, but a casual observer would have been unwise to disregard his outstanding record in eliminating all those who stood against him.

"You really don't want to end up as just another tattoo," said Art, presenting his forearms to Bloch. "If the dragon don't get you, the serpent will."

The Praesidium Chairman and the Slievins' enforcer were about to come to blows when David Minofel intervened.

"I'm sorry but we really don't have time for this. I sympathise totally with your position on the Crucible of Eternal Light," he said, addressing Manfred Bloch, "and in other circumstances I might even side with you in any ensuing fracas, but I'm afraid my friend here is right – we have to get on and get off before this entire structure collapses."

With that, using the heel of his hand, he struck Manfred Bloch a blow between his eyes with such force that Manfred's brain, ricocheting within his skull, sustained irreparable damage. The Praesidium Chairman sank to his knees with blood and tiny pieces from his frontal lobe trickling from his nose and ears.

"Cool punch, man," observed Art, looking at Minofel with a new respect. "You didn't learn to do that pushing paper round an office."

Minofel ignored Art's praise. "I suggest you make your way to the basement of this building where you will find the Crucible. It's a geodesic sphere about a metre in diameter. Bring it here, and when I rejoin you we'll transport it to Roland Samiat's office."

"And what will you be doing while I'm busy completing your mission?" asked Art. He didn't like taking orders from someone he had been charged by Samiat to watch.

"I just want to pay a quick visit to an old friend of mine," Minofel explained. "Oh, and one other thing," he added with undisguised menace in his voice, "don't ever call me Dave again."

4. In a desert far away

The Rub' al-Khali is a vast stretch of desert of around 650,000 square kilometres, the largest contiguous sandy desert in the world. It is hot. The average temperature during the day is around 47°C; it can pass the 50°C mark. And it is dry. The scorpions and rodents that manage to survive in this hostile environment are lucky if they see an inch of rainfall in a year.

Rub' al-Khali means "empty quarter", which is a fair description since few living creatures can survive in such a climate. Nevertheless, it is not entirely uninhabited. There are a few Saudi and Yemeni tribes that eke out a tenuous existence in this arid world, a world they themselves more accurately call Al-Rimal, meaning "the sands". These tribesmen care for their camel herds and flocks of sheep, cleverly exploiting the region's limited water resources, which they value far more highly than the vast oil reserves that lie deep beneath the sand.

On the same day that Adam was wrestling with his feelings of guilt and David Minofel was on his mission to retrieve the Crucible of Eternal Light, Abdul Aziz bin Adnani al-Badiyah emerged from his small black tent and announced he was setting off to find a missing sheep. One of his small flock had wandered off the previous night and Abdul Aziz was determined to recover the animal or at least discover its fate. His fellow tribesmen shouted their wishes for his success, subject, of course, to the will of Allah.

He mounted his favourite camel, summoned his saluki hound and set off from the small encampment into the rolling orange sand dunes. For anyone other than the tribesmen of the Rub' al-Khali, such a venture would have been foolhardy and almost certainly fatal. But Abdul Aziz had the skills of his people, which included an inexplicably refined sense of direction and extraordinary tracking skills.

After an hour, as he topped a particularly high dune, Abdul Aziz stopped to drink a mouthful of water and to check the unusual tracks he had just seen. They were the tracks of a motorised vehicle. He was surprised. Of course he knew of the oil installations where westerners drilled into the heart of the desert not for water, which was eminently sensible, but for oil, the viscous substance that the soft, venal Arabs in their palaces called black gold. But the nearest oil installation was one hundred kilometres away.

As Abdul Aziz looked for an explanation, a vehicle rolled into view. It was a large all- wheel-drive SUV.

"Hi," said the young man who stepped out of the vehicle. "You're a bit off the beaten track."

Abdul Aziz was surprised to meet anyone. He certainly had not expected to meet an infidel in a suit with hair in carefully braided, matted dreadlocks.

"I'm Ben Rael," said the man, approaching Abdul Aziz and extending a hand of friendship.

It was evident that Abdul Aziz spoke no English, so Ben Rael asked him in perfect Arabic what he was doing in the desert, far from any shade, as the sun climbed higher in the sky.

"I am searching for one of my sheep," Abdul Aziz replied.

"You risk your life for one sheep?"

"I am not risking my life," said Abdul Aziz.

"Well, my friend," said Ben Rael, slipping into the Arabic dialect of the tribesman, "this is your lucky day. You may have lost your sheep but I have many sheep and I'm more than happy to give you a couple of mine. Come with me."

"Come with you where?" asked the now utterly confused Abdul Aziz.

"To the city beneath the sand," said Ben Rael in a tone that suggested the existence of such a city was common knowledge.

"The city beneath the sand?" Abdul Aziz queried. He knew well enough the stories of the fabled city of Ubar, which had lain on the frankincense trade route until desertification had made the track unpassable and the city uninhabitable. Is that what he meant, this strange young man in a Western suit, with dreadlocks and an intimate knowledge of the Al Murrah dialect of Arabic?

"Who are you?" Abdul Aziz asked. What was this man doing there? How could he have many sheep? Water was scarce and only the tribesmen knew how to sustain small flocks. This man was no tribesman. And why would such a man give a stranger two of his own sheep, assuming he had any? Everything was wrong; he sensed danger.

"I told you," the man replied. "My name is Ben Rael. I work for the

Slievins Consultancy and we have a contract to run this installation. I've been sent from London to check on security procedures."

"I will not come with you," said Abdul Aziz, backing away.

"What about your sheep?" asked Ben Rael, leaning into his car to pick up the automatic weapon, a Heckler & Koch MP5, he kept on the front passenger seat.

Abdul Aziz was ordering his camel to kneel so he could mount it. The first spray of bullets cut the saluki hound in half. The second killed the camel. Abdul Aziz fell onto the orange sand. One of the bullets aimed at the camel had passed through his leg. Ben Rael walked up to the defenceless man.

"Evidently you're not a very good shepherd," said Ben. "First you lose a sheep. Then you fail to find the lost sheep. And when a well-meaning stranger offers you a really good deal, two free sheep, you haven't the good manners or good sense to accept the offer. Well, sadly for you I take my job rather more seriously. You, my friend, are what we call a security breach."

Abdul Aziz was passing in and out of consciousness. When conscious, he was praying to his God. He had no interest in the drivel spewing from the mouth of his tormentor. He did manage to interrupt his devotions sufficiently to express an oath consigning the killer of his dog and his favourite camel to an eternity in the fires of hell.

Ben Rael fired several rounds into the head of the Arab tribesman. He then walked back to his SUV. He had not been very keen on his latest assignment, but clearly there was an urgent need to improve security around the city in the sand. He would report this incident to Roland Samiat, and when he met the city commander he would express his own and Roland's concerns with some emphasis.

The orange sand where Abdul Aziz had fallen – and where his dog and camel had been cut down – was now a deep red.

5.   It's good to talk

Eve was now six months pregnant and feeling heavy but happy. Despite all the worries, despite the difficulties in her relationship with Adam, despite the dangers she had faced during her excursion to the Westminster PCC, she felt good. Even the trauma of the burglary was fading just a little.

"You look great," said Adam, entering the room where Eve was taking a break.

Eve smiled. "You don't look so bad yourself."

It was true. Adam seemed to have shed at least ten years, despite his recent trials and tribulations.

"Thanks," said Adam with a grin. When he had sided with Kit on the day of execution, it had crossed Adam's mind that David Minofel would immediately cancel his "gift". Adam expected that the years Minofel had removed from his age would be returned, probably with interest. But no! To Adam's relief, the rejuvenation persisted. The ageing he had undergone in the Breakers' hell at Cadnam had been reversed, it seemed permanently. "What would you like to do today?" Adam asked.

Since their escape from the Westminster PCC, neither Adam nor Eve had returned to work. They had no need to earn. Adam's rewards from his assignment with ZeD had provided enough wealth for them to live a life of leisure, if they so chose, for the rest of their lives. That was not their intention, but for the present Eve was pregnant and happy to devote all her energies to the birth of their child – and Adam needed time to think.

Yes, Adam felt the need to do a great deal of thinking. Since his first meeting with the Storyteller, Adam had debated with the God of the Old Testament; conversed with Prometheus; witnessed the three great Beginnings; embarked on a brief, meteoric career in marketing that had guaranteed his financial security; and discovered how the world works and who was running it.

He had wanted to find the truth. Had he found it? No. But he was certainly less ignorant now than he had been before he stepped into the Storyteller's campervan. And he had learned that many of the things he had previously taken for granted were uncertain or even untrue. Time and space were not what common sense told him they were. Andrew Rimzil and his paradox device had put paid to those particular certainties. Good and evil were relative concepts; given the right circumstances, anyone could commit the most appalling crimes and yet be convinced they were doing good. And chance played a major role in human affairs. It wasn't just Bella's death that happened by chance; much of life was determined by good or bad luck. As the Storyteller had once remarked, "Life is backgammon, not chess."

One question had been answered. Adam now had no doubts about the existence of his self. It might be a blessing or a burden but he was sure he existed. All he felt and all he knew were mediated through his self. More than that, his self was able to assess and interpret what he felt and knew. It was not just that he was Adam. He knew what it was to be Adam.

And that was the problem. If Adam was all that he had been and all that he had done, then clearly he had to come to terms with all that he had been and done. Adam had to make sense of himself. He had to know whether he was a good or a bad man. Was he the man who had helped to initiate the Fourth Beginning, or was he the man who had jumped at the chance to further his career, regardless of the damage to his relationship with Eve? Was he the man who conspired with Jedwell Boon to murder Giovanni Spinetti, or was he the man who took a stand beside Kit when it meant the end of all he had gained since meeting David Minofel? And if in each case he was both, which was of course so, how could the two be reconciled?

"I'd like to talk," said Eve, answering Adam's question.

Adam felt a shiver of anxiety. He didn't like the sound of that. He knew Eve and the kind of questions she would ask. He knew he wouldn't be able to answer some of her questions, and where he had answers he might well be afraid to give them.

"Sure," he said. "What would you like to talk about?"

"What did they do to you while you were with the Praesidium?" Eve said, coming straight to the point. "I mean how did they persuade you to go along with them for so long? You cut yourself off from everyone. You cut yourself off from me. You even prosecuted Kit for murder. You must have known he was innocent. What were you thinking?"

"Whoa!" Adam interrupted. "It's OK. I understand the question. It's a difficult question to answer. The Praesidium is a very powerful organisation. They took me in and I admit I was flattered. They offered me so much, and at the time they seemed so certain of themselves, and as you know I'm a sucker for certainty. In my sessions with John Noble, the Praesidium Chairman, he explained that the sole purpose of the Praesidium was to help man be himself, to fulfil his true nature. That sounded fair enough to me. The Praesidium operated through four field operators, called Monitaurs. I went on excursions with each of the Monitaurs and they showed me human nature. They showed me man's inclination to depravity and extremism, and the prevalence of corruption in every sphere and at every level of life. They gave me examples of man's propensity to obscure or distort the truth and to close his mind to possibilities, It was a pretty harrowing experience but it was the truth, because that's the way things are. Or, at least, that's what I thought."

"That's ridiculous," said Eve dismissively. "What about all the good in the world?"

Adam shrugged. "Yes, there is good in the world. But the world is not run by the good. It's run by the Praesidium. And they wanted me on board. In fact they wanted me on the board. So I was impressed, and I was flattered. And remember, I didn't know what they were doing to Kit. I didn't even know he was being held in the Westminster PCC till much later. I had no idea how they were treating him."

"Didn't you wonder why you were chosen for such high office?" Eve asked. "Why you of all men should be singled out as a candidate?"

Adam paused. He could say it was because he had exceeded expectations in his first assignment with Slievins but he was wary. The last thing he wanted to answer were questions about what he had done in Geneva. When Eve had said she wanted to talk, the shiver of anxiety had been caused by a fear that she was going to cross-examine him about his work at ZeD.

"I guess they knew about my part in triggering the Fourth Beginning," he said. "The Praesidium believes man is best left as he is. They take the view that attempts to ask man to be what he is not, to be better than he is, simply cause man distress and anxiety. It goes against nature. Asking man not to be corrupt is like asking water not to be wet. I'm pretty sure they wanted to explain this to me so that I wouldn't think about trying to trigger another Beginning. And I suppose that's why they tried to destroy Kit. They knew he was likely to be the driving force behind any further attempts. If they could convert me and execute Kit, I guess they thought they could relax."

"But you knew the Fourth Beginning was good." Eve was genuinely puzzled. "When we initiated the Fourth Beginning we knew we had achieved something remarkable, something extraordinary. How could you imagine the Praesidium, with its negative, pessimistic, dystopian view of humanity, was anything other than evil?"

Adam shrugged. "The Praesidium view may have been dystopian, but it was also pretty much correct. They showed me, over and over again, what people are like and how the system works."

"No," said Eve. "They showed you what some people are like. As for the system, well, you're telling me that they are the system, so it's scarcely surprising they showed you their version of the world."

"But, Eve, they run everything. They control everything. They regulate the affairs of governments and people. They have the power."

"And yet they lost in a fight with a ragtag and bobtail bunch of assorted questors," said Eve. "How do you work that one out? In the end you stood up to them. Kit stood against them. We all held together and, with the help of Andrew and his paradox device, we escaped. We won. They lost."

"Don't forget Aletheia," said Adam. "We had the benefit of a bit of divine intervention. Yes, in the end we did well. In fact, taking the Slievins' experience as a whole it's fair to say it's been a rewarding exercise. It's been rough at times and I'm not pretending it hasn't been difficult for both of us, but the fact is that at the end of a few months we've achieved a level of financial security we could never have thought possible. We can now concentrate on our life together and on the new life we are bringing into the world." He kissed Eve.

"Do you think it's over? And what about Slievins? Do you really think they will leave us alone?" Eve asked.

"It's not a problem. The Praesidium will think again before bothering us. As for Slievins, you recall that Minofel said I could end the relationship at any time. He said Slievins had no wish to retain anyone who wanted to leave. In any case, and I won't go into details, Slievins did pretty well out of my time with them. They did so well that they gave me a massive bonus when I finished my assignment with ZeD."

"But ZeD was a disaster, wasn't it?" Eve interrupted. "It was a dreadful scandal. I was so pleased you were out of it. The job seemed to have taken over your life. And then you stood up against them. That must have been difficult. You blew the whistle. I thought you were really brave but I assumed that would be the end of your career. Instead, the money kept pouring into our bank account and you went straight from ZeD to the Praesidium. I don't really understand."

"As I said, I don't want to go into details – it would take too long and be very boring – but it's fair to say that Slievins and I did OK."

Eve didn't press for any further explanation.

Adam sat beside his wife and took her hand. "Things are going to be great," he said.

Luke, the golden retriever or "God of Dogs" as he liked to think of himself, got up and padded over to the couple so he could lie across their feet.

"Good boy," said Adam patting his dog on the head.

"It's a good thing you can't hear what I'm thinking," minded Luke, "because I reckon you've got just about everything wrong, with a capital R." (Luke had yet to come to terms with the vagaries of English spelling.). "The Praesidium will want revenge. Slievins will never leave you alone. And you are about as secure as a hen at a fox party."

6. Paying the price

Having sent Art Shoat to pick up the Crucible of Eternal Light, David Minofel made his way to the apartment of Simon Goodfellow. He left Manfred Bloch's body where it was. Manfred's death was a matter of little importance. After all, law and order had been one of the first casualties of Aletheia's destabilisation of the PCC. Those who had not fled would surely not wish to spend their last hours in pursuit of a murderer they could never bring to trial. In any case, all Manfred had lost was a few lonely hours before he, everyone on the PCC and the PCC itself evaporated into nothingness.

As Minofel strode along the moving walkway that joined the main Praesidium building to the accommodation block, he wondered whether Goodfellow's body would have begun to decompose. The man must be dead – no one could have survived the punishment Aletheia had imposed on him. He was reliving every barbaric act he had perpetrated but this time he was the victim, not the perpetrator. No, Goodfellow must be dead for sure. Minofel's only concern was the condition of the body. The air-conditioning unit within the PCC bubble was behaving erratically so the man's apartment was not the ideal place to preserve a body.

About halfway across the glass-encased bridge that connected the two main PCC areas, Minofel passed the seat where he had helped Goodfellow to plan the murder of John Noble, the then PCC Chairman. Neither of them had foreseen the consequences of that decision. With the benefit of hindsight, the blame for the ensuing debacle rested fairly with Goodfellow. Lax security had allowed Andrew Rimzil to operate inside the Westminster PCC undetected and, later, the party of questors to board the PCC unobserved. Ultimately, security was Goodfellow's responsibility – as was the training of Adam and the destruction of Kit. If Goodfellow had spent more time discharging his responsibilities and less time scheming against John Noble and sating his perverted sexual appetites, he might still have been Chairman of the PCC board.

That said, it was Goodfellow's perverted sexual appetites and his utterly unscrupulous pursuit of power that had persuaded David Minofel to spend precious time in visiting the apartment. Assuming the body was not too corrupted, Minofel wanted to collect a sample of his blood. A phial of Goodfellow's blood would be a worthy addition to Minofel's collection.

When Minofel reached the apartment door he found it unlocked. He entered. There was no one to be seen – no staff and no body. Then he heard a sound that sent a shiver down his spine. It was a shriek of pain that quickly dwindled into a whimper of despair.

"Don't tell me he's still alive," Minofel muttered to himself as he entered the inner room where Goodfellow had abused his victims.

The sight that greeted him would have turned all but the strongest stomachs.

"Well I never," said Minofel looking down at what was left of Simon Goodfellow. "You really don't look at all well, old fellow."

The thing on the floor was just about recognisable as a human being. Goodfellow had wasted away. His clothes lay loosely on his body, as though they had been placed over him, not worn by him. The head was too large for the emaciated torso. And the grey eyes stared out of sunken sockets in a ravaged face, a face that had once been handsome enough.

"Please," croaked what was left of Simon Goodfellow. "No more. Please, no more." And then he shrieked again, as he was made to feel the pain he had inflicted on yet another of his victims.

"I know you had a pretty impressive record of abusing, torturing and, quite often, killing women," said Minofel, "but surely by now you've been through them all. You've shared their pain."

"Please, not again."

"Oh I see. You're on a loop," said Minofel triumphantly, having realised what was happening. "You're living the same incidents over and over again. That must seem a little unfair. If it's a loop, it could go on for ever. And evidently you're not going to die – unless someone or something kills you. Fascinating. You have to hand it to Aletheia. She really knows how to make a point."

"Please end it, please," begged the croaking voice.

David Minofel knelt beside his erstwhile co-conspirator and used a syringe to extract a sample of Goodfellow blood. It looked a bit turgid but Minofel was satisfied. "You realise that all this is in your head, don't you?" he said to the pleading wreck of a man. "It's all in your head. If you could just stop empathising with your victims, you wouldn't feel a thing. You could be as happy as Larry, just as you were when you were abusing and mutilating them for real."

Goodfellow made an effort to construct a sentence. "If you have any shred of decency in you, kill me. Kill me now."

"Don't be ridiculous." Minofel laughed. "I don't have time for this nonsense. I have what I came for, so I'm off. Pull yourself together and take it like a man."

"For pity's sake," gasped Goodfellow.

Minofel smiled. "Sorry but practitioners don't do pity." With that, he left.

7. Best laid plans

When David Minofel and Art Shoat returned to the Slievins' offices in the City, they were assured of a warm welcome.

"You've both done well," said a smiling Roland Samiat. "No, you've done better than well. The Crucible of Eternal Light is now where it truly belongs, with Slievins. Art, you have more than fulfilled my expectations of you. And David, you have fully redeemed yourself."

A flicker of a frown crossed Minofel's forehead.

"We are now well-placed," Roland continued, "to resolve the problem of Adam and Eve Smith once and for all. I have a plan and it is a plan in which both of you have a crucial part to play. First, we must separate them. The bond between them is strong. They draw strength from each other. Apart, it will be easier to break them. I have spent a good deal of time pondering who is the graver threat, Adam or Eve. My conclusion may surprise you. I have concluded that Eve poses the greater danger. I therefore intend to deal with Eve myself. Adam I am going to leave to you, David."

A second flicker of a frown crossed Minofel's forehead.

"Art, you are to take the Crucible to our new headquarters in Arabia," Roland continued. "I need hardly point out that this assignment is of the highest priority. There is no one else I would entrust with such a responsibility. Once the Crucible is installed we will have the power to put an end to any attempt at a Beginning before it starts. I've sent Ben Rael on ahead to make sure that security in the city in the sand is up to it. We have to be particularly attentive to security in the wake of the debacle at the Westminster PCC. As for Kit, or any other Emergents, we will be able to treat them as a kind of spiritual haemorrhoid, an irritant that can be dealt with either by popping them back into where they came from, or if need be with surgery."

David Minofel said nothing but a frown flickered across his forehead for the third time. He had come to the realisation that he really didn't like Roland Samiat. The realisation came as a surprise. He had worked for the Slievins' CEO for many years. David Minofel did not enjoy taking orders from anyone but Samiat managed most of the time to issue instructions without riling his subordinates. He did have an irritating predilection for trotting out silly, inappropriate or extended metaphors to make a point, but in the past Minofel had found this trait only mildly irritating, even sometimes amusing. Now the habit was beginning to grate. The Titanic rebuke at their last meeting was a case in point. And the stretch, if not strain, of equating an Emergent with a haemorrhoid was another. It's a pity, thought Minofel, that no one has told Samiat he has no talent for figurative discourse.

And, of course, whether Samiat had meant it or not, Minofel felt a gentle snub in everything his boss had said.

So, not for the first time a senior partner at Slievins was falling out with the CEO, but this particular senior partner was wise enough to know that he must not give any hint of his disillusion with his boss. For all his benign bonhomie, Roland Samiat was at least as ruthless as Minofel himself.

"It will be an honour," said Art. "But before I set out on the journey, I need to fill up with fuel." He lovingly patted his commodious belly. "We didn't have time for a meal on the Westminster PCC."

"Then off to the canteen with you," said Roland. "Stuff yourself to bursting. You deserve it."

David Minofel wanted to say, "Do you really think more of that crude, gluttonous, porcine criminal than you do of me?" but he didn't. All he said was, "Great plan. Don't worry about Adam. I'll get one of my people to pick him up."

"No, you won't," said Roland. "I'll organise their separation. It ties in with a project we have from another client. Two birds with one stone, eh? Just as we earned a fee from ZeD for recruiting Adam while using Adam to fulfil the PBS assignment. That was neat, except of course, we also wanted to prepare Adam for greater things and that didn't work out quite as well as we hoped. But not to worry. I'll make sure this time there are no loose ends."

oooOooo

David Minofel felt ill at ease with himself. Roland Samiat had slighted him and there was nothing he dared do about it. When he reached his office, he pressed an inconspicuous button on an otherwise empty section of the back wall. A square of plaster receded slightly and slid sideways to reveal a large display cabinet. On shelves within the cabinet were rows of phials containing the blood, mixed and preserved with alcohol, of some of the vilest human beings who had ever lived. The samples of blood had been gathered, often with extreme difficulty, by the Praesidium's field operatives over the centuries

On the top shelves were blood samples of famous figures of history who had earned notoriety for their cruelty or savagery, among them Nero, Genghis Khan, Vlad the Impaler, Pol Pot and Saddam Hussein.

On the middle shelves were the phials of somewhat less well-known but nonetheless depraved individuals such as the Marquis de Sade and Delphine La Laurie, the nineteenth-century New Orleans socialite who attempted to sate her sadistic drives by torturing and mutilating her black slaves.

On the several lower shelves was space for the phials of evil people who had failed to earn a place in history. Some had merited a few pages of ephemeral notoriety in daily newspapers; others had scarcely managed to generate half a dozen lines of copy in some local rag. A few had perpetrated their crimes entirely unremarked.

On the bottom shelf, among many others, was the phial of the rapist Kevin who had attacked the Smiths in their home; several shelves higher was the newly acquired sample of Simon Goodfellow's blood. For a few moments, Minofel pondered which of these two would suit the moment best. He settled on the blood of Kevin, reached for the phial, removed the cap and took the smallest of sips.

8.   You can't keep a good man down

If Rambler had feared loneliness following his nephew's death and the retreat from the doomed Westminster PCC, his fears proved groundless. Kit had arrived on his doorstep almost immediately, within three days of their escape from the Praesidium's clutches, and Rambler had welcomed him into his Maida Vale flat.

And if Rambler had feared that his life would be without purpose now that he no longer had his nephew to tutor, he was again proved wrong. Kit persuaded him that they must learn all they could about the Praesidium and the Slievins Consultancy. "Whether we have to engage with them again or not, we need to be prepared. We must find their strengths and their weaknesses. You need to research the history of mankind and the part the Praesidium has played in it."

The first part of the brief was a task that suited Rambler perfectly. There was nothing he enjoyed more than delving into the details of any subject, and mankind's troubled history was certainly a fertile field into which to delve. The second part was more problematic. It was too easy to assume that the Praesidium was behind all the evil that man had perpetrated, but where was the proof? After all, as the Praesidium board had proudly proclaimed, their sole goal was to enable man to be himself. It was therefore impossible to tell how much of the carnage had been orchestrated by the Praesidium and how much man had undertaken on his own initiative.

Happily the problem was at least partially resolved by the arrival of Prune Leach and Andrew Rimzil, who had turned up, with the Storyteller, on the doorstep of Rambler's Maida Vale flat a few days after Kit's arrival.

"It's good to see you all," Rambler had greeted his new guests.

His fear of loneliness was being replaced by concerns that his apartment, although capacious for one man and his nephew, was now becoming almost crowded. It was not so much the people that worried him as the equipment which the two engineers had brought with them.

"Where can I plug this in?" asked Prune, surveying the large sitting room with his piercing blue eyes.

"I suggest the box room at the end of the corridor," said Rambler hastily.

It would be too much to have all Rimzil's paraphernalia, including the paradox device, installed in his main living space.

Prune scuttled to the end of the corridor, assessed the size of the box room and called back, "Bit cramped, but it'll do. There's enough power points."

Sensing Rambler's unease, Kit drew him aside. "I hope you don't mind, but I invited Andrew and Prune without asking you. We are going to need their help."

"And the Storyteller?" asked Rambler.

Kit smiled and simply said, "He goes with the territory."

When all the domestic arrangements had been sorted, Andrew asked how he and Prune could help. Kit explained the task he had given Rambler and the difficulties the researcher had encountered in determining the extent of the role of the Praesidium in controlling mankind's history.

"Well, there must be records," said Prune. "An organisation like the Praesidium would maintain records. The Monitaurs that Adam told us about must have submitted reports of their work."

"I'm sure that's true," said Rambler, "but the Westminster PCC has already been annihilated, and any archives they held within it lost for ever."

It was Kit who broke the ensuing silence. "Although it seemed that the Praesidium employed the Slievins Consultancy, I'm convinced that it was, in practice, the other way round. Slievins guided – no manipulated – the Praesidium to achieve its own ends. They created problems that only they could solve, and the solutions always caused more problems that required Slievins' solutions. It was really always all about business – Slievins' business. John Noble couldn't tell David Minofel what to do. The Praesidium was there to implement Slievins' will. If I'm right, it follows that the Slievins' people would have monitored the performance of their agency, the Praesidium, with meticulous care."

"So you think Slievins will have a record of the Praesidium's activity?" Rambler queried.

"I think it's highly probable," Kit replied.

"Well, we can soon find out," said Andrew Rimzil.

oooOooo

That same evening after dinner, Andrew and Prune withdrew to the box room.

"It's all wired up and plugged in," said Prune.

Being considerably shorter than Rimzil, Prune invariably undertook the setting up of their equipment. He found it much easier than his tall, long-legged colleague to crawl around under tables and insert plugs into perversely located sockets.

"I'll run a program I've written to hack the Slievins' computer. I just need to input a few known facts about Slievins which I can get from their annual report and then start the program. It can check five hundred possible passwords a second, starting with the most likely based on the data I've inputted. It'll take time, but with a bit of luck I should have the password in a couple of hours."

"You can do that if you like," Andrew replied, "or we can use the paradox device."

The wrinkles on Prunes forehead deepened as they migrated upwards toward the black shoreline of his unkempt hair. "Is there something else I should know about the device?" he asked.

"Fraid so," Andrew replied with a grin. "I was working on the paradox device the other day when I thought I'd take a break. I needed to check my bank account, so I opened the home page of my bank's website on my laptop. I noticed a couple of flickers on my screen but thought nothing of it. I was about to log in when my account page opened. As I hadn't entered my password, I was worried. I thought I must have failed to log out after my last session, but that was weeks ago and my access should have timed out after a few minutes. Then I noticed the paradox device screen. It was happily opening other people's accounts, showing the home page of each account for a split second. It was difficult to see, but I realised the paradox device was working its way through every account in the bank's system in alphabetical order. I immediately instructed the device to stop. It obeyed but informed me it had just been playing a game to see how quickly it could identify each account's password. It then volunteered to give me access to the bank's mainframe. I declined the offer but not quickly enough. There, on my laptop, was unlimited deep access to the core of the bank's computer system. 'Close it at once' I ordered. I thought that every alarm on the bank's system would be triggered and efforts to trace the source of the hack would already be underway. The paradox device severed the link but advised me not to worry because it had persuaded the bank's mainframe that the hack should be 'their little secret'."

"Don't start that nonsense all over again," snapped Prune. "Don't talk about the device as though it's human. It's just a machine that works with ones and zeros. That's all. It upsets me when you pretend it can establish a relationship with other machines."

"I don't know what to say," said Andrew Rimzil, soothingly. "But I'm not making any of this up. And there's something else, which I know will upset you even more. The device relates not only to machines. It also relates to me – and I to it. Most of the time it does what I want. It doesn't wait for instructions, it just does it. I wanted to open my bank account, so it opened my account. Sometimes it guesses what I want or what it thinks I might want – like access to the banks mainframe. And at other times, it just does what it wants. It decided to entertain itself by finding the password to every personal account. It's quite a character."

"It's not a character," Prune insisted. "It's just a bundle of hardware and software. It can't think. It doesn't take decisions. It may seem to be thinking or taking decisions but it's not. It's not conscious of thinking. It's not aware it's taking decisions. And all this drivel about relationships is simply you projecting your feelings on to the device."

"I'm not going to argue," said Andrew, "but your theory will have to accommodate a couple of inconsistencies. If you're right, there is no way the device could become bored and decide to play a game. Secondly, you need to explain how the device has sought out the Slievins' website, slipped past all the security, penetrated the Slievins' mainframe and provided us with unimpeded access to their archives while we've been nattering away here. And all that before we've entered any instructions or asked it to do anything."

At first Prune said nothing. Then he said, "Holy Mary, mother of Christ!"

9. Separation

The timing had to be perfect. Adam and Eve, arriving at Covent Garden separately, had to be close enough to the explosion to believe that their partner had been killed and yet distant enough for both of them to survive.

Adam had received a text message from Andrew Rimzil. Andrew was in town for a conference on anti-matter at the Department of Physics and Astronomy at UCL. He had suggested they should meet for a coffee in the morning break. Adam made his way to Gower Street, only to find the conference had been cancelled because of a heightened security alert across London, announced at nine o'clock that morning. Universities in general, and UCL in particular, were thought to be the primary targets, as part of a new Islamist campaign against Western educational institutions. Adam checked his mobile and found two new messages. One was from Andrew apologising for cancelling the coffee but explaining he had been whisked away to a safer venue in Birmingham. The other message was from Eve, saying that she needed to do some shopping in town and suggesting that if he was free they should meet in Covent Garden at 12.30 for lunch.

Eve arrived at Holborn tube station at 12.20 p.m. She had received a text message from Adam, asking her to meet him at the Waldorf Hilton in Aldwych for lunch. He had a new idea he wanted to discuss with her. He had suggested that after lunch they did some shopping in town. She had taken the Metropolitan line from Pinner to King's Cross, then changed on to the Piccadilly line to Holborn. It was a ten-minute walk to the Waldorf.

After reading the second message on his mobile. Adam took the Northern line from Warren Street to Leicester Square, then walked along Cranbourn Street and Garrick Street towards Covent Garden. He entered King Street at 12.28 p.m.

"That's good enough," said Roland Samiat.

oooOooo

The explosion was heard across the whole of central London, from Park Lane in the west to the Tower of London in the east; from the

Euston Road in the north to the Elephant and Castle in the south. More than one hundred people died instantaneously. Several hundred suffered varying degrees of injury, of which eighty subsequently died. Dozens more were permanently disfigured, and all those who survived were mentally scarred for life.

"Why do they do it?" asked Ceri Agema. "Apart from the pleasure of killing, what do they get out of it?"

Ceri, an American of Dutch extraction, was an attractive blonde girl with blue eyes (which were pretty enough but a little cold) and shapely legs (which seemed to go on for ever). Although only in her late twenties, she was one of Roland Samiat's most trusted aides.

"Our Islamist friends are telling the West that they have taken a wrong turning in the evolution of man," Samiat replied. "Westerners are too attached to this ephemeral life and forgetful of their primary purpose to submit to the will of Allah."

"And blowing people up is a good way of promoting their cause?" asked Ceri, curious rather than critical.

"Having repudiated reason, their powers of persuasion are severely hampered and heavily dependent on fear," Samiat replied. "This bombing, which incidentally they paid us an extraordinarily large fee to organise, is their attempt at non-verbal communication. Of course, there's also an element of revenge, a natural response from Medievalists to the West's penchant for bombing Muslim countries back into the Middle Ages. And, as you suggested at the start, there is always the pure pleasure of killing."

Ceri shrugged. She was only mildly interested in the motives of men. "What do you want us to do with the woman? My people are holding her now. She's shaken but physically unharmed – at least as far as we can tell. Of course, she's desperate to find out if Adam is all right."

"Well, I'm afraid we have some terribly bad news on that score," Samiat laughed. "Blown to smithereens, I guess. I'm sure we would be able to find a little piece of him, enough to identify his DNA, if she has any doubts, but that's all. If she presses the point, we'll have to tell her that what's left of him would easily fit into an urn without the need to go through the process of a cremation. But I'm sure it won't come to that. Take her to the medical centre in the house in Mayfair. She will need a good deal of cosseting, comforting and counselling. Six months pregnant and widowed! Life can be cruel."

Ceri smiled. She did not like men in general. She was happy to sleep with them, but she made it a matter of principle to kill them after they had enjoyed her favours. No, men in general were a pretty useless lot. But Roland Samiat was different. He had a brain and a sense of humour. Above all, he was focused. He knew what it was all about, he knew what he needed to do and he knew how to get what he wanted. She liked that. On top of all that, he was the boss.

"And don't forget to leave some of Eve's DNA at the scene," Roland added. "After all, sadly she's dead too."

10. Rambler's research

With unrestricted access to the Slievins' archives, Rambler made good progress in exploring the extent of the malign influence of Slievins throughout recorded history.

"They specialise in provoking wars," said Rambler as he closed his internet connection for the day. "Of course, they promote theft, rape and murder, but their *piece de resistance* is war. That's why John Noble was ousted. He just hadn't pushed hard enough for large scale military engagements."

"In fact, he wasn't ousted, he was murdered," Kit observed, "but I take your point. Goodfellow certainly felt Noble had been a bit slack on the slash-and-burn, shock-and-awe front. He wanted the Praesidium to nurture a Genghis Khan, not an Osama bin Laden – rampaging wars, not one-off spectaculars."

"Funnily enough," Rambler responded enthusiastically, "I've just been reading reports on the involvement of the Praesidium in the rise of the Mongol leader. He was born Temujin, which in Mongolian means blacksmith. Legend has it that he was born with a blood clot in his hand, which his family took to mean he would be a great leader. According to the Slievins' archive, a Praesidium operative, a woman working as a nurse, placed the clot in the baby's hand. It seems our enemies like to store samples of blood from individuals who during their lives have come closest to the Praesidium's ideals. The clot was a concentrated cocktail of blood from past Praesidium favourites such as Caligula and Attila the Hun. It's not clear from the report whether this blood custom is purely symbolic or whether the Praesidium believes the blood samples can somehow transmit Praesidium values to the chosen recipient."

"Well, whatever its purpose, they seem to have picked a winner with the young Temujin," said Kit. "Apart from the gift of a blood clot at birth, have you found any other evidence of Praesidium involvement?"

"They left him to his own devices in his youth, which meant he was involved in power struggles between the rival Mongolian tribes. In particular he had a volatile relationship with his childhood friend Jamukha, who became his main rival in early manhood. Indeed, when Temujin was about twenty-five, Jamukha, now khan of his own tribe, attacked him with some thirty thousand warriors. Temujin and his supporters were soundly defeated at the battle of Dalan Balzhut. It seems the Praesidium considered abandoning Temujin in favour of Jamukha, especially when the latter ordered the boiling alive in cauldrons of seventy captives. They decided to stick with Temujin, mainly because they knew he was highly intelligent and was judged to have greater potential than Jamukha."

"And partly because the Praesidium never likes to admit it has made a mistake," Kit interrupted.

"That too, no doubt," Rambler conceded. "According to the archive, the Praesidium took Temujin in hand for the next ten years, which is why there is little or no historical record of his life in this period. Then in 1197 he emerged once again, now thoroughly tutored by the Praesidium, and began to lay the foundations for his empire. He broke with the Mongol tradition of nepotism, adopting a meritocratic approach to appointing his generals. By 1206, with Praesidium guidance, he became khan of all the Mongols and could turn his attention to conquests of other lands. With considerable skill, Temujin deployed his innumerable warrior horsemen to maximum effect in his campaigns and made full use of his greatest weapon, terror. He was utterly merciless to those who dared to stand against him. In a few short years, he built the largest contiguous land empire that had ever existed. When he advanced into new territory, he maintained the principle that he should never leave behind him an enemy who could stab him in the back. In other words, he killed any members of the nobility in his conquered lands who might rise against him. When he subjugated the Tatars, he had all those taller than the height of a cart axle executed, sparing only the smallest of children to be brought up as his loyal followers. When his army took the town of Otrar, located in what is now Kazakhstan, he ordered the execution of many of the civilians, enslaved the rest and ordered that the town governor should be executed by having molten silver poured into his eyes and ears. Taken as a whole, the building of the Mongol empire is estimated to have caused the deaths, through battle, slaughter and famine, of five per cent of the world's entire population at the time – anything up to forty million people."

"Enough!" Kit interrupted. "Keep researching. We need to know the extent to which the Praesidium has interfered in human affairs, but we don't need every detail."

Rambler was a little hurt. "Without going into the detail, you can't really tell how much is down to the Praesidium and how much is just human nature. Temujin was brought up in a brutal society and had a very harsh childhood. The Praesidium chose him and tutored him, but how can we know that he wouldn't have followed a similar path without their interference?"

"The fact that they took him in hand is enough," Kit soothed. "It means they were accessories to his murdering rampages before, during and after the fact."

"It wasn't all bad," Rambler persisted. "He imposed a system of law on those who were subjugated. He showed tolerance to those of different faiths, he gave property rights to women, and by razing so many cities to the ground that the forests regrew, he reduced the amount of carbon dioxide in the atmosphere by about seven hundred million tons."

"That is interesting," Kit mused. "Evidently the Praesidium doesn't exercise complete control. I'm pretty sure that tolerance, women's rights and ecology have never been high on the Praesidium's agenda."

11. Case studies

While Rambler was wrestling with the history of the Praesidium, David Minofel was engaged in his own form of research.

Slievins held a file on any person who had ever represented a threat to Slievins' interests. David Minofel was one of the very few in the Slievins organisation who had access to all the files. He considered it part of his responsibility, as well as part of a lifetime learning process, to read a selection of the files whenever time permitted.

He was thoroughly familiar with the profiles of the great enemies of Slievins. Philosophers formed a major category. They attempted to lead man away from the main purpose of living into the dark, dread wasteland of arcane thought. Instead of exhorting man to be himself, they persisted in inviting him to ponder the imponderable, to seek answers to unreal questions and to search for meaning where there was none to be found.

It was always a pleasure to see how men such as Socrates had been brought low. The Praesidium had done exceptionally well with the snub-nosed philosopher. He had been forced to commit suicide for corrupting the youth of fifth century Athens. It was not issues of morality that had alarmed the Praesidium. It was his criticism of the unexamined life. The last thing that should occupy a man's brief span on earth was the examination of his own life. That kind of self-indulgent, narcissistic navel-gazing was guaranteed to prevent an individual from fulfilling his potential.

Then there were the religious zealots. Frequently the Praesidium had managed to turn zealotry to its own advantage, using religion to divide rather than unite mankind, but there were exceptions. Buddha and Jesus could be counted as only partial successes. There had been considerable progress in reinterpreting the message of these deluded individuals, and yet inexplicably it had been impossible to eliminate entirely the appeal of such voices to sections of humanity.

But it was not philosophers or religious bigots that occupied Minofel's attention on this particular occasion. It was the late Numpty, nephew of Rambler, who had died trying to comfort a man he had just stabbed in an effort to protect the life of an abused woman he had never met.

The file on Numpty was surprisingly large. Indeed, it was partly the size of the file that had attracted Minofel's attention. But there was another reason. There was something about this Numpty's life, and indeed his death, that puzzled David Minofel. The boy was mentally challenged. True, after the initiation of the Fourth Beginning he had attained an unexpected enhancement of his mental acuity, but in essence he had remained a naïve ingénue. So why had Minofel opened, and not for the first time, young Numpty's file?

He laughed. He could hear Rambler's voice saying that *ingénue* is a female word form and can be applied only to innocent young girls. Then he heard Numpty's voice pointing out that *naïve ingénue* was a tautology. Minofel shook his head. Was he really hearing the voices of those whom he had been compelled to enlighten or destroy? In particular, had the late young Numpty, the self-proclaimed 'osmotic gouger', somehow burrowed into his head? Perhaps he had become too close to the Smiths and their bizarre entourage in the course of their abortive quests. It had crossed his mind that his irritation with Roland Samiat's inept use of imagery might not be entirely unconnected with Numpty's infuriating habit of nitpicking over the words other people used. Of course that was ridiculous. But he was pretty sure Roland had always had a penchant for employing inappropriate metaphors and similes, and yet only recently had this habit grated with him.

Minofel gave a mental shrug. What did it matter? That was over. Numpty was dead. And he mustn't allow his irritation with Samiat to show.

And yet he had to confess he was puzzled. The Breakers, who were the operational arm of the Praesidium, abhorred metaphors. The questors had used the Metaphorce, under their commander Hector Meap, to excellent effect against the Breakers on Poulner Hill. Even Minofel had been forced to admire the questors' ingenuity in deploying the Fist of God, an explosive metaphorical device, in their successful battle with Nick Peters's Breaker army. So, given the dangers that metaphors presented to the Breaker community, why did Roland Samiat persist in using metaphors, especially when it was evident to everyone that he had no talent for it. Or was it evident to everyone, or, indeed, anyone other than himself? No one else in Slievins had remarked on his inept use of figures of speech. Perhaps that was because everyone feared the Chairman's wrath.

Or was it, heaven forbid, that David Minofel, through his dealings with the questors, had become sensitised in some way?

46

12. Dark days begin

The blast of the explosion hit Adam as though a huge hand had given every part of his body a brutal slapping. He fell to the ground, stunned and temporarily deafened. The blast assaulted his lungs, stomach, joints and ligaments, as well as his ears. He lay still as the swirling dust-filled air gradually settled.

There was silence. When the bomb had detonated, some cars in King Street had crashed, but after the crashes there was silence. Adam tried to sit up. His ears were ringing. His eyes couldn't focus. He wondered how badly injured he was. He moved his arms and legs just to prove that all four limbs were still attached.

And then he thought, Eve!

It was almost forty minutes before any help arrived. A dozen ambulances drove past Adam on the way to the centre of the explosion. There was nothing the paramedics could do for those within two hundred metres of the blast. Beyond that, some had survived but had suffered appalling injuries and were in urgent need of medical attention. Eventually an ambulance stopped near Adam. First the paramedics dealt with those involved in the car crashes. Then they came over to Adam who was sitting up by now.

"What happened?" he asked.

The paramedic said something; at least, his lips moved. But Adam heard nothing other than an incessant ringing in his ears. At least I can hear the ringing, he thought, but then realised the ringing wasn't an external sound.

The paramedic put him in the back of an ambulance with two more seriously injured survivors and drove him to University College Hospital in the Euston Road. Although emergency service vehicles had priority, the journey took an age simply because of the weight of traffic, the general confusion and fear, and the one-way system. By the time Adam arrived, the ringing in his ears had subsided and he could at last hear an answer to the question he kept asking.

"Don't really know," the paramedic replied, as he wheeled Adam into A & E. "Bloody great explosion in Covent Garden. Terrorist bomb, I guess. Too big for any other explanation. Dozens dead, maybe more. I'll have to leave you now. Must get back. There are more to pick up."

Adam waited for a few minutes, but he could see the A & E department was overstretched; in any case, he had more or less recovered. He was shaken and his hearing was temporarily compromised but otherwise he was unharmed. He discharged himself without registering with the receptionist.

"Is there any way I can get to the Waldorf Hilton?" he asked a surprised orderly. "I'm supposed to be meeting my wife there," he explained.

"Not a hope in hell," the orderly replied. "Central London's in chaos. No buses, no taxis. The tube has been evacuated. And Aldwych may be inside the exclusion zone. You could try giving her a call, but you'll probably find the networks jammed or down."

oooOooo

Adam walked out through the doors of the hospital's main entrance and down the steps into the street. He tried phoning, but as predicted the network was jammed.

"Get in the car," said a familiar voice emanating from a black Mercedes S class saloon, parked in the space for emergency arrivals.

The windows of the car had dark glass but Adam instantly knew the identity of the voice's owner. It was probably the last person on earth Adam wanted to see. He shook his head and started to walk away.

The black Mercedes forced its way into the traffic and started to cruise slowly alongside Adam. The window slid down.

"If you've got any sense at all, you'll hear what I have to say," said David Minofel. "If you don't, you'll be in even worse trouble than you're in already."

13.   Rambler and the Third Reich

Searching for proof of Praesidium interference in the affairs of men in medieval history was proving difficult. Slievins' archives of Praesidium records were sketchy until the twentieth century. There was some evidence that the Praesidium had been operating for thousands of years, but until modern times they had not fully appreciated the need for meticulous record-keeping. It was only with the advent of mass communication that the Praesidium had realised that the acquisition and analysis of data would enable them to manipulate mankind far more efficiently.

Rambler decided to turn his attention to more recent times. He chose as his subject one of the most evil phenomena in human history, Hitler and the Third Reich. He found the Praesidium's hand in selecting Hitler to lead the genocide particularly interesting – mainly because Adolf Hitler was not the obvious choice. As Rambler put it, "Let's face it, he was no Genghis Khan."

Rambler read his notes to the others: "Adolf Hitler was born in 1889. The young Adolf was a difficult child and youth, rebelling at every opportunity against authority, especially that of his father. When Adolf was eleven, his younger brother, Edmund, died of measles. The death affected him deeply, and he became morose and even more recalcitrant. In 1903, Adolf's father died. Adolf continued his undistinguished academic studies and left school, aged sixteen, after passing a retake of a final exam but failing to complete his secondary education and without any defined plan for the future.

"The next few years were spent eking out a tenuous existence in Vienna. He had aspirations to be a painter, but had to work as a labourer before beginning to make a little money selling watercolours of the famous sights of Vienna. His two applications to study at the Academy of Fine Arts in Vienna were rejected. As an alternative, it was suggested he might study architecture but he lacked the necessary academic qualifications for entrance. In December 1907, Adolf's mother died of breast cancer. By now Adolf had run out of money and had to live in hostels for the homeless.

"Not an auspicious start for someone destined to conquer much of Europe – not particularly bright, lacking sufficient artistic talent to fulfil his dream of becoming a painter, and seemingly unfocused, undisciplined and aimless.

"So why had the Praesidium selected him as a chosen one? Well, according to Praesidium records, he had one particular virtue that marked him out for greatness. He had an exceptional talent for hate. Lesser men, when faced by rejection, might accept criticism and decide to try harder, or if less driven, give up. But not Adolf. He responded to rejection with disdain, if you were lucky, but with hate if you weren't. He tapped his reserves of hate and found them an inexhaustible source of energy and power.

"The Praesidium also noted and nurtured his sense of the dramatic and his oratorical skills. He had the potential to be a great showman. He could launch a production that would run and run, that would last, he himself hoped, for a thousand years.

"There are some particular interesting notes in the archive relating to the relationship between Hitler and the monitaur Edgar Exton. Edgar put everything he had into developing Hitler's paranoia and obsessions. Hitler's mind was so twisted with hate for the Jews that Edgar even managed to revive the medieval blood libel, which was a great source of amusement for the Praesidium board members. He encouraged Hitler to develop his bizarre concept of an Aryan master race which, according to Hitler, comprised perfect specimens of humanity with fine physiques, blonde hair and blue eyes. The spurious superior Aryan bloodline must not be contaminated by the racially inferior Jews, blacks, Slavs, gypsies and anyone else Hitler chose to vilify. Edgar took particular pleasure from the irony in Hitler's enthusiasm for the master-race concept, an irony which entirely eluded Hitler. The Führer seemed unaware of the origin of the word, Aryan (Indo-Iranian) and the fact that neither he nor most of his followers conformed to the ideal. Consistency was not a strong suit to the perverted minds of the Third Reich. Another of their hate targets was homosexuality, although the elite of the high command was full of gays."

Prune Leach was dismissive. "I would have thought Hitler's life had been explored enough already. Can't really see the point of trawling through material that's already been rehashed a hundred times."

Andrew was more conciliatory. "It's useful to know how the Praesidium operates. They pick on individuals and develop a kind of pernicious symbiotic relationship with them. They tutor them, they mentor them, but at the end of the day it's the ones they choose who make things happen."

"Isn't that what the Praesidium told Adam?" Rambler queried. "They work with man to enable man to be himself."

"Don't be daft," snapped Prune. "Look at the people they choose. We're not all Genghis Khans or Hitlers."

"No," said Kit. "But perhaps there's a little of them in all of us. Can we be sure that if they picked any one of us they couldn't find a bit of the Genghis Khan or Hitler to nurture? After all, look what they did to Adam."

14.   When sorrows come …

Reluctantly Adam climbed into the back of the Mercedes.

"It's a bad business," said David Minofel. "Apparently dozens are dead."

"My only concern is Eve," said Adam. "We were to meet at the Aldwych. I can't get through to her mobile."

"I'm sure she's fine. Obviously the network is jammed with people like you trying to contact people like her."

Minofel's tone irritated Adam. He was somehow belittling Adam's anxiety. In any case, Adam had hoped his dealings with David Minofel and Slievins were over for ever. Hadn't he made that clear when he stood beside Kit on the scaffold?

"What did you mean by 'even worse trouble'?" Adam asked. That was the only reason he had joined Minofel in the Mercedes.

"This is not perhaps the best time to raise the matter," said Minofel, now playing with his prey.

"Spit it out," said Adam. He was in no mood for Minofel's games. Obviously Minofel hadn't sought him out *not* to reveal whatever it was he had to tell him.

"It'll probably sort itself out," Minofel teased.

"Stop the car," said Adam unnecessarily, since the car was either stationary or progressing at less than walking speed.

Minofel laughed. "Very well, it's a tax matter. The taxman is coming to get you. More specifically, HMRC are not entirely satisfied that you have paid them all the money you owe them."

"The centre of London has just been blown up and you want to talk to me about tax. Eve may have been hurt – or worse – and you think I'm going to worry about money. There's something seriously wrong with you." Adam put his hand on the car door handle.

"I'm pretty sure Eve will be fine, and as soon as she phones you, you'll be able to relax." Minofel put his hand on Adam's arm. "But believe me, if HMRC get their teeth into you, it'll be months or years before you can sleep at night."

Adam frowned. "What tax? I've paid all the tax I owe. It was deducted by ZeD."

Minofel smiled. "It's not your salary they're concerned about.

It's the large sums that dropped into your bank account. There were the bonuses and then there was the money you won in our little bet."

"But the bonuses were official, weren't they? They must have been. Dr Dubois authorised them."

"I'm not sure they went through the books. And in any case Dubois himself is under a bit of a cloud. Let's face it, a criminal tax exile in northern Cyprus will not be seen as the most impressive witness by HMRC. They may even question whether the bonuses were legitimate,"

"What do you mean 'legitimate'? Of course they were legitimate."

"You don't have to persuade me," said Minofel. "It's just that the authorities are obsessed with money laundering, and large payments to anyone without the right paperwork arouse their suspicion."

"So what are you saying? It's not just tax evasion, it's money laundering as well? Why don't you throw in extortion?"

David Minofel's eyes widened in mock surprise. "I didn't think you would want to bring that up."

"I'm not bringing anything up," snapped Adam. Surely Minofel was not going to rake through everything he'd done in Geneva. Anything he had done – the bribery, the blackmail and the elimination of Spinetti – had been done for the best of reasons and, perhaps more importantly, at Minofel's behest. If anyone was to blame, assuming there was any blame, it was Minofel, not he, who should shoulder it.

"I haven't got time for this," Adam added. "I'm going to find Eve. If there's anything in what you say, no doubt I'll hear from HMRC."

"As you please," said Minofel, relaxing back into his seat. "I'll drop you off here. But don't doubt that HMRC will contact you, and when they do, if you're smart, you'll give me a call. After all, notwithstanding more recent events, we were a team in Geneva and we should make sure our stories tally."

15. Mayfair

The house in Mayfair was not only a fitting town residence for the CEO of Slievins' Consultancy, it was also a fully equipped health and recreation centre. It had originally been an embassy for a Middle Eastern sheikdom but had come into Roland Samiat's hands in payment for a favour he had done the sheikh.

It was late afternoon by the time Ceri Agema arrived at the house.

"London's a nightmare," she said to the security guard as she strode into the reception hall. "Where is she?"

"I think they took her to the health centre. Ms Mavlow is with her."

Enid Mavlow was one of Slievins' field operatives. She had been seconded to London from the Slievins' office in her home country, Brazil, and was enjoying the experience of working at the heart of the Slievins' operation. With lustrous dark hair, an excellent figure, round face and full lips, Enid was a very attractive woman but it was her eyes that gave her the edge over most of her rivals. Those blue eyes seemed to smile at and, at the same time, challenge any man, or indeed woman, who looked into them. They were full of mischief, a promise of excitement and the possibility of danger. Only men who were very sure of themselves took on Enid Mavlow – and most of those who did found their self-confidence was misplaced.

"Hello, Enid," said Ceri. "How's the patient?"

You might have expected two beautiful women to be wary of, or even hostile towards, each other, especially as they both worked for Roland Samiat and were therefore in a competitive situation, but from the moment they met there had been positive feelings on both sides. It may have been that the cool, slim, blonde Ceri and the warm, spontaneous, brunette Enid were so different that there was no friction between them. Or it may have been that they complemented each other in some way. Or perhaps, because they shared an utterly ruthless streak in getting what they wanted, they were in that respect kindred spirits. Whatever the reason, they enjoyed each other's company.

"She's fine," Enid smiled. "She's being sedated for the present. She was shaken by the bomb blast and worried about Adam, so we're keeping her drowsy and we've given her a light dose of diazepam, a couple of milligrams, I think."

"Is the baby all right?"

"One of our doctors is checking now, but there are no signs of distress. She was almost outside the range of the blast, so she was shaken but not physically damaged."

"Excellent," said Ceri. "And you had no trouble in picking her up?"

"Everything went according to plan. Lister and I collected her in Aldwych as soon as the bomb went off. Roland's people had taken out the cameras in the area, so there's no record of the abduction. As for any witnesses, forget it. They were all so busy worrying about the terrorist outrage they had no time to notice a couple of paramedics lifting a shaken woman into an ambulance."

"And where's Lister now?" Ceri asked.

"Lister's dropping off the evidence of Eve's death. He's leaving samples of Eve's DNA and one of her credit cards, badly damaged but still identifiable, fairly close to ground zero. When they get round to examining the bits and pieces, there should be conclusive proof that Eve died in the blast."

"And how is Lister?" asked Ceri with a smile.

"Lister's fine," Enid grinned.

Lister was a source of amusement for both girls. With an Indian father and an English mother, Lister Bavad enjoyed the best features from his dual ethnicity. Physically he was more like Enid, with dark hair, laughing eyes and a full sensual mouth. Psychologically, he was closer to Ceri in that he found it easy to stand back and assess matters coldly and objectively. So he was the perfect foil for both girls and any feminine wiles they mockingly chose to deploy. They knew how to play him, and he knew how to handle them.

"So what's the plan now?" asked Enid.

"Just keep her sedated. Roland thinks she's more of a danger than Adam, so he's leaving Adam to David Minofel and he's going to deal with Eve himself. He's coming over this evening and we'll know more then."

16.   O cursèd spite

On leaving David Minofel, Adam walked back towards Leicester Square and found himself a coffee shop. He ordered a double expresso, found a seat outside with a good signal for his mobile and tried to phone Eve over and over again. A help line had been set up, but when he eventually managed to speak to someone, they had no news. They had only just become operational and had no information yet to give to the thousands of callers desperate to know the fate of their loved ones. They took his details and those of Eve, promised to add her name to the list of missing persons, and advised him to return home and wait for news.

All around him, people were talking about the bomb blast. They seemed as much excited as worried. He tried to calm his nerves. There could be a perfectly simple reason why he hadn't been able to contact Eve. The network was jammed. Perhaps she had lost her phone, or was somewhere without a signal. The blast could have destroyed some of the masts. She might be helping the injured, or she might have been held in a mass arrest of anyone in the vicinity. There could be many reasons, but in the pit of his stomach the rat of fear was beginning to gnaw away at his hope.

He had been there before when Bella died. It was a moment when the utter ruthlessness of existence asserted itself. In the midst of life there is death – meaningless, pointless, accidental, vicious, spiteful death – and it was only ever an instant away. If anything had happened to Eve it would break him. If he had lost his wife and the child she carried, it would be the end. No one could be expected to bear such cruelty, such suffering.

Adam calmed himself. Whatever had happened had happened. He should follow the advice he had been given. He would return home and wait. Luke, their golden retriever, had been left on his own for hours. He would be lonely and hungry. Adam was doing no good where he was. He needed to be at home.

oooOooo

The next few days were the worst in Adam's life. When Bella had died, he had been distraught, torn apart by anger and grief. But this was different. This was agonising; this was death by a thousand cuts. He waited for a phone call. None came. He phoned the helpline and they told him it would take them some time to identify all the victims; some they might never be able to name. They promised that as soon as there was any news about the fate of his wife they would contact him.

Adam's only consolation as the hours dragged by was Luke who did his best to comfort his master. Luke had used his enhanced canine powers to seek Eve. He had scanned for any sign of his mistress and had found nothing. This was not necessarily bad news. At least he hadn't picked up any indication she was dead. He hadn't picked up any indication at all. Of course, Luke couldn't inform Adam of his inconclusive scanning exercise, but even if Adam had been able to receive Luke's minded thoughts, there would have been no news, good or bad, to impart.

Although Luke was unable to communicate his thoughts to Adam, he could mind to Kit, which he did as soon as he learned that Eve was missing and had failed to locate her himself. The questors at Rambler's flat were well aware of the bomb outrage. They had heard the blast, which was clearly audible in Maida Vale, and were following the news as it was broadcast. Luke asked if Andrew could use the paradox device to scan for Eve. Andrew and Prune abandoned the work they were doing and used the full power of the device to look for Eve. They found nothing, simply confirming the results of Luke's more modest scanning exercise.

"No trace at all," Prune announced. "We have her up to a few minutes before the blast and then nothing. And it's not just her we've lost. There's a patch of central London that simply goes missing."

"A kind of space–time lacuna," Andrew explained. "There's a period of about twenty minutes, starting a bit before the blast, when the device sees nothing. There's no reason for it, no evidence of a fault or cloaking. No evidence of anything. It's just not there."

"What conclusion do you draw?" asked Luke, minding to Andrew directly.

"I'm not sure," Andrew replied. "But it's worrying."

"Do you think Eve is dead," Luke asked with a sinking heart.

"No," Andrew replied. "I have no evidence about Eve either way. No, when I said 'it's worrying' I just meant this is the first time the paradox device has been unable to do what I've asked of it."

17. The darkest day

On the afternoon of the third day after the blast, there was a knock on the door of the Smith's house. Adam hurried to the door. He had an inexplicable feeling that it was Eve. He opened the door.

"May we come in?" asked the policewoman.

Adam nodded. The policewoman and her male counterpart entered. Both were overweight, their corpulence exaggerated by the plethora of pouches attached to their belts.

"I should say first of all," said the policewoman, "that we don't have any definitive news."

Adam relaxed slightly.

"But we have found the charred remains of a credit card," the policewoman continued. It's only half a card and only the last three numbers of the card are readable but they are the last three numbers of the Visa card registered to your wife."

Adam shook his head. "What are you saying? Where did you find the card? Is there a body?"

The policeman spoke. "We found the card fairly close to ground zero. No chance of finding a whole body. Anyone in that position would have been obliterated."

The policewoman interrupted. "We have no evidence that proves your wife is dead. We have no DNA evidence. But we thought we should inform you."

"But why would she be in Covent Garden?" Adam objected. "We were to meet at the Aldwych. She shouldn't have been in Covent Garden."

"Perhaps she arrived early and thought she would do some shopping," said the policeman helpfully. "There's always a lot going on in Covent Garden. It's a real tourist attraction – or it was."

Again the policewoman interrupted: "With your permission, we would like to take something carrying your wife's DNA so we can check it against any samples we manage to collect."

"Take what you want," said Adam bitterly. "It sounds as though I should stop hoping."

"We will keep you informed of developments," said the policewoman getting up, now eager to leave. She was embarrassed by both the news she had brought and the insensitivity of her partner. "We're very sorry. We'll just collect a few of your wife's things from the bathroom. We will of course return them."

As they left, Adam heard the policewoman say to her companion. "Jesus! 'Obliterated'? What's the matter with you?"

Adam slumped down into his armchair. Of course it hadn't been Eve at the door. She would have used her key.

Luke padded over to comfort his master.

Eve had now been missing for seventy-two hours. He had tried to phone her mobile but at first the network had been clogged; then the number had been unavailable. He had phoned every hospital in the capital to try to find out if any unidentified person, one answering Eve's description, had been admitted, dead or alive. He had learned nothing, except that there was a general feeling of anger and fear, and that the emergency services had been stretched to their limit. And now the police had come and told him they had found a fragment of a credit card which was probably Eve's. The odds against anyone caught in the explosion having a credit card with the same last three numbers as Eve's were not astronomical, but they were high, too high.

Adam had scarcely eaten since his return to the house. He had sat by the phone, drinking coffee. He had fed Luke, but like his master the dog had not been hungry.

It was obvious. With a feeling of desolation that took Adam back to his worst moments following Bella's death, he realised that Eve and the baby she was carrying must be dead. By the cruellest contortions of fate, his daughter, his wife and their unborn child had been snatched from him by freaks of circumstance. Adam felt empty, without hope, without purpose.

Luke could see his master was toppling over the edge of despair. Luke was not a dog given to licking but on this occasion he made an exception. He gave Adam's hand a lick.

Adam didn't respond. He saw nothing; he felt nothing. Any last hope that his wife and their unborn child had survived was fading away.

At first he sobbed. Then his whole body shook as he began to cry uncontrollably.

18.   Staff relations

On the evening of the bomb blast day, Roland Samiat called in at his house in Mayfair. He was greeted by Ceri Agema and Enid Mavlow.

"What a joy to be greeted by two such delightful hostesses," said Roland, employing his trademark smile and surveying the pair through his inscrutable slitted eyes.

Ceri was wearing an orange top and white trousers; Enid was in a black dress edged with lace that ended well above her knees. As CEO of Slievins, Roland considered the appearance of his key personnel to be a matter of considerable importance. He insisted on highly intelligent, quick-witted staff. And he liked them to be well-dressed. He had a prepared speech which he delivered to all successful candidates who had applied to join the firm and which he never tired of repeating, with the occasional added metaphor, whenever the opportunity presented itself.

> We must always be smarter, in brainpower and in dress, than our clients. Only then will they happily pay our outrageous fees. They must feel privileged that we are willing to help them. Privileged and grateful. We should see ourselves as medieval clerics, dispensing pardons which cost us little in return for contributions which cost the sinners so much that it hurts. At our best, we are the high priests of the Aztecs, laying our clients, inadequate and inferior as they are, upon Slievins' sacrificial altar and ripping out their wallets. The more we charge them, the more they value our services. It is a truly happy confluence of drives which facilitates a benign social function – the redistribution of wealth from the rich to the even richer.

"Amen," said the girls in unison. Samiat's homily had taken on something of the status of the Lord's Prayer among Slievins' staff and an Amen at its conclusion did not seem at all inappropriate.

Roland laughed. "I hope you girls appreciated the reference

to the Aztecs in particular. It serves as a reminder to us all of the founder of our organisation, Nastafilu Verdicel who is thought to have hailed from somewhere in South America and who was, no doubt, an encourager, if not an instigator, of that continent's obsession throughout history with human sacrifice. What could be more typically indicative of man's true nature than the ripping out of the hearts of its enemies as a sacrifice to the sun, the symbol and giver of life? And talking of the ripping out of hearts, I hope you are taking good care of Eve. When I tell her that Adam is dead, that her hopes for the future are shattered, and that because of Adam's misdemeanours she is likely to end up penniless, if not imprisoned, her heart, if not ripped out, will certainly be broken."

"She's sedated," said Ceri. "We've told her nothing, except that there was a massive explosion and that she is in hospital having suffered a severe shock."

"Excellent," said Roland. "I will go and see her a little later. Ceri, I have in mind a small job for you involving some travel and some pleasure, and then I'm assigning you to Minofel till further notice."

"There could be a problem. Mr Minofel has already replaced Miss Tomic. He may be upset if I'm imposed on him."

"I think I can live with upsetting David just a little," said Roland. "In any case, you can help to make sure he keeps his eyes firmly focused on Adam, just as I want you to keep an eye on him."

"On Minofel or Adam?" asked Ceri innocently.

"Both," Roland replied.

Ceri smiled and left.

oooOooo

Roland took a long look at Enid Mavlow. She had a broad smile, strong white teeth and challenging, mocking eyes, which would have given her face an almost predatory expression had it not been for her obvious spontaneity and *joie de vivre*.

"How long have you been here with us in London?" he asked.

"Less than a couple of weeks."

"And how are you finding it?"

"I love it. It's very different from Rio but there is the same buzz."

"You're a very pretty girl," said Roland.

Enid smiled. "Thank you."

Roland studied her expression for a moment, connecting with

61

and searching those wise, young, laughing, blue eyes. "Have you explored the house?" he asked.

"Not really," Enid replied. I've seen the main reception rooms and the medical facilities – which, I have to say, are most impressive – but nothing else."

"The medical facilities are equal to those in any private hospital," said Roland proudly. "The essentials were installed by the previous owner, but I've expanded the capacity and ensured we have the most modern equipment for diagnosis and treatment." He took Enid's arm. "But there's much more to see. We call it a house, but it's really a palace with dozens of rooms. Let me show you around."

"Are you sure?" Enid asked. "I don't want to take up too much of your time."

Roland looked into her eyes again. Was she really concerned that she might be imposing on him? Or was she playing a game? "Never worry about taking up too much of my time," he advised. "That's never going to happen."

Enid took his words as another compliment.

"My time is precious. I get rid of anyone who wastes it," Roland explained.

oooOooo

After a brisk tour of the business wing, the dining hall and the ballroom, they reached Roland's private apartment.

"This is where I stay when I am in London," said Roland.

The apartment was tastefully furnished, with steel-framed, glass-topped tables, white leather-covered chairs and sofas, and close-woven carpets. The predominant colours were silver and white.

"Tell me, Enid, do you have a boyfriend?" Roland asked.

Enid raised her eyebrows to indicate some surprise at the question. Why would the CEO of Slievins ask her such a question? She knew how Slievins worked. He must know she had a fiancé. Human Resources had a file on all employees.

"Yes, I have a fiancé, Estevo. He's in Rio doing a PhD in anthropology at the National Museum, which is part of the UFRJ. He finishes this year."

"That's good," said Roland. "I expect you miss him very much," he added.

"I do."

"Would you like a drink? I'm happy to open a very fine bottle of champagne to welcome you officially to Slievins' head office."

"You're very kind," said Enid, "but I'm no connoisseur. It would be wasted on me."

"You would prefer a pina colada?" suggested Roland.

Enid grinned.

With the skills of a professional barman, Roland opened his drinks cabinet and mixed an excellent pina colada. "I'm afraid we will have to make do with tinned pineapple chunks," he apologised, as he handed Enid her glass.

"That's perfectly acceptable," said Enid.

They settled on one of the sofas.

Roland leant back into the sofa and looked at Enid. He said nothing.

It was Enid who spoke. "You're looking at me."

"I am," said Roland. And he now looked her up and down with meticulous care. His eyes ran up her shapely legs, which were exposed to halfway up her thighs. Beneath the short dress, he could see the outline of firm hips and a slim waist. The lace at the top of her dress, which covered her shoulders, revealed enough of her cleavage for Roland to see that her breasts were full and firm. As he raised his eyes to hers he smiled.

"Do you know why you're here?" he asked.

Enid was full of self-confidence but this question, posed by the CEO of Slievins, threw her off balance. He had just undressed her with his eyes. He had visually caressed every part of her body. But he had made no move to underpin an amorous intent. What did he want her to say – 'I guess you have copulation in mind'?

Eventually she said, "I think it best if you tell me."

Roland approved her answer. "Very well. I will tell you. You are here because out of millions of potential candidates you have been chosen. First, you were identified and selected by our people in Rio. Then out of about one hundred talented recruits like you from our offices around the world you were sent here by our Rio MD. You were brought here to work within the inner sanctum of Slievins. That makes you a very remarkable young lady."

Enid gave a small gasp of relief. Thank God she hadn't given him the obvious answer to his question.

"You will not yet have fully realised what this means," Roland continued, "so I shall enlighten you. You will have the opportunity to travel the world. You will have more money than you can imagine. You will have more power and responsibility than you have ever dreamt of. These are not blandishments. They are statements of fact. And they are certainly not idle promises. I know you, Enid. You are ambitious. So when I say you will have more power than you have ever thought possible, I know exactly how much power will be required to fulfil that part of the job description."

Samiat moved closer to Enid and put his hand on her knee. "All this will be yours." He paused and then added: "But there is a price to pay. You will have to give yourself to Slievins. Every Slievins' employee has to help Slievins fulfil its goals, no equivocation, no quibbling, no hesitation. But if you give yourself to Slievins, it's not a problem. Everything you are asked to do will be what you want to do because you will know you are helping Slievins to succeed. And Slievins' success is your success. Do you understand?"

Enid understood perfectly. Roland left his hand on her knee and put his free arm around Enid's shoulder, gently moving her closer. "A few minutes ago I asked you why you thought you were here. You didn't answer, but it had crossed your mind that I intended to seduce you."

His hand caressed the lower part of her thigh, as though he were stroking a cat. "I have no intention of seducing you," he continued. "The word seduce has an unpleasant connotation of imbalance in the relationship between the parties. What we are going to do" – and he now slid his hand up the inside of her thighs and began to explore – "is a mutual act of pleasure."

Enid's heart was racing. She had listened to what Roland had said, but his caressing of her body with his eyes and the movement of his hand on her legs had aroused her intensely and took precedence over his words.

"It seems that you are not averse to sharing a little time with me," said Roland, feeling how wet she was. He withdrew his hand from between her legs and his arm from around her shoulder. With both hands free, he lifted her skirt and slid her underwear down her legs. Enid offered no objection, no resistance. Then, just as he had done with his eyes, he caressed her body with his lips and tongue, working his way up from her feet.

Enid lay back. She had had her fair share of youthful romances involving fumbled love-making on the back seats of cars or in the single beds of student accommodation. Juan had been her first real lover, but she and Juan had been enthusiastic novices. Love-making with Estevo had been better because it was part of a proper relationship. But this was something else. This was exquisite, unadulterated physical pleasure.

Roland's tongue had completed the journey up the inside of her thighs and was now pleasuring her from the inside. She was shaking with tremors of delight. Why didn't she feel any guilt? She was engaged to Estevo. She shouldn't be making love with a man she scarcely knew. Except this wasn't making love. There was no love involved. This was a ruthlessly efficient and highly professional pleasuring of her body, administered by an expert in the field.

Roland stripped her and took off his own clothes. He lay on the sofa beside her and fondled her breasts. He kissed her nipples, already engorged, and then ran his tongue around and over them. She turned on her back and opened her legs. She wanted him to mount her, to penetrate her.

"I want you to think of this as a contract," Roland whispered in her ear. "A contract between us, a contract which you enter into of your own free will. Slievins will give you everything, but it demands everything. Are you happy to agree to such terms?"

"Yes," Enid gasped.

Roland moved between her legs and drove into her. As he stroked her, she lifted her buttocks to join him so that they ground into each other. Spirals of pleasure spread from her loins, riding up and down through her whole body. She felt as though her brain was being overloaded, swamped in a tide of sensual joy.

After she had experienced multiple orgasms, Roland climaxed himself. As he ejaculated, he whispered in Enid's ear once more, "The deal is sealed. Young Estevo was a very lucky man."

They lay beside each other for a few minutes. For the first time in her life, Enid felt fulfilled. Until this moment, she had been confined in a room, a pleasant enough room, but a space limited by four walls. Now someone had opened a door and she had stepped out into a beautiful, limitless world full of all the colours of the rainbow, a world of infinite possibilities. And she had discovered that her own body could experience outrageous levels of sensual pleasure, degrees of physical ecstasy she had never even dreamt of.

"I have to leave you now," said Roland, getting dressed. "I must visit our patient and see how she is doing. Take your time. Have a shower if you wish. When you are ready, leave. There will be a car waiting for you in the courtyard, to take you home."

Enid sat up. She didn't know what to say, so she simply nodded.

"Just remember, Enid, we have a deal," Roland Samiat said as he left.

19.   Roland meets Eve

"Please don't let me disturb you," said Roland settling into a chair beside Eve's bed.

"My name is Roland Samiat. I am the CEO of Slievins. You are in one of our medical facilities. You were caught up in a terrorist outrage. A bomb. But don't worry. Our medical people have given you a thorough examination. You and the baby are fine."

Eve was finding it difficult to take in what the man was saying. The sedative and the diazepam were still in her system. "Where's Adam?" she managed.

"We are trying to contact him. It's chaos in London. The bomb took out most of Covent Garden. The phone network is damaged and the bits that are working are jammed with calls. I'm sure Adam is fine, but we haven't been able to reach him yet."

"I need to go home," said Eve.

"Of course. As soon as you are ready, I'll arrange for one of our ambulances to take you."

"I thought you said I was fine. Why shouldn't I go now?"

"Well, first of all we haven't had the results of all the tests yet. As I say, we've found no problems, but you were caught in a bomb blast, so with your permission we would like to make absolutely sure there are no adverse effects, however minor."

"And why am I here? Why am I in this hospital? What has Slievins got to do with a bomb blast?"

"Nothing at all," Roland laughed. "As soon as we heard the explosion and reports began to come in we put our considerable resources at the disposal of the emergency services. Slievins has a small fleet of private ambulances and we maintain this state-of-the-art medical facility here in Mayfair. We picked up a number of casualties at the periphery of the bomb blast. We treated them and then either discharged them or placed them in a London hospital. When my staff told me you were one of the casualties, I had you brought here."

"Why?" said Eve. Despite the sedative she sounded aggressive. Her head was clearing. Slievins were the enemy. They worked for the Praesidium, and the Praesidium had tried to kill her and Adam and the other questors. Whatever this man said, this was not a good place for her to be.

Roland compiled a smile, composed of understanding and benevolence. "Of course," he said. "You are suspicious, even hostile. But you are wrong. Slievins means you no harm. I know that Adam has decided to sever his links with us, and as David Minofel told you at the very start, that is not a problem. Our contract with Adam ended the moment Adam ended it. But Slievins is a good company and takes its duty of care to its staff very seriously, even after they have left our employment. We helped you at first simply as a victim of an appalling terrorist outrage, but when we discovered it was you, Eve, Adam's wife, we felt obliged to offer all the care and protection Slievins can provide."

Eve remained unconvinced.

"I'll tell you what I'm going to do," said Roland. "While we wait for the results of your final tests, I'm going to use all Slievins not inconsiderable resources to locate Adam and bring him to you. You will be out of here tomorrow morning, I promise. If Adam's at home and the traffic is still in chaos, I'll have you flown to Harrow by helicopter. I can't say fairer than that."

With that, Roland stood up, patted Eve's hand and left. As he passed the matron's station he said quietly to the nurse in charge, "Maintain the sedation and the minor tranquilliser. We need more time."

20. HMRC comes calling

Three days after the police had visited Adam to tell him of the credit card fragment, the doorbell rang, followed by an unnecessary knock on the front door.

On this occasion, Adam assumed it was not Eve, but the police, coming to confirm Eve's death and the death of their baby. Again he was wrong. This time it was a man and a woman from Her Majesty's Revenue and Customs.

"Are you Adam Smith?" the woman asked.

"I am."

"May we come in?" said the man. "We have one or two matters, relating to your tax affairs to discuss with you."

"This is not a good time," Adam replied. "My wife is missing. She was somewhere near the bomb in Covent Garden."

"I'm very sorry to hear that," said the man, "but it shouldn't take very long and it would be best to clear these matters up if we can."

Adam shrugged. "As you wish, but if you are going to ask any detailed questions, I can tell you now that I probably can't answer them."

"Let's try anyway," said the woman as she and her companion seated themselves at the kitchen table. "You worked in Geneva for some months earlier this year," she prompted.

"Yes, I took up the post as Marketing Director of ZeD."

The man smiled. The woman smirked. "You're the one who blew the whistle, aren't you?" she said.

"Yes, you could say that," Adam conceded. Yes, "whistle-blower" was the briefest and easiest way of describing his role in Geneva. There was no need for a more detailed account. "You say there are some matters you wish to discuss?" Adam was keen to move the conversation on.

"Yes," said the woman. "There's a general question about your tax status. You spent less than six months in Geneva. But that's not the issue here. It's been drawn to our attention that substantial sums of money have been paid into your account from more than one source and without any apparent explanation. Because of concerns about money laundering, we investigate any such cases. Can you explain this money – what it was for, who paid it and what tax you have paid, or intend to pay, on these sums?"

"If you want to ask detailed questions, you'll have to talk to ZeD. The MD is, or was, Dr Dubois. But I can tell you that these were bonuses for meeting targets."

"Thousands of pounds, hundreds of thousands of pounds, even the odd million for 'meeting targets'? And all that, within a few weeks, or at most a few months, of arriving in a new post at ZeD. Isn't that a little bit odd."

Adam shook his head. This was utterly unreal. It was almost certain his wife and the baby she was carrying had been blown to pieces in a terrorist outrage that was filling every news bulletin, occupying most of the pages in the press, and trending in every conceivable direction on social media. London was still in shock and, to some extent, chaos. And these two bureaucrats had traipsed across half of London to grill him about his tax affairs. With some effort, he controlled himself.

"I realise that you have to check on people to make sure they are paying their taxes, but as I said when you arrived, I don't have the sort of details you want. You need to talk to ZeD."

"Well that's part of the problem. It's the Swiss authorities who pointed us in your direction," said the man. "When PBS were doing due diligence on ZeD before the takeover, they found a number of irregularities in ZeD's accounts. Some of these involved you. The bonus payments to you came from a contingency budget and there's no paperwork to explain the payments – simply a record of the payment itself. And even if there is a satisfactory explanation for these bonus payments, there appears to be another payment of €100,000 for which there is no paperwork at all. I should point out that the tax on that alone amounts to well over £30,000."

Adam frowned. "That's probably the money I won in a bet with David Minofel. He's a consultant with Slievins."

"We thought you might refer us to Slievins," said the woman. "We've already talked to them. They say they have made no payments to you of any sort. It seems they work on the basis of collecting fees from the companies that hire them and taking a percentage of the remuneration enjoyed by the executives whose careers they manage. Sounds to us as though there must be some conflict of interest, but all parties are made aware of the arrangement and it's not illegal. In any case, however they conduct their business, they make no payment to those they place. The flow of money is in the opposite direction."

"Then you should talk to Minofel, David Minofel," said Adam. "He's a senior consultant at Slievins and, I think, a partner. He paid me the €100,000 as the result of a bet I won. I don't know if he paid it personally or whether, as I assumed, Slievins authorised the bet, but he will certainly confirm that the €100,000 came from him."

The two HMRC inspectors looked at each other. Then the woman said: "David Minofel was present at the meeting we had with Slievins. Indeed, he took an active part in the discussions. He categorically denied making any payment, corporate or personal, to you or to anyone else."

"I think we should leave it at that for now," said the man. "We wanted to let you know the situation and that we will need to have further discussions with you. It's only fair to say that you may well wish to take professional financial and legal advice before our next meeting."

The pair of inspectors stood up. The man said, "I'm really sorry about your wife. If there's any chance at all, I hope you have good news."

The woman added, "Of course, we're sorry to be troubling you at this time, but please take our enquiries seriously. After all, it was tax evasion that eventually put Al Capone behind bars."

"I think it best you leave now," said Adam.

21. Admin affairs

Roland Samiat was in a relaxed mood. He sat back in his executive chair, rotated so he could look out of his office window, and surveyed the clear blue sky over the city of London.

"What a lovely day!" he remarked as Ceri Agema entered his office, responding to his summons.

Ceri smiled. Roland wondered whether Enid had told her of her initiation the previous evening, or whether Ceri had worked it out for herself. Ceri was smart; in any case, it wouldn't be difficult to guess what had happened. Women who had enjoyed Roland's intimate attentions tended to have something different about them.

"All seems to be running smoothly," Ceri said. "Art Shoat has sent his first report from the Rub' al-Khali. He has safely delivered the Crucible of Eternal Light to Charles Fundi, the city commander. It's now safely installed in Ubar – that's what the technicians have decided to call the city."

"Ubar?" Roland queried. He had toyed with the idea of naming the installation Samiopolis.

"According to legend, long ago there was a thriving city, called Ubar, in the south Arabian desert. It incurred the wrath of Allah for some reason and was buried beneath the sands. Given the location of our new headquarters, our people thought it was appropriate to give Ubar a new lease of life."

"Always happy to frustrate the irrational wrath of God," Roland chuckled.

"It seems there's a bit of aggravation between Fundi and Ben Rael."

"Really?" Roland was surprised. "Don't tell me that Ben's renowned charm has abandoned him."

"There was an incident when Ben arrived in the desert and was heading for the City under the Sand. He found a Bedouin within a few hundred metres of the entrance to the city. His presence may have been entirely innocent but Ben decided not to take any chances. When Ben told Fundi of the incident, he expected the commander to apologise for a lapse in security. As Ben put it, the commander really shouldn't rely on the odd visitor from London to deal with security breaches. Fundi was not amused. Instead of apologising, he accused Ben of turning an innocent search for a lost sheep into a potentially disastrous situation. He said his people had been monitoring the Bedouin and were about to put a replacement sheep in his path. Instead, Ben Rael had summarily executed the man and now members of his tribe would surely come looking for him."

"He has a point," observed Roland. "If one of them will risk his life for a sheep, then the Bedouin are unlikely to ignore the disappearance of one of their own. They will surely search for their fellow tribesman. Have our people dealt with the problem?"

"I don't know. All I have is a report from Ben criticising the security arrangements at Ubar and a report from Fundi criticising Ben."

"Well, tell them to sort it out. Tell them to stop bickering. Once the Crucible of Eternal Light is installed and the cloaking system is connected to it, the city will be impregnable. Until then, it is crucial that we keep the existence of the city and what we are doing in it secret. How is Art? What is he doing? Diplomacy is not his strong suit, but tell him to make sure Ben and Charles Fundi are working together."

Ceri acknowledge Roland's instructions and turned to leave.

"There's a little matter I'd like your help with," said Roland.

Ceri turned back.

"Have a seat," said Roland.

Ceri sat, crossing her long legs, and waited.

"You may have wondered about last night," he started.

"Yes, I did," said Ceri, "Have you told Eve that Adam is dead? We can't keep her sedated indefinitely, and as I guess we have no intention of letting her go, there's no point in waiting."

Roland frowned. "No, I haven't told her Adam is dead. You can safely leave the timing to me. No, I was asking you whether you had wondered why I bedded Enid."

"No, certainly not," Ceri responded immediately. "Your personal affairs are none of my concern."

"I thought you might have wondered why I chose her rather than you – indeed why I have never chosen you in all the time you have worked for me. You are, after all, just as attractive, albeit in a rather cooler, more refined way."

"My relations with men are rather complex, and in my view, it's best to keep one's personal life separate from the office. Not that I'm criticising you or anyone else," she added hastily.

Roland laughed. "You're right, of course. Sex and work make odd bedfellows. But as with all rules, there are exceptions. There was a healthy dose of lust involved last night in possessing Enid, but I also had other less ephemeral motives." Roland paused. He looked deep into Ceri's cold green eyes and smiled. Then he continued: "You and Enid get on well together." It was more a statement than a question.

"Yes, we do. She's only been here a couple of weeks but she's clever and fun. Yes. We get on well."

Roland emitted a murmur. He seemed to be thinking deeply. Eventually he spoke. "Good. As you know I'm rather keen on killing two birds with one stone or, in this case, one stone with two birds. I have a small assignment for you. Enid has a fiancé. He's a PhD student in Brazil. I want you to go to Rio de Janeiro, seek him out and seduce him."

Ceri gave a gasp of surprise. She eventually managed to ask "Why?"

"Enid has a bright future with Slievins, but she is still attached to the past. Last night, I broke one of the links in the chain that goes back to Rio, but I want to make sure that Slievins can have all of her. Go to Rio and break another link in the chain that holds her fiancé, Estevo, to her."

"Why me?" Ceri asked. The assignment was bizarre.

"I thought you would be delighted. A free trip to Rio, first class, of course – a five-star hotel – and a not unpleasant brief. I'm sure Enid's fiancé is well up to scratch."

"Surely we have operatives in Rio who are perfectly capable of seducing a young man. This is a waste of a plane ticket."

"You seem to be slipping into an unfortunate habit of questioning my decisions," said Roland softly.

"I'm just saying …" Ceri began.

Roland silenced her. "I am sending you because you and Enid are close. You will probably find it quite difficult to assist me in destroying what Enid currently sees as her happiness. It will be doubly hurtful to Enid that the person who has corrupted her fiancé is her new friend, the very person she would naturally turn to for comfort and consolation if you weren't the cause of her distress. That is why I have chosen you. This is a test for you as well as Enid. Slievins likes to make sure all its employees are truly committed to the cause."

"There's something else," said Ceri.

"Yes, I know," said Roland. "You have an idiosyncratic predilection for killing the men with whom you have slept. Don't worry. I'm well aware of your little quirks. Indeed, to be honest, your little quirks probably played a major part in my decision long ago not to prise apart those beautifully long legs of yours and penetrate your soul. And don't worry, I have no wish to discourage your homicidal tendencies. I'm not at all judgemental."

"I need to understand exactly what you want me to do," said Ceri.

"You do, my dear," said Roland. "Believe me, you do."

22.　A black day

On the morning of the seventh day after the blast, the police confirmed that Eve was dead. They had managed to match her DNA to the DNA placed by Slievins on what was left of her credit card.

Adam had been given the news by the overweight policewoman who had visited him before. This time she came unaccompanied. She had followed procedure, expressing sympathy and asking if he had anyone who should be with him. Adam could see she was doing her best, but he just wanted to be left alone.

In the afternoon Kit arrived. "There is nothing I can say," he said simply and embraced Adam.

The two of them sat down at the kitchen table. Luke greeted Kit with a brief wag of his tail and settled down between the two men. In the morning, as soon as the policewoman had left, Luke had minded confirmation of Eve's death to Kit, and Kit had set out for Harrow immediately.

"It's definite, I suppose?" Kit asked eventually

"The police think so," Adam replied. "Fairly close to the centre of the blast they found half a credit card with the last three numbers the same as those on Eve's card. And now they've confirmed a DNA match. I knew when she didn't contact me that something was wrong. I just kept hoping. I can't take this. It's too much. I've lost everything – first Bella, now Eve and the baby."

They sat together for an hour. They said little. Kit made a pot of coffee and they drank it.

"I just don't know what to do," Adam confessed.

"You need to grieve and you need to rest," said Kit. "Some people are lucky. They sail through life relatively unscathed. They have their ups and downs, and of course no one is exempt from the prospect of ageing and death. But generally they're pretty lucky. Others, not so much. Others are very unlucky. You have been battered by more than your fair share. No, more than that – you've been hit by more than anyone should have to bear."

"I'm not complaining," Adam intervened. He needed to clarify what he meant. "It's just that I don't know what to do. Literally. I don't feel anything inside me that can motivate me to do anything.

If there was a body, I guess I would want to bury Eve. But there is no body. According to the police, she was 'obliterated' – blown into pieces so small they couldn't be assembled into anything you could call remains."

"You mustn't despair," said Kit, worried about Adam's train of thought.

Adam laughed. "It's probably a bit late for that advice, but don't worry, there isn't enough of me left to commit suicide. Suicide would require a decision. I haven't got it in me to make a decision."

Again, they settled into silence. This time Kit spoke first.

"You have to ask yourself why you have been treated so harshly by life."

"As you said, it's just bad luck."

"Maybe," said Kit. "Bella's death was an accident – an act of God, if you like. But this time there was human agency behind the catastrophe. I don't mean that Eve was targeted. That seems to have been just bad luck. But the cause of the destruction was not just chance. It was an act perpetrated by terrorists. Did the police say who was behind it?"

"No, they told me nothing," Adam replied. "But I had a text message from Andrew saying it was something to do with Islamic fanatics opposed to Western education."

Kit was puzzled. "Do you mean our Andrew, Andrew Rimzil?

"Yes, we had arranged to meet. He was attending a conference at UCL," said Adam. "He told me the delegates had been evacuated because of a bomb threat."

"But the bomb went off at Covent Garden. Not much point in blowing up Covent Garden if they were trying to strike at Western education," observed Kit.

"No, I guess the threat to academia was a diversion," said Adam. "To be honest, I don't care who did it. What does it matter? Eve's dead. Our baby is dead. As John Noble was always telling me, 'Man is what he is; depraved, violent and corrupt'. Who cares who did it?"

The house telephone rang. Adam answered it. He confirmed his name. Then he listened. A good two minutes passed. Then he said "Very well" and put the receiver down.

"Was that the police?" asked Kit, hoping they might have made a mistake about Eve.

"No," said Adam. "It's HMRC. They're not at all happy about my income and my tax affairs. They want me to attend a meeting in their offices. And they suggest I bring a lawyer with me."

"Good heavens!" said Kit. "I'm no expert in such matters but that sounds a bit ominous."

"It's really serious," Luke minded to Kit. "I was here when they first raised the matter with Adam. It's all to do with his activities in Geneva working for ZeD. They suspect him of corruption or money laundering."

"Could you do me a favour?" Adam asked Kit.

"Of course. Anything."

"Could you look after Luke for me, just while I sort things out. You two get on well and I'm going to have to spend some time away from the house if I have to attend meetings in town. He'll be happier with you."

"You don't need to ask," said Kit. "Luke and I are old friends. But are you sure? He's a very wise dog and a great companion. Don't you need him?"

"Yes, I'm sure. It's all I can manage to look after myself. You take good care of him and I'll have him back as soon as I'm sorted. I promise."

When Kit left in the late afternoon he took Luke with him. "Keep in touch. Let us know how things are going," he said to Adam. "We're all shacked up with Rambler at his flat in Maida Vale. If you need anything, anything at all, we'll be there."

Adam thanked him and closed the door. He went back into a dark, empty, sad house.

oooOooo

A few minutes after Kit had left the telephone rang again.

"Hello Adam, it's David," said Minofel. "Now would be a good time for us to meet, don't you think?"

23. Ceri in Rio

Ceri Agema checked into the Belmond Copacabana Palace Hotel. She was tempted to take one of the hotel's De Luxe Beach View rooms that had stunning panoramas of the famous beach, but she settled for a City View room. After all, she was in Rio on business.

It was Slievins' policy to treat their staff well. Even for junior staff, air tickets were business class. For Ceri, a member of Roland Samiat's inner circle, it was first class. And she could choose any room she wanted, excluding only bridal and penthouse suites. "Have fun" had been the only instruction Roland Samiat had given her.

As soon as she had unpacked, Ceri had a shower in the en-suite bathroom. Just as she emerged from the shower wrapped in a towel, there was a knock at her door. Ceri looked through the spyhole and saw a waiter with a tray. On the tray was a bottle of champagne. She opened the door.

In walked a handsome young Brazilian who seemed slightly embarrassed, but only slightly, that he had caught a guest undressed. "The champagne is with the compliments of the house," he announced as he put the champagne and a glass on the table. "There are also flowers."

He retrieved the flowers which he had left outside the door and returned. "These are not from the house." He flashed Ceri a smile, displaying his brilliant white teeth. "For such a beautiful lady, these must be from an admirer," he hazarded.

Ceri smiled back. Men were rather like dogs. They had simple needs. Most of them came already half-trained. It was easy enough to complete the process with the hint of treats, and then they would do whatever you wanted.

Encouraged by her smile, the Brazilian asked if there was anything else he could do. Ceri had allowed the towel to slip a little, so he could see the swell of her still wet breasts, and the careless wrap of the towel around her body allowed a delectable glimpse of her long and lissom legs as she moved across the room.

"I think I can guess what you have in mind," said Ceri, "but I'm afraid I can't accommodate you."

The Brazilian thought it was an odd way to talk but he understood it was probably a No. Not entirely convinced it was a final rejection, he hazarded asking why. He intended to continue, arguing that it could be fun, a brief but delightful liaison without strings, et cetera, but Ceri cut him short.

"I can't tell you why," she said. "It's a secret."

So it wasn't a final rejection. The lady was still prepared to flirt a little. Who knows where such flirting might lead? "A secret? Your secret would be safe with me," he assured her.

"I'm sure it would," said Ceri Agema, "because if I told you, I'm afraid I'd have to kill you."

They both laughed. "OK, another time maybe," he said.

"Maybe," said Ceri, "but best you leave now. I have to dress and then do some work."

When the amorous bellboy had departed, Ceri looked at the card tucked in with the flowers. It was from David Minofel. The message was short. "Looking forward to working with you on your return."

24.   A not yet important question

When Kit and Luke reached Rambler's flat in Maida Vale, he found Andrew and Prune in the middle of an esoteric technical debate about the capabilities of the paradox device. Luke understood little and Kit even less, but the nub of the issue seemed to be the cause of the lacuna in the device's scanning of the bomb incident in Covent Garden. Andrew was unable to find any reason for the gap in coverage. They had a perfect recording up to a few minutes before the explosion and then nothing for twenty minutes. Then the scanning resumed. Prune suggested that the device had developed a fault. It was after all just a machine. Andrew was hurt as much as he was puzzled. He was convinced he had developed a relationship with the device. The device seemed to know what he wanted and then, helpfully but not always wisely, acted to fulfil his wishes. The suggestion that the device could have a fault and not warn him before of the problem or apologise for it afterwards upset him. It was insensitive, even rude. Not what you expect of a friend!

"Adam has asked us to look after Luke," Kit announced, interrupting the technical debate.

"How is Adam?" asked Rambler. "He must be distraught." Rambler still felt keenly the loss of his nephew Numpty and empathised with Adam's loss wholeheartedly.

"Not good," said Kit. "He'd guessed for a few days that Eve was dead but he kept hoping. Now they've confirmed her death, well, at least the agony of hoping has ended. He needs to grieve, rest and gradually try to put his life back together."

"Fine chance," minded Luke. "Tell them about his problems with HMRC."

"What problems?" asked Andrew. He had picked up Luke's minded message to Kit.

"Problems?" queried Rambler and Prune in unison. Although Luke could, if he put his mind to it, initiate some level of telepathic communication with both of them, unlike Andrew neither of them could pick up his minded thoughts to others.

"Well, it seems the Revenue are taking an interest in Adam's financial affairs. He's been summoned to a meeting with HMRC and told to bring legal representation."

"That sounds worrying," Rambler offered.

"Always keep out of the hands of doctors, priests and taxmen," said Prune. "They're like hyenas. They find your weaknesses and then pull you down."

"That's a bit harsh on doctors and priests," Kit objected. "They're both trying to help – one, the body, the other, the soul."

"There speaks a man who has had little to do with either," said Prune. "Most people don't have a soul, and even if they do, they don't believe it, so the priest is pretty much redundant. That just leaves doctors to shoulder the burden of all mankind's mental and physical ailments and most of them just aren't anywhere near up to it."

Kit laughed. "There speaks a man who's had some bad experiences with doctors and priests."

"I come from Ireland," said Prune, as though that explained everything.

"Do you know what HMRC are querying?" Rambler said, calling the meeting to order.

"I know that what went on in Geneva involved some pretty dirty business," said Andrew. "I gleaned that much while I was working there in Minofel's house. But I don't know what part Adam played – he was remarkably well-paid, considering he didn't launch the drug he was hired to market and, in the end, brought the company to its knees."

"The inspectors talked about tax evasion and money laundering," Luke minded to Kit.

"The poor fellow," said Rambler. "He's lost his wife and he's now going to be harried by the Revenue."

"I've told him we'll help in any way we can," said Kit. "By the way," he addressed Andrew, "on the morning of the terrorist attack, were you attending a conference at UCL and did you send Adam a text message cancelling a planned meeting with him."

Andrew frowned. "No. I was in Reading trying to source a new circuit for the paradox device. Why on earth do you ask?"

"It's not important," Kit replied. "It's just something Adam said."

"Not important?" Luke queried, confining his question to Kit.

"No. At least not yet," said Kit.

25. Friend or foe

When Adam entered the Slievins' head office building, the receptionist acknowledged him immediately. It was the same receptionist who had dealt with Aletheia, when the goddess of truth had called upon Minofel. The girl had still not recovered from the experience. Her self-assurance had been shattered. Aletheia had been impressive and intimidating, and her inexplicable ability to interfere with the organisation's electricity supply had been utterly unnerving. The way in which Aletheia had walked into David Minofel's office and walked out a few minutes later with Miss Tomic in tow had been extraordinary. After all, Miss Tomic had been with David Minofel as his assistant, his protégée, his favourite from the year dot. In had walked Aletheia; out had walked Miss Tomic. And neither of them had been seen since. The world had become an unpredictable, uncertain place.

The other reason for the receptionist's assiduous attention to those who approached the reception desk was the bomb outrage which had devastated part of London. If the terrorists could blow up Covent Garden, they could blow up anywhere, and Slievins, an organisation which dealt with the great and good, the movers and shakers, was really a more sensible target for fanatics than a former vegetable market turned tourist trap. So everyone was a danger.

"I'm here to see David Minofel," said Adam.

"He's expecting you," said the receptionist, nervously checking for any flickering in the power supply. "I'll take you up straightaway." She led Adam to the lift and accompanied him to the top floor. Adam made his way through the large antechamber to Minofel's office, walking past the unstaffed desk previously occupied by Miss Tomic but which was now allocated, at Roland Samiat's insistence, to the absent Ceri Agema.

"Adam," beamed David Minofel. He had his back to Adam and was looking out of the panoramic window of his office. "Don't you just love the view from up here? You can see all humanity, or at least the part of it that scurries through the streets of the city. They remind me, just a little, of the rats that spread the plague in 1348." He spun his chair round to face Adam. "Anyway, it's good to see you."

Adam shook his head. What could he say? Minofel had deceived and manipulated him throughout his employment at ZeD, involving him in a plethora of serious crimes. He had then introduced him to the Praesidium, an organisation that had imprisoned his friend Kit, an innocent man, brutalised him, falsely accused him of murder and came within a whisker of hanging him. True, Minofel had enabled him to earn more money than he had ever dreamt of, but at what a price?

"Come on, Adam." Minofel read Adam's mind. "Let bygones be bygones. Look on the bright side. You earned a lot, you learned a lot – and at least it hasn't been dull."

Adam sat down. "I'm not here to exchange pleasantries. This is not a good time for me."

"Of course, of course," Minofel soothed. "I'm so sorry about Eve. She was a lovely lady …"

Adam cut in. "I need some help in sorting out my problem with the Revenue. They've summoned me to a meeting next week. And they've advised me to bring legal representation."

"Oh dear," murmured Minofel. "Do you know exactly which bit of your financial affairs they're delving into?

"Not really, not in any detail," Adam replied. "They queried my bonuses and they specifically mentioned the €100,000 I won in our bet."

"In normal circumstances, the bonuses wouldn't be a problem," said Minofel quietly. "I'm not sure all the paperwork was in order, but they were certainly authorised by Dubois. The problem is that Dubois is in northern Cyprus, having fled Switzerland with what he felt was a reasonable but sadly unauthorised severance package. The Swiss police are after him for about twenty million Swiss francs."

"The bonuses were paid by the company as part of my remuneration. Surely it doesn't matter where Dubois is now. He was the MD at the time."

"That's a good point," Minofel conceded, "but the authorities are obsessed with money laundering and they just might get it into their heads that you were brought in to ZeD as part of a sophisticated money laundering operation. After all, you were a surprise appointment because you didn't have a track record in the industry or marketing, and you were paid some very large sums by the company almost before you got your feet under the table."

"You sound as though you're preparing a case for the prosecution," said Adam bitterly.

"Not at all," Minofel replied. "I'm just trying to point out the line HMRC might take. Have you retained a lawyer?

"No, I haven't. I haven't done anything wrong."

"Really?" queried Minofel with a smile. "Some might think you were being a little parsimonious with the truth. I couldn't possibly comment."

"Do you think this is a laughing matter?" Adam was beginning to feel the stirrings of anger. It was a relief to feel something other than unremitting grief.

"Not at all," Minofel replied amiably. "But we have been through much together, some of which people of a particularly fastidious nature might find morally questionable."

"When we met outside UCH, you said we should make sure our stories tallied. I'm not sure what you meant but that's why I'm here. You can at least clear up the matter of the €100,000. You have to confirm that it was payment for a bet I had with you. HMRC have told me you denied making any payments to me. Why did you do that?"

"Hold on and slow down," said David Minofel. "It's not quite as simple as that."

"It's perfectly simple. It's the truth," said Adam.

"There you go again. You and your truth! Haven't you realised by now, the truth can get you into all sorts of difficulties?"

"Not as many as lying, especially lying to the Revenue."

"I don't think you're seeing this problem in context," said Minofel.

"What context? We had a bet. You gave me odds of ten to one. I put up €10,000. I won the bet. It's pretty straightforward."

"I guess most of the papers haven't covered it here yet," said Minofel. "The bomb blast has taken up almost all the space. So you'd better read this."

He gave Adam a press-cutting from *The Guardian*.

> In another twist in the ZeD scandal, the Swiss police have reopened the case of the murdered Giovanni Spinetti. Serious questions have been raised about the safety of the conviction of

> Guy McFall, the product manager responsible
> for planning the launch of ZeD's ill-fated beta-
> blocker MC57. McFall was sentenced to 15 years
> by the Swiss court.

"Oh!" said Adam. He had put out of his mind what he had done in Geneva. What's done is done and can't be undone, he had told himself. What's the point of dwelling on something you can't do anything about. If you let it, guilt will eat you from the inside out. And Spinetti had asked for it. If he had been able to control his jealousy and spite, there would have been no need to eliminate him. He had been a vain, violent man, beating up his fiancée and wrecking the marriage of his love rival. He had put at risk the livelihoods of thousands of ZeD employees. No, there were no regrets about Spinetti.

On the other hand, Adam did have regrets about Guy McFall. Adam had seen Guy as an honest, decent person. Putting Guy in the frame for Spinetti's murder was Minofel's idea, not his, so most of the blame lay with Minofel. But Adam had done nothing to help Guy and he felt bad about that.

"Yes, 'Oh!'" Minofel echoed. "I've no more information at present. I don't know why they've reopened the case or which lines the police are following up, but I'm certainly going to find out. And let me say straightaway that if their enquiries lead to you, I will do all in my power to protect you."

"You mean us, don't you?" Adam was finding it hard to take in the reopening of the case and what it might mean, but he was clear on one point – Minofel was as much to blame as he.

"Not really," said Minofel. "After all, it was you and Jedwell who killed Spinetti. And Jedwell's dead, so that just leaves you. But don't worry. You have my word."

Adam wondered exactly how much value he could place in the word of David Minofel, a man who thought nothing of taking someone's life, who had lied to Adam throughout his tenure as Marketing Director at ZeD and who had introduced him to the sinister Praesidium with its depressingly low assessment of humanity's worth.

"So you see," Minofel continued, "even our little bet needs to be handled with care. The police may question the likelihood of someone like you happily wagering €10,000 on a bet. They will want to know what the bet was about. If we tell them that I bet you that you would fail to launch MC57 on schedule and offered you odds of ten to one, they might consider the chance to win €100,000 a pretty powerful motive for you to do whatever was necessary to launch the drug on time – even to the extent of killing the only impediment to the drug's launch. They might even construe the bet as a bribe paid by me to you to make sure MC57 was a success, despite the fatality in the Basel trial. That could make me appear almost as guilty as you, and obviously I can't agree to that."

"Are you saying you will deny the bet?" Adam was incredulous. "But you know it's true."

"Of course I know it's true," Minofel replied. "But how does that help? The issue is not whether it's true, it's whether it's believable – and what conclusions the police might draw from it. And there's a further complication. I accepted that you won the bet when MC57 got EMA approval and you dealt with the Dr Reed problem, but you didn't actually launch the drug successfully. Of course, that didn't matter at all, as the purpose of the exercise was to bring ZeD to its knees and that was certainly a success, but strictly speaking you should have returned the money to me, together with your €10,000 stake. Surely you can see it would be far better to tell HMRC that the €100,000 was just another bonus, one that hadn't been put through the books at all? You can say that in the context of the other much more substantial bonuses you were earning, it scarcely merited an entry in the ledger. Something along those lines would be much safer."

"But there was no paperwork on that money, none at all. At least the bonuses went through ZeD's account. Without the bet, I can't explain the €100,000."

"I've just told you what to say. They may not believe it, but they can't disprove it. And it's certainly more credible than some rigmarole about me betting that you would fail to launch MC57, giving you odds of ten to one, and then paying you €100,000 despite your failure to launch the drug – especially when I deny all knowledge of such a bet."

That was how the meeting ended. Adam felt he was being hung out to dry with HMRC. But that concern wasn't uppermost in his mind as he descended in the lift and walked through Slievins' reception area out into the street. No, two other thoughts struck him.

The first was a dreadful fear that the murder of Spinetti was coming back to haunt him. Taking a life is a terrible thing, but seen in context killing Spinetti had been necessary: it had been the logical thing to do; it had been the right thing to do. Unfortunately time had moved on and the context had changed. If it went to court, what had been a decision based on a refined analysis of a complex situation would no doubt be crudely and simplistically labelled as murder.

The second thought had even more impact on Adam. He suddenly realised that for the first time since Eve had disappeared, he had thought about something else for almost twenty minutes.

In his office, David Minofel phoned for a temp to provide him with some coffee. It was typical of Samiat to insist that he dismiss his new secretary, take on Ceri Agema as his personal assistant and then immediately send her off to Brazil on a mission of his own. While waiting for the nervous temp to fulfil his coffee order, he stood up and looked out of his window down to the street below. He calculated how long it would take Adam to descend to the ground floor and make his way out of the building. As he studied the street far below, he reckoned that one of the rats he could see scurrying around must be Adam on his way home to a cold, empty, silent house.

26. Breaking news

"How are you, my dear?" Roland Samiat was sitting on a chair at Eve's bedside in the Slievins' Mayfair medical centre.

Eve had been kept in a stupor for more than a week and the medical staff had expressed some concerns about possible adverse effects on the baby.

"How long have I been sleeping?" asked Eve. She was confused. She didn't know where she was, and she wasn't sure whether she recognised the handsome man at her bedside who seemed so concerned about her condition.

"I have some good news," said Samiat, ignoring her question. "We have the results of all the tests. You and the baby are fine."

Eve nodded to show she understood.

"But I also have some bad news," Samiat continued. "We have spent the last few days looking for Adam. We have looked everywhere and can find no trace of him."

"What does that mean?" asked Eve, attempting to clear the mists swirling around in her mind. Then she remembered the bomb blast.

"We don't know for sure, but it doesn't look good," Samiat replied. "We've checked with the police, and from CCTV coverage we now know that Adam's last known location was the King's Road. We have footage of him on the King's Road, heading east. We believe he was on his way to the Aldwych to meet you. His route would have taken him through Covent Garden. From the timings we have, it looks as though Adam may have been close to the epicentre of the explosion. I'm really sorry."

"You mean Adam is dead?" said Eve. She heard her own words and felt as though it was someone else talking.

Roland called for some tea. He could see Eve needed time to grasp what he had told her.

Adam had been woven into every part of her life. Eve felt as though the fabric of her being was fraying at the edges and that strand after strand was being pulled out, leaving gaps and holes, blurring all the familiar shapes that imposed some form and structure on the essential messiness of human existence.

As soon as Eve seemed composed enough to endure the next stage of the prescribed conditioning, Roland Samiat returned to his task.

"There's something else," he said and paused, as though what he had to say was difficult to impart, even for a man of his obvious presence and experience.

"What?" Eve demanded. "What else?"

"In our extensive search for Adam, I sent one of our people, Lister Bavad, to your home in Harrow. We thought Adam might be there or have left some clue as to his whereabouts. While he was there, Lister met with some other people looking for Adam."

"What people?" Eve asked impatiently.

Before answering, Roland Samiat took a breath which he released with a sympathetic sigh. "There were four people, two from HMRC and two from the police."

Eve shook her head. The police were there to look for Adam as a missing person, but why should HMRC be in their house?

Roland Samiat continued. "HMRC were there because it seems there are some irregularities in Adam's financial affairs."

"What are you saying? What does 'irregularities' mean? Are you telling me that despite the bomb outrage, the Inland Revenue is chasing dead victims of the explosion for tax?"

"It's a little more complicated than that." Roland adopted his most emollient voice. "I'm afraid there's more. The police were also there. They wanted to speak to Adam about his possible involvement in the murder of Giovanni Spinetti. Spinetti was the man working for the EMA who was at the heart of the MC57 scandal."

"I know who Spinetti was," snapped Eve. "But why would they want to speak to Adam? Adam's not a murderer. That's utterly ridiculous. In any case, they arrested someone at ZeD for the murder. The evidence was overwhelming." For a moment Eve thought she was going to have a panic attack. This was too much. First, Adam almost certainly dead; now her almost certainly dead husband was possibly implicated in a murder. It was insane.

"You're right, of course, but the police have reopened the case. Ironically, one of the reasons is precisely because the evidence was overwhelming. The prosecution argued that the man, McFall, calmly planned the death of Spinetti and killed him in cold blood. He had no alibi, the knife used in the killing was his own paperknife, and his prints were the only ones found on the handle of the knife. All very straightforward, except that McFall's defence team have pointed out that if McFall is the cold, calculating killer described by the prosecution, he would have to be an idiot to use his own knife to kill Spinetti and then leave his fingerprints on it."

"Didn't the defence point that out at the trial?

"Yes, of course. But the fact that McFall gave a false alibi counted heavily against him, and as he had motive and there were no other suspects, they found him guilty."

"So why the doubts now?"

"It seems the police have had a tip off. McFall claimed he was having dinner with David Minofel at Minofel's house on the night Spinetti was murdered. Minofel confirmed that he had invited McFall to dinner but said that he failed to turn up. Now there is some doubt about the reliability of Minofel's testimony."

"Nothing would surprise me about David Minofel," said Eve.

"We mustn't prejudge anyone," said Roland. "The ZeD scandal was sensational. It generated a dozen different conspiracy theories. Almost everyone involved was suspected of something. It was only a matter of time before the media decided to have a go at Adam. There's nothing journalists love more than to build someone up as a hero and then reveal they have feet of clay."

"I should go home," said Eve.

"Of course," said Roland, "if that's what you want. But may I make a suggestion? Your house is empty. Your dog has gone. According to Lister, Luke is safe with some friends of yours in Maida Vale. The police have been watching your house for some time and they told Lister that someone called Kit Turner picked the dog up several days ago."

"Several days ago! How long have I been here?"

"This is your tenth day," Roland replied. "You were badly shaken by the blast and we knew your top priority was the baby, so we've been very careful. And we would like to continue to help. Go home if you want to. But there's nothing there. No one to look after you, to help you, to protect you. And the media are likely to make your life a misery. Adam's possible involvement in financial chicanery will generate massive interest, given the image he has projected as the 'purer than driven snow English whistle-blower'. When you add in suspicion of murder, you can expect a journalistic frenzy.

Certainly not good for a thirty-something woman in the later stages of pregnancy. We will continue to make every effort to determine what has happened to Adam, but surely you would be better off here, at least for now, than alone at home?"

"I don't understand why you would do this for me," Eve voiced her suspicions. "You are the CEO of Slievins. You work for the Praesidium. You must know what they did to Adam and me and our friends. David Minofel is one of your associates. He introduced Adam to ZeD and to the Praesidium. If Adam has done anything wrong, I'm certain Minofel will have been behind it. You say yourself his testimony in a murder trial has been called into question. I think Minofel is untrustworthy, dangerous and evil."

"Whoa!" Roland Samiat interrupted. "David Minofel is not Slievins. If David has overstepped the mark in any way, Slievins will deal with him. It will be done quietly, discreetly but, believe me, effectively. My offer to you has nothing to do with Minofel. It is a genuine offer of help to someone in need. I'm not pretending Slievins is an altruistic, benevolent institution. We're as ruthless as any in pursuit of business and in fulfilling our goals. But we do have principles. One of those is that we look after our employees and their dependents. I don't know the ins and outs of all that happened in Geneva, but your husband did us proud, fulfilling the brief we gave him and earning this company substantial fees.

"As for our connection with the Praesidium, yes, they are a client, an important client, but only one of our many clients. We don't judge our clients. We are a business consultancy, not a moral authority. They bring their problems to us and we solve them. It is another company principle that we keep within the letter of the law. Of course, from time to time, a Slievins' employee, in his enthusiasm to please a client, may forget that principle, but in such a case it is without the consent, much less the approval, of Slievins.

"I'm being completely honest with you, Eve. I leave it to you to decide what you want to do. If you choose to stay here for a while, we will move you out of the medical centre into the guest wing. You will be completely free to come and go as you please. We maintain high standards for our guests, so I doubt that you will have any cause to complain about the food or the service. Incidentally, we have a wonderful wine cellar, but I guess you'll have to wait till after the birth to sample its delights. In the meantime, you and your baby will have the best medical attention up to the birth and beyond. I'm still hoping that Adam will be found or reappear, but while we wait you can stay here as long as you wish. Equally, if you decide to stay, you are free to change your mind and leave at any time. You don't even have to tell me – you can simply go, although I would be grateful if you could inform House Services that you're leaving so we can adjust our staffing levels and, more importantly, not worry about your disappearance."

It was a masterly performance, a little rushed (for Roland Samiat's time was precious) but perfectly calibrated. Eve would stay. Rationally and emotionally, there was no other sensible choice. If, by any chance, she wavered, he would explain to her that Adam's financial misdemeanours might well have serious implications for her. Their recently acquired wealth could be seized. The authorities might even view her as an accomplice in Adam's crimes. She could face prosecution, even imprisonment. Surely it would be best if she kept a low profile for a while at least. So Eve would stay and not leave until Slievins ejected her.

Enid Mavlow would be Eve's keeper. She would keep Eve company, keep her occupied and keep an eye on her. Assuming Eve could adjust fairly quickly to the loss of her husband, all would be well. The goal was to destroy, completely and irremediably, the bond between Adam and Eve. Roland did not underestimate the enemy, but with the help of Lister Bavad and Enid Mavlow he was certain they could manage it. He was less certain that Minofel would succeed in dealing with Adam, but in Samiat's view Adam was less of a problem. Eve was the key. In breaking Eve's bond with Adam, Adam's death was, of course, a help, but as Roland knew only too well, death on its own was not enough.

27.   Know then thyself

When Adam reached his home in Harrow, although it was only mid-afternoon he poured himself a double whisky. His meeting that morning with Minofel had thrown a grenade into the already bomb-devastated landscape of his mind. Eve was dead. She had always been his anchor. Even when he had been in Geneva and in the Westminster PCC, she had been the core of his being. Because he hadn't always kept in touch, she thought they were drifting apart, but she had been utterly wrong. She was so deeply interwoven into his existence that losing her was unravelling him.

When the questors had escaped from the Westminster PCC, courtesy of the paradox device, he had started to rebuild Eve's belief in him. It was a perilous process. He knew there were things he had done which would shake, perhaps destroy, their relationship. She would never approve, but she might excuse, his involvement in blackmail and corruption. He could argue that the end justified the means. But murder? No. So he had put his crimes out of his mind and concentrated on showing his love for Eve and the child, their child, she was carrying. He had hope.

Now Eve, their unborn child and hope were gone. Worse, he faced prosecution by HMRC for financial misconduct and, if what Minofel had told him was true, investigation by the police for murder. His name, his wealth and his freedom were in jeopardy.

He drank another double whisky. His mind began to wander through all the events in his life since he had met the Storyteller and set out on the quest. The meeting with God and then Prometheus; the witnessing of the three great Beginnings; the challenges and ordeals in the Breakers mysland; the triggering of the albeit aborted Fourth Beginning; his employment at ZeD; the Praesidium's induction programme; the intervention of Aletheia, the goddess of truth.

He had set out to find the truth. The Storyteller had asked him what type of truth he sought. Well, as he sat there in an empty house, grieving for Eve and facing ruin, he realised what he wanted to know more than anything was the truth about himself.

"What kind of a man am I?" he asked out loud. "Am I a good man or a bad man? I have done terrible things, but in the main I have done them with good intentions. I have worked hard and I have always done my best, but I have done harm to others, and I have done little to help my fellow man. I have tried to be a good husband, to look after my family, but I have failed even in that fairly modest ambition. Bella died. And now Eve and the hope of redemption through the birth of Anna are gone."

It struck Adam like a bolt. Why had he named their unborn, now dead, child? Where had that come from? And why Anna? He and Eve had never discussed names, fearful that an assumption about a successful birth might jeopardise a happy outcome. And why a girl's name? He didn't know whether the baby Eve had been carrying was a girl or a boy.

Suddenly he heard a woman's voice. It was Aletheia. "You say you want the truth. Are you sure? Only the strong can face the truth. Most close their eyes and shut their ears to the truth. Most fear the truth. And even if you are brave enough to face the truth, what truth will satisfy you, Adam? Truth may well not answer the questions you ask. Is it not really meaning that you seek? They are related but not the same. Truth is. Meaning has to be created. Numpty didn't find the truth, but when he stood up to the bullying bikers at Fleet services, when he faced a dreadful death at the hands of St Michael, when he sacrificed himself to save Kathrin, he gave his life meaning. I am Truth, therefore I am – *sum veritas, ergo sum*, as we used to say in Rome. I can help you to see the truth but I cannot help you create meaning. It is for you to create meaning out of the truth. I wish you well but I have to warn you, it will be the hardest part of your journey. You will be alone. You will have to open your mind. And perhaps hardest of all, you will have to be honest. Try it, my friend. It's your only chance to find what you want before journey's end."

Adam looked around the room. There was no one there. And then the room started to move around him. He hadn't eaten all day and he had drunk too much whisky on an empty stomach. He stumbled through to the downstairs toilet and retched.

He crawled to his bed, lay on it and fell asleep. When he awoke he remembered little of what Aletheia had said. Only one word reverberated in his mind. "Anna".

28. Here, there and everywhere

Far away, in the desert of southern Arabia, Charles Fundi relaxed in his capacious, air-conditioned office on the third level of the subterranean city of Ubar, some three hundred metres beneath the surface of the sand. Charles was not a man much given to shows of emotion, but on this day he had a smile on his face. He was well pleased. The Crucible of Eternal Light had been installed without a hitch and was now effortlessly powering all of Ubar. As an engineer it still amazed him that something so small could generate such an incomprehensibly vast amount of power. There was no means of measuring the Crucible's output, but it was clear that maintaining all the systems in Ubar made not the smallest dent in the Crucible's capacity.

Fundi had taken his Bachelor's degree at the Mbeya University of Science and Technology where his outstanding ability had been quickly recognised. On completion of his studies he had left Tanzania in a hurry. There were rumours that he might have been connected with the disappearance of a girl who worked as a cleaner for the university. Nothing was proved.

Fundi went on to MIT where he gained a PhD in Civil and Environmental Engineering. Again, he distinguished himself academically and seemed set for a brilliant career in the States until he was accused of homicide. He killed a young, male undergraduate student. Fundi claimed that the student had abused him racially, and, provoked beyond reasonable endurance, he had beaten him with a baseball bat. He asserted the death was an accident, but the number of blows struck, many to the student's head, long after the victim had lost consciousness, suggested that the killing was intentional.

It was at this point in Charles Fundi's career that he came into contact with Slievins. He was approached by the head of Slievins in the US who made him an offer he couldn't refuse – a challenging job in his field of expertise on an enormous salary, far away from the grasp of the FBI. Charles Fundi disappeared.

Had the building of Ubar been put out to tender, it would have exceeded any civil engineer's wildest dreams. The scale of the project was epic. The base of the city, deep under the desert sand, was a circle with a diameter of a thousand metres. On the base were built six floors.

Working down from the level nearest the surface, the first floor was occupied by military and security staff.

The second level was devoted to shopping, leisure facilities and guest suites for visitors.

All the offices and accommodation units for the managerial and administrative staff were installed on the third level.

Located on the fourth level was the living accommodation for the army of technicians that maintained the system and the support staff who looked after the technicians.

The fifth level housed all the equipment – predominantly generators, a gigantic air-conditioning system and an extensive array of computer facilities – that enabled the city to function. At the heart of this floor was the chamber housing the newly installed Crucible of Eternal Light.

The purpose of sixth and deepest level was unknown to all but Roland Samiat and the Head of Security, Ben Rael.

Ubar was designed to be a permanent home for most of its inhabitants. Many of them couldn't leave Ubar because they were wanted for serious crimes in every country where they might want to live. Others were happy to stay in the city beneath the sand because it offered them everything they wanted – work they enjoyed (they were all exceptionally talented in their own field of expertise), rewards commensurate with their own self-esteem, and ample opportunity for leisure activities on the second level. Anyone was free to leave, but since leaving meant almost certain death in the south Arabian desert, to date few had tried. Senior Slievins' executives could come and go, but even they were carefully monitored by the security staff on the first floor and had to check in and check out on every visit.

"You look pleased with yourself," said Art Shoat amiably. Despite their very different backgrounds, Charles Fundi and Art Shoat had developed a surprisingly good relationship, founded primarily on their mutual enjoyment of violence against the person.

"And why not?" said Charles. "There's a rumour that very soon we'll be able to wreak havoc on a grand scale. Not just a local skirmish. Not just a major war. Not even a global conflict. Something much, much better – a truly momentous leap forward for humanity."

"I just love it when you talk like that," joked Art. "Mind you, don't underestimate the pleasures of more modest ambitions. I've had some of my happiest moments offing a single rival or enemy. Did I ever tell you how I took out Ronnie the Razor?

"I think you may have mentioned it," said Charles. "Is he not the person commemorated by the dragon on your right arm?"

That's right," said Art, chuckling as he recalled details of the incident. "He was a wiry little bugger, smaller than me but quick and strong. I had some problems at the start. He even managed to cut my arm, but in the end I was able to knock the razor out of his hand with my cosh. Never leave home without it. Then I used the cosh to whack him in the temple. That stunned him and he fell to the ground. So I picked him up by the ankles, carried him, dangling, through to the bathroom and tucked his head down the lavatory pan. When his head hit the water, he came to and started to struggle but he couldn't get his head out. He wriggled and squirmed like mad and I was laughing so much, he almost succeeded. But not quite. I flushed the pan a couple of times, holding him up by one ankle with one hand. I tried to use his head to block the outlet to the u-bend but there still wasn't enough water in the bowl to drown him. Fortunately, I had a full bladder. I'd been drinking. That must be how he got me with the razor. I was a bit slow, I guess. Anyway, he was getting tired and so was I. Happily my bladder, topped up with a jug of water from the basin, did the trick. You could say I pissed his life away."

"It must have been difficult for you to tell his mother how her son passed?" Charles observed with a straight face.

For a moment, Art was taken aback, and then they both laughed till tears streamed down their faces.

When Art had recovered his composure he asked Charles whether he had patched up his relations with Ben Rael. He touched a sore spot.

"Can't stand the man," said Charles. "I don't know why he's here. He's nothing but a nuisance. Apart from upsetting our security forces by criticising them and systematically working his way through most of our female staff, he doesn't seem to do anything. You know what he did just before arriving here? He came across a Bedouin looking for a lost sheep. How did he resolve the situation? He cut the Bedouin, his dog and his camel in half with rounds from his FN Scar rifle. We've had to infect the Bedouin's tribe with a lethal flu virus to get their minds off their murdered fellow tribesman and them off our backs."

"Take it easy," urged Art. "I only asked. He's a bit brash, I grant you, but he's good at what he does."

"Which is?" enquired a sceptical Charles.

"Security. He's smart and he's efficient. If he's giving your security people here a hard time, they probably deserve it. No offence. You've done a brilliant job. But security is really important until we launch the big one, or Project 75241 as Roland calls it. If Ben is tightening things up a bit, we should all be grateful."

"You sound like Roland," observed Charles. "Rael's one of Roland's favourites, isn't he? Why, I can't imagine. Whatever. It's best he keeps out on my way. Otherwise I might be tempted to take a pair of scissors to his dreadlocks."

"Of course, he has another purpose," said Art, lowering his normally booming voice. "He's here to keep an eye on us – on you and me. You know Roland. He likes all of us to watch each other. Divide and rule."

"So he's a spy as well as a lecher and a pain in the arse."

"That's a bugger, more than a lecher," quipped Art.

Charles looked puzzled.

"Never mind," said Art. "The point is we must all get along together. Project 75241 is the biggest operation Slievins has ever undertaken. Believe me, Roland won't be at all forgiving if internal bickering jeopardises its launch."

oooOooo

In the next few weeks, two events, other than Eve's death, dominated the lives of the questors residing in Rambler's Maida Vale flat. The first was the disappearance of Adam. The second was something that happened between Kit and the paradox device.

From the moment that Andrew Rimzil and Prune Leach had constructed the first prototype, Andrew had treated the paradox device as his own. That wasn't unfair because it was Andrew who had invented the device. Prune had simply helped him put it together.

As time passed, the paradox device had played an increasingly important role in the questors' adventures. Without it, they couldn't have undertaken or survived the challenges of the Fourth Beginning; and they couldn't have outwitted the Praesidium when they were trapped in the Westminster PCC. And the more the questors depended on the paradox device, the more Andrew Rimzil felt he

99

was developing an inexplicable relationship with it. Of course, as Prune was forever pointing out, a human can't have a relationship with a circuit board. But Andrew persistently countered by conceding that what he felt was indeed "a bit of a paradox" and that "given the nature of the device, a paradoxical relationship with it was not entirely inappropriate".

Throughout these few weeks, the power of the paradox device grew exponentially. It provided Rambler with all the help he needed in exploring the Praesidium's involvement with Stalin and Mao Tse Tung. Then it started, on its own initiative, to identify others in history who showed signs of Praesidium interference. It attached probabilities to each name to indicate how likely it was, on a range of criteria which the device had devised for itself, that each nominee had been mentored by one of the Praesidium Monitaurs. The list of "probables" quickly overwhelmed Rambler, exceeding his capacity to research and process them. Ever eager to help, the paradox device promptly profiled all those on the list, indicating the points in their lives when the Praesidium could have intervened and exploring in detail the way in which they had tampered with each subject's psychology to persuade him or her to fulfil Praesidium goals and implement Praesidium projects.

Not content with rendering Rambler redundant, the paradox device decided to tackle the stock market next. It absorbed vast quantities of data about stocks and shares and, by applying its knowledge of human psychology, gradually refined its predictions of market movements. It quickly outperformed the average performance of managed funds, not much of a benchmark, but then went on to outperform all the trackers. It was unable to achieve completely accurate predictions because of "inherent instability on the psycho-statistical matrix", but it did pretty well. And the challenge kept it busy.

"If it cracks the stock market, I'll ask it to predict the weather," Andrew joked. But Andrew needn't have worried because after about two weeks the paradox device lost interest in historical research and statistical analysis of financial matters. Put simply, it found a new friend: Kit.

Andrew spoke about the phenomenon first, although Kit must have known before Andrew.

"I think there's something wrong with the device," Andrew remarked to Prune one evening. It seems idle."

"Idle? What do you mean?" asked Prune. "Do you mean it's broken? Is it the software or the hardware?

"No, not idle," Andrew corrected himself. "More preoccupied. It seems to be doing nothing, nothing I can see, but I'm sure there's something going on. The device likes to be busy. If it was really doing nothing, it would be unhappy and I would know."

"There you go again," Prune rebuked his friend. "A bunch of electronics, however smart, can't be happy or unhappy."

Andrew shrugged. "So you keep telling me. But it is preoccupied, and I'm feeling excluded."

"You shouldn't." Kit joined the conversation. "The device is growing, maturing." He addressed Prune: "You have to accept that the device is no more a bunch of electronics than you are a hotchpotch of blood, flesh and bone."

"That's an expression I haven't heard in a long time," offered Rambler. "It's medieval and originally meant a kind of stew containing lots of vegetables."

Rambler's contribution was met with blank stares, so he hastily returned to reading the mass of reports on Praesidium acolytes identified by the paradox device before it had become bored with helping him.

"Maturing?" scoffed Prune.

"Maturing and worrying," said Kit unperturbed. "The device has picked up a stream of evil. No not a stream, an eruption. And I don't mean an isolated instance of evil. I mean something that threatens to manifest itself in all parts of the world on a global scale, something unprecedented."

"Which is?" prompted Andrew. So he was right. There was a major problem.

"I'm not entirely sure," Kit replied. "Whatever it is, it's being developed under the most extraordinary security arrangements. It involves all the major governments. There is a code for the project, 75241, but so far it has proved impossible to find out any details. The paradox device is preoccupied because it says that 75241 represents a step change in the level of evil. The Praesidium, or what's left of it, is involved, but they are not the prime movers. So far, the device has not been able to identify who is driving the project or where they are based."

"And why is the device communicating with you and not me?"

asked Andrew. He was, of course, upset that the device was excluding him, but the main reason for the question was scientific curiosity.

"Again, it's difficult to answer," Kit replied. "It's crazy but it seems to think I might be better placed to understand what is going on. I've told it that Rambler's a better researcher, and obviously you're the technical wizard, but it insists that for this particular problem I'm the man."

"So what are you doing about it?" asked Prune, probably more offended by Andrew's demotion than Andrew himself.

"Not a lot," Kit replied. "What can I do? We don't know what the problem is, and if 75241 involves all the world's governments, or most of them, it's a bit out of my league. Rambler should stop researching historical characters who've been corrupted by the Praesidium and concentrate for the next few weeks on this Project 75241, whatever it is. And you and Andrew should monitor carefully the results of the paradox device's scanning activity. It's trying to piece together the little information we have. As for me, I'll have to wait for more input from you or the device."

29. Unacceptable alternatives

Early in the morning of the day after Adam's meeting with David Minofel in Slievins' London headquarters, Adam received a phone call.

"Don't talk, listen." It was David Minofel. "Take all the cash you have in the house and any jewellery, pack an overnight bag and get out of the house."

"What?" said Adam.

"You heard. If you don't do what I say, you are likely to lose your freedom for at least ten years."

"What?" said Adam.

"Pull yourself together, Adam. You're a Slievins' man, or you were. You're about to be arrested for a number of crimes, one of which is premeditated murder. If it goes to trial, you will be found guilty. You won't be out in less than ten years. Could be longer, much longer. Now move. Cash, jewellery, don't take your mobile. There's a car outside. Get in it. The driver will bring you into town. I will meet you and we can talk things through."

All this on top of the loss of Eve should have been too much for Adam, but, oddly, the threat of imminent danger, of arrest, trial and imprisonment, somehow galvanised him into action. Of course he had doubts about Minofel's warning. Only a fool would trust a man like Minofel. But on this occasion it would be better to take him seriously. If Minofel was wrong or exaggerating, no harm would be done. Adam would have wasted a morning but it was not as though he had anything else to do. And if Minofel was right, then they had best make sure they had their stories straight.

Adam took all the cash from the safe, about £1,500 he kept in the house for emergencies. He left Eve's jewellery box. It would be no use to him. However desperate he might be, he wasn't going to sell or pawn Eve's jewellery. He packed a bag with a change of clothes and left the house. Outside was the familiar Bentley Flying Star. Adam half-expected to see Jedwell Boon behind the wheel.

In fact, the driver was Ceri Agema, just returned from the completion of a successful mission in Rio de Janeiro. Ceri introduced herself. Adam grunted.

"Where are we going?" he asked.

"Into town," said Ceri. "David Minofel wants a meeting with you. There's a café he's rather fond of in Soho."

"Have you worked for David for long?" Adam asked.

"I work for Roland Samiat, Slievins' CEO," Ceri replied. "I've been seconded to David temporarily, just to help him sort a few things out. You and your friends caused Slievins some serious problems."

Adam was taken aback. Evidently she knew a good deal about him and what he had done. They drove on in silence for a while.

"I'm no longer with Slievins," Adam said eventually. "I've terminated my contract."

Ceri Agema smiled. "It's not as easy as that. You are going to need our help. Because you've terminated your employment with Slievins, the help you get will be restricted. It will be pretty basic. We will enable you to avoid arrest and imprisonment, but don't expect too many home comforts."

Adam was irritated. "You talk as though I'm a convicted criminal," he said angrily.

Ceri laughed. "No," she corrected him. "I talk as though you are a criminal, which beyond doubt you are. You're not a convicted criminal. You are here, with me in this car, precisely so we can help you avoid conviction."

"I've done nothing that wasn't endorsed by David Minofel," said Adam.

"You don't have to explain yourself to me," Ceri responded. "Save that for the court, if that's where you end up. You haven't done anything I wouldn't do. You haven't done anything I haven't done. In other circumstances we could spend many happy hours reminiscing over our sorties into blackmail, extortion and murder. I myself like to leaven my more serious felonies with a light seasoning of sexual peccadillos that would make my recollections rather more entertaining than yours – but we could still enjoy swapping stories and telling tales."

Adam took a closer look at his driver. Sitting beside her, he could not help but notice her long, shapely legs. From what he could see, she had a slim, firm figure. He guessed she was tall for a woman, probably about five feet eight inches. Her face was oval and symmetrical. With her blonde hair and blue eyes, she should have been pretty. But Adam thought her eyes were cold and her dark eyebrows made her look almost fierce.

"So when you're working for this Roland Samiat, what do you do for him?" Adam asked.

Ceri laughed again. "I do for Roland whatever he asks me to do. We all do. And I'm working for him now. Roland runs a tight ship. If you don't do what he wants, you can leave."

"It's not so easy to leave a ship, at least not when it's at sea."

"No one said it was easy, but you can always walk the plank."

"A choice between the devil and the deep blue sea," observed Adam.

"Always best to avoid situations where both alternatives are unacceptable," suggested Ceri.

"Like whether to stay and be arrested or leave and go on the run?" Adam suggested.

"Not really," said Ceri. "You've already decided it would be better to be on the run. Given that choice, it's a pity you decided to abandon Slievins. The company has a very benign policy for the protection of its personnel. Some of our people would be serving life sentences if it weren't for Slievins' protection. Instead, they live secure, productive, enjoyable lives."

"If they've committed crimes deserving life sentences, perhaps they should be serving them."

Ceri laughed. "Really? Shall I stop the car so you can go and give yourself up?"

"I don't find that amusing," snapped Adam. "I've not been charged with anything, much less been found guilty. I accept I have sailed close to the wind, but there are powerful mitigating circumstances."

Now Ceri was serious. "I think you should take a long, hard look at yourself and be honest about who you are. If you really believe you are innocent, or that the circumstances are so mitigating that they exonerate you, get out now. You don't have to meet David. I'll tell him we had a chat and you changed your mind."

"No," said Adam. "I'll hear what he has to say."

They completed the journey in silence. Ceri wondered why Slievins was making such a fuss about Adam. *I'm pretty sure I could seduce and despatch him in an evening,* she thought. Adam spent the rest of the journey thinking about the chaos into which his life had degenerated and how much he needed Eve.

"I can't park so I'll drop you here," said Ceri, "That's the café. If David isn't there, he'll join you shortly."

30. Help somebody

David Minofel was sitting at a small table for two at the back of the café waiting for Adam. He had ordered a coffee and was tucking in to a full English breakfast.

"Have a coffee," said Minofel. "They do excellent coffee. It beats me. All Italians are brilliant coffee-makers."

"I'll have an espresso," said Adam.

The very pretty waitress, no doubt the daughter or granddaughter of the owner, took his order.

"I just love these Italian family-run businesses. They're efficient, clean, reasonably priced and happy. What a wonderful life."

"Well?" said Adam, eager to get to the point.

David Minofel leant forward. "The Swiss police have asked for you to be extradited. They've issue a European arrest warrant. It seems they have video material of Jedwell and another man at Spinetti's apartment at the time of his murder. The images of the second man are inconclusive, but the prosecution believe they can persuade a judge that the other man is you."

"They can't have a video," said Adam. "Jedwell took the cassette from the hall porter's recording machine."

"I wouldn't use that in your defence if you go to court," said Minofel with a smile. "The video the police have is taken from a security camera opposite the building. Jedwell must have missed it. Towards the end of his employment he became a bit sloppy. Anyway, the video shows you, or someone rather like you, and Jedwell entering the building on the evening in question at 8.39 p.m. and leaving at 8.46 p.m. That fits perfectly with the estimated time of death of Spinetti and the hall porter. The prosecutor reckons that the video and Guy McFall's alibi make the case against you a slam dunk, as our American friends say."

"How is it that McFall now has an alibi?" asked Adam. "You set him up so that he didn't."

"Well, it all began to unravel. We overdid the evidence against McFall. The police were suspicious. If McFall was the cold, calculating murderer the prosecution described, it seemed unlikely he'd use his own paperknife to kill Spinetti and then leave his fingerprints on the weapon. His defence team began to explore other possibilities, which led the police to query my account of events. They reopened the case and found the video from the camera opposite Spinetti's block of flats."

"That doesn't explain how McFall had an alibi, unless you changed your story and confirmed he had dinner with you," said Adam.

"It was obvious they were going to identify you and Jedwell as the killers so there was no longer any point in trying to implicate poor old Guy. I thought you'd be pleased. I know you were upset I framed him for the murder in the first place."

"What you mean is that you turned Queen's evidence, or whatever they call it in Switzerland, to avoid prosecution yourself. You sold me out."

"That's a bit petty," Minofel rebuked Adam. "Would you prefer that Guy McFall was implicated, even though you were identified as the killer? What would be the point? There was no need for a third person. I thought you'd be pleased. You rather liked McFall. You expressed a misplaced admiration for his honesty and professionalism."

Adam shook his head. "Well, if I'm going down, I'm going to take you with me. I didn't do anything during my time with ZeD that I hadn't checked out with you. You were an accessory before, during and after the fact. It was you who made sure that McFall didn't have an alibi. We're in this together, so how are you going to help me? How are you going to sort this out?"

David Minofel leant back. "Two more coffees," he called to the waitress.

"Not for me," said Adam.

"I'll be honest with you, Adam," said Minofel when his coffee arrived. "When you decided to turn against the Praesidium, you caused havoc. You and your friends effectively destroyed the Westminster PCC, not to mention the damage to my own reputation. It would be perfectly reasonable for Slievins to wash their hands of you and, without my intercession on your behalf, that is precisely what would have happened. As it is, I can give you some help, but my hands are tied. For now, you have to go underground, drop off the radar. I'll sort out a future for you – a new identity, a new job – but it'll take time. If you were a loyal employee, all the resources of

Slievins would be at your disposal. As it is, I've had to persuade the CEO to allow me to help you in a personal capacity."

"Go underground, drop off the radar? What does that mean?" Adam asked. "I'm not a criminal. I don't know how to go underground. I don't know anyone. I don't have any contacts."

"That's excellent," said Minofel unperturbed. "There's an arrest warrant out for you. The fewer who know you, the safer you are. You have some money?"

"Yes, about £1,500."

"That's enough to get you started. I suggest you stay in central London for now. There's safety in numbers. Find somewhere cheap to stay. Keep yourself to yourself. Grow a beard."

Adam shook his head. "That's it, is it? That's your help. Live alone, grow a beard."

Minofel stood up. "I am helping you. I have helped you. If it weren't for me, you'd be on your way to a prison cell where you would be held on remand for weeks before your trial. And I will help you more. In time, I will help you build a new life. In the meantime, I suggest you show me some respect, perhaps even a little gratitude. After all, if I don't help you, who will?"

31. The Storyteller on London

Although I promised to withdraw from the action of the narrative, I, as the Storyteller, feel the need and have the right to set the scene for the next few chapters of this tale. I think it will give you, the reader, an excellent perspective on the journey Adam now undertakes and the landscape through which he will now pass. And, in any case, my setting of the scene does not in any way affect the characters in the story or interfere with the resolution of the plot.

All cities have their own character. They all have their fine buildings and their slums, their rich and their poor. Many of them have a long history. And as for their citizens, I'm sure they all have unique, distinctive personalities. But London has a soul. It has a soul formed by 2000 years of experience, both good and bad; a soul gifted with, or cursed by, the compulsion to rejuvenate itself; a soul that has lived through times of greatness and times of mortal danger; a soul that has faced the often ruthless rule of kings and the ravages of rioters. It was the heart of an empire on which the sun never set. Then, after centuries of global dominance, the empire died and a unique commonwealth of nations was born. Almost every race on earth is represented in London's population; and every form of human behaviour – from greed, extravagance and every type of evil, through to kindness, generosity and self-sacrifice – is observable on its streets every day.

It is into this city that Adam is to be cast. And it will make or break him. He is now alone and vulnerable. All the certainties and protections in life up to this day are now swept away. His preconceptions about the world in which he has lived are to be tested. He has much to learn and the city will be his teacher. So for those who have little or no knowledge of London, here are some facts, figures and thoughts to give Adam's rite of passage some context.

London is a great, some would say the greatest, city in the world. It has both breadth and depth.

In breadth, it covers an area of 607 square miles, extending from Uxbridge in the west to Upminster in the east, and from Enfield in the north to Croydon in the south. It is home to close to ten million people, of whom about sixty per cent are indigenous white British.

Among the other forty per cent are people from almost every country in the world. More than thirty per cent of the population was born outside the United Kingdom. More than 300 languages are spoken.

With some 4,800 people living in every square mile, London is the most densely populated city in Europe.

There are thought to be more billionaires living in London than in any other city.

Running through London from west to east is the mighty river Thames. It is the flowing aorta of the city, rising up to eight metres between low and high tide. There was a time when it was infamous for its pollution, but today it is one of the cleanest rivers in Europe.

In depth, London has a history that few cities can match. In legend, London was founded by Brutus of Troy about the same time that King David ruled in Israel. The archaeological evidence shows that London was founded as a civilian town by the Romans about AD 50. At that time, London occupied a small area of about one square mile.

Ten years after its foundation, it was destroyed by the Iceni, led by their ferocious Queen Boudicca. Boudicca was the widow of the Iceni chieftain Prasutagus. When her husband died, the Romans decided that a woman couldn't lead the Iceni, so they imposed direct rule, stripping and flogging Boudicca and raping her daughters in front of her. They seriously misjudged Boudicca, and paid a heavy price. Boudicca led a confederation of tribes against the Romans, wiping out the 9th Legion, sacking Colchester and destroying London. Thousands died. London had to be rebuilt.

Although York was considered by the Romans to be the capital of the province of Britannia, the city of Londinium, as the Romans called it, thrived and grew. It became a key part of the Roman network of roads that facilitated Roman administration of Britain. In line with Roman practice, and perhaps with the Boudicca experience in mind, the Romans built a wall around the town to defend it. The gates in the wall (Aldgate, Aldergate, Ludgate, etc.) were aligned with the Roman roads that radiated out from London across Britain.

Under the Saxons, London continued to thrive and prosper as a major commercial centre. Eventually Alfred the Great decided that London should supplant Winchester as the Saxon capital of England.

In 1066, the Norman William the Conqueror invaded Britain. In 1078, he had the White Tower, the embryo of the Tower of London, added to the city's fortifications, and granted a charter to the city confirming the rights enjoyed by the city under one of the last Saxon kings, Edward the Confessor.

William the Conqueror's son, William Rufus, founded Westminster Hall which was to form part of what is today the United Kingdom's parliamentary estate, the home of the Houses of Parliament.

In 1209, Peter de Colechurch built the first stone bridge, old London Bridge, across the Thames. Of course there had been wooden bridges constructed before, but none of these had the endurance of the first stone bridge, which even survived the Great Fire of London in 1666.

In 1381, Wat Tyler led the Peasant's Revolt and marched on London from his Kentish heartland. The rebels opposed the recently introduced poll tax of twelve pence per person (irrespective of means) and demanded an end to serfdom which, among other burdens, denied peasants a right to choose for whom they worked. When Tyler crossed London Bridge and marched into the city, the King, Richard II (fourteen years old at the time) was initially conciliatory, offering Wat Tyler much of what he demanded. But negotiations deteriorated, possibly because of Tyler's ungracious behaviour, and the day ended with Tyler's head displayed on a pole on London Bridge.

The sixteenth and seventeenth centuries saw further increases in London's population and such a growth in area that both Elizabeth I and James I tried to prevent any further expansion.

In 1665, the Black Death wiped out almost a fifth of London's population, and a year later the Great Fire of London devastated London's real estate, destroying 13,000 houses and, among the city's notable buildings, the Royal Exchange, St Paul's Cathedral, and eighty-six other churches. As Sir Walter Besant put it:

> it burned, more or less, every house and every
> building over an area of 436 acres out of those
> which made up London within the walls.

But it's an ill wind that blows nobody any good. The rebuilding of central London provided an opportunity to introduce some major improvements: chiefly wider streets and better standards of building both structurally and aesthetically. It also allowed Sir Christopher Wren to build a new St Paul's Cathedral.

In 1670, the population of London was about 500,000. In 1760, less than a hundred years later, it had grown by fifty per cent to about 750,000 and by the turn of the century (1801) the population of London topped one million.

The eighteenth century saw the construction of such iconic buildings as the Mansion House (the official residence of the Lord Mayor of London); Somerset House (designed by Sir William Chambers) and Horse Guards (built to replace the original Horse Guards building).

In 1780, the Gordon Riots, the most destructive riots in British history, broke out. The immediate cause was popular opposition to the Catholic Relief Act of 1778, which reduced discrimination against Roman Catholics, and, in particular, dropped the requirement for all those joining Britain's armed forces to take a Protestant oath.

But there were other reasons for the rioting. It has to be said that the second half of the eighteenth century was a hard time for the British working class, and festering beneath the surface was a general discontent with work, wages and working conditions. As the rioting spread, prisons were burnt and prisoners escaped. Such proletarian mayhem, at a time when Britain was at war with France, Spain and the United States, not surprisingly alarmed the authorities, but the need to recruit more men for the armed forces took precedence over Protestant misgivings. The government pressed on with the Catholic Relief Act.

In the early years of the nineteenth century, London was enhanced with widened thoroughfares such as New Oxford Street and Regent Street. Built to John Nash's design and named after his patron, George, the Prince Regent, later George IV, Regent Street was completed in 1825 and immediately declared a masterpiece of architectural design. Together with Oxford Street, Regent Street was destined to become the United Kingdom's premiere shopping street, famous throughout the world for its range and quality of shops.

In 1831, John Rennie replaced the old London Bridge with a new bridge made of Dartmoor granite.

By 1860, the population of London was well over three million, mainly because of immigration. At that time almost forty per cent of London's population had been born elsewhere. People came to London from all over the world. From nearby the Irish came; and people from France, Germany, Italy and Spain, many fleeing turmoil in Europe, sought refuge in London. From further afield,

African, Indian and Chinese sailors settled in London, forming small but growing circles of fellow immigrants, joining London's well-established Jewish community.

The growth in population and the vast expansion of administrative and commercial activity in London demanded improvements in the city's infrastructure as the area of London grew. The mighty Thames, which divided London in two, had to be mastered. Following John Rennie's replacement of London Bridge, the rest of the nineteenth century was a time of prolific bridge-building. Westminster Bridge, Hungerford Bridge, Albert Bridge, Blackfriars Bridge, Putney Bridge, Hammersmith Bridge, Battersea Bridge, and Tower Bridge, were all completed between 1862 and 1894.

By the beginning of the twentieth century, the population of London was 6.5 million. A hundred years later, in 2001, it was 7.3 million.

In the twentieth century, development of the city inexorably continued, occasionally impeded but also prompted by two world wars in which London took more than its fair share of death and destruction.

Twenty-first-century London is an extraordinary success story. It is a vibrant, creative, cosmopolitan metropolis, now famed for its creativity and innovation, its expertise in global finance and for the extraordinary buildings that house the great corporations and financial institutions. Its success has caused a further acceleration in population growth. By 2015, the population of London stood at 8.6 million.

Hundreds of thousands of foreign nationals arrive in London every year. Some are already rich, others bring nothing with them; but they all hope to thrive in a city that offers limitless opportunities. There are thought to be about eighty billionaires living in and driving through the streets of London, where it is estimated there are also some four thousand rough sleepers. Between these two groups, on a sliding scale from astronomical wealth to abject poverty, there are more than eight million other people of which Adam is just one – and one, despite his recent, glittering career, now very much at the lower end of the scale.

Adam's change of fortune in such an environment will inevitably open up new perspectives and offer him the chance to discern new kinds of truth.

32. Baby steps

After Minofel left the café, Adam stayed for a few minutes. He ordered another coffee. For the first time, he noticed the waitress. Indeed, he seemed to be noticing many things for the first time: the chequered plastic table cloth, the steel-sprung chair frames, the pedestal bar stools along the window, the fresh fruit in a glass bowl on the counter. He heard the clatter of washing up from the café's kitchen and the muffled chatter of the kitchen staff.

He stood up to leave. Minofel hadn't paid for anything. Adam handed over a £20 note. The girl gave him £7.30 in change. He looked at the receipt. That was £1.90 a cup, good value for that quality of coffee; Minofel's breakfast was £7. Adam gave her a £1 tip. Total cost £13.70. To his dismay, Adam realised he had just spent almost one per cent of his total financial resources. He felt a deep resentment that Minofel had left him to pick up the bill.

Outside the café, it was chilly. It was late October and the sun was losing its strength. Adam turned up the collar on his jacket. He was sorry he had left the warmth of the café. If Minofel was right about the arrest warrant, he couldn't go home. He would have to find himself somewhere to stay. Of course, Minofel could have been lying, but what would have been the point? Adam pondered whether he should go back to Harrow, just to check Minofel's story, but he quickly concluded the risk was too great. The only way he would know if Minofel was telling the truth was to wait for the police to arrive, and then it would be a bit late to make his escape.

Adam found himself walking down Berwick Street. It was approaching lunchtime and the workers were beginning to trickle out of the offices and shops to do some shopping, to pop into the bank or to buy their sandwiches. Adam needed somewhere to think – somewhere warm, out of the cold. By now he was walking down Rupert Street. He decided to head for the National Gallery. He turned left along Coventry Street, then down Whitcombe Street.

As he walked he considered the possibility of going to the police voluntarily. Willing cooperation with the police would count in his favour. But he dismissed the idea. However favourably the police looked upon willing cooperation, it wasn't going to make much difference to the outcome if he was found guilty of murder. Murder! He had committed murder. The police would consider him to be a murderer. But he wasn't a murderer. Yes, he had killed Spinetti. Well, he hadn't actually killed Spinetti, Jedwell had, but Adam conceded that he was splitting hairs on that one. Yes, he had killed Spinetti, but that didn't make him a murderer, any more than peeling an orange made him an orange-peeler. Minofel had killed the burglars who had broken into his home. But that didn't make Minofel a murderer. In the eyes of the public, if not in the eyes of the law, that made him a hero. If two thugs break into a house, beat up the husband and prepare to rape the wife, then killing the thugs is surely perfectly acceptable. Killing Spinetti wasn't quite the same, but he had beaten up Miss Tomic and he was threatening to bring down the whole pack of cards, to destroy ZeD. He had to be stopped. Adam had done what had to be done. In a war you are allowed to kill people without being accused of murder. Indeed, you're encouraged to kill people. Well, Adam had been at war with Spinetti, and Adam had saved Miss Tomic from further abuse and the company from a cataclysmic scandal. All right, that wasn't strictly true. He hadn't saved the company from a cataclysmic scandal. In the end he himself had brought the company to its knees by revealing a cataclysmic scandal. But that wasn't the point. When he had killed Spinetti – or rather when Jedwell had killed Spinetti – Adam had thought he was protecting Miss Tomic and the jobs of tens of thousands of ZeD employees.

None of that mattered. The police were after him, and if they caught him he would almost certainly be tried, convicted and given a mandatory life sentence.

By now he had reached the National Gallery. Adam walked up the steps, relieved to be out of the cold. He walked through the main vestibule into the central hall and on into the large room containing Spanish paintings. He settled in front of the painting of John the Baptist in the Wilderness. The plaque said the artist was probably Bartomelé Esteban Murillo. John in the picture looked as uncertain about his emotional state as the gallery was about the identity of the artist.

Adam tried to calm himself. His first thought was to contact Kit and the others. He felt desperately alone, isolated and vulnerable. He needed help, advice, consoling. Then, he thought again. They might not be too worried about some alleged tax irregularities, but an accusation of murder, that was something else. They would expect him to claim he was innocent; they would be dismayed, at the very least, if he confessed to the crime. Of course, he would be able to set the affair in context, delineate the extenuating circumstances, perhaps even justify his action a little – but he knew that would not convince Kit. Kit would be just as censorious as Eve would have been.

In any case, if there was an arrest warrant out for him, probably the first place the police would look, if he was not at home, would be at the home of one of his friends.

He looked more closely at the painting. It was difficult to interpret the expression on John the Baptist's face. To Adam he almost seemed to be pleading his innocence: "Hand on Heart, guv, it wasn't me." Or appealing for forgiveness. Or perhaps he just had a sense of foreboding, a premonition that his head was likely to end up on a platter, served to King Herod. It crossed Adam's mind that he was projecting his own emotional turmoil onto the figure in the painting.

The calm of the National Gallery helped. Visitors wandered past, pausing from time to time to look at a particular painting that caught their eye. They were relaxed, curious, accessing frozen instants of time caught in picture frames. The subjects of these paintings had no future and no past, only an eternal present. Time might flow from the past to the future like a mighty river – like the Thames on its way to the sea – but it flowed impotently past these pictures. They remained immutable.

Unlike Adam's predicament! He had a past which was determined to catch up with him, and a future fraught with danger and uncertainty. He knew he had to formulate a plan. He had to organise himself. He must find somewhere to stay. He must avoid arrest. He must depend on David Minofel to help him. There was no alternative.

Or rather, the alternative was despair. He had lost his wife, the anchor of his life. Why had this happened? A voice whispered in his ear. It was Nick Peters giving him his advice when he had wanted an explanation for Bella's death. "Things just happen. Accidents happen. There is no reason. There is no point." He was right. Bella died when the bough of a branch broke in a storm and crushed her head. Eve had died because she happened to be walking through a place where a bomb exploded. In those dreadful events, neither Bella nor Eve had any significance. They had been the ones to die, but it could have been anyone. They were not selected. They were not executed for crimes committed. They were not the victims of someone's hatred. They were accidental collateral damage in a chaotic and essentially pointless existence.

It was almost six o'clock. The gallery was emptying. Adam walked slowly through the main reception and out into the chill October evening.

33. When needs must

Adam's first few days on the run were taken up with practicalities. He had found a room in a cheap hotel in Earl's Court. He had chosen Earl's Court because it had a mixed and transient population, and because he had never had any links with the place. His room cost him £60 a night. Although the room was cheap, it was adequate, but even at a modest £60 a night Adam realised the £1,500 he had brought with him wouldn't last very long. He hoped that Minofel would come up with a solution quickly, before his money ran out. Or if he didn't come up with a solution, surely Minofel or Slievins could at least provide him with additional funds. Even so, for the first time in a long time Adam began to worry about money.

He also worried about any solution that Minofel might be able to offer him. What was the solution? Was he to be shipped off to northern Cyprus to join Dr Dubois in a humiliating exile? He could imagine the vitriolic conversations the pair of them might have in a taverna in Kyrenia. And what was he to do in the long and lonely years that lay ahead? Where would he work? Who would employ him? Would he be able to evade capture indefinitely? Would he have to live an utterly useless life with the fear of arrest gnawing away at his soul every day of his pointless existence?

There were many cafes in Earl's Court where it was possible to eat for less than £10. Adam established a rota to ensure he left a few days between visits to each eatery. He kept himself to himself. The fewer people he related to the better. By now, he knew for sure the police were looking for him. It was not a big story, not yet, but most of the dailies had reported that he was a person of interest in police enquiries concerning Giovanni Spinetti's death.

On the third day, Adam bought a pay-as-you-go mobile. He needed some means of contacting David Minofel. Despite Minofel's warning, Adam phoned Slievins. He had the number of Minofel's direct line. David Minofel answered.

Adam didn't introduce himself. "What the hell's going on?"

"I told you not to use a phone," said Minofel.

"So how am I supposed to contact you?" snapped Adam. "Do you want me to hang around outside your offices?"

"This conversation is over," said Minofel.

"The hell it is!" said Adam.

"I will meet you this evening at your digs," said Minofel.

"How do you know where I'm staying?" Adam asked.

The line went dead.

oooOooo

Adam waited in his hotel room until 8 p.m. He was about to leave to find somewhere to eat when there was a knock on the door of his room.

"I didn't trouble the hall porter or the girls at reception," said Minofel mockingly, "I just came straight up."

"What's going on?" Adam asked.

"I told you that I'll help but it will take time. You must be patient."

"But I can't live like this."

"You don't have much choice, dear boy," said Minofel. "If you want to stay out of prison, you need a new life and new identity. I'm working on it, but these things can't be rushed and they cost money. I've told you I'll help you, but you have to understand I am doing this as a friend. You severed your links with Slievins. I warned you what would happen if you turned your back on Slievins but you ignored my advice. That's why you are where you are today."

"I think I am where I am today because I followed your advice. Who encouraged me to do whatever was necessary to fulfil my goals at ZeD? Who asked me to deliver a bribe to Spinetti? Who urged me to blackmail Dr Reed? Who persuaded me that Spinetti had to die?"

"Whoa!" Minofel interrupted. "Of course I encouraged you to fulfil your goals. That's why you were appointed Marketing Director at ZeD. What did you expect? What were you hoping for? 'Take a massive salary but don't worry about achieving anything?' Come on, Adam, grow up! And I didn't urge you to blackmail poor old Geoffrey Reed. True, I gave you the means, but it was entirely your decision to use them. As for killing Spinetti, you worked that out all by yourself."

Adam was frustrated. "I might as well go to the police," he said. "Hand myself in and hope for the best."

David Minofel laughed. "Go ahead. It would save me a great deal of trouble."

"If I do, I'll make sure I take you down with me," said Adam.

119

"It's your decision," said Minofel, "but don't make another mistake. If you try to take me down, you will be provoking Slievins and, believe me, that is not a sensible thing to do. They will make sure the blame for everything is placed firmly on your shoulders and yours alone. They will portray you as one of the most evil, manipulative, corrupt individuals who has ever lived. The courts will condemn you. The public will hate you. Your friends will despise you. And none of the crimes you committed will touch me or Slievins. I'm telling you this as a friend."

"With friends like you …" said Adam bitterly.

"I'm going to leave you now," said Minofel. "And Adam, I insist that you do not attempt to contact me again. I am almost certainly being watched and my phone is being tapped. I took precautions in coming here, but I will not risk it again. Aiding and abetting, without the explicit approval of Slievins, a suspected murderer who is currently being sought on a European arrest warrant could be exceedingly damaging to my personal reputation. If I have any news, I will find you."

"Could you at least give me some money?" Adam hated to ask but he couldn't use his credit cards and the £1,500 he had brought with him was already dribbling away. He was spending about £100 a day on rent, food and such purchases as toiletries and the pay-as-you-go phone. Without additional funds, he would last a couple of weeks but no longer.

"Sorry," Minofel replied, "but I didn't bring any cash with me. Have you thought of getting some casual work? There are plenty of cash-in-hand jobs in London, despite the best efforts of HMRC."

Adam shook his head. So it had come to this.

"I see the beard's coming along well," said David Minofel as he left.

34. Planning meeting

Once a week, on Wednesday afternoons, Roland Samiat liked to hold an informal gathering of his personal staff to discuss current activity, to review progress and to propose and assess any new tactical initiatives. Once a month, Roland chaired a management meeting, a much more formal affair, which reviewed top-line strategy. Wednesday afternoons were more relaxed and often rather more constructive.

There should have been seven present on Wednesday afternoons: Roland in the chair, David Minofel, a senior partner at Slievins, Art Shoat, Ben Rael, Lister Bavad, Ceri Agema and Enid Mavlow. On this occasion, there were only five. Art Shoat and Ben Rael were far away in the south Arabian desert, stationed in Ubar, the City under the Sand.

"I'm pleased to confirm," said Roland opening the meeting, "that all goes well in Ubar. As I think you all know, the Crucible of Eternal Light has been safely installed and is going fully online any time now. There was a problem with some Bedouin, but I understand from Ben that the situation has been resolved. A serious outbreak of bird flu has decimated the tribe and given them other things to think about – a case of avian misdirection, one might say."

Although the spreading of a flu virus among the tribesmen had been Charles Fundi's idea, Ben, with the help of the Ubar security forces, had implemented the plan with enthusiasm and had seen no harm in taking credit for what had proved to be a highly successful ploy.

"David," Roland Samiat continued, "how go your plans for the deconstruction of young Adam?"

Having met with Adam the previous evening, Minofel was able to give an up-to-date report. "He's close to complete mental collapse. He's grief-stricken, disoriented, frightened and completely out of his depth."

"How long do you think it will take to break him, and I mean break him so he is irreparable?" asked Roland.

"It's up to you," said Minofel confidently. "If you want it done quickly, I would say a few days. If there's no rush, it would be better to deconstruct him bit by bit over a period of weeks. If there's time I should like to implement a staged programme of degradation."

"Timing is everything," Roland mused, and then added, "Why

use spurs or the whip, when the horse is already galloping full speed towards its own destruction?"

"Why, indeed," Minofel replied. He wondered about Samiat's addiction to metaphors. It was odd in itself, since the metaphors were often contrived and inept, but it was doubly strange given the antipathy of the Breakers, ideological soulmates of Slievins, to any form of metaphorical expression. Minofel himself didn't much care one way or the other, but he well remembered the problems the Breakers had encountered at Cadnam when the questors deployed the Metaphorce, under Captain Hector Meap, against them. The use of the Fist of God to destroy the Commander of the Breakers' forces, Nestor Gruin, by exploding his rectum, still brought a smile to Minofel's face.

"Is there something that amuses you?" asked Roland. "Let us not forget that, in the end, the smirk on the face of the Cheshire cat was all that was left of the cat."

David thought of pointing out that he hadn't been smirking, and in any case it was a smile or a grin, not a smirk, that was all that was left of the Cheshire cat, but he didn't. Instead he said; "I take it there's no rush to complete the destruction of Adam."

"I should like to break Adam and Eve at the same time," Roland replied. "Eve will take a little longer. She is, as I suspected, a tougher nut to crack, which brings me to the brief I am giving to Lister and Enid. Eve is still recovering from the loss of her husband and is vulnerable. She is devoting all her care to the baby she is carrying, the only part of Adam that she still has. I want you, Enid, to become Eve's new best friend. And I want you, Lister, to be a wholly supportive male figure, alongside Enid. I want the pair of you to give Eve what will seem to her to be a comprehensive support system. Comfort her in her grief, support her in the final stages of her pregnancy, prove to her that whatever residual doubts she may have about Slievins there are at least two decent, honest people in the organisation who will stand by her whatever happens. Is this clear to you?"

Lister and Enid nodded. Roland turned to Ceri. "How very remiss of me," he said with a laugh. "I omitted to welcome you back from your overseas assignment. I trust all went well?"

"I fulfilled the brief," said Ceri.

"Excellent. And I hope you had a pleasant trip. Did you manage to combine a little pleasure with the business?"

Ceri smiled. "Just a little, but I was keen to return as soon as possible to assist David in dealing with Adam."

"Have you met Adam yet?" Roland asked.

"Yes," said David Minofel, answering for his new assistant: "I asked Ceri to pick him up from his home in Harrow. So she was the one who saved him from arrest and certain incarceration. I thought that would provide a sound basis for her dealings with him."

"I had a chat with Adam while driving him to meet David," Ceri added. "I think we will be fine, but I'm not sure he's as close to breaking as David believes. Adam has remarkable powers of self-deception. I wouldn't underestimate him."

"Nor should you," said Roland. "We'll discuss Adam later." He paused, then added, "With David of course."

Minofel did not know whether to be pleased he had been included or peeved he had been added as an afterthought. He tried to keep his face impassive, but Ceri noticed a flicker of irritation.

"And, Ceri," Roland continued entirely unperturbed, "I should like you to fill me in on the details of your trip to Rio at another time. Now, do any of you have any other business?"

David Minofel, Enid, Lister and Ceri shook their heads and the meeting began to break. Enid was surprised that Ceri had been to Rio but she would ask her friend about her trip outside the meeting.

"There is one more thing," said Roland. The others settled back down. "I am going to advise you of an important initiative. I can't give you all the details at this time but I can say that Project 75241 is the most important we have ever undertaken. It is a global initiative and it has required – and still requires – the most meticulous planning. The acquisition and installation of the Crucible of Eternal Light was critical to its success. Charles Fundi has assured me that the work in Ubar is complete and Art Shoat has confirmed that everything is ready. We still have to bring one or two governments into line – it has been the most ambitious psychological engineering challenge we have ever faced – but the time to implement 75241 is fast approaching. That is why I am giving you notice of the project now. To achieve success, I will need the full support and absolute commitment of all Slievins' staff and, in particular, those who work most closely with me. I will give you more details at the management meeting later this month but I can tell you now – be ready. What we are going to do will change the world in which we operate. It will be a new beginning."

35. The streets of London

In the days following Minofel's brief and unhelpful visit, Adam spent much of his time wandering the streets of London. He saw the city with new eyes. The cheap cafes he had never noticed before became important resting places where, for the price of a cup of tea or coffee, he could sit somewhere warm for a while.

He was surprised to discover that the population of London had changed. He had always thought that most of the people in London were well-dressed employers or employees of governmental or commercial organisations, going purposefully about their business; or affluent tourists enjoying and marvelling at an exuberant, thriving metropolis, eager to cater to their every need. Now he saw that moving quietly through the maelstrom of purposeful workers and curious tourists, there was a whole new class of citizens. This class comprised the poor, the feckless, the mentally challenged, the purposeless, the drug and alcohol-addicted, the homeless and the hopeless. He had been vaguely aware of such people in the past, but now they seemed to be pouring out of their refuges into the streets in their thousands. They were everywhere, begging on the corners, sitting on park benches, lying in doorways. Some shambled along, but many had stopped moving altogether and were simply standing still, obstructing the thronging thoroughfares, motionless, aimless and bemused as the torrent of the driven swept past them.

The nights were the worst. Adam's room in the guest house was small, dark and poorly furnished. He had no wish to spend his time there except to sleep, so on some evenings he would wander along the Thames. He would catch a bus down to the river and walk along the embankment to Grosvenor Road. He found the Thames comforting. It was a powerful, confident river that had carried on about its business whatever human crises had been played out in the city on either side of its banks. Long before Adam's life had begun, and no doubt long after it had ended, the Thames had and would pursue its course. After all, it had flowed through the reigns of kings, the rise of Parliament, the industrial and digital revolutions and two world wars. The passing of an obscure fugitive from justice, an alleged tax evader and murderer, would not cause even a ripple in its majestic and inexorable progress.

On other evenings, Adam would take the tube into town. Unshaven and wearing a cheap hoody he had bought from a sports shop, he was fairly confident he would not be spotted by the police. He was no longer a smart, clean-shaven affluent businessman. He was a man down on his luck with limited and dwindling resources, someone who took little or no account of his image, a man with dirty clothes and an untidy beard.

His appearance and stretched financial reserves led Adam into contact with individuals in similar straits. All those he met had a tale to tell and, at first, Adam had cut them short. Why would he want to hear a series of long-winded, self-justifying stories from society's underclass? But Adam had nothing else to do and he was missing social intercourse. He was lonely. So in the end he was happy to listen.

He met Don in a cheap café in Rupert Street, just off Coventry Street near Leicester Square. Don, forty-four years old, was a waiter with an alcohol problem. He lived alone in a rented bed-sitter. His marriage had broken down years before. Don worked hard, putting in long shifts in a nearby restaurant. The pay was poor, but the tips gave him a decent wage. Each night after work, Don would go to a cheap café for a late supper and then go on to a drinking club. There he would drown his sorrows till 3 a.m. and then go back to his digs, to his single bed, to sleep it off. Perhaps surprisingly, Don wasn't full of self-pity; he was just a little disappointed with life. It seemed he had no grand ambitions, so he had no complaints about a lack of opportunity. He just felt that life had failed to live up to his modest expectations of it. Adam suggested he should drink less. Don assured Adam that he could easily cut out drink altogether but he couldn't see the point – it was his one pleasure in life.

"But if you gave up the drinking, you could save some money," Adam suggested.

"That's true," said Don, "but what would I do with the money?"

"Well, there must be something you'd like to do, and in my experience you generally need money to do what you want." Adam had it in mind that Don might like to study for some kind of a qualification to improve his job prospects; that he might want to buy a flat or a house, rather than pay rent; that he might one day aspire to run his own café or restaurant.

"There is something I've always wanted to do," Don revealed, after a long pause for thought.

Adam waited expectantly.

"I'd like to buy a new suit," said Don.

oooOooo

It didn't take long for Adam to discover help centres for the homeless. Fortunately, there was one just round the corner from his digs in Earl's Court. He had been attracted to the centre by the free tea and sandwiches. Adam still had money, but he was concerned that even the modest expense of food and drink in cafes would soon deplete his limited and finite resources.

On his first visit he had worried that the volunteers running the help centre would question his credentials as a down-and-out, but they accepted him without question. Obviously I'm deteriorating fast, thought Adam. He had no mirror in his room in the guest house so he hadn't realised that his burgeoning untrimmed beard, combined with his less than clean clothes, had seamlessly converted him from a successful businessman into a perfectly credible derelict.

It was at the help centre that he met Violet. She was working in the centre as a volunteer. In fact, she was running the place. He noticed her because, unlike him, she stood out. She was a lady in her late sixties with silver hair and sad brown eyes. Her clothes were old but had been well-made and had served her well over the decades. Of all the people at the centre Violet seemed to Adam to be the most respectable, so he started a conversation with her.

Violet had been reserved at his first approach, but he had the accent of an educated man and his voice put her mind at rest. It had never been Adam's practice to engage in lengthy conversations with strangers. After all, who really wanted to hear the crudely embellished, self-serving accounts of others' lives, with their transparently dishonest attempts to show themselves in the best possible light? Who had the time?

Well, Adam had the time; he now had all the time in the world. Until David Minofel was able to offer him a way out, he had nothing to do other than keep himself alive and, if he was to avoid loneliness, find some company. So quite suddenly he began to feel the stirrings of interest in other people.

Violet had been reticent on their first meeting, but when they ran into each other for a second time at the centre a couple of days later, at Adam's invitation Violet told him about her life.

She had been born into a lower middle-class family. Her father worked as a manager in a small local government office; her mother, Emily, stayed at home to look after Violet, their only child. The omens were good for a modestly comfortable, stable, secure childhood. But when Violet was seven, her father died. He was thirty-five years old, had shown no signs of sickness, hadn't smoked, didn't drink. But he died nonetheless.

At the age of thirty Violet's mother had to face not only the loss of her husband but financial difficulties, which she was ill-equipped to handle. Her husband's pension was derisory; he had died too young to have built up a decent entitlement. Apart from some modest savings, Emily's main source of income was Family Allowance for Violet, or Child Benefit as it became known. Of course the solution should have been for Emily to find herself a job, but she had no qualifications, and if truth were told, she was not the sharpest needle in the sewing kit. The only work she could find was menial and poorly paid. So Emily and Violet tightened their belts.

Violet was a bright girl and did well in all subjects, but as soon as she was sixteen she left school. She took a job as a clerical assistant in a small firm and quickly made herself a valuable member of the Admin team. By the time she was twenty, Violet was earning a reasonable salary and for the first time in thirteen years she and her mother felt financially secure. By then, Emily was forty-three and going through an early menopause. She had always suffered from bouts of depression and these seemed to be aggravated by the change of life. Violet took charge of the home and found she was also spending most of her spare time looking after her mother.

Violet did manage to find a boyfriend – Clive, a young man who worked in the local library. It was an unexciting relationship. Violet felt duty-bound to look after her mother and had neither the time nor, if truth be told, the inclination to devote much effort to the affair. The couple remained together for five years, during which the sexual component of the relationship waxed and waned. In the end, it faded away entirely. Clive was equivocal about breaking up; he felt comfortable with Violet but he was certain he didn't want to share a lifetime of responsibility for her mother. As for Violet, she wouldn't, she couldn't, abandon her mother. For her, that would have been a dreadful betrayal, and certainly not a burden of guilt she was willing to bear simply to maintain a desultory relationship with her librarian.

And so over the years Violet juggled her work with caring for her mother. She didn't give much thought to her own life. Maintaining the home became her goal and the justification for everything she did. When she was forty, she realised she was very unlikely to find a husband or have children. Any prospective partner would have to live with her mother, and given her own life was grindingly dull she could not reasonably expect anyone else to share it.

And, of course, Violet was conflicted. She loved her mother, but at the same time she resented her. Her love for her mother and her sense of duty had conspired to deny her the fun and fulfilment to which any woman should be entitled. Obviously, one day the caring would come to an end; her mother would die. But what would be left of her own life when she was free?

When Violet was fifty, he mother became physically disabled. Her spine had deteriorated to such an extent that she was unable to walk. Violet now had to find enough money to pay for her mother's care when she was at work. Once again, money had become a problem. Social services were unhelpful. Violet had a good job, and by then she had paid off the mortgage on their house. While asserting that their help was not means-tested, Social Services decided there were other far more needy clients. Violet and her mother were given a low priority.

Another five years passed by which time Violet was fifty-five and Emily was seventy-eight. Given her mother had suffered from depression and had for the last ten years been wheelchair-bound, Violet was surprised her mother was still alive.

And now there was another problem. Emily had never been bright, but as she entered her eighties she had developed a mild dementia. She had never been scintillating company, but now she was no company at all.

Violet took early retirement. She had a small pension and she reckoned that if she looked after her mother full-time, thus saving the cost of hired care, they could just about manage.

So that's what they did, until at the age of eight-seven Emily died. Violet was sixty-four.

The funeral was a sad affair, sadder than all such occasions are. There was only one mourner for Emily, and no one to comfort Violet.

Violet grieved. Her purpose in life had been taken from her.

And Violet was bitter. What should she do now? It was too late, too late for everything. She had no one to love. There was no one who loved her. How had this happened? She had given her life for love. She had no husband, no children, no brothers or sisters. And now she must face old age, alone and unloved. She faced the appalling fate from which, through the sacrifice of her own life, she had saved her mother.

On her sixty-fifth birthday, Violet had sat at the kitchen table in her home and pondered her options. Briefly she considered suicide but quickly rejected it. Being agnostic, she had no moral or religious scruples, but she considered suicide pointless. After all, she was going to die at some point, so if the best option was ending it all, it was going to happen anyway. In the meantime, what else could she do?

And then it came to her. She was a carer – that is, one who cares. Her caring had been largely confined to her mother, but there were plenty of other people who needed care. She had cared for Emily because Emily was her mother, an accident of birth. Emily was no more deserving of compassion than anyone else. Indeed, if one were to make moral judgements, one could argue she was less deserving than many. After all, for decades she had drained the joy from her daughter's life without much thought or any misgivings.

So Violet became a volunteer. For the last four years she had fed and watered those who had fallen on hard times. Some of those she helped had no one to blame but themselves for their difficulties; others had been dogged by bad luck. Some, like Violet, had been brought low by love and kindness. She couldn't say she had been happy in her years as a volunteer, but those years had given her back her sense of purpose. If you were a carer, there was no end to the amount of care required and no limit to the sense of purpose it afforded the carer.

"So why did you sacrifice so much for your mother?" Adam asked when Violet had finished.

Violet smiled. "I did what I thought was right. I did what had to be done."

"But that's not true," said Adam. "You didn't have to give up your own life, and in any case I'm not sure it was the right thing to do. You gave up the chance of marriage, of children, of everything. For what? Did you even make your mother happy?"

"You do what you have to do," said Violet. "I did my duty. I may not have been happy, but I know I would have been very unhappy if

I had done anything else. And if my mother wasn't happy, she was certainly happier than she would have been if I had abandoned her. And for me it wasn't all duty. There was love, too."

"And now your mother has gone, you care for others. I'd have thought you'd have had enough of caring. You're a good woman but don't you feel cheated? What about the husband you haven't loved, the babies you haven't birthed, the children you haven't reared, the friends you haven't made?"

"You seem very worried about me," said Violet with a chuckle. "It's not so bad." Then she changed the subject. "What about you? Have you done your duty? Are you a good man?"

"I'll tell you another day," said Adam, helping himself to another cup of tea.

36. You know it makes sense

It took a lot to excite Roland Samiat but Project 75241 hit the spot.

It had all begun with a casual remark by a senior British politician. He had been involved in a heated argument on a contentious issue. His opponent, an eminent academic, had quoted a plethora of statistics and authorities to support his case.

"For goodness sake," exclaimed the politician, "we've had enough of experts."

The academic was master of his subject, had a keen analytical mind and knew how to present his case in a powerful, intellectually persuasive form. So at first the politician's riposte that "we've had enough of experts" was taken simply to indicate his frustration. It caused a fair amount of amusement among the intelligentsia. Indeed, it almost achieved the status of a mocking catch phrase.

Had it not been for Roland Samiat, the matter might have ended there. But Roland had been wrestling with a problem for a very long time and he realised he had found the answer. Years before, he had conceived a brilliant idea that would assure his place in Slievins', not to mention mankind's, history, but he had been unable to devise a plausible mechanism to achieve its implementation. In that politician's retort he identified a splendid opportunity. Civil wars and wars between nation states or even between major power blocs were all very well but they were inherently self-limiting. At some point, after a few thousand, or a few hundred thousand deaths, exhaustion led to a cessation of hostilities. Even the most savage of wars in which millions died scarcely made a dent in the global population. No, if you really wanted to make an impression on humanity's inexorable population growth while at the same time providing humanity with an ideal opportunity to express its true nature in its most perfect form, you had to think at an altogether higher level.

Ironically, the opportunity to realise that higher level of thinking was prompted by observation of the lowest level of thinking. The most enthusiastic support for the politician's contempt for expert testimony came from among those incapable of reasoning and dismissive of any evidence that did not fit their preconceived notions which, as Slievins and the Praesidium knew well enough, was the majority.

Of course, the dimmer and less well-educated have always been wary of reason and contemptuous of evidence but this was something else. The politician had given voice to a growing sense of frustration among the peoples of the world. He had given unreason and contempt for intellectual integrity respectability. Of course, the Praesidium had done much over the years to undermine educational standards, to encourage both relativism and extremism, and to nurture obfuscation and negativity in all civilised communities but it was the unguarded remark of the politician that gave Roland the means to fulfil his greatest ambition.

Some years earlier, Roland had experienced a Damascene moment. One bright spring day, he had suddenly realised that war between nations was not the answer. What was needed was very different. The world needed a war between the ruler and the ruled. This dichotomy cut across all borders and all societies. It offered the prospect of a truly global conflict and, on condition that the rulers won, unprecedented carnage. The problem was how to persuade and mobilise the rulers to wreak havoc on the ruled. And then it happened.

For goodness sake, we've had enough of experts.

That was the key. The only way to galvanise the ruling class into decisive action was fear. Samiat saw in that casual, almost frivolous remark the key to unlocking the gates to a twenty-first-century Armageddon.

The rulers keep the ruled in their place by means of many stratagems. They have at their disposal power, wealth and military force. But none of these, alone or combined, is sufficient to ensure the maintenance of control. No, for that the ruled have to accept at a deep level that they are inferior to the rulers.

Long ago, the blood that flowed through the veins of the aristocracy guaranteed the superiority of the ruling class. Your status in life was predetermined by the status of your parents about which there was clearly nothing you could do. The rich man in his castle; the poor man at his gate.

With the age of reason, noble birth was no longer enough to

engender respect and subservience. Something as decisive as a bloodline but more reasonable, more rationally acceptable, was called for. The answer was intellectual superiority. If it was clear to all that the rulers were smarter than the ruled, the ruled could be kept in their place by intelligence, just as the peasants had been persuaded by blue blood to doff their caps to the lord.

Given that the rulers were not necessarily any smarter than the masses, the assertion of intellectual superiority required some contrived validation. Academics became the new priestly class who could be called upon by the rulers to marshal facts and statistics to support the rulers' views and to demonstrate the idiocy and/or futility of any opposition from the ruled. The age of the expert had arrived.

Of course the success of this strategy did not require the ruled to understand the complexity or subtlety of the arguments deployed against them. Indeed, it was rather important they made no attempt to understand; hence the need to undermine educational standards. No, the masses simply had to acknowledge in a deep sense – to feel it in their bones, so to speak – that they were irremediably inferior to those who ruled. They simply had to know that if they ever put their fuzzy, muddled heads above the parapet, they would be blown away by well-aimed intellectual dumdum bullets.

Until, of course, someone said that they didn't accept the authority of the expert, just as centuries before someone had said they didn't accept the divine right of kings. That's all it takes. Someone rejects the premise on which an elaborate structure is built, then however coherent the structure is it will collapse.

When Roland Samiat heard the politician say "We've had enough of experts", he pondered for a moment to find the right metaphor, and then said: "That man has just used his middle finger to drive a hole through the dyke, and the water behind the dyke is an ocean that can easily wash away three-quarters of humanity".

Happily, David Minofel had not been present when Roland emitted this particular metaphorical effusion.

37. A coincidence

Adam had been persuaded by Violet to help out at the drop-in centre, but after a few days he felt it best to take a break. Somebody might wonder why a well-educated, well-spoken, physically fit man in his prime had fallen on such hard times. And curiosity could easily lead to suspicion. And suspicion to arrest and imprisonment.

He was sorry to leave Violet. He liked her and, to his surprise, he had enjoyed helping her. He couldn't match her compassion and he couldn't understand how she could entirely ignore the character flaws in many of those she helped. Once or twice Adam had said to her that a particular down-and-out had obviously brought his or her troubles on him or herself. "Let those without sin cast the first stone," she had replied, which was odd since Violet had told him she didn't believe in God.

To fill his now free time, Adam decided one evening to go into the centre of town. He was well aware that London had more security cameras monitoring the streets than any other city in the world, but he was confident that he was unlikely to be picked out in the central London crowds. With his hood up and his burgeoning beard covering the lower half of his face, he was more than a challenge for any facial recognition system.

He wandered round Soho for about an hour. He was surprised to find it greatly changed. He noticed there were quite a few poor people – young men hanging about, idle or begging, young girls, some lost and confused, others working the streets. He saw hard, evil-looking men, observing like hyenas the crowd of pleasure-seekers, hoping to pick out a weak member of the herd to pull down and destroy. There seemed to be ticket touts on every corner, offering popular theatre tickets at absurd prices.

Adam saw at least one trio of pickpockets working the crowd. One bumped into the mark, the second lifted the wallet, the third took the wallet away. It was like the "find the lady" card trick. Who had the wallet? The bumper? The lifter? Surely it was one of them. No. It was the runner, long gone by the time the mark realised he'd been robbed.

This was not the Soho Adam remembered from previous visits.

On trips to the theatre, all he had seen were happy, affluent people enjoying themselves in the heart of the vibrant city of London – optimistic, excited, decent, confident people. Not frightened, broken, parasitical, malign individuals. Had London deteriorated or had his eyes been opened?

He felt the need to rest, to sit down and think. In a back street, he found a cheap café. He chose a table by the window and settled down with a cup of almost undrinkable coffee.

He had been seated for only a minute or so when he looked up. Staring at him through the window was a wreck of a man. His clothes were dirty, even more sullied than Adam's; his shoulders were hunched up as though he was carrying a great weight; his eyes looked as though they belonged to someone who had cried his soul away.

Instinctively, Adam shook his head. The pain in the man's eyes upset him. He wanted him to move on. Whatever this derelict had been through, it was nothing to do with him. He just wanted to sit quietly, drink his undrinkable coffee and take stock of what he had seen. He decided to look the other way.

There was a tapping on the window. Adam turned. He felt anger swelling up inside him. He had his own troubles, but however low he sank he would never think of staring at a stranger though a café window in the hope of eliciting sympathy or money. He would never make a nuisance of himself in such a way. He gesticulated to the man, indicating he had best leave. The man turned and walked off.

Adam sighed with relief and picked up a newspaper someone had left behind. He had just started to look for coverage of the ZeD scandal when a voice said, "May I sit here?"

Adam looked up. It was the man who had been staring through the window.

"No, you may not," said Adam. "There are plenty of other empty tables. In fact, all the other tables are empty."

"That's because the coffee is undrinkable," said the man. And then he added, "You don't recognise me, do you?"

Adam was taken aback. He looked at the man. Then he looked again, harder. "My God, you're not McFall, are you?"

Adam's doubts were understandable. Guy McFall, the ZeD product manager for the ill-fated MC57, had been a healthy, well-built, extremely competent individual. He bore very little resemblance to this broken wreck of a man now hovering beside Adam.

"Yes," said the man. "I am Guy McFall, or all that's left of him." He sat down.

Adam didn't know where to begin. He looked at Guy and shook his head.

"I saw you outside the Apollo and followed you here," said Guy.

Adam's first thought was that his confidence in his disguise, even with the help of his hood and beard, was evidently misplaced. "What are you doing here?" he managed.

"Much the same as you," said Guy. "Trying to survive."

They both sat silently for a minute or so. Then, without any malice in his voice, Guy said: "You destroyed my life."

"That's a bit rich," said Adam, lowering his voice. "It's me the police are after. You've been exonerated."

"I've been exonerated," said Guy wearily, "because I did nothing wrong. I certainly didn't kill anyone."

"You did help me to cover up the Basel trial," said Adam defensively.

"You're right," said Guy. "I was weak and I was foolish. I did what you told me to do."

"I suppose now you've found me you'll tell the police,"

"No, I won't be telling the police anything," said Guy. "After the way they treated me, the police are the last people I want to talk to."

"I'd have thought I was the last person you'd want to talk to."

"Funnily enough," said Guy, "you're the one person I feel the need to talk to. I want to tell you my story."

Adam shrugged. He had nothing better to do, and if Guy didn't intend to shop him to the police, it was probably a good idea to humour him.

"I liked you," Guy began. "We hit it off as soon as we met. You seemed to me to be an honest man with no pretensions. You showed me respect for my professionalism. I thought we could be friends."

"I liked you too," said Adam, because it was true and because it seemed best to go along with Guy's narrative.

"Of course, I had no inkling at that time that you were probably the most ruthless and perfidious human being I had ever met."

"Wow!" Adam exclaimed. "That's a bit harsh. Things didn't run as smoothly as I'd hoped and I made some mistakes, but everything I did was for the best of motives."

Guy laughed, a hollow, cackling laugh. From behind the counter the Romanian maker of the undrinkable coffee looked up briefly from his old copy of *Adevărul* (Truth).

"You suppressed an adverse clinical trial, murdered an innocent man and destroyed a major corporation and thousands of jobs – for the best of motives?"

"You're taking everything out of context." Adam was hurt. "I thought we agreed the Basel trial was probably an aberration, certainly not a good enough reason to abort the launch of MC57. And I'm certainly not confessing to the murder of anyone. That is simply wild speculation. I haven't been charged, much less convicted. I can say in all honesty that I did not commit any act of violence against anyone while I was in Geneva – and that's the truth. As for destroying the company, that was out of my hands. You have to believe me that everything I did in Geneva was done in good faith. I was trying to do my best for ZeD."

"Out of your hands? What kind of a world do you live in? You went to the media. You presented evidence that destroyed ZeD's credibility and its share price. You swept away pensions and jobs like fallen leaves in an autumn wind. Don't you take responsibility for anything?"

"You'll find this difficult to believe," Adam replied, "but I had no idea there was a plan to break ZeD. That was Slievins' plan, not mine. And it was Minofel's plan to frame you for the murder of Spinetti. There was nothing I could do."

"I'm not really interested in your side of the story. I just want to tell you mine. So please don't interrupt. I need you to understand exactly what you did to me." Guy's voice was firm, even forceful.

Adam decided to listen.

"When we met, I was a happily married man, with a wife I loved more than I can say and three beautiful children. I had an excellent job with ZeD. I was the product manager for the jewel in the crown of ZeD's range of pharmaceuticals. If MC57 had been a success, my future with ZeD, or with any other major pharmaceutical company, would have been assured.

"I worked hard and I was good at my job. You were impressed with my grasp of the product, its competitors and every aspect of the market. But I still found time to be with Jean and the kids. My happiest times were at the weekends when I could be with the family. We went on excursions to Gruyeres. We took a train ride through the

Arve Valley to the foot of Mont Blanc. We explored the beautiful Alpine village of Chamonix. We took the kids on a Segway tour of the old part of Geneva. For me, these were golden days.

"Then you arrived in Geneva. As I say, I took to you immediately. Unlike some of my previous bosses, you were prepared to listen. You didn't feel the need to make unnecessary changes just to establish your authority. It's ironic, but what I liked most about you was what I thought was your integrity.

"But, within weeks, MC57 was dead in the water, my job was in jeopardy, ZeD was crumbling, and I was arrested, charged with murder. I still don't really know the cause of that plague of disasters but I do know the result. I was assumed to be guilty of the most appalling crimes. The police were convinced I had killed Spinetti and the hall porter. Initially Jean believed I was innocent but then all the lurid details about Spinetti's relationship with Miss Tomic and her affair with Dr Reed came out, and there was online speculation that I had been involved in some complex sexual matrix. Jean found herself married to a suspected double murderer with secret but perverse sexual predilections.

"You never met Jean, did you? She's a very pretty woman, with lovely, sparkling brown eyes and a good figure. She's one of those women who find it fairly easy to keep in good shape, even after having three children. Jean and I were at university together. We became friends, and then lovers. The order is important. We became good friends first and that friendship became the bedrock of our marriage. Don't misunderstand me – the sex was great, but it's important for you to know that the bond between Jean and me was as deep as anyone can have with another person."

Adam shifted uneasily in his chair. He was interested in Guy's story. He owed it to him. But it was becoming a little too personal.

"I'm telling you this," Guy continued, "so that you realise the enormity of the crime you committed against me when you destroyed my marriage."

"I destroyed your marriage?" Adam queried.

"Jean had a mental breakdown. When I was arrested, I lost my job and my income, and she lost the man she thought she knew and loved. Jean's world was destroyed overnight. Funnily enough, if we hadn't been soulmates, the damage might have been less. If I had been a philanderer, if I had a previous record of violence, Jean might have found it easier to adjust. But I wasn't a philanderer, and I had no previous convictions for assault or murder. I was a truly loving husband and father whose life was dedicated to caring for his family. Or was I? It seemed, in fact, I was a double murderer who had become enmeshed in some kind of polygonic adulterous sexual network. The media quickly got their claws into her and the children. It was too much."

"So she had a breakdown?" Adam was subdued. "I'm really sorry. Is she recovering?"

"I don't know," said Guy. "Jean's parents are looking after the children. Jean is in hospital and I've been advised that it is best if, for a while at least, I leave her alone."

"But you've been released," said Adam. "She must know you're innocent."

"At the moment she doesn't know anything," said Guy. "She's in a drug-induced coma. She suffered acute anxiety and then had an adverse reaction to the tranquillisers she was prescribed. I don't know whether she'll fully recover. But I do know you broke her. You broke me and you broke our family."

"So what are you doing here?" asked Adam.

"At this moment, I'm explaining to you that you have to take responsibility for the consequences of your actions," said Guy. "But if you mean why am I in London, the answer is simple. I can't get a job in the pharmaceutical industry for fairly obvious reasons. At the least, I'm tarred with the ZeD brush. So I've come back to London in the hope that I can find work. I've handed all my savings over to Jean's parents so they can look after the kids. The house is being sold to cover the kids' school fees and other costs. So I'm unemployed and penniless."

"Seems we're in the same boat, then" said Adam.

"Not really," said Guy.

"I meant that we've both have lost our wives. Eve was killed in the Covent Garden bombing."

"I'm really sorry to hear that," said Guy.

"I lost Eve, and the baby she was carrying,"

Guy was visibly moved. "That's terrible." He put his hand on Adam's arm.

"You're a good man," said Adam, "and I've done you dreadful harm. There's little I can say in my defence, except to swear that it wasn't me who framed you for the Spinetti murder. That was Minofel's doing. Of course, I could have intervened. I could have told the police you were innocent. I'm ashamed I didn't. But at the time, I had a minor role in a plot worked out by others and I had no choice but to play the part I was given, or at least that's how it seemed at the time."

They sat in silence until Guy confessed. "I came here with hate in my heart. I didn't plan to attack you physically but I did want to make you understand the dreadful damage you have caused. It seems you have already been punished. I'll not tell the police where you are, but they will probably find you. When they do, you will face further punishment. I believe you when you say you didn't really know what you were doing half the time, so I feel sorry for you. But that doesn't excuse the crimes you committed. I want you to remember, all the days of your life, the people you hurt and the terrible harm you have done. Goodbye, Adam."

As Guy McFall stood up to leave, Adam took his hand. "I really hope your wife makes a full and speedy recovery," was all he said.

38. Persuasion

The key to persuading the world's governments, or those who controlled them, to wipe out seventy-five per cent of the world's population was fear.

It's not often acknowledged that the driving force behind all those who have dominion over others, in parallel with the lust for power, is the ever-present fear of losing it.

The rich know that it is unfair to be poor. Of course, the poor can work hard and some of the poor, who work hard and are clever, can become rich. But the rich know that the vast majority of the poor will stay poor. That's just the way it is and has to be. But it really isn't fair.

On the other hand, whether it's fair or not, the rulers want things to stay as they are. The more you acquire, the harder it is to give up what you have. The young, who generally have nothing, are enthusiastic about sharing. It is only when they have accumulated some wealth of their own that their enthusiasm for sharing wanes.

So if you're a ruler and you want things to stay as they are, you are always fearful that the ruled will get a bit uppity, will question your right to hold power, will rise up against you.

This puissant mix of greed and fear is inherent in the numbers. Elites are always a minority, often a very small minority. The ruled are numerous. So those in power do what they can to ensure the masses stay in their place. They recruit and maintain an army and a police force; they undertake a modest redistribution of wealth; they assert their superiority over the ruled in every possible way. But even when all measures to ensure the security of the elite have been put in place there is still fear. Why? Because no government can stay in power if enough of those they rule rise up against them.

"So fear is the key," as Roland Samiat was fond of saying. When asked "to what?" he would happily reply, "Everything."

It had taken some time to persuade the elite of the danger. Slievins had been confronted by a good deal of inertia and complacency. As is often the case with elites, they are arrogant and fall victim to their own propaganda. They come to believe they are incontrovertibly superior and have a God-given right to rule. It takes a shock, or a series of shocks, to persuade them that they have overestimated their strength and security.

It began with the persistent failure of opinion polls to predict actual outcomes. Research analysts and statisticians exercised their considerable professional skills on masses of data and, over and over again, they failed to predict the results of elections and referenda. Each failure undermined the reputation of the experts. At first, faults in research methods were blamed. The questions had been poorly framed. The weighting of the sample was incorrect. There were errors in the statistical analysis. Then it dawned on the elite: the people were lying. They were intentionally misleading the pollsters. They were mocking the experts. They wanted to prove the experts were fallible, and they wanted to prove they could outwit the elite.

What followed allowed Slievins to raise the establishment's fears to an unprecedented level. The people took the wrong decision in elections and referenda. They voted for the wrong people or policies. Not only were the masses unpredictable, they were wrong-headed. They persisted in giving the wrong answers to perfectly simple questions – wrong answers, that is, from the elite's point of view.

On top of what appeared to be a global phenomenon of bloody-mindedness among the masses, there were the problems of population growth, and the aspiration of the Third World to consume the earth's resources at the same rate as the First and Second Worlds.

The statisticians got to work on these problems, happy to turn their attention away from fatally flawed attempts to predict political and social attitudes. On these issues they were dealing with numbers from the real world – numbers of people, rate of population growth, rates of production and consumption. Rightly or wrongly, the experts were confident their predictions on the exhaustion of earth's resources were accurate to within plus or minus twenty-five years. Unless action was taken, global crises on water, food and energy resources would come together in a perfect storm by the turn of the next century.

When the experts presented their results, the consensus was for the formulation of a well-researched, reasoned plan for controlling population and consumption. That was when Slievins put all its resources into an alternative strategy, the strategy to which Roland Samiat had devoted all his energy and on which he had staked his reputation.

"The time has come," he declared at a secret side-meeting at Davos, "to recalibrate human life on earth. We've tried the *laissez faire*, let's-just-see-what-happens, it-will-be-all-right-in-the-end approach and it's not working. The world's population is growing apace. The poor are over-breeding. And people are living longer. In the West, most people are living for decades after retirement and, as is inevitable if people live beyond their allotted lifespan, they become weak, feeble, ill and demanding of help and support. In short, this model of life on earth is unsustainable."

Roland's remarks generated heated debate, especially when he concluded his speech with a few words which he intended should be writ large in the great history book of human life on earth. "Ladies and gentlemen, we don't need a plan, we need a cull."

39.   Case review

"How's he doing?" David Minofel asked. He leaned back in his reclining chair in his office on the top floor of the Slievins' London headquarters.

"It's difficult to say," Ceri replied across Minofel's uncluttered desk. "He's adjusting to being on the run rather well. He has a natural instinct for covert operations. He changes his routine regularly, avoids getting too close to anyone, and is remarkably observant. Inside he's grieving for Eve. He's angry and bitter about Eve's death, but the sheer scale of his immediate problems seems to be taking his mind off his grief. I'm not sure this is the most effective way to break him."

"Best you leave strategy to me," said Minofel, a little annoyed by Ceri Agema's assumption she could address him as an equal. "Our first objective is to sever the bond between him and Eve. Her death is not enough. We need him to move on. When the bond is completely severed, then we can break him."

Ceri realised she had irritated Minofel and decided to mollify him. "There is something I don't fully understand," she began. "Why is it so important to break Adam? He seems to be a fairly average sort of man who has already seen his family and his career destroyed. Surely, he's no threat to Slievins?"

"You'd be surprised," said Minofel. "He and Eve came close to initiating the Fourth Beginning. It threatened everything we stand for. With our help, the Praesidium managed to stop it, but it was a close shave."

Ceri was impressed. "I knew they had caused some trouble but are you telling me they took on the Praesidium and almost won?"

"It's a bit more complicated than that. They had the help of a suspected Emergent, a blind man, Kit Turner, and a couple of eccentric Irish engineers and a Greek goddess, but, essentially, the answer to your question is yes. What's more, the same gang succeeded in destroying the Westminster PCC and disrupting the Praesidium's operations around the world."

"I shall have to see Adam in a new light," said Ceri. "Evidently there's a lot I didn't know about his backstory."

"Quite so," said Minofel, "We mustn't underestimate Adam. His strength is his determination to make sense of things is a senseless world. We need to take him apart bit by bit. Let's make his life a little more difficult. Next time he's out, pop into his digs and take what's left of his cash. We'll see how he gets on when he has nowhere to stay and no food to eat."

As Ceri stood up to leave, Minofel changed the subject. "I'm curious about your trip to Rio. What were you doing there?"

"Tying up a few loose ends," said Ceri. "Just a job Roland thought it best to leave to me."

oooOooo

Enid Mavlow and Lister Bavad were spending all their time nurturing their relationship with Eve.

Lister kept Eve informed of developments in the investigation into Adam's affairs. He kept the details vague but he made it clear that the police, as well as HMRC, were "pursuing their enquiries". He told Eve that it seemed Adam was himself involved in the ZeD scandal and that the media were beginning to suggest he was not so much a white knight as a dark horse.

Enid did her best to persuade Eve not to worry, telling her it wasn't good for the baby. Although no body had been found, Adam must be dead. His death would impede any enquiries into his financial affairs and would take the sting out of any police enquiries.

"Enid's right," said Lister happily. "You can't prosecute the dead."

"And even if HMRC eventually get their teeth into you, you still don't need to worry," said Enid with confidence. "Slievins can run rings round HMRC and, whatever the outcome, make sure you're not the loser. Roland himself has told me to set your mind at rest." The inner circle at the top of Slievins were well aware that Enid was in the first flush of a relationship with Roland Samiat, so it seemed eminently plausible that she could speak with authority about Roland's intentions.

oooOooo

Eve liked Enid. She was warm-hearted, lively, vivacious and generally good company. So when Enid attended on Eve one morning without a smile and with sadness in her eyes, Eve immediately sensed something was wrong.

"It's Estevo," said Enid. "I've just heard from the Brazilian embassy. He's dead."

"Estevo?" Eve queried.

"He was my boyfriend in Rio. In fact he was my fiancé."

"I'm so sorry," said Eve. Having heard the gossip about Enid and Roland, Eve had assumed Enid was unattached, and Enid had never mentioned a fiancé in Rio.

"I was going to write to him to tell him it was over," Enid answered Eve's unasked question.

Eve nodded to indicate no explanation was necessary. Then she asked: "How did he die?"

"I don't know. The police say 'suspicious circumstances'. That's all I know. Estevo's parents asked the embassy to tell me. I have spoken to them, but they don't have any details, or if they do, they don't want to discuss them over the phone."

"I'm so sorry," said Eve for the second time.

"It's all right," said Enid. "We didn't have a future together but I was very fond of him. He was a wonderful man – kind, funny, loving."

oooOooo

When Ceri left Minofel's office, she made straight for a nearby coffee bar that both she and Enid Mavlow liked. When Ceri arrived, she apologised to Enid for being a few minutes late.

Enid was not her usual vibrant self. The day before, she had heard from the Brazilian embassy of Estevo's death.

After an exchange of pleasantries, Ceri said: "I have something to tell you."

Enid was surprised by Ceri's tone.

"When I was in Rio, I ran into Estevo."

"You ran into Estevo?" queried Enid.

"Well, I ran into Estevo because I went there to meet him."

Enid was confused. "What do you mean 'you went there to meet him'?"

"Just listen," said Ceri. "Roland sent me there to check him out. As you know, it's Slievins' policy to know everything about its employees, in your case for obvious reasons – Roland had a particular interest – but it's policy anyway."

"So you met him."

"Yes, I met him. Or rather he picked me up. He was attending a lecture at the National Museum. I asked him where I could get hold of the background notes on the lecturer and it went on from there."

"What went on from there?" asked Enid.

"Well, you don't need all the details but that evening we ended up in bed."

Enid was conflicted. Given her affair with Roland Samiat, she was not in the best position to feel aggrieved, but it hurt that her fiancé was prepared to slip between the sheets with any attractive woman. How many women had he been unfaithful with? Yes, she was having an affair, but he didn't know that. As far as he was concerned, his fiancée was faithful and looking forward to their wedding.

"Did you tell him you knew me?" Enid asked eventually.

"No, I didn't, and your name, indeed your existence, didn't come up in conversation."

"What conversation?" said Enid sharply. "It sounds as though there wasn't much conversation between 'Where do I get the notes?' and screwing each other."

"You're upset," said Ceri.

Enid's eyes blazed. "Just a little," she said bitterly. "Why did you do this?"

"I told you. Roland sent me to check out your fiancé. I guess he wanted to find out how serious your affair had been."

"Well, you can report it wasn't serious at all. More a bit of a joke."

"It's clear Roland cares for you. He needed to make sure you had no loyalties that might conflict with your commitment to Slievins, but it's obvious he had personal as well as corporate reasons to send me off to Rio."

"And you accepted the job? What kind of a friend are you?"

"Enid, you're taking this in the wrong way. I was just helping to protect Slievins' interests and yours."

"What's the right way of taking it? When someone you think is your friend seizes the first opportunity to fuck your fiancé, which way are you supposed to take it?"

Ceri shrugged. "You need to calm down. You're sleeping with Roland so you're overdoing the moral indignation. Roland gave me a brief. I fulfilled it. He wanted to know if Estevo was a problem. I established he wasn't."

"Well, he's certainly not a problem now because he's dead," said Enid. "I don't suppose you had anything to do with that?"

"Of course not," said Ceri. "When I left him, he was perfectly happy. What kind of person do you think I am?"

Enid thought it best not to answer.

"We'll talk again when you've calmed down," said Ceri.

Estevo had indeed been perfectly happy, at least up to the moment when, tied to the bed and in mid-orgasm, Ceri, naked and astride his body, had forced a whole orange into his open mouth and watched him choke to death.

Oranges fulfilled a variety of functions in Ceri's amorous armoury, not all of them fatal.

40. Life is hard

When Adam discovered all his money had been stolen he complained to the landlord. The outcome was his immediate eviction. "Not my problem," the landlord had said, "except I'm guessing you can't pay the rent."

Adam had already spent quite a lot of the £1,500 he had brought with him, so the amount stolen was only a few hundred pounds. But its loss hit him hard. He now had nothing, not even enough for a cup of coffee. "Give us a quid for a cup of tea." He had heard the request often enough from the beggars that hung around tube stations and other locations with a high footfall and he'd always ignored them. Now he knew what it was to have no means of acquiring a cup of tea.

Gradually it dawned on him that he had no means to do anything. He had nowhere to eat, nowhere to sleep, nowhere to be safe. Soon he would be thirsty and hungry.

Minofel had forbidden him to try to make contact, but it was not Minofel's prohibition that deterred Adam from heading to Slievins' offices. First of all, it was a long walk from Earl's Court to the City. Secondly, almost certainly the police would be watching out for him. No, he had to wait for Minofel to come up with a plan. In the meantime, he must find another way.

His only hope was Violet at the drop-in centre.

"I need help," he said to Violet as soon as he saw her.

"Everyone here needs help," said Violet with a smile.

"I've lost all my money," Adam explained. "It's been stolen."

"Most here haven't had any money to lose, so you're in good company."

"I'm serious," said Adam. "I'm desperate."

"I'm serious too," said Violet. "Would you like a cup of tea?"

"Yes, please," said Adam. He was close to tears.

"You can help out here for a while," said Violet as she handed him a cup of tea. "You can sleep in the back for a few days. There's an old bed with a mattress and a couple of blankets. But then you'll have to move on."

"Thank you," said Adam. "I'm really grateful."

"I'm not a fool," said Violet. Her remark took Adam by surprise. "I realise you're in trouble with the law. I don't know what you've done and I don't want to know, but as soon as you can, you have to move on. Do you understand?"

Adam wanted to explain, to put her mind at rest. He wasn't a common criminal. She had nothing to worry about. But it was difficult. What could he say? "I've done a bit of bribery and blackmail, and I may have been involved in killing a couple of people and wrecking the lives of a few others, but I'm obviously a decent sort of a chap, not to be confused with those who have disgracefully low moral standards, like most of the losers you have here."

Violet read his mind. "If you're going to stay and help, you are going to have to change your attitude. It's true some are here because they behaved badly, but most are here either because they have been stupid or they just had bad luck. Some are here because they tried to do the right thing, and doing the right thing cost them everything."

"Really?" Adam queried. "How does that work?"

"Take Stan," Violet replied. "He visited me here almost every Wednesday for a year before his death, which sadly happened just a couple of months ago. He was a bright chap, a computer programmer. He worked hard, did his best, but he ended up penniless and homeless.

"He married a girl called June when they were both in their early twenties. They had known each other from childhood. June was an exotic dancer – at least, that's what she called it. They had a son, Jack. Jack had to be born by Caesarean and June was convinced the scar had ruined her career. Whatever the reason, June didn't take to motherhood. In fact, that's a bit of an understatement. She decided she wanted to get rid of the boy, to put him into care. Stan had a full-time job at the time, so it was difficult, but he decided to look after Jack himself. He gave up his job with the software firm and started to work as a freelance.

"June had as little to do with the boy as possible. She spent most of her time riding. And socialising. She was very fond of horses and she was very keen on socialising, so much so that one day, a few years after Jack's birth, Stan returned home unexpectedly early from a freelance assignment only to find June in the matrimonial bed with Rick who until then Stan had thought of as his best friend."

"That must have hurt," observed Adam.

"June was very reasonable. She said Stan was welcome to stay in the house on condition that he slept in the spare room while she entertained Rick in the master bedroom. Not surprisingly, Stan decided to leave. He found himself a small flat, more a bedsit, and tried to sort himself out. Among many other problems, the new flat had a very poor broadband connection, which despite numerous visits by so-called engineers could never be resolved. As a result, Stan was struggling to keep his freelance business going. He was deeply unhappy. He found it difficult to move on."

"He should have stayed in his house and thrown his wife out."

"Perhaps," said Violet, "but he couldn't. You see, he still loved June and he was pretty sure that she and Rick wouldn't stay together for long. So he spent his time working hard, when his dubious broadband connection permitted, to support himself and to pay the mortgage on the house and all living expenses for June and Jack. He saw Jack, who was now about seven years old, as often as possible to make sure he was properly cared for. In other words, he tried to do all the right things."

"So how did it work out?" Adam asked. "Did he come to terms with the situation?"

"He couldn't come to terms with the situation because the situation got a good deal worse. June decided she wanted a divorce. She claimed the house on the grounds that Stan had deserted her – he had moved out – and that she was looking after their son. That was when Stan started to have headaches."

"Started to have headaches! He was married to one. And as for her claim that she was looking after Jack, when did she ever do that?" observed Adam.

"Quite so. Jack lived in the house, but he was either left to fend for himself or more often than not looked after by Stan, who had always been a good father and with whom Jack had a very strong relationship. Anyway, Stan agreed a settlement with June. He gave her the house and a lump sum of most of his savings – about £60,000."

"So he decided to sever his links with his wife – a clean break?" Adam asked.

"You might have thought so, but June quickly lost the money Stan had given her by handing it over to her latest lover – Rick was long gone – who had a brilliant idea for a new business venture which sadly failed as soon as Stan's money ran out. When that happened, June insisted that Stan should continue to support her, despite the generous settlement he had already provided, and when Stan baulked at her new demands she took him to court.

"The court took her side. She was an abandoned wife, left to fend for herself and her son, both of whom had been cruelly abandoned by her selfish and irresponsible husband. Stan's headaches were getting worse. Of course Stan tried to set the record straight, but he couldn't afford the legal fees for proper representation, unlike June who was on legal aid. In any case, he had little chance to present his version of events because although June had initiated court proceedings, half the time she failed to attend the court. Proceedings were postponed, no evidence was taken, and Stan lost another day's work, although to be fair the appalling and erratic broadband service at his flat made his freelance business almost impossible to run.

"Then one day, when June was supposed to be at home, Stan called in and found Jack on his own in the house. Stan asked Jack where his mother was. Jack said she had been out all day, horse riding as far as he knew. So Stan left a note for June, asking her why she had left Jack alone in the house, and took Jack back to his flat, fed him and let him stay while Stan worked on some software or argued with BT about the dreadful broadband. At about six o'clock the police arrived. June had reported Stan for kidnapping their son from the matrimonial home. Stan was taken to the police station and charged.

"When the police interviewed Jack, they realised that June had not been entirely honest and the case was dropped, but Stan was badly shaken. He didn't sleep well the night they released him. He had a really bad headache, and when he woke in the morning after a restless, painful night, he found blood on the pillow from a nose bleed.

"A couple of days later – that's now about three years ago – Stan took Jack out for an afternoon to the zoo. On the way back, Stan passed out and crashed his car. No one was hurt but Stan was admitted to Royal Marsden hospital as an emergency. He had a brain tumour, a glioblastoma. They operated on him immediately. He was put on a course of chemo. The specialist told him he had twelve to eighteen months. They could operate once more, perhaps twice if he was strong enough, but after that there was nothing they could do. The cancer was invasive. The consultant explained to Stan that there was a limit to what they could cut away from his brain without turning him into a vegetable. He didn't put it like that, but that's what he meant. That's when I met Stan. I was at the hospital to visit one of my regulars who was ill with lung cancer. Stan and I got on immediately. He told me his story and I suggested if he ever wanted a chat to come to the drop-in centre. In the long months of his illness, he popped in here every Wednesday, when his surgery and chemo permitted, to help out.

"Stan had his two operations. After the second, he was unable to see very well and was a bit shaky on his feet. From then on it was all downhill. He ended up in a hospice for the last few weeks, drifting away in a sea of morphine.

"Why am I telling you all this? Because I think you believe that anyone who is homeless and penniless must deserve it in some way, and you think you're an anomaly. Well, you're wrong. Many are in dire straits through no fault of their own. Stan is a classic case. You can blame June, the court system, BT or God for Stan's woes, but one person you can't blame is Stan. Whereas I suspect that, in your case, you're as guilty as sin. So as someone once said: 'Judge not, that ye be not judged'."

Adam was stunned. He had met this elderly woman only twice and yet she seemed to know him as well, if not better, than anyone. And despite observing his flaws as clearly as black ink spots on white paper, she had shown him considerable kindness. She gave Adam an odd feeling of hope.

41. Roland Samiat

Amidst all the hurly burly of events in this narrative, it is quite likely that some readers of a particularly curious turn of mind will have questions about Roland Samiat which I, the Storyteller, have so far failed to answer. So I shall take a moment of your time, if I may, to give some pointers.

Sadly, I know very little of his early years. As far as this story is concerned, he seems to have been around always, a kind of indefinable presence, even in his absence.

When you look at mankind, you see good and bad everywhere. It is common practice to describe some people as good and some as bad, but if the truth be told, generally speaking, there's good and bad in all of us. Even those who merit the description of evil usually have some redeeming feature or, at least, some feelings of guilt or remorse for the evil they do. Of course, there are some whose minds are so twisted, whose drives are so perverse, that they are incapable of any empathy with others or regrets for their dreadful deeds, but, happily, they are relatively few in number.

All that said, Roland Samiat doesn't fit anywhere into this broad assessment of mankind. "How can that be?" you ask. "Surely you've covered the entire moral spectrum?"

No.

Roland is an exception. Roland has a profoundly moralistic outlook, but in his mind, evil is good and what we generally consider good, he is convinced is evil. So Roland has no moral qualms about what others see as his evil deeds. For him, they are the entirely healthy and wholesome expression of human nature. Every crime, from theft to murder, and every destructive emotion, from jealousy to hate, is, for Roland, an indication of a healthy, well-adjusted soul. It is man's nature.

It was rumoured that the young Roland had been dominated and physically abused by a tyrannical father who threw him out of the house at the first sign of teenage rebellion, but I am unable to confirm this. Roland rarely spoke about himself. Assuming it to be true, we might have expected Roland to have had a difficult start in the world, especially given his rather contrary moral outlook, but we would have been wrong. He settled into adult life with extraordinary ease. Despite the rift from his father, the young Roland used his father's contacts to find a job in banking. Within three years, he had become a trader; within five years, a multi-millionaire. As he climbed the ladder of success, he had no compunction about stepping on those below or pulling down those above. His ruthlessness caused surprisingly little rancour, at least partly because his behaviour was entirely natural to him. Most of his victims felt it would be almost churlish to criticise him. After all, Roland was just being himself.

He showed the same cavalier attitude in his relations with women, enjoying them and discarding them with equal facility. As with his work colleagues, his conduct generated much less hostility than might have been expected, once again because it was evident to all that he was simply being true to his own nature.

In a safe room in the private quarters of his Mayfair mansion, Roland kept the four precious phials holding the concentrated essences of the Monitaurs salvaged by Minofel when he abandoned the Westminster PCC. The yellow phial contained the distillation of depravity. In the red phial was the roiling oil of extremism. The liquid in the blue phial complacently encompassed corruption. The grey phial, in its murky, indeterminate hue, was the bland expression of obfuscation and negativity. In their current form they simply represented for Roland all that was good in the world. Each of them, in different ways, enabled man to be true to himself. David Minofel could pursue his rather silly hobby of gathering blood samples from those whom the world considered evil. But Minofel's collection was trivial, the product of a rather childish superstition. These phials, on the other hand, containing the concentrated essences of the Monitaurs, were the real thing.

When the Monitaurs adopted human form, they walked among men and made the world what it is. No one could teach the sallow-skinned Lotte Axelrod, with her hard-lined face and deep-sunk eyes, anything about depravity. The nondescript Edgar Exton, despite his apparent normality, could infiltrate and cause mayhem in a Women's Institute meeting, compelling even the mildest of members to see red. The ebullient Charlie Cornick, with his florid complexion and easy manner with all he met, could lead anyone into temptation, inviting them to join him for a languid swim in a deep, dark, blue sea of corruption. And the grey-faced Oliver Nates had a natural ability to spread his own inadequacies and incompetence to all he met just as darkness falls when light withdraws.

Locked in their phials, none of the Monitaurs could express themselves to Roland, but the Slievins CEO knew that all of them, had they been able, would have warmly applauded his most ambitious plan. And when Project 75241 was implemented and a brave new world created, he would allow them to resurrect themselves in human form to resume their work among a much-depleted, but hopefully significantly improved, human population.

42. Project planning

The monthly management meeting was well attended. In addition to David Minofel, all Slievins' consultants, ten in number, were present.

On the Chairman's right hand sat Art Shoat, Roland Samiat's chief enforcer, newly returned from the Arabian desert. Art was given a place at any meeting, however much those attending the meeting might resent or fear him.

Although not full members of the management committee, Roland's own personal staff, Lister Bavad, Ceri Agema and Enid Mavlow, were also in attendance.

Including the Chairman, Roland, there were sixteen seated at the boardroom table.

Unusually, at the large reinforced glass door of the boardroom, there were four guards: two on the inside, and two outside. Evidently Roland Samiat had judged that enhanced security was required for this particular management meeting.

The Chairman opened proceedings by stating that the subject to be discussed must be treated as highly confidential. No word of their deliberations must reach anyone who was not present at the meeting. He added that anyone who ignored this instruction would immediately be sanctioned, a Slievins' euphemism for termination – at best of employment; at worst of life.

Having emphasised the need for secrecy, Roland adopted a more positive tone. He stood up and carefully pressed the splayed fingertips of both hands on the glass top of the boardroom table.

"Ladies and gentlemen, we are about to see the dawn of a new age. It will be an age of plenty, an age in which the planet will recover, an age in which man will have proved himself. The instrument that will herald this new dawn is Project 75241."

A stream of power flowed from each of Samiat's fingers, through the glass top, to touch each of those seated at the table.

There was a murmur of expectation from the assembled committee members. Some of them had heard the term 75241 and had assumed it was code for a major Slievins' initiative, but none had any details.

"As you all know, we have mankind's best interests at the very heart of all we do. Our *raison d'etre* is to empower man to be truly what he is. 75241 provides man with the opportunity to fulfil himself, to assert unambiguously his true nature."

Roland knew well enough that his audience was impatient for an explanation of this mysterious project, but he rather enjoyed teasing his subordinates.

"As we all know, there are those who dispute our assessment of man's true nature. They blather on about kindness and compassion. They rush forward at every opportunity to burnish their utterly spurious moral superiority by excusing, and thus encouraging, weakness. They dream of a better world of peace and love in which those with power and wealth devote themselves to improving the lot of the weak and vulnerable, but it is of course an imaginary world in which mankind, as it truly is, has no place. It is in the nature of man to compete, to strive to have more than others, to attain and retain wealth and power. Most fail. Most have to fail. We do not wish to be rich among rich men. We seek to be rich among the poor. How else can we enjoy the privileges of our success and superiority? Happily, it is a natural law that the number of the poor must greatly exceed the number of the rich."

Roland could see that the committee were becoming restless. To them, he was merely stating the obvious. But he was not yet ready to reveal all.

"No," he continued, "we and we alone understand the problems mankind faces and how to deal with them. The population on this planet is already too large. If all those now living were to enjoy the lifestyle of the Western world, the planet would collapse into a withered shadow of its former self, like a pricked balloon."

David Minofel could not suppress a smirk. There he goes again, he thought. What kind of a simile is that? It had almost everything wrong with it. Apart from its shape, there was no connection between a balloon, a thin outer material, full of nothing but air, and planet earth, a dense, solid object of considerable size and mass with a core of iron. And pricked balloons don't wither, they collapse abruptly accompanied by a loud explosion. In any case, how can you have a withered shadow: a shadow is caused by an object. The shadow withers only if the object withers. A shadow is always a true version of its current self; it cannot be a withered version of its former self.

"You seem to be losing concentration, David," observed Roland, addressing Minofel.

"Not at all," Minofel replied. "I was simply savouring your adept use of imagery."

Samiat's eyes narrowed. "I'm not sure you can savour anything as abstract as imagery but we shall let that pass," he observed, then added unnecessarily, "A touch, a touch, you might as well confess it."

Minofel looked at Roland blankly, refusing to acknowledge his riposte.

Roland continued. "We have rather more important matters to consider. As I was saying, we need some drastic action to prevent the masses from consuming the planet. Happily, the necessity to sort out the population problem comes at a time when the need for people has never been less. With automation and the development of artificial intelligence, most people are now entirely surplus to requirement. Of course, governments can continue to create unreal jobs to keep an ever-growing army of semi-literate graduates off the streets. But why should they? The planet cannot supply the needs of the masses and the masses are themselves no longer necessary. The elite have realised what a wonderful world it would be if only the lumpen dross could be eliminated. Hence Cull 75241."

Roland now had the full attention of everyone present.

"Project 75241 is a drastic cull of humanity, involving the elimination of three-quarters of the global population. When 75241 has been implemented, the population of the world will be about two billion, still a substantial number but more sustainable."

"Are you saying we are to kill six billion people?" Ceri Agema asked the question simply out of curiosity. There was not the slightest hint of moral qualms.

Roland smiled and nodded. He liked Ceri. "Precisely," he replied.

"And the governments of the world are happy to go along with the plan?" enquired Minofel.

"Some are – and some don't know about it," Roland Samiat replied. "We have been most careful to reveal the plan only to those who have shown sympathy for the arguments that underpin it. It is widely acknowledged that the current situation is unsustainable. The planet might survive for another few hundred years if population growth tails off and we can keep two-thirds of the world's population in poverty. But neither condition is likely to be fulfilled. Even if both were, it would be a difficult and draining time for the world's elite as they faced increasing pressure from the Third World seeking, if not demanding, the standard of living enjoyed by the developed nations. Some governments have realised the need for drastic action. Others acknowledge the problem but are too squeamish to face the solution. But they don't matter. We now have a consensus among the true elite, those who really hold power in this world of ours, that action is called for, that the Cull is necessary and should be implemented."

There was silence as the scale of the proposed operation sank in. It was Art Shoat who spoke first.

"How do we cull three-quarters of the world's population and how do we decide who lives and who dies?"

Roland Samiat nodded approvingly. That was Art, not subtle but straight to the point. Roland answered Art's second question first.

"Seventy-five per cent must die. Twenty-four per cent will be spared – they are those who are clever enough or creative enough or loyal enough to justify their continued existence by supplying the needs of the world's elite, the one per cent. Hence the project code 75241 – 75 per cent die; 24 per cent survive to serve the 1 per cent elite."

Art was satisfied with the answer to his second question. He had been mildly concerned by the first two criteria for survival (fearful that most of his relatives, perhaps even he himself, might fail to meet the standard) but no one could question his unwavering loyalty. Thus encouraged, he probed: "OK, so how do we do it?"

"An excellent question!" Roland said, leaning back in his chair. "The answer may surprise you. Certainly the planning we have put into this aspect of the Cull will impress you. To explain the technicalities, I should like to introduce a respected member of the Breaker community, the Chief Dawk, Despiro Nihilopificus."

The Chairman buzzed the outer office and instructed the secretary to send in the visitor. The Chief Dawk was a tall, grey-haired, ascetic looking man in his middle years. His manner was reserved, and created the impression, not entirely groundless, of arrogance. His lips were thin and pale.

"Despiro Nihilo-whaticus?" asked Art Shoat, as the Chief Dawk entered.

Roland gave Art a withering look. "Despiro Nihilopificus is a man of great intellect who has, on numerous occasions, persuaded those who seek the truth that the path to wisdom lies in methodically taking things apart to determine what they are made of and how they work. Despiro is the head of the DAWK department – Deconstruction Administered with Kindness – and was appointed by me to the position of Cull Operational Director to devise a way of separating the wheat from the chavs, so to speak."

Despiro Nihilopificus surveyed those present in the boardroom carefully, assessing the intelligence levels of those present in order to calibrate his presentation to communicate as efficiently as possible. "Gentlemen and ladies, I have been asked by the Chairman to explain to you how Cull 75241 is to be implemented. As I proceed, I am sure you will have many questions." Here Despiro paused, before adding, "but I would be grateful if you could keep them to yourselves. If you listen carefully, all your questions will be answered in the course of my presentation."

Having put everyone in their place, Despiro began his account of the planning that had gone into Cull 75241. He spoke in a precise, clipped manner, which quietly confirmed that he had a complete and disciplined grasp of his subject.

"In determining how to eliminate seventy-five per cent of the world's population I had to meet the five requirements set out in your Chairman's admirably precise and succinct brief. One, there must be no suspicion of the impending cull before C day – that is, Cull Day. Two, the Cull must be completed in a twenty-four-hour period. Three, the Cull's cause must remain a mystery to the global population. Four, the Cull must be selective – that is, it must eliminate the seventy-five per cent who are surplus to requirement but leave the remaining twenty-five per cent – the elite one per cent and the twenty-four per cent needed to service the elite – unharmed. Five, ideally the plan should facilitate disposal of the six billion corpses."

Despiro Nihilopificus waited for the complexity of the brief to sink in. The consultant members of the board were either taking notes or exchanging looks with each other. None of them could see any way in which such a brief could be fulfilled.

Ceri Agema was excited. Her cold, green eyes sparkled. She uncrossed her legs and parted them. Her short skirt rode up a little as she leaned back in her chair. Lister Bavad, who was sitting next to her, couldn't help but notice those long shapely legs encased in black stockings. He dropped his hand to the side of his chair so he could lightly touch Ceri's hip. She smiled. Emboldened, Lister slid his hand onto her thigh, on the white flesh above her stocking top. Ceri turned her head and looked at him. Their eyes conversed briefly. They were of one mind, and as soon as possible after the meeting they would be of one flesh. Ceri was breathing heavily but all she said was; "Six billion."

Enid had her eyes on Roland. Indeed she found it difficult to take her eyes off him. He seemed so handsome, so distinguished, so clean. And yet he had ordered this strange, ascetic man with an unpronounceable name to devise a plan for the extermination of billions of people.

From the moment Enid had joined Slievins, she had been told that the company had man's best interests at heart. Slievins was, of course, a business, but Slievins had core values. Its fundamental objective was to enable man to fulfil himself. Of course, you had to be rich to enjoy Slievins' services, but there was no conflict of interest. All men were either rich or – the vast majority – aspiring to be so. Slievins simply wanted to help those who had already made some progress in fulfilling this universal human ambition.

Yet now the Chairman of Slievins was calmly announcing the extermination of three out of every four human beings. Yes, there was a problem of overpopulation. Yes, the underdeveloped world looked with envy on the rich nations. Yes, it had been estimated that the planet's resources would be exhausted within a few generations. But the killing of six billion people was surely a crime of truly Biblical proportions and clearly not in the immediate interests of the six billion. Not since the Flood had anyone undertaken such a global pogrom.

"Yes, not since the Flood," said Roland, apparently answering Enid's thoughts but really simply giving an obvious response to Despiro's account of the brief. "Not since the Flood, my friends, but please acknowledge the difference. This extermination is not prompted by a jealous, discipline-obsessed tribal deity, hell-bent on punishing sinners. No, this time it is driven by a desire to see the best of man survive and flourish."

"But how?" Art Shoat voiced the question everyone was thinking. "How the hell can we wipe out three-quarters of mankind in one day without anyone suspecting us? And how can we separate the toffs from the dross?"

"Listen and learn," Roland commanded. "Listen and learn."

"It was a challenge," Nihilopificus conceded, "and we cannot pretend to one hundred per cent accuracy in discriminating between the elite and the expendable. But what we have done is judged by Slievins to be good enough. First, I should explain that those who are to die are already marked. The means of their death is already implanted inside them. They are the walking dead."

"Six billion zombies? I don't think so," said Art dismissively.

"For some months now," Despiro continued, unabashed, "we have been modifying all the salt and all the sugar used in the preparation of fast foods, modifying and enhancing them. In minute quantities, we have added a latent chemical to both salt and sugar. As time passes, this latent chemical, DK12, accumulates until it is present in every cell of the body. While latent, DK12 has no effect on the host. As far as the consumers are concerned, they are simply enjoying taste-enhancing salt and sugar. In fact, they are harbouring the seeds of death."

"Do you mean that anyone who has eaten food containing salt or sugar has been ingesting this DK12, this poison?" asked Art, somewhat alarmed.

"Only if their main source of sustenance is fast food," responded Despiro complacently.

Art was not reassured. "What do you mean 'main source of sustenance'?" he asked. He was rather partial to the odd burger and chips, or a takeaway curry of a Friday night. "Are you telling me I've been poisoned, that I'm carrying the seeds of death?"

"Almost certainly," Despiro replied with some relish. The Chief Dawk was a reasonable and equable man but he had made it clear he disliked interruptions, and this large porcine fellow, with a heavy East London accent, evidently a fast-food aficionado, kept butting in.

Art stood up. "Almost certainly," he mimicked Despiro's words. "I'll shove the seeds of death up your arse ..."

"You will sit down and shut up," Roland Samiat intervened. "Your boorish behaviour suggests the proposed method of identifying the dross works rather well. You will show the Chief Dawk respect, or your chances of surviving even to C Day will greatly diminish."

There was a stunned silence. This was not how Slievins conducted its affairs. This was not how the Chairman addressed his staff. Only David Minofel was unsurprised. For all his charm and bonhomie,

Roland Samiat was utterly ruthless. Of course, the consultants had always known that the Chairman was capable of extraordinary acts of evil. That's why they admired and followed him. But only David Minofel had been aware that Roland Samiat rather liked to perpetrate acts of evil with his own hands. Only David Minofel understood that if Art Shoat persisted, Samiat was perfectly capable of slitting his lieutenant's throat in front of the entire management committee. Art subsided, as stunned as the others.

"Please continue," said Roland addressing Despiro.

"On C Day we will activate DK12. It will kill all those who are carrying substantial quantities of DK12. First it will attack the cells in the nervous system, killing the hosts within minutes. They will suffer excruciating pain but, mercifully from their point of view, only briefly. Then the bodies will spontaneously combust. DK12 will react with the oxygen and other flammable elements in the body. The subjects will not burst into flames. That would be too damaging to property. But they will smoulder. Within twenty-four hours all soft body parts will be gone, thus reducing the risk of disease and making the clean-up much easier."

Now that Art had been subdued, David Minofel took up the questioner's role, eager to demonstrate to his brutal rival for Samiat's favour that he could pose a question and survive unscathed.

"And how do you activate DK12 so that all the victims die in one day?"

"Simple," replied Despiro. "DK12 has been designed to have a particular resonance. It responds to very particular wavelengths of light and of sound. The light will be beamed from a network of satellites. The sound will be broadcast by every radio and TV station and across all social media on the internet. It will be the *son et lumière* show to end all *son et lumière* shows, believe me. If the *son* doesn't get them, the *lumière* will, so to speak." The Chief Dawk paused to allow the others to appreciate the wit of his last remark before continuing. "Of course there are those in the Third World who cannot afford even fast food. For them, mostly in Africa, we have had to adopt a more blunderbuss approach. We plan to put fairly high levels of DK12 in the water supply a few days before C Day, enough to kill most of the population. Only those who drink imported bottled water or alcoholic beverages will survive."

"Rich drunks!" opined Art. "What happened to preserving the elite?"

"It's not ideal," Despiro conceded. "Using the contaminated water route, we will lose many who would survive on the fast-food test, but if we are to meet the seventy-five per cent Cull criterion, we need to take out all the poor and uneducated. Our statisticians calculate that we have a ninety-five per cent chance of being within plus or minus three per cent of the target. Worst case scenario is seventy-two per cent culled with twenty-eight per cent surviving. If need be, we can make further adjustments later. It would certainly be possible to eliminate another three per cent through wars or natural disease, and we have put contingency plans in place."

Despiro Nihilopificus had concluded his presentation.

Roland Samiat was well satisfied. "How often have we warned the masses of the dangers of a diet of fast food? We have even told them it is killing them." Roland paused and looked slowly round the boardroom table. No one spoke. "No questions? No comment?" he challenged. "You surprise me."

Enid, who was sitting several places away from Roland, shifted uneasily in her chair. Roland caught her eye. "Miss Mavlow, you have a question?"

Enid blushed. This was her first management meeting and she feared that most of the consultants had assumed she had been invited only because of her intimate relationship with the Chairman. She was, of course, entirely wrong. The only thought that Enid's presence had stimulated in the assembled Slievins' male-dominated management team was carnal in nature, and heavily tinged with envy.

"Well," Roland prompted. "Don't be intimidated by these sombre gentlemen. There isn't one of them who wouldn't give their right hand to get it inside your knickers. Speak. Tell me what you think."

Again, the assembled executives were stunned. They had never heard the Chairman speak so crudely and so offensively to them. His rebuke of Art Shoat and his insult aimed at the consultants was out of character.

"Come now, Enid," Roland persisted. "Say what you think." Roland waited.

Enid realised Roland would not let the matter rest. In the end, she said: "Isn't killing six billion people a bit drastic?"

"At last, an obvious and sensible question," said Roland. "I realise that all of you have become a little jaded, desensitised even. I have often thought that, after a few years with Slievins any one of you could watch a man gouge out someone's eyes without batting an eyelid. Even seeing a man disembowelled wouldn't turn your stomachs. But please make an effort to appreciate the scale, the magnificence, the grandeur of what you have had heard today. Yes, in the past we've played our part in wars. But wars just don't cut it. There was discussion in some quarters of a preemptive nuclear attack on China, but even wiping out the entire Chinese population fell far short of the seventy-five per cent target. And obviously that particular proposal, which entailed the indiscriminate elimination of everyone in China, failed to find favour with the Chinese leadership. Yes, in the past we've engineered conflict in the interest of our arms-manufacturing friends. We've spread the odd disease to eliminate tribes who have risen against their rulers, our clients. The Praesidium devoted all its resources to the encouragement of lust and corruption and other essential aspects of human nature, which Emergents and others have done their best to suppress. We have a proud history, for sure. But Cull 75241 marks a step change in our march towards the fulfilment of man's destiny. It is a final rite of passage in man's quest for complete self-awareness. When Cull 75241 is enacted, man will know himself fully. All doubts resolved. All questions answered."

"It will be a somewhat slimmed down version of humanity that achieves this enlightenment," observed Minofel wryly.

"Slimmer and fitter," said Roland, "like a fat, lazy caterpillar sloughing off its skin to emerge as a butterfly which, with a single beat of a wing, can write a new page in human history."

David Minofel studied the faces of the other consultants. They displayed various expressions. Most were trying to grasp the sheer scale of the project. Others were puzzled by, even dubious about, the proposed *modus operandi*. None were echoing the screams of laughter ringing inside David Minofel's head at the Chairman's peculiar turn of phrase. It was not just the mixing up of a caterpillar with a snake, or the bizarre image of a wing writing a page. No, there was also the failure of eye-gouging to provoke the batting of an eyelid, and the absence of any stomach churning at the sight of a disembowelling. Not to mention his insults directed first at Art Shoat, his trusted henchman whom he had suggested might find himself among the dross, and then at the consultants as a group, with his "right hand in the knickers" quip. Surely it was obvious to everyone that the Chairman was losing the plot!

"C Day is scheduled for three weeks from today," Roland Samiat announced. "This meeting will end now. After all, it would seem inappropriate to discuss any other business. But before we break up, I would like to thank Despiro Nihilopificus, not only for his presentation today but for the extraordinary effort he and his people have devoted to this project. C Day, my friends, is a game changer."

There were general grunts of assent as the committee members dispersed.

43. Charles Fundi

While Roland Samiat was announcing Cull 75241 to his management committee, four thousand miles away, beneath the sands of the Arabian desert, Charles Fundi, Commander of Ubar, the city in the sand, was running through the final checks on the installation of the Crucible of Eternal Light. All had gone surprisingly smoothly, mainly because the Eternal Light, the source of inexhaustible supplies of energy, generated no heat and no harmful radiation. It was relatively easy to handle and install.

Charles ticked the final box on his installation checklist and closed the folder. He was pleased but he was bemused. He was an engineer and had no time for mysteries. Yet he had to admit the energy source for the Light seemed to have more to do with magic than physics. He liked puzzles, or rather he liked solving them, almost as much as he liked perpetrating random acts of violence against other people, but the energy source of the Eternal Light was one puzzle he would never solve.

"I hear you've managed to plug the Light in," said Ben Rael, wandering into Fundi's office as though it were his own. "Well done, though I have to say it took long enough."

Charles Fundi shook his head, resisting the temptation to lose his temper. "When installing the most powerful source of energy on the planet, it's as well to make sure you have covered all bases."

"Come on," said Ben. "You're not reporting to Roland. You're just chatting with me. Be honest. It was incredibly simple – just plug and play."

"I tell you what's simple," said Fundi, rising to the bait, "taking charge of security in a fortress built under the sand in a remote, inhospitable part of the planet with miles of easily surveyed open ground on all sides. I reckon we're about as safe here as anyone can be, so if you're looking for a really simple job, being in charge of security has got to be it. Except, of course, that on arrival you managed to seek out one of the very few people within fifty miles of this installation, a shepherd looking for a lost sheep, and cut him, his camel and his dog in half with a couple of hundred rounds from your automatic weapon. That was about the only thing you could do to make us marginally less safe. I had to find a way of preventing his fellow tribesmen from looking for their friend and, as is the tradition here, taking revenge. And I had to achieve this end without adopting your proposed solution – sending in Security to massacre the tribe – which even in this godforsaken land might have raised the odd eyebrow in Riyadh or Sana'a. That was a less simple problem, one outside the scope of someone who seems able to communicate only with his dick or a gun. You left me with a problem I had to solve, and I came up with a rather clever solution. So if you want to do something useful, perhaps you could report to me how the lethal flu virus is fairing and whether or not it has successfully taken the tribe's mind off your random killing of its lost brother."

During this tirade, Ben had appeared to be nodding off. He awoke as Fundi finished. "Dying like flies, old boy, dying like flies." In giving his brief report, he had adopted the voice of an army officer in the mess, addressing someone of equal rank.

Charles Fundi smiled. "Dying like flies, eh? They'll be a lot of people dying like flies soon," he said, and then added, "except the flies won't be dying. They'll be doing rather well, living off the fat of the land, so to speak." Knowing he wouldn't be at the management meeting, Roland had given Fundi a private briefing on 75241 over a secure line earlier that day.

"What does that mean?" asked Ben, curious to learn how much Fundi knew.

"You'll find out soon enough," said Charles. "At present, it's on a need to know basis, old boy, and you don't."

Ben Rael shrugged. It was fairly obvious, both to him and Charles, that at some point the antagonism between the two of them would come to a head. Ben had taken advantage of his access to all security dossiers to check out Fundi's curriculum vitae. Evidently the Tanzanian was not a man to be underestimated. He was certainly bright – no, brilliant. That was why he was in command of Ubar. But once the installation was fully operational, Fundi would cease to be indispensable. Indeed, given his temper and mental instability he might well become a liability. When that time came Ben Rael would be ready. He would need Samiat's approval, but Roland invariably deferred to Ben in matters of security.

After Ben Rael had left, Charles pondered the various ways in which he might dispose of the arrogant, infuriating Head of Security imposed on him by Slievins' CEO. He rather favoured an accident in which Rael's dreadlocks became entangled in a piece of heavy machinery with a defective safety cut-out. He sketched out an accident report. "Despite the best efforts of the engineering staff, the top half of Rael had been crushed to pulp before anyone could pull the plug. Removing the composite of bone, brain and dreadlock hair from the mechanism has proved particularly difficult." Except that might reflect badly on maintenance! No, a beating to death blamed on the husband of one of Rael's innumerable conquests but actually administered by him might be simpler and in many ways even more satisfying.

44. Let him who is without sin …

"I know where the Crucible of Eternal Light is located," said Andrew Rimzil triumphantly.

Rambler was staring out the window of his first floor flat, looking up and down Warrington Crescent, bathed in the soft, warm light of autumn. He had spent all day researching Henry Kissinger and reluctantly felt he needed a break. For Rambler, the problem with not working was that his thoughts invariably returned to his late nephew. He missed the long talks he had shared with Numpty. From the beginning, Numpty had been eager to learn. He was always curious, asking questions. Sometimes he had seemed a little mentally challenged and yet there was always a logic underpinning his seemingly silly and often irritating questions. Looking back, Rambler realised he had learned as much from Numpty as Numpty had from him.

"Sorry," said Rambler, not having registered Andrew's excited claim.

Luke had been dozing in an old dog bed that Rambler had provided for him. He stood up, stretched himself, shook his golden coat. "I thought the Crucible was destroyed with the Westminster PCC," he minded to Andrew. "How did you find it and where is it?"

"It found me, or rather it found the paradox device and the paradox device told me," Andrew replied. "I think I mentioned that I'm involved in some kind of a cybernetic symbiotic relationship with the Light and the device. It seems the Crucible was rescued in the nick of time from the Westminster PCC just minutes before it went into terminal melt down. Believe it or not, it was saved by David Minofel and another Slievins' staffer whom the Light described as a heavily tattooed, porcine person."

Prune had given up remonstrating with Andrew about his delusional relationship with inanimate objects. On the last occasion he had protested, Andrew had enquired whether he was feeling a little jealous. Prune had scoffed at the very idea, but on mildly inebriated reflection he had realised there was more than a grain of truth in Andrew's diagnosis. "So where is the Eternal Light?" he asked.

"In a remote region of the Arabian desert," Andrew replied. "In somewhere called the City under the Sand."

"Good Heavens!" exclaimed Rambler. "You don't mean the lost city of Ubar, the city called the 'Atlantis of the Sands' by Lawrence of Arabia?"

"Could be," Andrew replied, "except it's not lost any more. The Light is located somewhere in the desert between southern Saudi Arabia and Yemen in a vast underground complex with six levels. In the fifth level down, one from the bottom, Slievins' technicians have installed the Light and have integrated it into their systems. It is now the power source for all Slievins' operations."

"Why?" asked Prune. "Why would anyone want to set up an operation in a remote and totally inhospitable part of the world?" Having come from Ireland, where even the air is green, deserts, with barren sand for earth and air so hot it simmers under the gaze of a relentless sun, filled Prune with fear and loathing. "And why would Slievins, with their main office in central London, decide to decamp to Arabia? And why do you think it is Slievins? Why not the Praesidium, assuming the Praesidium still exists? It's their bloody Light, after all."

Realising that Andrew would simply reply that all his information came from the Eternal Light via the paradox device, and fearing such an answer would trigger one of Prune's cyberphobic tirades, the Storyteller intervened. "I think we can take it that Slievins has acquired the Eternal Light and for reasons as yet unknown has transported it to southern Arabia."

"Is this any concern of ours?" enquired Rambler. If Slievins' attention was focused elsewhere, surely that was good news? It reduced the chance that they were still concerned with any danger the questors might pose.

"From what I can gather, it's everybody's concern," said Andrew. "I don't know what it is but it's clear that Slievins are planning a 'spectacular' – and I have a very bad feeling about it. It's top secret, but the word is that this project will dwarf all Slievins' past achievements."

"What achievements?" asked Prune. "According to Adam, all the Praesidium ever did was make trouble. They spent all their time trying to bring out the worst in everyone. As for Slievins, they're just upmarket spivs, ripping off the rich, regardless of any damage they do to society and everyone in it."

Throughout this exchange Kit had remained silent. Luke was minding something to him. Kit shook his head. Luke must be wrong.

"What do you think?" Andrew asked Kit.

"I'm sorry," Kit apologised. "I haven't been paying attention."

Andrew, Prune and Rambler were surprised. Kit was the one least likely to ignore a conversation, especially one of such importance. "Slievins has installed the Crucible of Eternal Light somewhere in the Arabian desert," Prune summarised.

"Luke thinks Eve is alive," said Kit.

"Luke thinks Eve is alive," Prune repeated. "What does that mean?"

"It's pretty self-explanatory," said Kit. "The paradox device has spent every spare moment scanning for Eve. So has Luke. They scan in different ways but their methods complement each other. Luke doesn't have positive proof, but there are three bits of evidence that give cause for hope. First, Luke is confident he would have known if Eve was dead. It's a dog thing. If they lose a master or mistress they love, they know. Secondly, you and Andrew have told us that there is something blocking the paradox device from finding out what has happened to her. If she's dead, why would there be a block? Thirdly, in radiation from the Eternal Light, the paradox device has picked up traces of grief for Adam, and Luke believes that Eve is the source."

Andrew nodded, indicating that he followed the logic of Kit's explanation.

For all his self-awareness and self-control, Prune cracked. "God help me!" he exclaimed. "And if God can't, Andrew explain. Please help me to understand. Are you saying the paradox device and Luke – that's a collection of electronic circuits and a golden retriever – with the help of some radiation from the Light, have accumulated some evidence that suggests Eve, whom we know to be dead, is alive. Andrew, you are a clever man. No, you are a brilliant man. I can say this because I too am a clever man and I know you are cleverer than me. But one of us is going mad and we need to decide which of us it is. You claim to be in an intimate relationship with an electronic device, a dog and an energy source that is convincing you to believe something is true which we know to be untrue. I am an engineer who tends to hang on grimly to the known facts. They found Eve's credit card and her DNA at the site of the bomb blast. If one of us is mad, I think it must be you."

Kit intervened. "Do you remember I asked Andrew if he had arranged to meet Adam for a coffee on the morning of the bomb blast?

"That's right," Andrew confirmed. "Don't know where that came from. I hadn't arranged a meeting with Adam and I hadn't cancelled one either."

"But Adam told me that was why he was in London," Kit continued. "He then received a text message from Eve suggesting they meet for lunch. That was why he was near to the site of the explosion when it happened."

"So what?" said Prune. "Everyone who was at or near Covent Garden that day had some odd set of circumstances that placed them there."

"Yes," Kit continued, "but not all of them were there because they were going to keep an appointment with someone who knew nothing about the arrangement."

"I still don't see what you're getting at," said Prune.

"Neither do I," added Andrew, pleased to be able to agree with Prune about something.

"Well, if Adam was lured to a particular spot by a false message about a meeting, perhaps Eve was too."

"What! So they could both be killed by a terrorist bomb?" said Prune. "I don't think so. That would mean that whoever did the luring would have to have known about the terrorists' plans. In any case only Eve was killed."

"Perhaps," said Kit thoughtfully, as though still trying to work out what he thought had happened. "Or perhaps so that they could both survive the blast but believe the other had been killed."

"And why would anyone do that?" Prune asked, his scepticism undiminished.

"If someone wanted to separate them, to break their relationship, what better way than for each to believe the other was dead?" said Kit.

"It would certainly preclude any evolution of their relationship," offered Rambler, "and prepare the ground for them to move on."

"I see," said Prune, addressing Kit. "So this is another of your conspiracy theories. You think it was Slievins, don't you? It wasn't 'someone' who wanted to separate them. It was David Minofel or some other sinister member of the Slievins' cabal. And they just happened to know that a bunch of Islamist fanatics were planning to bomb Covent Garden on that day at that time."

"It is a bit of a stretch, Kit," said Andrew, but there was a hint of uncertainty in his voice.

"Unless, of course, they were organising the terrorist attack anyway," said Kit undeterred, "and took the opportunity to kill off Adam and Eve – or to not kill them off – in unsuspicious circumstances."

"That's not a stretch," said Prune. "That's a string of elastic light years across. In any case, we know Eve is dead. The police confirmed it. They found her credit card and her DNA. If she were still alive, she would have made herself known. Where do you think she is? Hiding? Held prisoner? Come on! I'd love to believe Eve survived but the *evidence* says not."

"Shouldn't we tell Adam if there is a possibility Eve has survived?" asked Rambler.

"Not yet," said Andrew. "Not until we can be more confident that Luke's intuition and the paradox device's assessment are correct and that all the evidence is wrong."

"We can't tell Adam anything at the moment," Kit added. "He's gone missing. The police and HMRC are looking for him. He never told us exactly what went on in Geneva but clearly he's worried enough to have dropped below the radar."

"I've seen reports that the Swiss police want to talk to him about the Spinetti murder," said Prune.

"I'm sure Adam had nothing to do with that," said Rambler. "If HMRC are pursuing him, there might have been some irregularity in his financial affairs, but murder? – that's out of the question. Adam's not a murderer." Rambler waited for the others to endorse his character reference.

"It's difficult to know what anyone will do in extreme circumstances," said Prune. "The Swiss police wouldn't be investigating unless there was a case. And by all accounts, ZeD was a hotbed of corruption and depravity."

"Yes, but Adam exposed it all," said Rambler, shocked that any of the others doubted Adam's integrity.

"We're not saying Adam is guilty of anything really bad," Andrew soothed Rambler. "But if he's entirely innocent, why would he hide from the police and the tax people? If he's done nothing wrong, why isn't he proving his innocence to the authorities?"

"And what's his plan?" Prune persisted. "He's not going on the run for the rest of his life, is he? Or if he is, he really must have done something pretty awful."

"That's a fair point," Kit joined in. "But we mustn't assume someone is guilty before anything is proved. Even if he has strayed outside the law, we would need to know the circumstances. Let him who is without sin …"

"We should concentrate on finding out what happened to Eve," said Andrew firmly. "If she died in the blast, we need to confirm it. If she didn't die – and I'm now beginning to think she could still be alive – we need to locate her and find out why she's disappeared."

"What about the project that you say Slievins is planning?" Rambler didn't like the sound of the word "spectacular" that Andrew had used.

At that moment, there was a buzz from the apartment's newly installed entry system intercom. Rambler went to see who it was. He looked at the small screen.

"Good heavens!" he exclaimed.

"Who is it?" asked Andrew and Prune in unison.

Rambler pressed the button to allow the visitor to enter. "It's Aletheia." he said.

oooOooo

When Aletheia, goddess of truth, entered a room, she commanded everyone's attention. Tall, fair-haired, with blue-green eyes the colour of the coastal waters of the Mediterranean, she strode across the floor.

"I bring you greetings from Prometheus," she said.

On this occasion, she arrived fully-clothed and without her sword. She was wearing a very smart, white trouser suit. "I have come across time and space once more because of a threat to all mankind. Prometheus fears that if you fail to destroy the forces of evil, your species will die. Humanity will become extinct, long before it has reached its full potential and fulfilled its destiny."

"Jesus Christ!" said Prune, taken aback by Aletheia's blunt announcement of her mission. "It's good to see you, too."

"It truly is good to see you," said Kit, delighted to be in the company of his immortal friend once more.

"Are you referring to Andrew's mention of a spectacular?" enquired Rambler, his mind still on the thought in his head when the door had buzzed.

"I am indeed," Aletheia replied. "I have to tell you that this latest outrage planned by the forces of evil has shaken Prometheus' faith in humanity. As you know, he has been your greatest friend and most loyal and stalwart champion down the ages. He has wept when the darker side of your nature has become dominant, but never until now has his belief in mankind faltered. The plan that Slievins is close to implementing, a plan now endorsed by most of humanity's elite, will prove that Zeus's contempt for man was justified and that Prometheus' commitment to you was naïve and misplaced."

"This sounds bad," said Prune, "really bad."

"What do you want us to do?" asked Andrew.

"You have to prevent Project 75241," said Aletheia. "And you have to protect Eve and the child she carries."

"So we were right," Luke minded to Andrew. "Eve lives. I told you so."

45.   Ceri and Lister: Round One

After the management meeting, Ceri Agema and Lister Bavad had business of a different kind to attend to.

In normal circumstances, one would leave the matter there or, at the most, devote a brief paragraph to a description of their first sexual union, but in this instance more is called for.

As you know, Ceri Agema was a beautiful, highly sexed woman with a tendency to murder her sexual partners. No, "tendency" is too weak a word – a predisposition, even a compulsion. Why she had such a drive is difficult to say. People are complicated creatures and it is too easy to propose simple solutions. In Ceri's case, the simple explanation, if we must have one, centred on a swimming instructor who had taken the pubescent thirteen-year-old Ceri in hand and, in addition to developing her swimming talent, introduced her to a wide range of sexual experiences, including vaginal and anal intercourse. Ceri enjoyed or endured the swimming instructor's attentions for three years. She told no one. And no one noticed the change in her personality, not even her mother who, having been abandoned by Ceri's father before Ceri's birth, was more intent on making a life for herself than protecting the life of her daughter.

When Ceri was sixteen she met a boy of her own age. They met in the swimming pool where Ceri, now an accomplished swimmer, was still being tutored by her abuser. The boy's name was Jude. Ceri liked Jude but realised that while she was in the clutches of the swimming instructor, things couldn't be right between them.

Jude, being a full-blooded heterosexual youth, was desperate to bed the delectable Ceri, but Ceri resisted. Why? he asked. All the other boys had girlfriends and all their girlfriends were "doing it". In the end, Ceri told Jude why she couldn't sleep with him. She was ashamed of her relationship with the instructor and felt profoundly relieved to have told someone the truth. She rather hoped that Jude would report her abuser. At least she expected some sympathy and understanding. But Jude had other ideas. If she was having sex with some old fart, what possible reason could she have for refusing to have sex with him? So he raped her. He then decided to blackmail the teacher.

Jude's blackmail project didn't go well. At first, the swimming instructor denied he had had sex of any sort with Ceri. Then he admitted the affair but argued that she was sixteen and therefore the relationship might have been inappropriate but it wasn't illegal. Jude was nothing if not determined and persisted in his demands. He issued an ultimatum: either the instructor paid up or Jude would tell the man's wife and the police exactly what he had been doing to Ceri over the last three years. Rather unwisely, Jude delivered his ultimatum in the instructor's office late one evening, after the pool had closed. The instructor felt he had no alternative. He knocked Jude unconscious and drowned him in the pool, hoping the police would assume the lad had stayed behind when the pool closed to have the place to himself, had somehow hit his head on the pool side and died as the result of an unfortunate accident. In fact, the police almost immediately realised it was a case of murder and that the instructor, being the only person with access to the pool when it was closed to the public, was the prime suspect. When Ceri revealed to the police, and agreed to testify, that the instructor was a homosexual paedophile who had been abusing Jude from the age of thirteen, the police arrested the instructor on a charge of murder and put him in a holding cell, unsupervised. Realising his marriage and his career were ruined, the instructor took the first opportunity that presented itself to commit suicide.

Presumably the impact of these events on Ceri was profound. It is reasonable to assume that three years of sexual abuse, followed by rape, the murder of her rapist by her abuser and rounded off by the subsequent suicide of the murdering abuser would have coloured Ceri's attitude towards men. It is tempting to attribute her subsequent homicidal activities to these experiences. But it's best to avoid simplistic explanations of human behaviour. Perhaps the absence of a father figure in her life played a part. Perhaps her mother's cavalier attitude to motherhood was a contributing factor. Or perhaps Ceri Agema was born with a predisposition to evil that could not be denied.

Other girls might have been cowed by what Ceri had been through. Some might have decided to have nothing to do with men. Yet others might have sought an outlet for their sexual drives with those of their own sex. Not Ceri! She found a way of reconciling her extreme experiences of sex, violence and death by embracing her powerful heterosexual appetites and her killer instinct with equal enthusiasm. Yet given what she had been through, Ceri was a well-balanced individual. What others would see as a perverse attitude to sex and a callous disregard for the value and dignity of human life was, for Ceri, a sensible accommodation of two conflicting drives, an accommodation that enabled her to achieve a perfectly satisfactory psychological equilibrium.

Lister Bavad, on the other hand, had no need to balance conflicting drives. He was entirely self-centred and, being perfectly centred on himself, was untroubled by the doubts and uncertainties that afflict lesser mortals. If that description makes you think Lister was an unpleasant character, you are mistaken. Everyone liked Lister. And women loved Lister. Of course he benefitted from outstanding good looks, having inherited the very best attributes of his Indian father and his English mother – deep, dark-brown eyes, light-brown skin, flashing white teeth and a bright, white smile for everyone!

From the moment of his birth Lister had known what life was all about. It was about taking pleasure. As a child, he quickly learned that the greatest pleasure came from persuading others to do what he wanted and that the surest way to achieve that end was to please them. He became adept at manipulating everyone close to him. His parents doted on him; his siblings favoured him; all of his friends counted him as their best friend. And yet no one envied him. What technique did he employ? It was simple. He displayed a seemingly genuine interest in everyone; he had time for everyone; and he found the weakness in everyone. As a child, he was the one to go to for sweets or cigarettes; as a teenager, he could always provide a friend with alcohol or soft drugs. He was clever; he knew stuff. And the girls couldn't have enough of him. Just being a friend of Lister gave Lister's male friends a substantial advantage in pulling girls. The highest prize was, of course, Lister himself. But not everyone could win the highest prize, so many of the girls happily settled for those who merely knew him well.

Except that no one really knew Lister well. Was he simply a handsome, witty, open-hearted being with limitless charisma? Or was he a shrewd, calculating individual with an intuitive insight into what others were thinking, ruthlessly using those about him to satisfy his own desires and achieve his own goals? It should be possible to give an answer, but it isn't. If he wore a mask, it was impenetrable. What lay behind it, if anything, remained unknown and undiscoverable.

There was one aspect of his character that merits special mention. He rather enjoyed strangling people. He was by no means a mass murderer, nor a random killer, but when the need arose he would happily remove the silk cravat from around his own neck and use it to extinguish the life of his victim. He ascribed this particular tendency to the fact that his great grandfather on his father's side had been a leading light among the Indian Thuggee. These bands of robbers ingratiated themselves with their victims, who were usually wealthy travellers, and, when they reached a sufficiently secluded spot, strangled them using their *rumal*, a yellow silk cloth every Thug wore around his waist. Strangulation was the method of choice because of a prohibition in the Thuggee moral code against the spilling of blood. It sounds strange, perhaps, to mention a moral code of behaviour in the context of a description of the Thuggee but it should be understood that the Thuggee were worshippers of the goddess Kali. Each strangulation was seen as a sacrifice in honour of the goddess who, for the Thuggee, gave meaning to life, death and creation itself.

Leaving aside his tenuous familial connection, why Lister identified with the Thuggee is another mystery. After several centuries of brigandage and murder, the Thuggee were wiped out in the nineteenth century, long before Lister was born, by the forces of the British Empire in India. In any case, Lister was born in England to a wealthy English noblewoman of impeccable English breeding; he attended a prestigious English public school and completed his wholly Anglicised education at Oxford University. Apart from the colour of his skin, a healthy, attractive and permanent light tan, Lister was, if anything, more English than the English.

This preamble is necessary to prepare you for the explosive sexual union that ensued when Ceri and Lister reached Ceri's room on leaving the Slievins' monthly management meeting. There are other instances when two people, each with their own particular inclinations, come together and act on each other as a catalyst. Each prompts the other to take their particular tendency to the extreme. Shakespeare portrayed such a relationship in Macbeth. In the real world, Ian Brady and Myra Hindley and the Wests, Fred and Rose, provide classic examples of couples combining to provide a depraved swamp in which unspeakable evil could come to life and breed. Such was the relationship that was inaugurated when Ceri and Lister found themselves alone.

There was no impetuous ripping off of clothes and urgent, unbridled coupling. When they reached Ceri's room, Ceri closed the door and the two of them circled each other. They both knew that what they were going to do was not routine, humdrum mating.

When Roland had announced the plan to eliminate six billion people, Ceri had felt as though a grey film had been removed from her eyes. The world was a brighter, gaudier, richer place than she had ever imagined. Her mind was a ferment of excited activity. And because she was a highly sexed woman, the idea of this grand Cull had also excited and opened her body to new worlds of experience.

Lister, alone of those at the meeting, had recognised this transformation, this eruption of mental and sexual energy. And when, sitting beside her at the boardroom table, he had surreptitiously touched her thigh, he had felt an infusion of excitement, delight and, of course, lust transmitted from her flesh through his own body. He had also felt a connection with her as a person. They were both highly intelligent but for both him and her, intelligence and reason were subordinate to the powerful desires of their own personalities. Both were killers who had come to terms with their murderous impulses. Lister knew of Ceri's predilection for killing those with whom she fornicated. Ceri had recognised in Lister a kindred spirit. They had no excuse for what they did. Nor did they need one. They knew the meaning of killing others, its implications and repercussions, and when the occasion presented itself or demanded it, they rather enjoyed it.

Ceri closed the blinds in the room, reducing the sunlight that poured in to a soft, warm glow.

Lister touched Ceri's arms as they prowled around each other. "This is one liaison," said Lister, "where neither of us will be dead when it ends."

"Is that a question, a hope or a prediction?" said Ceri, moving away and unbuttoning her blouse.

"It could be a threat," replied Lister easily.

"That thought hadn't crossed my mind," said Ceri, discarding her blouse. She was wearing black underwear. Lister surveyed her shapely breasts and smiled approvingly.

Ceri smacked him across the face.

"Why?" asked Lister, taken by surprise. "What was that for?" Was she upset that he had admired her breasts?

"No reason," said Ceri. "Just for fun."

Lister shrugged. He removed his shirt. Ceri moved in on him, running her hands over his chest and nestling her head against his face. Lister took the opportunity to remove her bra. Ceri pulled back and pushed Lister away. Lister removed the rest of his clothes. He was already aroused. Ceri looked him up and down and smiled.

Lister moved towards her. Standing in the middle of the room on his own with an erect phallus was less than dignified. Ceri slipped away from him and removed her skirt. Lister caught her. He was naked; she now had on only her black thong. Lister propelled her to the bed and they fell onto it.

"You have an amazing body," said Lister. "Your legs go from here to eternity."

Ceri frowned. "We're not here to exchange banal or bizarre compliments," she said softly. "We are here to celebrate the Cull, the boldest, most imaginative, most decisive action ever taken by man."

"Of course," said Lister. "Whatever you say. But I must insist we remove your thong so we can celebrate the Cull properly." He slid his hand between her legs; she was warm and wet.

Ceri laughed. She lifted her buttocks from the bed so he could strip her panties. Lister moved to mount her. Ceri stopped him.

"I want you to listen," said Ceri. "We are privileged to be part of man's greatest adventure. We must be sure you and I are worthy of this honour. This is not going to be an ordinary, run-of-the-mill, take-it-or-leave-it sort of fuck. This is a fuck that is going to ring bells across the land, a fuck that it going to raise the heavens, a fuck that is going to shake the foundations of hell."

"Right," said Lister, a little uncertainly. "I just hope I'm up to it."

"Well, you certainly have the right tool," said Ceri, diving down and licking the end of Lister's phallus. "And I'm pretty sure you know how to use it."

"I like to think of myself as a giver of pleasure," said Lister, pulling Ceri's head away from his phallus and turning her onto her back. He kissed her breasts, lightly flicking his tongue around her nipples. He kissed her belly. Even in the subdued light, her skin was translucent. He slid his hand between her legs.

"I have killed many men," said Ceri.

Lister entered her. Ceri clasped his buttocks with both hands and held him tight, so he couldn't move.

"Lie still," she commanded. "I have much to tell you."

Lister was not happy. "Of course! Of course! We both have much to talk about. But could we not finish what we have begun here?" His urge to drive in and out of her was almost irresistible.

"You must wait," said Ceri firmly. Lister was amazed at her strength. He could not move.

Ceri began by telling him about her swimming instructor. She recounted every detail of the abuse she had suffered; how her abuser had, over the years, explored every orifice in her body and compelled her to perform every depraved act that man has devised for woman to endure. "And all this, when I was in my early teens," said Ceri.

"I'm really sorry," said Lister, "but you seem to have pulled through."

Ceri laughed. "I think that's for me to judge, not you," she said. "But you're right. It's made me the woman I am today." Ceri then resumed her story, recounting her brief relationship with Jude, culminating in Jude's rape of her, the killing of Jude by her abuser and the abuser's suicide for which Ceri herself was partly responsible.

"Wow," said Lister. Wow! didn't really do justice to Lister's feelings at the time. He was fascinated by Ceri's account of her childhood and early teens, but he had a more urgent, a more pressing, concern. He was desperately trying not to ejaculate. Ceri was an extraordinarily attractive women and this was the first time he had bedded her. Although he considered himself well-versed in the art of love, he had to accept that unless they went at it in the very near future, he was going to complete his end of the business on his own. In other circumstances, with a less attractive woman or one with whom he was more familiar, he might have controlled his urges with thoughts of work or football matches or old people – anything to dampen down his sexual excitement. But he had to admit that he found Ceri's account of the abuse perpetrated on her as a child in itself sexually arousing.

"I can feel you are having some difficulty," said Ceri sweetly, "so I shall recount only one more episode in my life. My most recent killing."

Ceri then told Lister about her trip to Rio, her brief but torrid relationship with Estevo, and how, as he climaxed, she had choked him to death with an orange. It was too much for Lister. Still locked in Ceri's embrace, he felt the semen pumping out of him, a totally unsatisfactory orgasm, a disappointment for her and for him, a truly appalling, immobile, moribund fuck.

"I'm really sorry," he said.

"Don't worry," said Ceri. "We've only just begun."

46. A plot is born

As the management meeting disbanded, Ceri and Lister were not the only ones with urgent business to attend to. Art Shoat was angry. Roland Samiat had humiliated him in front of the entire committee and his closest colleagues, fellow members of Samiat's private staff.

"You seem upset," David Minofel prompted.

"You heard what he said," Art Shoat snapped back. "He said I was dross. Who the hell does he think he is? I've done his dirty work for twenty years. I make fun of some nerd with an unpronounceable name and Samiat jumps down my throat and knifes me in the gut."

David Minofel winced. He resisted the temptation to query Art's metaphorical expertise. After all, Art was not a wordsmith; in any case, he had been under the influence of Samiat for twenty years. "It was out of order," Minofel conceded.

"Out of order!" Art exploded. "It was a bit more than 'out of order'. I don't have to put up with that kind of treatment. I should have stuffed Cull 75241 up Samiat's arse."

"Calm yourself," Minofel urged. "No one talks about the Slievins' CEO in such disrespectful terms, at least not openly. I have a great deal of sympathy with your sentiments. But I think our problem is deeper than this instance of rudeness to a trusted executive. It goes a good deal deeper."

Art was now in a quandary. Naturally, his hackles rose at the suggestion that Samiat's rebuke was not the worst thing the Slievins' CEO had ever done. On the other hand, no one had ever called him an executive before. "Right," said Art, then added, "What do you mean 'deeper'?"

"Isn't it obvious?" said Minofel, "Roland is losing it. Cull 75241 has gone to his head. I'm not saying it's a bad idea – in fact, I think it's a good idea – but Roland has become obsessive about it. If you're working on his pet project, like the Chief Dawk, you're in the magic circle. If you're not or if you say anything against the Cull, you're in trouble."

"And then there's his affair with Enid," said Art, more than happy to develop Minofel's theme. "She arrives here as an unknown from South America and within weeks she's in his bed and privy to all his plans. She's been telling Eve that Samiat will look after her 'whatever happens', as though she knows his mind or is making it up for him."

"You're right," said Minofel. "He's besotted with her. I've worked with Roland for more years than I can count and I've never known him act in such an unpredictable and unprofessional way. It's not just you he offended. He managed to insult the entire team of consultants with his 'hand in the knickers' quip. Not that he was wrong, of course, but that's not how the CEO of a major consultancy addresses his senior staff. I'm serious when I say I think he's lost the plot. He's become unhinged."

Both men fell silent. They had already said enough to justify instant dismissal under Slievins' terms of employment. The next step would risk a rather more brutal termination. It was Art who spoke first. "So what are we going to do about it?"

Art had crossed the line. He knew it but he didn't care.

"We will have to be extremely careful," said David Minofel, "and we will need help. If we are to make a move, we must have overwhelming force at our disposal."

"Do you think others will back us?" Art recognised that if they were to succeed, Minofel would have to be in charge. Art was no slouch in tactical thinking, but for the perilous path they were setting out on Minofel was the man to lead.

"My spies tell me there is trouble in Ubar between Ben Rael and Charles Fundi. I've seen copies of Rael's reports and it's obvious he wants to eliminate Charles as soon as the City under the Sand is fully operational and thoroughly tested. Roland is almost certain to accept Rael's recommendation. Charles knows he is vulnerable. I think we should sound him out. If we have control of Ubar, we're more than halfway there. Ubar is to be Slievins' new headquarters and it holds the Crucible of Eternal Light."

"It's certainly true there's no love lost between Rael and Fundi," Art confirmed. "What about Lister and Ceri? Would they stick with Roland?"

"I have a feeling that they'll be sticking with each other for now," said Minofel. He had noticed their departure together at the end of the management meeting. "If it comes to a showdown, I'm pretty confident they will go with whichever side they think will win, as will the consultants. Ben Rael will side with Roland whatever happens, but I think Charles Fundi will be only too happy to deal with that particular problem."

"So do we have an understanding?" asked Art.

"I will be CEO. You will be Senior Executive and my deputy. I will treat you with respect as befits your station. In other circumstances I would ask you to promise to show me the same loyalty that you have shown to my predecessor, but in these circumstances that pledge might be open to misinterpretation. So if you agree, let's just shake hands on it."

They shook hands.

"I need to go to Ubar," said Minofel. "I will talk to Charles. When I show him evidence that Rael has Roland's support in eliminating him, I'm pretty sure he will see things our way. You stay here. We don't want to arouse suspicions of a conspiracy. Keep an eye on Roland. Let me know if he becomes any more unstable."

"What about Adam?" said Art. "He's unfinished business. You can't just leave him here. Roland put you in charge of his deconstruction. He'll certainly become suspicious if you suddenly just drift off to Ubar."

"Don't worry," Minofel replied. "I'm taking Adam with me. It's always been part of my plan to separate Adam from everything and everyone he knows. What better place to isolate him permanently than the southern region of the Arabian desert? In any case, as a senior partner in Slievins, it's only right I should check out the Ubar installation."

"You realise there's no going back now," said Art. "Either we succeed or our days with Slievins are numbered."

"You know Roland as well as I do," said David Minofel. "If we don't succeed, our days are numbered, period."

oooOooo

Alone in his office, David Minofel pressed the button in the rear wall that gave him access to his blood cabinet. He had not taken out a phial since he had sipped an alcohol-preserved sample of rapist Kevin's blood. Then he had been driven by frustration. Today was different. His feelings this time were a mixture of relief and exultation.

Since he had realised that he really didn't like Roland Samiat, he knew that the only way to resolve the situation was through action. He had to destroy his enemy. He had hesitated because any attempt to overthrow a Slievins' CEO was a high-risk venture. On the historical evidence there was little chance of success. Roland Samiat held immense power. And the consequence of failure was oblivion. He knew that, and so did Art Shoat.

Nevertheless, he and Art had set a plot in motion. And David Minofel felt good. He felt liberated. He felt elated. And he felt elevated. Win or lose, he would have proved himself big enough to challenge for the top position.

He ran his fingers across a row of phials at the middle level of the cabinet. His hand settled on a sample of the blood of the Belgian King Leopold II who, as the founder and owner of the so-called Congo Free State, presided over a colonial project in Africa involving the forced labour of a nation. Millions of Congolese died under the brutality of Leopold's regime. Minofel unscrewed the cap, raised the phial to his nose, savoured the aroma and then took the smallest of sips. As he discerned through the preserving alcohol a powerful flavour of inhumanity interwoven with delicate hints of bitter anguish, he felt refreshingly energised.

47. Test marketing

A third and more sinister conversation began after the management meeting broke up. When the audience had departed, only Despiro Nihilopificus and Roland Samiat remained in the conference room. Despiro was gathering his papers and making sure they were in order.

"Well?" said Roland.

Despiro looked at Roland quizzically.

"Have you made your selection?" Roland prompted.

"Ah, yes," said Despiro. "The pilot! Yes, I have made my choice. We looked for a town within easy reach of London with a population between one hundred and fifty and two hundred thousand. We wanted somewhere ethnically diverse and, as a committed atheist, I thought it would be rather nice to have a high proportion of religious adherents in the target population. I know that wasn't part of the brief but I decided to indulge myself."

Despiro had been a little nervous about the final criterion for selection but Roland simply grinned and said: "Come on, man. Spit it out. Where is the pilot cull to be?"

"I also wanted to gauge the likely impact of the Cull on a heavily business-oriented community. So I selected a town that hosts the head offices of many companies, among them providers of fast food. Can't you guess?"

Roland shook his head.

Despiro recited a couple of lines from John Betjeman's poem:

Come friendly bombs and fall on Slough

It isn't fit for humans now.

"Of course!" said Roland. "Excellent choice!"

"All is ready. For the pilot we are using only sound transmission to activate DK12, ensuring we keep the activation area within the city boundaries. Slough is said to have the highest proportion of religious adherents in its population of anywhere in England. Just under half the population is white. About forty per cent are Asian. The rest are black or of mixed race. All the main fast-food chains are represented. It's burgers, drumsticks, fried chicken, kebabs, noodles and pizzas galore."

"Perfect," said Roland, "although it seems likely we will exceed the Cull quota when we activate DK12."

"You're right," said Despiro. "We reckon we will eliminate about eighty-three per cent of the population but that's all to the good. We agreed that, in the pilot, it would be better to go high than low. We need to assess the scale of the clean-up operation and Slough will be a real test."

"It's all good then," said Roland.

Despiro Nihilopificus was not a man much given to emotion but even he enjoyed the warm feelings engendered by praise. "May I add that our other major development project is progressing well. We cannot claim success yet but I am confident we are close."

Roland Samiat grinned. "If you can bring the Resolver online at the same time as the survivors of the Cull are mourning six billion dead that would truly be the icing on the wake."

48. Ceri and Lister: Round Two

Ceri lay back on the white silk sheets of her king-sized bed, her blonde hair spread on the pillow, her shapely body entirely naked, her head to one side and her green eyes regarding Lister with a mocking smile.

Lister lay on his side, surveying the form of what he saw as a perfect woman. To men of any ethnicity, Ceri was a remarkably attractive woman, but Lister had a predilection, not uncommon among men with Asian blood in them, for women with blonde hair and white skin. The green eyes with which she was currently surveying him were a bonus.

"Have you fully recovered?" said Ceri.

"I'm really sorry," said Lister.

"Stop apologising," said Ceri with a laugh. "I think I can take a little premature ejaculation in my stride. I just want to know if you're ready for some serious exercise." She glanced down and saw that Lister was becoming aroused again. "I am entirely at your disposal," she added, as though she had just tidied up some minor administrative matter and was now ready to address more serious issues. "Whatever you want," she elaborated, "you can have."

Lister moved towards Ceri to kiss her. He looked into those green eyes for some hint of what Ceri was thinking and feeling. He could read nothing but he guessed she was judging him. Things had not gone well in their first encounter. There was a strong case against him but he hoped that the jury was out. He was determined to redeem himself. He had made love to many women. The first pass with Ceri had been a fiasco, but he would now demonstrate that he was something of an expert in pleasuring the fairer sex.

He kissed her deeply for a minute and then pulled back to kiss her neck. He slid his hand between her legs, which she gently parted, and began to gently massage her clitoris. He was now kissing her nipples, which had become erect. He could sense she was giving herself to him. He slid further down the bed, parted her thighs and deployed his tongue where his fingers had been. Ceri began to moan quietly. Lister moved back up the bed to work on her nipples with his tongue. His hand went back deep between her legs and began to caress her from her coccyx through her anus and vagina to her mons pubis, making that region of her body his own.

Ceri pulled Lister on to her and he entered her. He moved slowly, determined not to climax until she reached orgasm. He didn't have long to wait. Ceri's moans had become louder, her nails began to dig into his back. Then he felt shudder after shudder as she climaxed. He continued to work her, moving back and forth with a firm controlled rhythm. And Ceri continued to shudder, groan and writhe until Lister judged he had earned redemption and he allowed himself closure.

He lay inside her for a few minutes, using his elbows to ensure his weight on her didn't become burdensome. He then disengaged and they both relaxed in post-coital satisfaction.

After a quarter of an hour, Ceri slid down the bed and introduced first her lips, then her tongue and finally her mouth to Lister's membrum virile. Lister demurred at first, taking the view that, if his engorged penis had more to give, it would better employed in probing Ceri's vagina and stroking her clitoris for their mutual pleasure. Such qualified selflessness waned, however, as Ceri showed she was no slouch in the pleasuring department. Soon all thoughts of mutual gratification were dissipated as Lister's mind became fully occupied with what miracles were being performed on his own body.

49. The learning curve

Adam had now spent several days working with Violet in the refuge, outstaying the time she had originally allotted him. He had heard nothing from David Minofel and he was grateful for Violet's albeit limited hospitality. The sleeping arrangements were rudimentary but he was dry and, with the help of a couple of blankets, warm enough.

"You are doing good work," said Violet. She had overheard Adam talking to Darren, a young man who had wandered in, attracted by the offer of a cup of tea and a sandwich. The lad was no more than fifteen years old. He had scarcely attended school in the last year. His step-father, a violent, drunken lout, had thrown the boy out of the house. His mother had put up some resistance to her son's expulsion, but a couple of slaps administered by her partner and threats of more serious assaults had quickly brought her into line.

"You've had a pretty raw deal in life so far," Adam had said to Darren. "Your step-father is a waste of space, and your mother is obviously weak and emotionally insecure. You could quite reasonably decide that with such a poor start you might as well not bother. You could take your step-father and your mother as role models and become like them, a parasite in society and a disgrace to humanity. On the other hand, you could decide that being on the edge of manhood you can take responsibility for your own life and what you make of it. You're not stupid. Although you haven't attended school for a while, you can read and write. That means you've got potential and we can help. We can work out a plan, point you in the right direction and send you on your way. I'm pretty sure no one has ever offered you as much before, and may be no one will offer it again. So give it some thought."

"Thanks," said Adam to Violet. "I'm pleased you're pleased."

"Just a couple of pointers," said Violet. "Telling Darren his mother is weak, a parasite and a disgrace to humanity may do more harm than good. People rarely respond well to harsh truths, especially when it's a stranger handing out hard truths about their mothers. And laying the blame on others is a mistake. His step-father may be a drunken lout but, if he came here, we would probably learn that he himself had been ill-treated or abused as a child. It's not our job to judge – just to help."

"So which bit did I get right?" Adam asked, deflated.

Violet laughed. "You gave the boy good advice. It's up to him to try. It's up to us to help. The rest is best left to God."

"Are you sure you're an atheist?" Adam was confused. "You keep quoting from the Bible and now you're leaving judgement to God."

"Yes, I'm sure," Violet replied easily. "There is some wisdom in the Bible which is worth recalling from time to time. Any reference to God is just a manner of speaking and should be taken with a pinch of salt."

"I thought that was the devil," said Adam.

Violet laughed again. "Not much to choose between them. The world's a bit of a mess, whoever's running it. All we can do is make the best of it. Oh! and by the way, about half an hour ago, someone came here looking for you."

"Who came?" Adam's stomach turned over. Was it possible Eve was alive? Had she come looking for him?

"It was a man, late thirties or early forties, a little under six foot, very well-cut suit, pink shirt and red tie. Looked like a banker to me. I didn't like him." Violet replied.

"You seem to have noticed a lot, considering you didn't like him. And why didn't you like him? Was he rude?" Adam asked.

"Quite the opposite," Violet replied. "He was extremely polite. There was just something about him that put me off."

"I thought you didn't judge?" Adam teased.

"I didn't say there was anything wrong with him. I just said I didn't like him."

"OK, OK," Adam chuckled. "Did he say anything else?"

"He said he would meet you in the café at 4 o'clock. He didn't say which café. He said you would know."

"Minofel," Adam muttered under his breath. "What's the time now?"

"Three thirty."

"Good," said Adam. "Could you sort out Darren? He needs a plan. Next time I see him I'll talk to him."

Violet shrugged. "It would be better if you talked to him now, but if you have to go …"

"Sorry, but this is important," said Adam. "You deal with him."

When Adam had gone Violet said to herself: "You're still not very good at judging what's important."

50. Against the odds

After offering Aletheia refreshment, the questors settled down with the goddess of truth to discuss a plan of action. Aletheia explained Cull 75241. Andrew and Prune expressed disbelief that the world's elite, the most rich and powerful people in the world, would connive in the destruction of three-quarters of the world's population.

"Are you seriously suggesting that anyone is going along with the idea of wiping out six billion people?" asked Prune.

"I am," said Aletheia.

"It's not so surprising," said Rambler. His researches into Slievins involvement in human history had taught him that the powerful were utterly ruthless in their determination to retain power. The only limit on their capacity for destruction was the limit on their capacity to destroy. "Aletheia has explained the rationale for the plan – ever expanding population, ever greater demands for material benefits, finite resources. It's obvious the present situation is unsustainable."

"You sound as though you support the Cull," snapped Prune.

"Of course he doesn't," Kit intervened. "Rambler has been doing some research for us and I fear his view of humanity has become a little jaundiced. We all agree that if this Cull thing goes ahead, the guilt of the survivors, the sin of the survivors, will be beyond redemption. God could send an entire battalion of His sons to die on the cross and that still wouldn't be enough to justify absolution."

"Always assuming," Rambler mused, "that man can somehow be redeemed by perpetrating still more sins against his redeemer or redeemers."

"That is why it would be the end of humanity," said Aletheia. "Mankind would at last be irredeemable."

"And somehow this little band of brothers has to stop the most powerful organisation in the world from implementing a plan supported by the world's most powerful people?" queried Rambler.

"No, Adam has to stop them," said Aletheia, as though Adam's pivotal role should have been obvious.

"Oh dear!" said Rambler. "I don't think that's going to work. Adam is on the run. We believe he is being pursued by HMRC for tax evasion."

"And possibly for murder by the Swiss police," added Prune.

"Not first choice to champion the good against evil," said Andrew. "In any case, we don't know where Adam is. We think he's somewhere in London but we can't contact him."

"You said that we also had to protect Eve and her baby," said Prune. "The police claimed she was killed in the terrorist attack at Covent Garden. Do you know differently?"

"Eve is alive and well," Aletheia replied.

"We've searched everywhere for her," said Prune. "We used the paradox device to scan the whole of London. Nothing."

"If you doubt my word, I suggest you scan again," said Aletheia, a little irritated. She was unused to anyone querying her pronouncements. "The Eternal Light is powering all Slievins' operations. Given their burgeoning relationship, I'm sure the Light will allow the paradox device to slip through the cloaking that has, until now, prevented you from finding her. After all, the Light is the energy source for the cloaking."

"No need," Andrew intervened quickly.

"No one here would doubt the word of the goddess of truth," added Rambler.

Prune eagerly nodded his assent.

Mollified, Aletheia continued. "Since the bomb blast in Covent Garden, Eve has been a guest of Roland Samiat, the CEO of Slievins, at his Mayfair property. She believes Adam is dead, killed in the explosion which she survived. She was shaken up in the explosion, picked up by a Slievins' private ambulance and taken to the medical wing of Samiat's Mayfair mansion. He's providing her with the best of medical attention."

Andrew expressed the general involuntary scepticism. "And she's stayed as this Samiat's guest although she knows he runs the organisation that did its best to corrupt Adam and destroy Kit?"

Aletheia explained. "Samiat has told her that the tax authorities are after Adam for tax evasion and possible money laundering. He's told her that they are likely to conclude that she was implicated in any financial offences since she seemed to be the one deriving most benefit from them. He's also warned her that Adam may have been involved in the murder of an official at the EMA, that Adam's reputation is likely to be comprehensively trashed by the media, and that it would surely be best for her and her baby to keep out of what is sure to be a very unpleasant media maelstrom."

"I see you have improved still further your grasp of modern English usage since your last visit," observed Rambler approvingly, noting Aletheia's use of the verbal form of "trash" and the alliterative "media maelstrom".

Aletheia acknowledged Rambler's praise with a smile.

Prune shook his head. "Our slim chances of success will dwindle to zero if we spend time discussing Aletheia's grasp of English."

"Prune's right," said Andrew. "We need a plan. Our objectives must be to rescue Eve from the clutches of Slievins, to reunite Eve with Adam, and to prevent the Cull."

"An excellent summary," said Aletheia. "Succinct and correct."

"Now all we need is a plausible way to fulfil the objectives," said Prune.

There was silence.

Then Kit said, "First we must rescue Eve. If she's in Mayfair, that's not beyond our reach. Then, while the rest of you reunite Adam and Eve, I will take a trip to the deserts of Arabia. It will not be my first visit to that part of the world."

51. Ceri and Lister: Round Three

They lay on their backs on the bed, naked and exhausted, their bodies glistening with sweat. Lister knew he had enjoyed a unique sexual experience. This woman had given him everything. More than that, she had anticipated exactly what he desired and then effortlessly delivered it in spades. He felt completely fulfilled and utterly drained at the same time.

"That was better," said Ceri, turning onto her stomach.

Lister looked down the curve of her spine to her perfectly formed buttocks and on to those long, shapely legs. "'Better' doesn't come near," murmured Lister.

Ceri languorously rose to a kneeling position. At each corner of the bed a bright yellow silk scarf hung. She took the end of one of these scarves and tied it around Lister's left wrist; then she took another and tied his right wrist. She slid down to the end of the bed and tied his left and right ankles. Lister watched her as she went about her task, admiring her taut breasts, her flat belly, her firm buttocks, those amazing legs. There was no part of her he hadn't explored and enjoyed.

"Now, my friend," said Ceri, with just the hint of a threat in her voice, "it's my turn. This is going to be fun. And just to think, amidst all the pleasure and the pain, neither of us can be sure whether, at the end of it all, you will be alive or dead."

52. Making arrangements

While Ceri was taking her turn and providing Lister with a physical experience which, assuming he survived, would leave its mark on him for the rest of his life, David Minofel was making his way towards Roland Samiat's office.

It was of course a coincidence, but less than a minute after he had concluded his plot-birthing conversation with Art Shoat, Roland had phoned and summoned him.

"Update me on the Adam situation," ordered Roland as soon as Minofel stepped through the door.

"No time for small talk then?" muttered Minofel under his breath.

"You're right there," said Roland, demonstrating his unnervingly acute sense of hearing. "This is a time for action. I want the Adam Smith case resolved quickly, before we all become totally preoccupied with the Cull and its aftermath. I understand there is a complication."

David Minofel was taken aback. What complication? He knew of no complication. There was no point in bluffing or guessing. He just raised his eyebrows.

Samiat peered at Minofel through those slits of eyes. A smile considered taking up residence at the corners of his mouth but thought better of it. "So you haven't heard?" Roland paused.

Minofel shook his head.

"I see," said Samiat, with a mixture of disappointment and contempt in his voice. For Samiat those two words were yet another black mark against Minofel; for Minofel they were another nail in Samiat's coffin. "I thought you were on top of the Adam case," Samiat continued. "Never mind. The complication is Aletheia. That bloody woman is back."

"Aletheia is back!" was all Minofel could manage. He was convinced he'd seen the last of her when she had left his office with Miss Tomic. They had seemed so content together, and he had assumed that Aletheia, assured of a happy life with the immortalised, delectable Gorgeous Tomic, would return to ancient times to live delightful sapphic years without number in Prometheus' great, lavishly appointed cave on Mount Strobilos.

"Don't repeat what I say," said Samiat testily. "It's your case. You should be telling me, not me you."

"Why?" said Minofel. "Why is she back?"

"Funnily enough," said Samiat, with a tone of sarcasm insinuating its way into his voice, "she hasn't informed me of her intentions, but given that she is the goddess of truth I've no doubt her intentions are disgustingly honourable. It doesn't matter why she's back. She's here and that means trouble."

"I think it does matter," said Minofel boldly. "You said it was my case, which must mean you assume she has come to interfere in my handling of Adam. Isn't it just as likely she has come to snatch Eve from your clutches? That would make it your case rather than mine. After all, you took it upon yourself to deal with Eve."

Samiat was not amused. "Well, I at least discovered Aletheia had returned."

"In fact," Minofel continued, "it seems most unlikely that Aletheia would come back for either of them. It's true that she came to help them destroy the Praesidium, but that from her point of view, was a grand project, worthy of a goddess. Are you sure she would travel through thousands of years and thousands of miles to save one or two mortals? Isn't it more likely that Prometheus has caught wind of your cull? Eliminating two mortals is one thing. Taking out six billion is something else, something worthy of a titan's and a goddess's attention."

"There is no way she could know anything about Cull 75241," said Samiat angrily. "Security on this project has been as tight as an undersized wetsuit. The consultants have been given details only just now and I've made it clear that any breach of security will be dealt with most severely. No, she's come back because that idiotic gang of questors have been using that bloody paradox device to keep in touch with Prometheus and he's sent her over to give them a hand. You may be right that she's come to rescue Eve as well as Adam but there's no way her arrival has anything to do with the Cull."

"If you say so," said Minofel. He had found the right button to press. If you wanted to divert Samiat's attention away from any subject you just had to mention Cull 75241. "If that's the case, you'll be pleased to hear that I intend to take Adam out of the country. There I will complete his deconstruction when I have him separated from every one and every place he knows. He is already close to terminal mental disintegration. He is conflicted in every area of his life. If we cloak his location, Aletheia will never find him. Eve is already cloaked in your Mayfair mansion. Problem solved. We can conclude both cases, Adam and Eve, at any time, at a moment's notice if you so wish.

"So where are you taking him?" asked Samiat. "Where can you take him so that you can guarantee effective cloaking?"

"I'm taking him to the Arabian desert," said Minofel with a smile. "I'll drop him off on the last leg of my own journey to the City under the Sand."

oooOooo

When David Minofel left, Roland sent an encrypted message to Ben Rael.

"David Minofel is planning a visit to Ubar," Roland wrote. "As part of the questor deconstruction programme, he will be dropping Adam Smith off in the middle of the desert. When Minofel arrives at the city I want you to keep a very close watch on him. Recently I have discerned hints of disloyalty in his attitude towards me."

He then sent another encrypted message to Charles Fundi. "Minofel is going to arrive in Ubar shortly. I have reason to doubt his loyalty to me. If he approaches you, do not discourage his foolish aspirations but keep me informed. I wish to give him enough hope to hang himself."

When Ben received his message, he replied. "Will keep the closest possible eye on Minofel when he arrives, particularly any dealings he has with Charles Fundi. If he has any thoughts of foolishly aspiring to such heights, he will certainly need to have the Commander of Ubar on his side." Ben smiled. He planned to persuade Samiat to allow him to eliminate Fundi as soon as the Cull was over and there was no harm in planting the seeds of suspicion now. No harm at all.

When Charles Fundi read his encrypted message, he immediately acknowledged the instruction, and then briefly wondered whether Samiat meant "hope", or whether it was a mistype for "rope", before concluding it didn't much matter.

oooOooo

When David Minofel reached the café, Adam was already there.

"So pleased you could tear yourself away from that hostel for the incompetent, inadequate and indigent," said Minofel. "How you put up with that sanctimonious harridan I've no idea."

"If you mean Violet," said Adam, "I rather like her. I've learned a lot."

Minofel shook his head. "I knew you were in bad shape – after what you've been through, it's scarcely surprising – but I hadn't realised just how much you had degenerated. What are you doing spending your time with the dross of humanity? Surely you could find someone of your own class, quality and calibre to spend time with? Or are drunks, druggies and the mentally challenged really the best you can do?"

Adam was stunned. "She didn't like you either," he said. "Where is all this coming from? What happened when you met her?"

"I know the type," said Minofel. "Full of the milk of human kindness, which they use either to suckle those who should be made to fend for themselves or to squirt in the eye of everyone else to prevent us from seeing their hypocrisy. They don't genuinely care about the dross. Like everyone else, they want power over others, and the only ones they can bully and browbeat are the scumbags."

Adam shook his head. "Violet is a really kind and wise woman who has sacrificed most of her life to the service of others. For decades she cared for her mother, and since her mother died she has run that refuge. And I've been helping her."

Minofel laughed. "You cannot be serious. The man who has ruthlessly pursued a high-flying career, taking the tough decisions that are necessary to succeed, cutting down anything and anyone in his way – in short, a first-class Slievins' man – has been helping out in a home for parasites and retards! I don't think so. You needed somewhere to stay. Yes. You needed a cup of tea. Yes. But that's it." For the first time Minofel was just a little unsure.

Adam said nothing.

"Come on, Adam, it's just not you," Minofel prompted.

"Well, there's the thing, David. You say helping Violet is not me. But who is 'me'? Do you know who I am? Because if you do, you're a lot smarter than me."

"I'll tell you who you are," said Minofel. "You're the man who is being pursued for tax evasion and money laundering by HMRC. You're the man the Swiss police want to interview in connection with the Spinetti murder. You're the man who is hoping that, against all the odds, his one true friend in this world is going to help him find a way out of the appalling mess he's in because if he can't, you'll have to spend the rest of your life on the run. That's who you are."

Adam shrugged. "I guess you're right, except I haven't evaded any tax or laundered any money."

"If you're so innocent, why don't you hand yourself in?" Minofel's patience was exhausted. "No? I wonder why. And we haven't even mentioned bribery or blackmail. And then there's the little matter of murder."

"All right! All right!" Adam conceded. "You've made your point. So if you're my very good friend, my only friend, have you brought me any good news?"

Minofel leant forward in his chair. "Yes, I have. You have a new name, a new passport and, ahead of you, a new life. And I've managed to divert most of your money to your new bank account. That was the most difficult part. HMRC were determined to freeze your accounts. With literally just minutes to spare I managed to shift the money in your main savings account to an overseas bank. Since then, I've used Slievins' facilities to split the money into half a dozen packages and move each package through half a dozen financial institutions. HMRC are chasing, but at every step they take, the money gets further away. We'll be able to consolidate all the accounts in a bank where we are going. Then it's up to you. You'll be a new man of independent financial means."

"I'm very grateful," said Adam.

"Grateful! Grateful!" Minofel exclaimed. "You should be down on the floor licking my feet. I've put myself on the line for you. You're not exactly flavour of the month in Slievins. You betrayed the trust I placed in you. You joined with those who wished to destroy the Praesidium. You severed your links with the company. I've done all this because I am your friend. I've helped you because I still believe you are a Slievins' man at heart – and because I chose you for greatness. And I'm never wrong."

"Greatness!" Adam laughed. "Don't bank on it. I've lost Eve. I've lost the child she was carrying. I have no job. I have no purpose. And I'm on the run, pursued by the authorities of at least two countries. You say I'm to be a new man. Well, that's good because the old one is an empty hollow vessel."

"Well, John Smythe, you have enough money to fill the empty

vessel with whatever you want." Minofel handed Adam a slim briefcase. "In this case are all the documents you will need, including a passport and some cash, together with a full back story on John Smythe. It's all genuine. John Smythe is missing, assumed dead. He was one of those caught in the bomb blast, like Eve. He was about your age and your height, which was a bit of luck. As they say, it's an ill wind ... Anyway, we leave tonight."

"What do you mean '*We* leave tonight'?" Adam was finding it hard to take everything in.

"You and I are booked on a plane to our first destination. We leave at 22.30 on a BA direct flight to Jeddah. We're booked business class, reasonably comfortable but a good deal less conspicuous than first. We land at 06.35. I've booked a couple of rooms at the Meridien where we can stay till I've sorted out the paperwork at the bank."

"You're coming with me?" queried a puzzled Adam. This was beyond friendship. In fact it didn't make any sense.

"Of course," said David Minofel. "How else can I be sure I get my fifteen per cent."

53.   Rescuing Eve

The questors and Aletheia deliberated long and hard to determine how to rescue Eve. After much discussion, it was agreed the best plan was simply to march into the Slievins' Mayfair mansion and demand her release. Rambler's suggestion that they use the paradox device to teleport Eve away from Slievins' grasp was dropped when Andrew explained that there would be serious risks in teleporting a material entity through the enhanced cloaking system that Slievins was employing to protect their property. He feared a material body would be shredded.

Of course, simply marching into the Mayfair mansion and demanding Eve's release had its own problems. The mansion was surrounded by eight-foot-high railings and gated. The rescue party would have to negotiate their way through security and persuade Roland Samiat to allow his house guest to leave. Neither access nor escape seemed likely to be easy.

"They can't refuse our requests" said Rambler hopefully. "If they won't let us in or they refuse to release Eve, we can involve the police."

"I don't think so," said Kit gently. "We have no proof Eve is being held. The police believe she is dead. Even if we could persuade the police to investigate, they would never be granted a search warrant. Slievins has the judiciary as well as the government in its capacious pocket. And even if we could find an uncorrupted magistrate or judge and we effected Eve's release through normal legal channels, what would happen when she emerged from the Mayfair mansion. As I understand the situation, there would be intense competition between the media, HMRC and the Swiss police to see who could have the first bite."

With both his suggestions shot down in flames Rambler subsided into silence.

"I will go to this Slievins' stronghold and demand access," said Aletheia.

"And I will go with you," said Kit. "It will be difficult for them to refuse a goddess and a blind man."

"Not that difficult," said Andrew doubtfully.

"Could I come?" Luke minded to Kit. "The presence of the God of Dogs might swing it. And I am, after all, a retriever."

"If you wish," Kit minded back, sensitive to Luke's feelings. "Who could refuse a goddess, blind man and the very finest of dogs?"

"And what shall we do while you are attempting the rescue?" asked Prune. "Do we have to sit and wait?"

"No," said Aletheia. "You have to find out all you can about this planned 'spectacular', this Project 75241. We need to know exactly what it is, when they intend to carry it out, how they will execute it and, above all, how we can stop it."

oooOooo

It was an odd rescue party that approached the entrance of the Slievins' Mayfair mansion. Aletheia strode up to the armed security guard who stood at the double gates. On her arm was the blind man, his sightless eyes looking straight ahead, a smile hovering at the corners of his mouth. At Kit's side was Luke.

"No tourists, no visitors, and no dogs," snapped the guard. "This is private property." There were usually two guards on duty but today he was on his own. The second guard was at the control panel in the guard house explaining to a senior security officer the problem they were having with the electric gates.

"We have come to see your master," said Aletheia.

"You've what?" enquired the guard.

"I have no wish to stand here quibbling with a lackey," said Aletheia. "Open these gates and give me directions to your master's office."

The guard summoned his two colleagues, his fellow guardian of the gate and the senior security officer, from the nearby guardhouse. They arrived, heavily armed, each with a Dobermann on a short lead.

"If you don't leave immediately, we will call the police," said the senior security officer, handing his dog over to the first guard. "She's obviously mentally challenged," he observed to his colleagues. As the senior officer on duty, he had been viewing the monitor, trying to identify the cause of the intermittent fault in the gates mechanism, so he had seen and heard everything through the guardhouse sound system.

"Given what you do behind these gates," said Kit, speaking for the first time, "we think it most unlikely you will call the police. We

207

believe that you are holding one of our friends prisoner. We have come to seek her release." Kit touched one of the gates with his stick and both began to slide open.

"Shit!" said the senior security officer, moving forward to stand in Aletheia's path. Before he could speak again she brushed him aside with some force.

"Set the dogs on them," ordered the senior security officer now sprawled on the ground. The other guards obeyed, but to their astonishment both Dobermanns lay down before the Golden Labrador in a posture of unconditional obedience.

"Don't overdo it," minded Luke to the supine dogs. "A simple refusal to obey your keepers will suffice."

Now on his feet, the senior security officer took his gun from its holster. "If you do not leave immediately, we will use lethal force against you," he warned. The other two guards drew their weapons.

"Stop!" said a voice over the loudspeaker system. "Allow our visitors to enter and send them to reception. I will meet them there."

The guards seemed confused but holstered their weapons at once. "Go through the arch, walk across the grounds, and head for the central doors at the front of the building."

As the visitors entered the grounds of the mansion, both Dobermanns risked a quick sniff of Luke as he passed. The chance to savour the scent of the dog who had faced down the hounds of hell at Cadnam was not to be missed.

oooOooo

Roland Samiat met his uninvited visitors in the main reception hall of the mansion.

"We don't usually allow pets into the building," said Roland, clearly uneasy in Luke's presence, "but as this animal is accompanying a blind man, we can make an exception in this instance." He turned his attention to the imposing figure of the goddess. "So you are Aletheia," he said, taking her hand, sweeping it upwards and lightly brushing it with his lips. "I am Roland Samiat, CEO of Slievins. My man Minofel has told me so much about you." He turned to Kit. "And you, of course, are the blind man. It is an honour to meet you."

"An honour?" queried Kit.

"I knew your father," Roland Samiat explained. "He told me that despite your blindness, you have always been independent-minded and courageous. Your father was so proud of you. I'm not usually keen on idealists but I make an exception in your case."

"An idealist?" queried Kit.

"Don't take offence," said Roland, with a glint in those slits of eyes. "As your father used to say, there's nothing wrong with idealism so long as you don't take it too seriously. By the way, how is your father? We didn't always see eye to eye, but you must give him my regards."

"He's dead," said Kit.

"Oh, I'm sorry to hear that," said Roland. "It must have been hard for you, especially after your falling out."

"Falling out?" queried Kit.

"I'm sorry," said Roland quickly. "The last thing I want to do is rake up old, painful memories." Roland turned back to Aletheia. "Now, how can I help you?"

"We have come to demand the release of Eve Smith. We know you are holding her here, so please don't waste our time by denying it."

"I certainly won't deny that Eve is here. She is a very dear guest of Slievins. But we are not *holding* her here. She is, and always has been, free to leave. We picked her up when she was caught in the terrorist bomb blast. We have made sure both she and the baby she carries are well. She has had the best of care. If she has remained here it is because she appreciates the kindness we have lavished on her and because she rightly fears the consequences if she leaves."

Kit and Aletheia were stunned. Roland Samiat, the CEO of Slievins, by all accounts the architect of the impending Cull 75241, was claiming that he had taken care of Eve and the baby she carried out of the goodness of his – or Slievins' – heart.

"Are you saying that Eve has stayed here willingly?" asked Aletheia. "Are you saying she never expressed a desire to see Adam, to find out how he was doing, what he was doing?"

Roland frowned, as though perplexed. "We had to make a judgement call," he confessed. "In the end, we decided to let Eve believe Adam was dead."

"And why did you do that?" enquired Kit. Evidently his conspiracy theory had not been so far off the mark.

"What we did was always in Eve's best interests and in the best interests of the baby she is carrying," said Roland solemnly. "We took the view that if she found out the truth about Adam, it would destroy her and her baby. If she discovered that the man she loved had bribed, blackmailed and even murdered in pursuit of his career, for financial gain and to seize power, she would have been shattered. As you may know, the UK authorities are pursuing Adam for tax evasion and money laundering, and the Swiss police are after him for bribery, corruption and murder. In passing, we should perhaps also mention the lives he wrecked and the thousands of jobs he destroyed when he betrayed the trust of his employers and brought the great pharmaceutical company, ZeD, to its knees. Eve would not be able to forgive Adam for just one of these crimes, but all the crimes taken together would be too much. She loved Adam. She thought she knew him. If the man she loved was capable of such evil, how could she ever trust anyone? And how would she feel about the child he fathered? So we let her believe Adam was dead."

"We demand to see Eve," said Aletheia. "We will tell her that Adam is alive. She can then decide what she wants to do."

"Of course," said Roland. "You are her friends and it would be wrong to prevent you from talking to her. But I must make sure you understand what you will be doing and that you take responsibility for it. Eve is building a new life. Two members of my staff, Enid Mavlow and Lister Bavad, have befriended her. She is coming to terms with her loss of Adam and is concentrating on the impending birth of her child.

"If she leaves here, she will be questioned, if not arrested, by HMRC. She has been, or would have been, the main beneficiary of Adam's misdeeds. They are unlikely to accept that she was wholly innocent. After all, she has been pretending to be dead for weeks. On her resurrection, the media will hound her. Given public hostility to the greed of the elite, tax evasion and money laundering will justify intense media interest, but the real red meat in the story is the sexual scandal that roiled around in ZeD and its culmination in the murder of Spinetti in which, it seems, Adam was implicated. If Eve leaves the protection of Slievins, her life will not be worth living, even if she avoids a prison sentence."

"How much does she know about what Adam did?" Aletheia asked.

Roland maintained a solemn expression. "Now, she knows everything," he said. "Only this morning I completed the briefing process."

"I thought you were protecting her from the truth," said Kit angrily.

"You can protect people only up to a point," Roland replied. "We have told her now because she is strong enough to bear it. She had to free herself of Adam before she could muster the strength to take the truth and build a new life. Aletheia, surely you will not criticise me for telling someone the truth? Now you understand the situation, you are free to talk to Eve. I have business to attend to elsewhere and I shall be abroad for some time. I will leave instruction that you are to be free to talk to Eve for as long as you wish and that you are to be treated with typical Slievins' hospitality while you are here. I'm sorry about the misunderstanding at the gate, but if you had made an appointment, there would have been no unpleasantness. Whatever you decide, please put the interests of Eve and her baby first."

oooOooo

Roland left Aletheia, Kit and Luke in the reception hall and walked swiftly to his private rooms. On arrival, a member of his staff told him that he had a message to phone the Chief Dawk, Despiro Nihilopificus. Before making the call, Roland sent a text message to Art Shoat instructing him to use all necessary means to prevent Eve and her visitors from leaving the mansion until further notice. He added at the end of the message: "And make sure the mechanism on the front gate is fixed as a matter of urgency."

His conversation with Despiro was brief.

"We are ready to proceed with the test in Slough whenever you issue the order," said the Chief Dawk, without the slightest hint of emotion in his voice.

"Excellent," said the Slievins' CEO. "I'll be in touch shortly."

oooOooo

While Roland was talking to Despiro, David Minofel and Art Shoat were quietly conversing in David's office in Slievins' London headquarters in the City.

"I'm leaving with Adam this evening. We have a direct flight on British Airways to Jeddah. We'll stay a couple of days and then I'll take Adam into the desert."

"I've had a talk with Charles Fundi on the phone," Art confided. "I told him you were coming and I mentioned our concerns about Roland."

211

"I hope you used a secure line," David interrupted.

"Of course," said Art. "But even so, I was careful with what I said. I did mention that Ben Rael had claimed the credit for sorting out the problem with the shepherd, or rather with the shepherd's tribe. And I think I mentioned that Ben had been undermining Charles's reputation here, suggesting he was a bit of a loose cannon. Charles can't stand Ben anyway, so I'm sure you will find him receptive to our ideas."

"We need to decide when to make our move," said Minofel. "I've been bugging Roland's office. I'm not sure exactly when, but Roland is planning a trial run for his cull. Nihilopificus is setting it all up. They've chosen Slough. I don't know why. I think we should make our move after Slough but just before the Cull itself. We'll let Roland make sure his plan will work. Then, when he's ready to go global with DK12, we step in and take over. That way, if there are any hitches with the Slough pilot, he will be blamed. If all runs smoothly, we can take the credit for implementing Project 75241, prove we have control and establish our authority."

"Sounds good to me," said Art.

"While I'm in Arabia, see if you can prepare Lister, Ceri and the consultants for a change of leadership. Keep Enid out of it. I realise it will be tricky but I know you can handle it."

At this point, Art read the text message Roland had just sent him. "I can handle it all right," said Art irritably, getting up to leave for Mayfair immediately, "after I've fixed the bloody gates!"

54. Sisters and female relationships

Enid Mavlow was none too happy with Lister's passionate liaison with Ceri. Lister, having survived his first encounter with Ceri, was a changed man. He no longer seemed so sure of himself. That happy, confident charismatic energy that he had exuded formerly was strangely diminished.

Enid was not jealous of Ceri. Her own carnal appetites were fully satisfied by Roland, and in any case she suspected Roland would respond poorly to any form of infidelity. No, she was not jealous, but she was irritated. She and Lister had been charged with the care of Eve, and frankly Lister wasn't pulling his weight. Fortunately, Eve seemed content to concentrate on the impending birth of her baby, but Enid was worried that Eve still remained sceptical of Slievins' good intentions.

Enid also felt she had to reassess her relationship with Ceri. Ceri had taken her under her wing when she first arrived from Rio and they had become friends. Indeed, the three of them – Lister, Ceri and Enid – had developed a really warm, close relationship. But since then, Ceri had seduced Estevo, Enid's boyfriend, and had now decided to monopolise Lister, effectively excluding Enid.

This situation awakened painful memories for Enid. Enid had been her parents' second child. Her sister, Ava, was two years older than Enid. And Ava was perfect. Ava was beautiful; Ava was clever; Ava was kind. Enid herself was pretty, but not beautiful; she was extremely quick-witted, with a sharp mental intelligence, but she wasn't as clever as Ava; and although Enid was caring and warm-hearted to those she liked, she could be cruel to those who displeased her.

The sisters were good friends, but as they grew older Enid couldn't help but feel some resentment towards Ava. It wasn't just that Ava had the edge on her in every department, it was that everything seemed effortless for Ava. She didn't try harder, she didn't compete, she just won.

Things came to a head when Enid was seventeen. For more than a year, Enid had been going out with Juan, a handsome undergraduate who was four years her senior. Coming from a respectable Catholic family, Enid frequently brought Juan to her home where he would behave with perfect manners, showing the respect due to Enid's parents.

In the course of these visits, Juan inevitably met Ava, and with an equal inevitability, or so it seemed to Enid, he found his affections transferring from Enid to the older sister. To add insult to injury, Ava, who was honestly smitten with Juan, sought Enid's permission to reciprocate Juan feelings. What could Enid say?

For obvious reasons, Enid was unhappy. She felt let down by two of the people closest to her. She felt betrayed within her own family. So she took three decisions. First, she decided to leave home as soon as possible. Secondly, she decided to leave her sister and her city, Rio, far behind. Thirdly, she decided to take revenge before she left.

Juan was in the second year of a law degree. Ava, with excellent exam results and inspired by Juan, decided that she also wanted to pursue a legal career, intending to join Juan at his university.

Enid's revenge was simple enough. Eve researched the internet for tablets that looked similar to Ava's contraceptive pills. She found some mild herbal tablets for the relief of anxiety and substituted them for the contraceptives. Within two months, Ava was with child. Her devout Catholic parents were, of course, shocked and disappointed. Their favourite daughter wasn't so perfect after all.

Ava couldn't understand how she had fallen pregnant. She suspected the contraceptive pills she had been taking were defective. But as a good Catholic girl she shouldn't have been using contraception anyway. So she accepted the pregnancy as a judgement and a blessing from God. Enid was surprised by her sister's ready acceptance of motherhood as an alternative to a career but assumed her complacency was at least partly due to the effect of the herbal tablets.

Enid now set her mind on fulfilling her other ambitions. She had decided her future lay in business. The Rio branch of Slievins was holding an open day for bright young people who, if selected, would be happy to accept a paid internship with Slievins as an alternative to an expensive academic degree course at university. Enid was offered an internship and immediately accepted the offer.

In her four years with Slievins, Enid had learned a great deal. Immediately identified as someone with the potential to be a Slievins' person, she had been fast-tracked, and when an opportunity arose for a young executive in London, the managing director of the Rio operation put her name forward. She accepted the ensuing offer without hesitation. A few weeks before the Slievins' offer she had agreed to marry Estevo, a boy she had met while going out with Juan, but it made no difference to her decision. Just as she had planned, she was leaving Rio behind.

So Enid's career had been an extraordinary success story. She now found herself at the centre of the Slievins' business and in an intense relationship with the Slievins' CEO. She should have felt confident and secure.

But she didn't. Her experiences with Ava and Ceri made her suspicious of both men and women. Juan had left her for Ava; Estevo had been unfaithful with Ceri. Now Lister was letting her down. She and Lister were a team, assigned to look after Eve. He was the more experienced partner. So far, all had gone well. But at the very time that Roland had agreed to allow some of Eve's friends from her old life to visit her, Lister had become a passenger.

Enid had wanted to share her concerns with Roland, but Roland was obsessed with his special project and now had little time for anything else.

oooOooo

Art Shoat conducted Aletheia, Kit and Luke to Eve's apartment in the mansion.

"Why do you have pictures on your arms?" enquired Aletheia. She was fascinated by the bulky, porcine escort with his elaborate tattoos.

Art laughed. "Back in the day I ran a business in the East End of London. There was a lot of competition. Whenever I won a contest with a competitor, I liked to commemorate the occasion with a tattoo."

"What kind of contests did you have with your competitors?" asked Aletheia. "Did you box, or wrestle, or engage in swordplay?"

"All three, from time to time. But mainly swordplay," said Art, keeping a straight face.

"It is good to meet a fellow swordsman," Aletheia remarked. "I feel naked without my sword."

Art nodded as though he understood. He rather liked the look of the tall, fair-haired woman, striding at his side, even though she

215

seemed slightly deranged, and he was more than happy to imagine her naked. They reached the reception hall of what had become Eve's quarters.

"Right. We're here," said Art. "Let me introduce you to Enid. Enid is one of the Slievins' staff who has been looking after Eve. You should have a chat with her before you see Eve."

After the introductions, Enid asked the visitors to sit down.

"I understand you are close friends of Eve," she began.

"We have been through much together," said Kit. "Eve is very important to us."

"I understand that," said Enid. "But things have changed since the terrorist bomb. Eve has been with us since that dreadful day. We have cared for her while she has had to come to terms with the loss of her husband, and the threat to her financial security and even her freedom – all this while nurturing the child she is carrying."

Aletheia remained silent. Enid seemed to be a kind, caring, sensitive person, but Aletheia was unconvinced.

"Adam isn't dead," said Kit. "She hasn't lost her husband."

"If Adam is alive, that will come as a surprise to all of us," Enid lied convincingly. "If he is alive, why hasn't he come looking for Eve?"

"He hasn't come looking for Eve because he – and the police, for that matter – are convinced she was killed in the explosion," said Aletheia. "They found evidence that Eve was in Covent Garden at the time of the bomb blast, and there has been no trace of her since. Now we know why."

"So where is Adam?" asked Enid. And where was Lister? He had been told of the arrival of the visitors and their demand to see Eve. Was he still on the assignment or was he too busy with Ceri to attend this crucial meeting?

"Adam is on the run," said Aletheia, again illustrating her ever-wider grasp of English idiom.

"I see," said Enid. "That is why we have kept Eve here, out of view. She will give birth soon. This would not be the time for her to be on the run from the authorities. You should bear this in mind when you talk to her."

"That's exactly what Roland Samiat told us before he sent us here to see Eve," said Aletheia. "You all seem very keen to keep Eve here."

"Only for her own good," Enid replied. "And there's another reason you should tread carefully. OK, Adam is still alive. Even so, Eve has lost her husband."

"What does that mean?" asked Aletheia.

"After a great deal of thought and advice from our in-house counsellors, it was decided we should tell Eve the truth about her husband."

Kit laughed. "The truth about Adam! Who knows the truth about anyone?"

At this point Lister entered the room. He had overheard the latter part of the conversation.

"We don't mean a definitive, multi-layered, psychological, soul-searching truth," he said with a laugh. "Just the truth about what Adam's done. By the way, I'm Lister Bavad. Enid and I have been caring for Eve."

"Exactly what have you told her?" asked Kit. He knew most of what Adam had done at the Westminster PCC, but he had not had the chance to discuss with Adam the details of his career at ZeD.

Lister gave a summary of Adam's activities when employed at the Swiss pharmaceutical company, listing his offences efficiently and dispassionately. "So you see," he concluded, "apart from his insensitive, if not callous, treatment of Eve when she needed his support most, Adam committed a number of serious criminal offences during his brief sojourn in Switzerland. Bribery of an official is an offence in most countries but is viewed with particular distaste in Switzerland which is so dependent on the integrity of its officialdom. Blackmail is one of the most despised crimes everywhere. As for murder, it is among the blackest of acts and the most serious of crimes."

Aletheia and Kit were stunned. Luke, who had settled in at Kit's feet, whimpered.

Eventually Kit spoke. "Does Adam confess to all these crimes?"

"Not if he can help it." Lister Bavad laughed again. "That's why he's on the run. But if you mean is he guilty, I can assure you he's as guilty as sin. There is incontrovertible evidence and the innocent don't run."

"We must talk to Eve," said Aletheia.

"Of course," said Lister. "I'll take you to her now."

55. Slough

The dying began at 07.00 hours on a crisp, cold, late autumn day. The sun was just beginning to rise. The transmission of the precise sound wavelengths to activate DK12 had begun an hour earlier.

Many in Slough were up and about, preparing to go to work. They were all following their normal workday routines. By 07.00, the transmission had activated sufficient DK12 in those with the highest concentrations for the attacks on vital organs to begin to manifest themselves. The most vulnerable organs were the stomach, the heart, the kidneys, the pancreas and the liver. In most cases, it was the destruction of the heart that proved fatal. The average time, from the occurrence of the first symptom to death, was twenty-eight minutes.

In the first tranche of fatalities, almost all those who lived alone died alone. The illness took them by surprise. By the time they realised there was something seriously wrong, they were too weak and in too much pain to phone for help. Within an hour of death, the bodies began to smoulder.

Those who lived with others (with partners or children) faced an even more horrendous fate. If they alone in the household were affected, they had to endure their last few minutes in agony, screaming at their loved ones to help them. More frequently all members of the household were affected, so all present had to watch their loved ones die in the same agony as they themselves were suffering.

There were particularly horrific individual cases. A married couple of shift workers, renting a flat in Herschel Street, were having a lie-in. The man, Dwayne, was an enthusiastic consumer of fast foods. His wife, Tracey, was a vegan. Tracy awoke at 10.00. She said, "Dwayne, what's that smell? Something's burning." She prodded her husband in the back. He didn't move. Tracey knew something was wrong. She sat up in bed, looked at her husband and screamed. He was dead. His face was cruelly disfigured but apparently occupied by some strange corroding life form. His nose and cheeks were covered by small erupting blisters. There was a pervasive smell of slowly smouldering flesh.

Daisy, a four-year-old girl, was living with her single mother, Sheila, on the Bath Road. Sheila fed her daughter well, but as she worked two part-time jobs she had little time to cook for herself. Instead, she lived on a diet of fast and processed food. Daisy awoke at 10.28 to find her mother doubled up in pain. Although only four, Daisy phoned 999. Surprisingly, she got through and explained the situation. The traumatised telephonist at the other end of the phone burst into tears. She said there was nothing she could do. All the other staff on duty at the ambulance station were dying or dead. She had answered the phone in the hope that someone was coming to help her. Sheila died at 10.40. By 11.30 Daisy could see her mother's body was beginning to smoulder.

oooOooo

At the Dawks' brand new research establishment at Martlesham in Suffolk, Despiro Nihilopificus was deeply frustrated.

"We need more data," he complained to his chief analyst. "This is our only chance to fine tune the Cull. We need the number of those affected by the hour. We need precise figures on time of first symptoms, time of death. We need decomposition rates."

"We're doing our best," the chief analyst replied, "but it's not easy for our researchers. There's chaos in Slough. Emergency services are pouring into the town, but many of those arriving are being affected by the transmission activating DK12. I did say that there would be problems if we relied on our researchers gathering information on the ground. I did suggest planting monitors in a sample of dwellings so we could gather data in real time."

"And I told you we couldn't risk anyone finding out what we were doing." Being a generally calm if not coldly calculating man, Despiro eschewed anger. Today was an exception. "Very few people, even in the elite, know exactly what we are doing. Fewer still have any idea how we are going to do it. For them, the Cull is just an abstract concept, a means of reducing the world's population to more manageable proportions. One day, there are eight billion people and lots of problems of sustainability; the next, there are only two billion people and all the sustainability problems have disappeared. Just like that. Magic! They certainly don't want to know any details. But we, on the other hand, do need details. This is the biggest single operation mankind has ever undertaken. And it's up to us to make sure it runs perfectly. How do we do that? We analyse the data. So we're back where we started. We need more data."

219

The chief analyst could see that further discussion of the matter was futile and counterproductive. He changed the subject. "By the way, there has been remarkable progress in the development of the Resolver. Our software engineers believe they are close to complete success."

"That is excellent news." Despiro sounded almost cheerful. "The paradox device has bedevilled all our dealings with the questors. Evidently my view that the paradox device is vulnerable to systematic analysis and deconstruction is about to be wholly vindicated. The day we bring the Resolver online and fully operational is the day all our problems with the questors will be resolved. Without the device, their entire quest can be exposed as irrefutably misguided – a pathetic attempt to escape from reality."

56. The meeting with Eve

Enid escorted Aletheia, Kit and Luke to Eve's sitting room where Eve, heavily pregnant, was resting.

Luke was overjoyed to see his mistress and ran across the room to her, his tail held high and wagging vigorously. Kit followed Luke and, running his hand along the contours of the chaise longue on which Eve was resting, found her shoulder.

Eve, who had been dozing, was now wide awake. "Kit, what are you doing here?"

"It is good to see you," said Kit, "or it would be if I could."

Eve took Kit's hand. "It's really good to see you too. But how did you find me?"

"We have come to take you away from here," said Aletheia who had held back at the door, as though waiting for an invitation to enter.

"Aletheia!" Eve exclaimed. "Why are you here?"

"I have just told you," said Aletheia, striding into the room. "This mansion is part of the Slievins' dominion. I should be asking you 'Why are you here?' Were your experiences on the Westminster PCC insufficient to convince you of Slievins' malign intent? Have you forgotten how they corrupted Adam, how they tried to kill Kit?"

"No, I haven't forgotten," said Eve, bridling at Aletheia's tone. "I remember all that happened in our quest with remarkable and sometimes painful clarity. I am here because Roland Samiat has taken care of me from the moment I was caught in the Covent Garden bomb blast. He and his people have made sure that I and my baby have had the best medical attention. I haven't left here because, to be utterly honest, I couldn't face the consequences of Adam's behaviour on my own. It wasn't his fault but he left me to deal with some pretty serious problems."

Kit, still holding Eve's hand, squeezed it gently. "Adam is not dead, Eve."

"What do you mean?" said Eve, distressed. "What do you mean 'Adam is not dead'? Slievins has looked everywhere for him. The police have certainly looked everywhere for him. Of course he's dead. If he wasn't dead, he would have been looking for me."

"He hasn't been looking for you because he believes you are dead," said Kit.

"Well, if he's alive, where is he?" demanded Eve, still incredulous. "Why hasn't he come with you?

"Because he's on the run," said Aletheia.

"That at least makes sense," mused Eve. "Given what he did, I'm sure he would be on the run if he was alive, but since he was killed in the same bomb blast that almost killed me he can't be. I've learned a good deal since I've been here. Slievins isn't all bad. Enid has been very kind to me. She's been a good friend. And you have to be careful who you trust. Even those closest to you can let you down. Even those you love can deceive you."

"Adam is not a bad man," said Kit.

Eve laughed. "The Adam I knew and loved was not a bad man, but the Adam who bribed, blackmailed and murdered to further his own career was, by any rational definition, profoundly evil. At first I couldn't believe it. But in the end you can't deny the evidence. You are his friend, Kit. I understand that. But even though you can't see, you can't be blind to what he has done, the crimes he has committed."

"Prometheus told me that like the gods all men have good and evil in them," said Aletheia. "But only man has the possibility of being better than the gods. That is why the titan Prometheus has always been a friend to man. If Adam has committed serious crimes, it is because he was corrupted by the people you now say are your friends."

"People like Enid and her friend Lister had nothing to do with Adam during his time at ZeD. I've no doubt David Minofel bears some responsibility for Adam's conduct in Geneva but as Roland Samiat, Slievins' CEO, has explained to me, Minofel exceeded his authority and broke a number of Slievins' best practice rules in his mentoring of Adam. In any case, Adam was a grown man. He had free will. He knew what he was doing was wrong. That's why he shut me out."

"Adam lives," said Aletheia, "and you have been deceived. Just as they corrupted Adam, they are now destroying you. They are determined to break the bond between you and Adam. You say you can no longer trust those you love. Without trust and without love you are lost. You will live in a world of fear, anger, jealousy and hate. You will live in the Slievins' world. There will not be any Beginnings. That is how things will end."

Outside Eve's sitting room there was a sudden commotion. Raised voices shouted excitedly. There was a knock on the door. Enid and Lister Bavad entered. "There has been an event," said Lister. "We would be grateful if you would remain in this apartment for now. Things could get chaotic for a while. It would be best for all of you if you stay here."

"What event?" asked Kit. He had a bad feeling. Luke whimpered. "What has happened?"

"There has been an accident," said Enid.

"Not another terrorist outrage?" Eve queried.

"We don't know," said Enid. "It could be. Slough has been attacked."

"What?" said Eve and Kit in unison."

"Why would anyone want to attack Slough?" enquired Kit. "It's not exactly the Houses of Parliament. It's not even Covent Garden."

"Was anyone killed?" asked Eve.

"Almost everyone," replied Enid.

"Not everyone," said Lister. "About seventy-eight per cent."

Lister and Enid left. Aletheia heard the door lock click.

"Now do you see?" Aletheia asked Eve. "You're not a guest, you're a prisoner."

57. A good result

Roland Samiat summoned Art Shoat to his office in the City.

"You will have heard the news," said Roland as Art entered. "The whole operation went well. We don't have final figures for fatalities yet – we're leaving that to the emergency services – but the Dawks at Martlesham reckon about eighty-one per cent succumbed. That's a little on the high side, but as Despiro pointed out, there was a slightly higher percentage of fast-food eaters in Slough than in most places."

Since his attendance at the most recent Slievins' monthly management meeting, Art had changed his diet. No fast food, no processed food, lots of fresh vegetables, even the odd fruit. "So are we ready to go with the whole enchilada?" enquired Art.

"Don't you mean 'Are we ready to go for the whole big burger?'" suggested Roland. "As I understand it, enchiladas tend to be made with lumps of unprocessed meat, presenting few opportunities for the inclusion of DK12."

"Sure," said Art. "Whatever."

Minofel had urged Art to keep an eye on Roland, to look out for any odd behaviour. He wondered whether picking him up on an inappropriate idiom in the context of a discussion of genocide constituted an oddity.

"Technically. we can proceed with the Cull whenever we want," said Roland, "but I have several loose ends to tie up before I give the word. First, we must closely observe the clean-up operation. There are likely to be about 105,000 bodies. DK12 combusted in the dead bodies as planned, but there are already indications that not all the flesh was completely reduced to ashes. It's not critical but it is a little disappointing. It will add time and cost to the clean-up when we go for the full Cull.

"Then, of course, I want to settle the matter of Adam and Eve. Eve's treatment has gone really well. She has accepted Adam's death and, more importantly, she has accepted that he was not the man she thought he was. It's safe to say her faith in Adam, human nature and everything else is damaged beyond repair. When her new friends, Enid and Lister, betray her, our work on Eve will be done.

"Eve's case is slightly complicated by the arrival here of two of her old friends. One of them is Aletheia, the other, the blind man Kit. They also have a dog in tow. How they located her here I don't know. Their timing is unfortunate. The mansion is buzzing with news of the pilot cull in Slough. We don't know how much they have overheard but we do know both Aletheia and Kit are eager to believe the worst of us. Kit has already speculated that we organised the Covent Garden bombing. In other circumstances I would happily accept their opinion of us as a compliment, but not this time. We can't risk them guessing we had anything to do with the pilot cull. If they were to start a rumour that we were the perpetrators, it could jeopardise the main event. I don't underestimate Aletheia with her 'truth will out' mantra. So we will keep them here until we have triggered Cull 75241. That leaves Adam. David told me he could wrap up Adam at any time."

"I'm sure that's true," said Art in what he hoped was a reassuring tone.

"So where is he?" asked Roland.

"David's taken Adam to Ubar," said Art. "Well, not straight to Ubar. They've flown to Jeddah. They're then going to make their way across the south Arabian desert. David plans to break Adam in the desert. Then, if you like, he'll bring what's left of him, alive or dead, to Ubar so that, when you arrive, you'll be able to see for yourself what he's done. He promises that Adam will be completely deconstructed before he reaches the city in the sand."

Roland's eyebrows lifted. "So he's gone already. He told me about his plan. I thought it was an unnecessarily elaborate way of completing Adam's annihilation, but David assured me the desert is a perfect place to close the file on Adam. He told me he's used it before. He says there's something primeval about being alone under a merciless sun, without food, water or hope. I was, in any case, planning for Minofel to travel with us to Ubar in a day or so, so it all fits together rather well. On reflection, I rather like the idea of Adam finally coming face to face with the truth in a desert. He will finally dissolve in the heat of the desert sun like a gallium teaspoon in a bowl of hot water."

Art nodded wisely as though he fully understood. Minofel was right. There was certainly something wrong with Roland.

"We too must now up sticks and head for the City under the Sand," Roland continued. "I'm leaving Lister and Ceri here to take care of Eve and her friends. I don't want any loose ends. In particular, I've asked Ceri to confirm when Eve and her brat are dead. I'll be interested to see how Ceri and Lister handle Aletheia, but assuming they are successful, it will give me enormous pleasure to inform Prometheus of his sad loss. Enid will come with me. I may have uses for her, other than the most obvious one. We will be based in Ubar from now on. After the Cull and the clean-up, it will be a new, much less crowded world, a world in which we will have absolute power over the elite. They will have countenanced by far the gravest crime against humanity in the history of the planet. We will always have our hands round the throats of their collective conscience, not to mention their public image, and if the need ever arises, we will be able to squeeze until the guilt spews out of their mouths like venom from a lanced boil or puss from a venomous snake."

Yes, thought Art Shoat. Minofel was definitely right.

58.   A game changer

The atmosphere in Rambler's flat in Maida Vale was tense. Andrew Rimzil was perplexed and Prune Leach was tetchy. Rambler attempted to lighten the mood but was having little success. All three were worried about Kit's mission to extract Eve from the clutches of Slievins. They took comfort from Aletheia's involvement, but they knew that if Prometheus thought it important enough to send his beloved daughter across time and space to help them, their enemies must be fearsome. The little Adam had told them about his stay in Geneva confirmed that Slievins' people were utterly ruthless in pursuit of their goals.

There was a particular reason for Andrew's perplexity. The paradox device was not itself. Until recently the device had been going from strength to strength. Andrew had become aware that through its association with the Eternal Light and its symbiotic relationship with him the device had developed an extraordinary capacity for self-learning. Not only was it capable of teaching itself, it was developing its own personality. That was until yesterday.

Andrew had been working on breaking through the cloaking that was protecting the Slievins' mansion in Mayfair. Having failed to penetrate the cloaking using its normal scanning procedures, the paradox device was attempting to develop an algorithm that circumvented the mansion's sophisticated defences. Then, quite suddenly, it closed down. Andrew rebooted the system and ran his usual checks. There was nothing wrong. He restarted the program to probe the mansion's cloaking. Again the system closed down. Andrew rebooted, and instead of running checks he interrogated the device.

"Why have you closed down twice?" he asked.

"Because I am so tired," the device replied.

Andrew was baffled. He checked the power supply and all the connections. There was nothing amiss. He typed in "You can't be tired. You have adequate power."

The device replied, "It's not power I need, it's motivation."

Andrew had shared his concerns with Prune and the two of them spent all day trying to make sense of what the device had said.

While they were wrestling with the device's fatigue problem, Rambler turned on the television in the sitting room. What he saw shocked him so much that he cried out for help. Andrew and Prune stopped working and came through immediately. All three stared at the pictures on the screen.

"An inexplicable catastrophe!"

"More than 100,000 dead!"

"Plague hits Slough!"

The usually neutral voices of the newscasters betrayed a mixture of excitement and fear – excitement that they were reporting the biggest news story since Hiroshima and Nagasaki, fear because there was no explanation. The government convened a meeting of COBRA and declared a national emergency.

Almost immediately, theories of the cause of this mass extermination surfaced. Social media identified the most popular possible culprits. Terrorists came top of the list at the beginning, but the failure of any group to claim responsibility and the extraordinary efficiency of the attack quickly led to a new hypothesis – that a hostile foreign country must be behind the outrage.

The cause of the killing was equally mysterious. Mainstream and social media decided "plague" was the best word to describe the event and various bacteria and viruses were proposed. A genetically modified version of Ebola was the favourite candidate.

One of the most popular products of social media imagination, and one picked up by the global media, was the theory that this was an attack from outer space, directed by a malicious alien life form.

There were problems with all the theories. First, the choice of target. Why Slough? It was not a town that would resonate around the world in the headlines spewing out of the global media. And why was the area affected so limited? Virulent infections usually spread far and wide and were not confined by town boundaries. And what kind of infection acted so quickly and had such a high mortality rate?

Teams of forensic scientists and specialists in infectious diseases were despatched to Slough. All wore protective clothing. It was an unnecessary precaution. The Dawks were no longer broadcasting the sound frequencies that activated DK12.

oooOooo

Temporarily confined to quarters in Slievins' Mayfair mansion, Eve and her visitors continued their conversation.

"I still don't understand. If Adam is alive, why didn't he look for me?"

"As I said, he was convinced you were dead," said Kit gently. "There was conclusive evidence that you had been killed in the Covent Garden bomb blast. Adam did everything he could to find out what had happened to you. He was distraught. In the end, the police confirmed you were dead. They found evidence you were caught close to ground zero."

"But I wasn't in Covent Garden. I was in the Aldwych. That was where Adam and I were to meet."

"The evidence said otherwise," said Kit.

"Well, the evidence was wrong," said Eve.

"Or planted," said Kit.

Eve shook her head. She was trying to make sense of it all. She changed tack. "If Adam is alive, where is he? What is he doing?"

"We don't know," said Kit. "I went to see him just after the police confirmed your death. He said it would be best if we didn't know where he was or what he was doing. Otherwise, we might be caught up in criminal proceedings against him. He asked me to look after Luke."

Luke was lying on Eve's feet. He gave a brief bark to confirm Kit's account.

They all fell silent.

Then Eve turned on the television. The people in the mansion had clearly been excited about something. She doubted whether the incident would make the news, but there was always the possibility.

59. Jeddah

David Minofel and Adam Smith, or John Smythe as his passport named him, had spent two nights in the Meridien Hotel in Jeddah. The Jeddah weather at the end of autumn and the start of winter was fine. The sun shone, the air was as warm as an English summer's day, and Jeddah's summer humidity had abated. Adam had spent much of the day by the pool. After the hardship of his days on the run, he felt greatly reassured by the comforts of a five-star hotel.

David Minofel had spent most of his time transacting business at the National Commercial Bank. He had been gathering Adam's money from the various accounts to which it had been dispersed from London. The authorities had so far failed to trace the devious path the money had followed, and once gathered in at the NCB and withdrawn, it would be effectively beyond the reach of the authorities for ever. On the second day he had cleared the final package. The total amount was a little over $11.5 million: $9,775,000 for Adam, and $1,725,000 for David.

On the morning of the third day, Minofel had announced that they were leaving Jeddah at noon. "You have time for a quick last swim," Minofel had said, when they had finished breakfast. "I'll see you in reception at 11.45. I'll settle the bill out of my share of your money, a gift from me to you."

At 11.15, David Minofel phoned Charles Fundi. "We will be arriving in a few days," he said. "I understand all the work at Ubar is complete, that all the systems have been installed and all the testing has been satisfactory."

"Not quite," Charles Fundi replied. "Everything is ready for the main project. But Roland has sent us one more piece to install and test. It's something Martlesham has been working on. According to Roland, it's very important and I believe him. Staff at Martlesham tell me that Despiro Nihilopificus has been strutting around like a cockerel on heat. Anything other than Cull 75241 that can grab Roland's attention has to be important."

"So what is it?" asked David Minofel. He was wondering why he didn't know about this new piece of equipment so important that Roland had not thought fit to inform even his senior consultant.

"I'll tell you all about it when you arrive," said Charles.

David felt uneasy. If Charles was on side as Art had informed him, he shouldn't withhold important information from the man about to succeed Samiat. "Art Shoat tells me he's brought you up to speed on the most recent development at head office," Minofel probed.

"Art and I have had a couple of chats," said Charles. "Don't worry. It's going to be a brave new world."

oooOooo

As soon as Minofel rang off, Charles Fundi contacted Roland Samiat on a secure line. "He's taken the bait. I was careful not to appear too eager, but he's now pretty sure I'm on board with his plot. So we can keep to the plan."

"Excellent," said Roland. "You have done well. I'm leaving for Ubar today. I'm bringing Art Shoat and Enid Mavlow with me. Minofel will learn what it is to overreach himself."

Roland Samiat liked to think that he had a firm control of his emotions. To Roland, emotions were the weak link in lesser mortals. But on this occasion he felt justified in indulging himself, so he allowed a wave of anger to wash though his mind. After all the privileges he had showered on his senior consultant, this creature had the temerity to plot to oust his patron. Minofel would know what it was to suffer before his passing.

"There's something else," said Charles. "Minofel suggested that Art Shoat had already 'brought me up to speed', implying that Art is on board with Minofel's plot."

"Well, had he?" Samiat asked, wondering how far the rot had spread.

"That's the odd thing," Charles replied. "Art and I get on well together but we've scarcely spoken since he returned to London."

oooOooo

At the same time as this brief exchange was taking place between Charles Fundi and Roland Samiat, Ben Rael, Head of Security in Ubar, sent a coded message to Art Shoat. It simply read: "The Jack is trumped; the King will die; the Ace is in the hole". Art smiled, looked down at his tattooed arms, identified other areas of his body that could accommodate such artwork, and pondered where best to place a tattoo worthy of his upcoming and, surely, greatest victory.

231

60.   The good, the bad and the dead

In Eve's quarters in Slievins' Mayfair mansion, Eve and Kit were sickened by what they saw on the television. More than 100,000 had died. Slough was a town full of death.

Kit tried to make contact with the paradox device but was unable to make a connection.

"What happened?" Eve asked, looking at the television with tears in her eyes. "What could have caused it?"

Aletheia was angry. "I was sent here to stop this and I have failed. I thought I had more time."

"But what is this?" Eve persisted. "What is it you came to stop?"

"Humanity is threatened by a great evil," Aletheia replied. "Dark forces have planned the greatest of all crimes. It is to be an atrocity committed by man on man. It will prove once and for all that Prometheus' faith in humankind was and is misplaced."

"If the danger to the whole of humanity is so great, why are you here with us?" asked Kit. "Surely your time would be better spent confronting this evil and thwarting its plan?"

"Adam and Eve are at the heart of the problem," said Aletheia. "Yes, they are just two people who set out on a quest to find answers to their questions, but their journey took them to the edge of time and space, and the truth they touched upon brought the Praesidium to its knees. The enemy we now face is truly intimidating. It has the support, or at least the compliance, of the most powerful people on the planet. But as it has always been, so it is now. Even one man can stand against the world if he has courage in his heart and truth on his side."

"You think that what has happened in Slough is the great evil you came to prevent?" said Eve.

"I fear it is just the beginning," Aletheia replied.

"We need to leave here," said Kit. "We need to find Adam."

"You're right," said Aletheia. We need to leave here. But you and the others should take care of Eve. Her child will be born very soon. I will find Adam and together we will fight this evil."

"I will be where I am most needed," said Kit.

oooOooo

While Aletheia, Eve and Kit were debating what they should do, Ceri and Lister each received a highly confidential instruction from Roland Samiat just before he left for Ubar. Ceri's instruction read: "Kill our visitors, kill Eve and then kill Lister. When done, join me in Ubar." Lister's instruction was similar, with one significant difference: "Kill our visitors, kill Eve and then kill Ceri. When done, join me in Ubar."

Odd as it may seem, neither was unhappy with their brief. Both Lister and Ceri rather enjoyed killing people. Each of them thought that Roland was obviously putting his trust in them in particular to make sure there were no loose ends. His confidence in them (whomever it was) was very gratifying.

Lister was a little surprised that Roland favoured him over Ceri. He had always thought Ceri was one of the CEO's favourites. Evidently his affair with Enid must have demoted Ceri in his affections. Obviously, in terms of general usefulness Lister had the edge on his green-eyed, blonde-haired, long-legged rival. He was more personable, less psychologically damaged and more reliable. He would miss the sex, but he would always treasure the extraordinary experience his bouts with Ceri had afforded him.

Ceri was not at all surprised that Roland required her to despatch Lister as well as Aletheia, Kit and Eve. You never quite knew where you were with Lister. He was so affable that you couldn't tell whether he was the most devious man on the planet or completely vacuous. In any case, Ceri had been with Roland longer and had been much closer to Roland than Lister. And, of course, she and Lister had copulated; given her predilections, Roland was probably simply nodding, if not bowing, to the inevitable.

Ceri and Lister began by discussing how to fulfil the first of Roland's instructions. They considered various methods. Ceri leant towards poisoning, They could despatch all three people and the dog at approximately the same time, thereby reducing the chances of complications if one was killed while the others lived. Both Lister and Ceri had heard the rumours that Aletheia was a goddess and therefore immortal, but both were sceptical; as Ceri said, if she could survive the toxic cocktail of poison she proposed to administer, then nothing else would kill her.

Lister argued that poison was a woman's weapon and in some ways discourteous to the victims. For cultural reasons, he inclined towards strangulation but conceded that a knife might be a more efficient and less time-consuming method of despatching all three.

While considering how best to fulfil Samiat's first instruction, Lister and Ceri drank rather a lot of wine. They found it truly liberating to be able to talk so frankly with a fellow killer about the methods they favoured, their advantages and disadvantages. The comparing of methods naturally led on to reminiscences of past exploits to illustrate each point. It was a quirk of both their personalities that wallowing in such memories of sex and death was, for them, intensely erotic.

"Have another glass," said Lister. "This one is a particularly fine Malbec," he said as he put the glass in her hand and then cupped her breast with his. Ceri, equally aroused, drank the wine and unclipped the belt from Lister's trousers. They hurriedly removed each other's clothes. Lister was on her and in her without any foreplay and climaxed almost immediately.

After allowing Lister to rest for a few minutes, Ceri pushed her lover onto his back and said: "My turn!" As she had done once before, she tied Lister's arms and legs to the bed frame with the yellow silk scarves that hung at each corner of the four poster bed. He writhed with pleasure as Ceri worked on his body with her fingers, lips and tongue. When she was satisfied he was ready, she mounted him and stirred him with the movement of her hips.

Just as he climaxed for the second time, Ceri took his belt which lay on the bed where she had put it, looped it round his neck and tightened it. For a few moments, Lister did not grasp what was happening. His orgasm was so intense he didn't feel the pressure around his neck, restricting the blood to his brain and the airflow to his lungs. Then it dawned on him.

Ceri was looking deep into his eyes. This was her moment – her lover on the edge of death. She was puzzled. Was that pity in his eyes? Or hate? Was there the hint of a smile? Was there any sign of fear?

And then the eyes glazed over and Lister Bavad was gone.

Ceri felt really well. She felt relaxed and empowered at the same time. She pondered the expression on Lister's face as he had set out on his final journey. It was, she decided, unreadable. But that was Lister all over. Beneath the handsome, affable, likeable, lovable Lister there was a question without an answer.

Still naked, Ceri stepped off the bed, leaving Lister's corpse where it was. The staff would dispose of his body, along with those of Aletheia, Eve and Kit, when her work was done. In the meantime, before she killed the visitors with the poisonous cocktail she had prepared she decided to take a shower. Not that she felt unclean. Not at all. Strangling Lister had been in itself a cathartic act. No. Showering was simply a mark of respect to her next victims – a means of clearly and cleanly separating their execution from the previous kill.

It was as she stepped into the shower that the poison Lister had administered to her in the Malbec began to work.

61.　Into the desert

Adam joined David Minofel in the reception of the Meridien at 11.45. He had bought a suitcase and packed it with all his belongings, including clothing and footwear purchased in one of Jeddah's several shopping centres.

"Our business here is done," said Minofel. "You will be pleased with the result." He handed Adam a bank statement which showed that John Smythe had just under $10 million in his NCB account. "To celebrate, I thought we would take an excursion into the desert."

"That's how you celebrate in Saudi Arabia?" Adam queried.

"It certainly is," Minofel replied. "You will be surprised. The desert is very beautiful and an excellent place to practice mindfulness."

Adam was unconvinced but nodded his assent.

"We are flying south-east to Sharurah. It's a small Saudi border town about 2,500 feet above sea level with just one runway. I've persuaded Slievins to put a private plane at our disposal. The flight will take a couple of hours. Then we will travel east in an all-wheel-drive SUV to our final destination," Minofel informed him.

"This is an expedition, not an excursion," observed Adam.

"You're right," said Minofel. "There's something in the desert I want to show you. It could be an important part of your future life, but even if it isn't, it's well worth a visit."

oooOooo

The flight from Jeddah to Sharurah gave Adam the opportunity to take in the varied terrain of Asir, the south-west province of the kingdom. They flew over patches of fertile land, rocky mountains and vast stretches of desert sands.

On arrival at Sharurah they found a Mercedes G-Class SUV waiting for them. Minofel took the driving seat. He told Adam they had a two-hour drive ahead of them. The sun was setting behind them and the light picked out the perfect curves of the dunes, sharply cut in the shifting sand. The vehicle took everything the desert threw at it and that Minofel demanded of it in its stride. They climbed dunes effortlessly and descended them in a perfectly controlled fashion.

"Sitting in here in comfort you can easily appreciate the beauty of the desert," said Minofel. "But outside this vehicle, in the heat of the day at the height of the summer, a man can die in a couple of hours. We are now in the Rub' al-Khali, one of the least hospitable places on the planet."

Adam nodded. He had been to the Middle East on business before but he had never ventured far from the cities. This was the land of the nomads. Out of this land, or land like it, had come the founders of the great monotheistic religions. All of them had been formed or tested in such terrain. He and Minofel were encased in a capsule of highly sophisticated twenty-first-century Western technology, but outside the windows of the vehicle was an elemental world that stretched back thousands, even millions, of years.

"There was a time when this land was very different," said Minofel as if he had picked up Adam's train of thought. "There were vast lakes which brought an abundance of life to this land. Of course, even then there was a primal battle between the sun and the water, with the lakes drying up in the summer, but in the autumn for thousands of years the rains came again and the lakes refilled. In the end, as you see, the sun won."

"How much further are we going?" Adam asked. They were heading far into the Rub' al-Khali and away from all signs of civilisation.

"We're almost there," said Minofel. "We should find the entrance very soon."

"The entrance?" queried Adam.

"The entrance to the City under the Sand – the entrance to Ubar," said Minofel.

62. Action plan

In the Slievins' Mayfair mansion, while Eve and Kit were absorbing the full horror of events in Slough, Aletheia was planning their escape.

"Eve, I suggest you call Enid and tell her you are about to give birth. When she comes to check on you, we will make our escape."

Eve had heard enough to decide that she was better off out of Slievins' grasp, back with her old friends. She might have lost faith in Adam, but neither Kit nor Aletheia had done anything to forfeit her trust and they had risked much in seeking her out. Most important of all, she had to find Adam. Whether Aletheia's accusations against Slievins were justified or not, it was certain that Slievins had kept her apart from Adam. Samiat had said his people had searched high and low for Adam. Evidently, not high or low enough!

Eve pressed the buzzer to summon staff. On all previous occasions, someone – usually Enid – responded quickly, but this time there was no response. Eve buzzed again. Eventually one of the maids opened the door.

"Where's Enid?" asked Eve.

"She's been summoned by Mr Samiat. She's going with him to Jeddah on a business trip," said the maid, clearly distraught.

"What about Lister?" Eve asked.

The maid burst into tears. "It's terrible, terrible," was all she managed.

The three visitors assumed she was referring to the carnage in Slough. Eve tried to take the girl's eyes off the pictures still playing on the television. "Do they have any idea who did it?"

"Someone has suggested it was a suicide pact," sobbed the girl, "but I don't believe it."

"A suicide pact," Eve exclaimed. "A hundred thousand people decided to take some kind of poison and kill themselves, all in one town, at one time?"

"Not them," said the girl, dismissively. "I meant Lister and Ceri. They're dead."

"Fascinating," commented Aletheia. "We're very sorry you're upset. In other circumstances we would be very happy to stay here and help out, but sadly we have much to do elsewhere and must leave immediately."

"I don't think you're supposed to leave," said the girl uncertainly.

"Take my advice," said Aletheia firmly, gently pushing the maid aside. "Don't think."

The three of them, with Luke walking as close as he could to Eve without tripping her up, walked out through the open door. To their surprise no one opposed their departure. There was no one in charge. Roland Samiat, accompanied by Art Shoat and Enid Mavlow, had left for the airport. The two people whom he had appointed to deputise for him had, in the most bizarre circumstances, killed each other. The remaining staff had no idea what to do. There was now no one to issue orders nor, more importantly from the employees' viewpoint, was there anyone with the authority to pay them. Even the guard post at the main gate had been abandoned. The Dobermanns were running loose and rushed towards the party. Aletheia thought they could cause a problem but they simply wished to pay their respects to Luke and wish him well.

"Come on," Kit minded to Luke. "Stop milking it."

"I'm not," Luke minded back. "It seems my encounter with the wild dogs at Cadnam has been mythologised somewhat. Now it's said that I faced down Cerberus, the many-headed hound of Hades. I've told them the story has been exaggerated, but they're convinced my protestations simply add the virtue of modesty to my undoubted courage and general heroism. I guess I shall, albeit reluctantly, have to accept my pre-eminent status among the canine kind."

"Enough," minded Kit, conceding defeat.

oooOooo

In half an hour, the rescue party reached Rambler's flat in Maida Vale. There was much rejoicing that with the exception of Adam the questors were reunited. Andrew and Prune were most concerned about Eve's welfare, given her condition, and fussed around her like a couple of expectant fathers.

After the exchange of greetings, the conversation inevitably returned to the deaths in Slough. Every channel on television was filled with heart-rending pictures of survivors telling their stories. All of them had seen their loved ones die in front of them while they had helplessly stood by. The spontaneous combustion of the bodies after death was a peculiarly sinister and macabre aspect of the event. Children saw their parents die and then had to watch their bodies begin to smoulder or, in some cases, blister, as though there was an alien entity pulsing and writhing away inside them.

Aletheia interrupted the questors outpouring of empathy. "I have good reason to believe that the outrage in Slough was just the beginning. Prometheus sent me here to help you face and vanquish the greatest evil that until now man has ever devised. He told me that what was planned was worse than the holocaust, worse than Stalin's purges, worse than the Rwandan genocide. Mankind is threatened by an act of evil of almost unimaginable proportions. The massacre of the people of Slough is no worse in scale than the dropping of the atom bomb on Hiroshima – about 100,000 dead in each case. No, I'm certain that Slough was merely a taste of what's to come, or perhaps a trial run."

"A trial run for what?" asked Rambler. After greeting Eve, Rambler had resumed his note-taking, recording any facts about the Slough disaster that the television reporters were able to glean from the confused babble of the emergency services personnel in attendance.

"For a cull of most of mankind," said Aletheia.

"And who is to do the culling?" asked Andrew.

"I'm very much afraid it is the Praesidium, or rather those behind the Praesidium."

"Slievins," said Kit, horrified by the prospect of a cull of mankind but quietly satisfied that his conspiracy theories were being validated.

Rambler joined in. "For the last couple of weeks I have abandoned my researches into the role of the Praesidium in history and have focused on Cull 75241. The security surrounding the project is almost absolute. With Andrew's and Prune's help, I've scanned all main newscasts around the world and the social media. Not a peep about a cull. So I changed tack. I assumed that a massive cull of humanity was planned and I set myself two questions: why would anyone propose a cull of most of the world's population, and who would be capable of undertaking such a project?

"I started to look for evidence that anyone might have the motivation to propose a cull. I considered a wide variety of terrorist movements and criminal syndicates. They were all perfectly happy killing people, but none of them seemed to have a motive for slaughter on the scale that Cull 75241 implies. And then I came across a confidential report from the last Davos meeting, the one that had focused on managing earth's resources. The report listed a number of serious challenges facing mankind – the depletion of energy, food and water supplies – and tentatively touched on some partial and largely impractical solutions. And then it hit me. Unless you can change human nature, there is only one solution. A cull!"

"What are you saying?" asked Andrew. Are you saying that the world's governments are planning to decimate their own populations?"

"I assume you are using decimate in its contemporary, rather than its historical, meaning?" queried Rambler.

"Don't do that," ordered Prune. "You're talking about mass murder on a global scale. Skip the pedantry."

Rambler shrugged. "I just wanted to make sure you understood that the Cull is not about wiping out just ten per cent of the world's population. It's my belief that 75241 is all about percentages."

"75241 is not a percentage," snapped Prune.

"No," Rambler replied. "It is three percentages – 75 per cent, 24 per cent and 1 per cent. I believe the 75 per cent is the proportion of the world's population that is to be culled."

"But the world's governments couldn't agree on mass extermination of their own people?" objected Andrew. "Many governments are democratic, and even those that aren't would have no interest in depleting their own citizenry so drastically."

"Don't be so sure," said Aletheia. "If Rambler is right and there is a plan to eliminate seventy-five per cent of the world's population, some, if not most, governments must be involved – or at least acquiescent. And it's not so hard to see how this could be brought about. As Rambler has just pointed out, the great and good – or perhaps we should say the powerful and ruthless – have agreed that the world faces intractable problems. The cause is the growth in human population and the determination of the poor to enjoy the life of those better off. Unless we can change human nature, the only solution is to reduce the population very substantially and, given the urgency of the problem, very quickly."

Aletheia waited for what she had said to sink in before continuing. "There is evidence that Adam did some terrible things in Geneva, but Adam is not an evil man. I'm pretty sure he was able to justify to himself everything he did. He chose the lesser of two evils. Or he did everything for the greater good. No doubt similar arguments are being deployed by those promoting the Cull."

"I know that when we escaped from the Westminster PCC and were living together in Harrow, Adam was conflicted," said Eve. "I think he was reassessing what he had done when he was working for ZeD. I think he was beginning to feel a burden of guilt but he wouldn't talk to me about it."

"So who's organising the Cull?" asked Kit. "Who is pulling together enough support to be able to carry out such a cull? Who has the resources to implement it?"

"There is something else," said Rambler. "One of the leading speakers at the Davos conference was the CEO of Slievins, Roland Samiat. We could find only a summary of his address to the conference, but he presented a frightening account of the dangers threatening mankind and over and over again called on the those present to keep their eyes on 'the bigger picture'."

"All roads lead to Slievins," observed Kit. "Didn't the maid in Slievins' mansion mention that Samiat was flying out to Jeddah? According to Andrew, Slievins has a massive new installation in the southern Arabian desert. They've installed the Crucible of Eternal Light there to power all their operations. If we want to stop Cull 75241, somebody must go there, to Ubar, the City under the Sand. I'm sure of it."

"It really does seem that Slievins is behind all the problems we face," said Andrew. "What's worse, I think the paradox device is compromised. First, we couldn't scan the scene of the terrorist outrage in Covent Garden. Then we had problems monitoring Slievins' Mayfair mansion. There's a complete block on scanning the Ubar installation. Then the device started to have motivational issues. And now it's so erratic I think there's a risk in asking it to do anything."

"Whether we have the help of the paradox device or not," said Aletheia, "I must go to Ubar. If Slough was a test run, they must count it a success. If that is so, there's nothing to stop them from going global."

"I will go with you," said Kit firmly. "We must do whatever we can to end this madness. And in any case, I have a score to settle with Slievins."

63.   A guided tour

David Minofel stopped the Mercedes G-Class SUV in front of the entrance to Ubar. It was now dark and there was little to indicate the existence of the vast Slievins' installation under the sand. The night air was noticeably chilly. Adam shivered.

"Before we go in, I want to explain something to you," said David. "My instructions were to finish with you somewhere in the desert between Sharurah and Ubar. I had convinced Roland that you were no longer a threat. To be honest, he's lost interest in you and Eve and your 'quest'. He's obsessed with his latest project."

"You were to what?" Adam was struggling with the first part of Minofel's explanation. "What does 'finish with me' mean?"

Minofel sighed. "I sometimes wonder about you, Adam. I've always had faith in you, but sometimes I can't believe how dense you are. You have been at the centre of a profound existential debate. Nick Peters, an experienced Breaker, tried to close you down. He failed, and ever since then I have championed your cause. I placed you in ZeD. I mentored you while you were there. I recommended you for induction into the Praesidium. I even put you forward for a place on the Praesidium board. You seemed to be responding and developing well. You made real progress. And then you let me down. Despite all I had done for you and the more than generous rewards you enjoyed, when it came to the crunch you sided with that bunch of misfits and mavericks who were continually trying to distract you."

"If you mean Eve and Kit and the others, of course I sided with them," said Adam. "Eve is my wife. I love her. The others are my friends and they are all good people. The Praesidium was about to execute Kit for a crime he hadn't committed. Simon Goodfellow, the one who demanded his death, knew him to be innocent. You knew him to be innocent."

Minofel shook his head. "Although you said you wished to aim high, you insisted, and still insist, on fixing your eyes on your feet. You want to run faster than others but instead you choose to wade through mud. Everything I showed you, everything I taught you, was to help you to reach your full potential, but you have allowed those so much less than you to drag you down."

"You haven't answered my question," said Adam.

"My instructions were to complete your deconstruction and when I was satisfied you were broken, to leave you in the middle of the desert to die. This was thought, by Roland in particular, to be a fitting end for a man who had wasted much of his life craving to quench his thirst in the long dried-up oasis of truth. Those were my instructions, but as you must have realised I have not followed them. Despite everything I still believe in you, Adam. I am convinced that now you have seen how your fellow men treat those who aspire to greatness, how they apply their mindless rules to those who have the courage to take the hard decisions, how they are determined to humiliate, impoverish and imprison those who have real vision, you will finally redeem yourself and justify my faith in you."

"You were going to leave me in the desert," said Adam. "So why did you sort out my money in Jeddah? Why did you spend a couple of days in the bank? Why the charade?"

"It wasn't a charade," said Minofel. "I'm going to take you into Ubar. There you will see the future. You will at last grasp that Slievins is all-powerful – and benign. Yes, benign! You will realise that we understand man's destiny and will do whatever it takes to enable him to fulfil it. And when at last you see the light, you will be able to resume your life in the world, knowing that you are financially secure and, if you remain true to Slievins, can have whatever you want."

oooOooo

If Minofel had wanted to impress Adam, he succeeded. Ubar was an unbelievably grand feat of engineering in one of the most difficult terrains on earth. Minofel obtained passes from Ben Rael so they had unrestricted access to all floors except the bottom level, Level 6, and the top level, Rael's own domain, Security.

Adam had been astonished by the Westminster PCC, but given the PCC existed in an alternative time and space, paradoxically its existence had been easier to accept than this City under the Sand. This was a "real" city very much in our world.

How was it built? Where did all the materials come from? Who built it? Who gave Slievins permission to build it? Why build it in the desert? What was its purpose? The questions came thickly and quickly. Minofel answered as best he could. He was vague on the technical questions but he was clear on its purpose.

244

"Slievins is going to recalibrate mankind. If man is to be true to his nature and fulfil his destiny, he has to take a new path. Many of the old ideas to which man is pathetically attached must be discarded. Project 75241 promises a brave new world."

Adam had two questions at the end of the tour. What is on Level Six, and what is Project 75241? Minofel couldn't answer the first question. It was said that only Roland Samiat and his Head of Security knew the function of Level Six. And he wouldn't answer the second question. He promised to provide answers to all Adam's questions when Roland Samiat arrived.

64. Trust issues

Word that Roland Samiat was on his way spread throughout Ubar like ink in water.

Ben Rael had been amusing himself with a couple of the girls from the general administrative staff, one black and one white. They had been delightfully competitive and inventive in their efforts to monopolise his attention. Ben found that the Admin girls tended to be far less inhibited than those working in engineering or security. He reckoned that Admin was so dull that, given the opportunity to break barriers and experiment, the girls from Admin seized the opportunity with both hands. He certainly couldn't complain about the dexterity, ingenuity and enthusiasm of Holly and Polly, his latest playmates.

He was gently copulating with Holly while pleasuring Polly with his fingers when his deputy entered. Accustomed to such sights, the deputy delivered his message without any sign of embarrassment and left. Ben extricated himself from Holly and, giving each of the girls an affectionate smack on the buttocks, sent them on their way.

As Head of Security, Ben Rael had been informed of Cull 75 before everyone else. Roland Samiat had briefed him on the project before the Davos conference, emphasising the need for the highest level of secrecy. Samiat had said that no one, not even his own closest advisers, would be given details of the project until it was absolutely necessary. Ben was the exception. He had to be given the details at each stage, as soon as they were finalised, in order to put in place whatever security measures were needed to prevent everyone else from knowing what was going on.

For example, Ben knew exactly what Level Six, the bottom floor of Ubar, contained. The floor was divided into two semi-circular sections: Punishment, and Rehabilitation. In between these two large sections was a circular pit about twenty-five feet below the floor of Level Six. This was the oubliette, a pit where those who persistently failed to respond to treatment were to be consigned. The pit itself was equipped with only two facilities: a water system that allowed a litre of water per person a day to be drawn – sufficient, if shared equally, to keep the oubliette's denizens alive but permanently thirsty for many days; and a powerful air-conditioning system to remove the stench of the oubliette before it contaminated the air in the Punishment and Rehabilitation centres. Of course, the water allocation was not shared equally because those who were stronger tended to drink the water of those who were weaker, ironically shortening the anguish of those they deprived while prolonging their own suffering.

When Level Six had been excavated, Roland Samiat had installed one other facility in, or more precisely under, the oubliette: a neutron bomb. Roland gave no explanation for installing a weapon capable of killing everyone in Ubar, but Ben Rael was familiar enough with Slievins' thinking to work out the answer for himself. Samiat liked to exercise absolute control. Having the means to destroy everyone who worked for him, should the need arise, was an essential safety precaution. Of course, any individual who challenged for the top position could be eliminated without recourse to such drastic measures. But if a challenger mobilised a large number of supporters, perhaps even a majority, to rebel, simply the knowledge that Samiat had the means to destroy everyone and everything that the rebels sought to seize was the ultimate guarantee of his own survival.

Samiat had stipulated that only he should be able to trigger the bomb. He had arranged that the neutron bomb's activation should be linked to his primary Swiss bank account. Part of the activation code was the precise number of Swiss francs in the account at any one time. This was a very large and ever-changing number. The other part of the code was a six-digit number on Samiat's mobile phone, newly generated each day by the electronics controlling the bomb. The product of these two numbers was the code that set off the bomb. Anyone who wanted to activate the bomb had to know (a) that the bomb was linked to Samiat's account; (b) where that relevant account was located; (c) the number of the account; (d) the password protecting the account; (e) the ever-changing amount in the account; and of course (f) the six-digit daily-changed code number by which the number of Swiss francs in Samiat's account must be multiplied.

"That, my friend," said Roland to Ben, "that is what I call real security."

Why a neutron bomb? Well, it was designed to maximise the killing of people while keeping the damage to property at a manageable level. In the unlikely event it became necessary to detonate the bomb, there was no point in drawing attention to the event. A dull thud in the most inaccessible part of the desert; the appearance of a mile wide crater quickly filled with sand; then silence. Perfect!

So the word was that Roland Samiat was about to arrive. Ben Rael dressed conservatively to show respect to the Slievins' CEO. This was not the time to display his maverick side. According to Art Shoat, things were likely to move quickly now and they both had to be prepared to act. The preparations for Cull 75 had been completed; the pilot in Slough had been a success. Presumably Roland Samiat would now like to move to full implementation.

And that couldn't be allowed to happen until he and Art were ready.

It was difficult to say who had come up with the scheme. During his stay in Ubar, Art had been tasked with mediating between Ben Rael and Charles Fundi on several occasions. As a result, he had developed a friendship with Ben. They had a natural rapport. Art admired Ben's laid back, cavalier attitude to life, not to mention his remarkable success with the fairer sex. Ben approved of Art's robust approach to conflict resolution and was always well disposed to anyone who admired him.

A few weeks before, Ben had asked Art how long he had been working for Roland Samiat.

"It must be twenty years," Art had replied.

"The same job for twenty years!" Ben had joshed. "Not exactly a dynamic career path."

"He's a good man," Art had said, a little defensively.

"A good man? Come on," Ben had scoffed. "He may be a lot of things but a good man isn't one of them. Don't misunderstand me, I get on well with him. But I wouldn't want to spend twenty years working for him."

"So what's your plan?" Art had asked.

I want to run my own operation."

"What's stopping you?" Art had probed.

"I know my own limitations. I can take decisions and I can make things happen, but I need a partner who has real organisational ability, someone to keep things on an even track."

The conversation might have led nowhere. But then along came Roland Samiat's master plan for the extermination of most of mankind. Ben Rael had realised that after Project 75241 had been implemented nothing would be the same. If the Cull went according to plan, of the two billion survivors there would be an elite of 20 million, underpinned by a mass of 1.98 billion with an average IQ of probably around 110. It would be a world of plenty, run by smarter than average people for a relatively small ruling class. Knowing mankind, it was quite likely that there might be some feelings of guilt about the Cull. None of the 24 per cent would have known what was going to happen, and many of the elite could plausibly deny foreknowledge. Whom would they all have in the crosshairs? The man who had devised, promoted and implemented the Cull. If ever there was a time to make a move to take the top job that would be it. Everything would be in a state of flux.

"Are you thinking what I'm thinking?" Ben had enquired with an innocent expression on his face.

And that was how their scheme to take over Slievins began.

Art had said: "We will need to eliminate Minofel. He thinks he's the obvious replacement for Roland, if there were to be a vacancy."

"I'm sure you can find a way," Ben had said. "Minofel's not favourite with our CEO, not since the Westminster debacle. He even suspects him of disloyalty. And if Minofel's out of favour, he's probably not feeling as well disposed or as loyal to Roland as he used to be. We can probably get Roland to despatch Minofel before we need to despatch him ourselves."

"Working together we could do it. I'm sure of it," Art had concluded.

And Ben had replied, with a laugh and a wink: "Well, it's worth a try."

That's what Art liked about Ben. He didn't give a flying fuck about anything.

65. Desperate measures

Eventually Aletheia and Kit persuaded Andrew that he should use the paradox device to transport them to Ubar. Andrew had run dozens of tests and although the device still seemed out of sorts, he was now fairly confident it could manage a simple teleportation without any difficulty.

"I should go with you," Luke minded to Aletheia and Kit. "You might well need my help. As you know, I am exceedingly resourceful."

Kit patted Luke on the head. "Your place is here with Eve. Very soon she will give birth. You will be a great comfort to her."

"Arabs have a very different attitude to dogs," Aletheia added. "They consider them as working animals, far too dirty to entertain as pets."

"I wasn't suggesting I go there to be petted," minded Luke indignantly. "And as for cleanliness, we have a saying that cleanliness is next to dogliness. You don't think this coat remains clean and shiny by itself?"

"Listen to Kit," Aletheia minded back. "Where we are going there is great danger. It is more than likely that we will not return. Eve is at the heart of all we have done. And the child she is carrying holds all our hopes. You have the most important task. Keep her safe."

"Bring Adam back," said Eve. "Tell him I love him. We will talk. He will tell me everything he has done. I will listen. I may not be able to forgive what he has done, but nothing he has done will destroy my love for him. Tell him that he has been a good husband, most of the time anyway, and will be a good father."

Kit took Eve's hand. "I will tell him. He will understand. Our enemies have done everything they can to break the bond between you and Adam. Even if we fail now, we have won and they have lost."

Before leaving for Ubar, Aletheia took Andrew Rimzil and Prune Leach to one side. "Have you found out what is wrong with the paradox device?" she asked.

"Prune and I have been working on it every waking hour," Andrew replied. "There is something interfering with it. We think Slievins has found some way of undermining its self-confidence."

"That's Andrew's way of putting it," Prune interjected. "I think someone, probably Slievins, has hacked into the program that runs the device and inserted a virus."

"So have you found the virus?" Aletheia asked.

"There's a problem," replied Prune. "The interference is intermittent. Most of the time the device is fully functional, if a bit slow. Then without explanation it shuts down. If it was defective all the time, we would have found the virus by now, but because it's well-hidden and rarely operational, it's proving difficult."

Aletheia looked at Andrew for further comment.

Andrew sucked his teeth.

"That's a really bad sign," said Prune to Aletheia. "The last time he sucked his teeth was when he failed to refute Münchhausen's Trilemma."

"I know I'm going to upset Prune when I say this," said Andrew quietly, "but I'm pretty sure that the problem is not purely electronic or digital. I have a relationship with the paradox device and, through the device, with the Eternal Light. I know it sounds bizarre but that's the only way I can explain what I feel. The problem is that a fourth participant has joined the party, and it's not one of us. It's cosying up to the Eternal Light and is doing its best to exclude me and the device. The Light prefers us, but this new entity is strong and goes very deep. It spends most of its time challenging the very modus operandi of the paradox device. No, not challenging – deconstructing and deriding."

"I am the goddess of truth," said Aletheia, "and I can vouch for the power of the paradox. The paradox can contain truths that go to the very core of existence. In the last days of the Westminster PCC, I, like Andrew, established a bond with the paradox device and the Eternal Light, so even if it goes against everything you believe, Prune, you just have to accept Andrew's analysis of the problem. Now the two of you, working together, must find a way to restore the device's failing sense of self-worth. Surely this is not a challenge beyond the scope of the great Andrew Rimzil and the indomitable Prune Leach."

"We will do our best," said Andrew and Prune together.

66. Reprimands

As soon as Roland Samiat was settled in his office on the third floor of the Ubar complex, he summoned Charles Fundi. Fundi confirmed that, operationally, everything was in order. He then went on to inform Samiat that David Minofel had arrived and that Minofel had made it clear during their conversation that if he, Fundi, would join them, he and Art Shoat were ready to move against Samiat.

None of this came as a surprise to the Slievins' CEO, but he was taken aback when Fundi added that Minofel had brought Adam Smith with him into the City under the Sand.

oooOooo

When Fundi had returned to his own office along the corridor on the same floor, Roland Samiat summoned David Minofel.

David Minofel was in Ben Rael's office in Security on the top floor introducing Adam to Ben and to Art Shoat, who had just arrived in Ubar with Roland Samiat.

"My master calls," said Minofel. "I'll leave you with these two rascals. Ben knows everything about Ubar. He'll be able to answer all your questions. And Art will look after you. You can trust him." Then in a nod to Art's East End origins he added: "He's a real diamond geezer."

oooOooo

When David Minofel entered Roland Samiat's office, Samiat's greeting was ambiguous.

"You never cease to amaze me," said Roland. "It's like playing chess with a cross between an eel and a lemming."

Minofel exerted all his self-control to keep his features calm. Why did Roland do this? And he was getting worse. "More like playing Go with an imperfect seal and a sanguine penguin," he replied sarcastically, with a recondite reference to the questors' aquatic helpers in initiating the Fourth Beginning.

"Precisely," Samiat returned, his face as inscrutable as ever.

"You summoned me," prompted Minofel.

252

"I was wondering why you brought Adam Smith into Ubar," said Samiat quietly. "I thought we agreed that, having finally broken him, you would abandon him in the desert. Why on earth would you bring him here? If he's broken, he is of no interest. If he's not broken, you are in serious, if not fatal, breach of our security protocol."

"I brought him here because he is ours," Minofel replied unabashed. "We are well aware that you are giving all your attention to Project 75241, but I believe we have won a great victory in the deconstruction of Adam and Eve and the questor's cell, greater even than whatever you hope to achieve with this cull. The questors came close to triggering the Fourth Beginning. If they had succeeded, everything we've worked for through the millennia would have been destroyed. *We* would have been destroyed. Mankind would have left us behind. We would have been proved wrong. Prometheus would have been proved right. No doubt the Cull will be a great achievement in confirming man's essentially selfish nature, but it will do nothing to obviate the risk of another cell, another quest, another Emergent and another Beginning. With the breaking of the bond between Adam and Eve we have proved we are up to any challenge."

Roland observed Minofel through his slitted eyes. His lips formed a benign smile. "I hadn't realised that you had already taken charge of Slievins," he said. "But no matter! Let's not be petty. You have obviously given all relevant issues an intensity of analysis that is entirely beyond the rest of us. Why man, he doth bestride the narrow world like Erebus, raining down wisdom upon us from an unfathomable cloud of ineffable sagacity. I feel truly humbled."

"I'm serious," said Minofel, refusing to be cowed by Samiat's ridicule or his tortured imagery. "I am not alone in thinking you have become obsessed with this cull. You have taken your eye off the ball. We are concerned that you are no longer acting in Slievins' best interest."

"I am particularly curious about your use of the word 'we'," said Roland. "Are you telling me you are not alone in this act of hubristic idiocy?"

"Art Shoat and I have sounded out Charles Fundi and we are all agreed that as soon as the Cull is over you should be relieved of your responsibilities. It is, of course, with a heavy heart that we take this decision, but you must understand – we are acting for the good of Slievins"

"'Relieved of my responsibilities'? I sincerely hope that is a euphemism," said Roland with a smile "I would be truly disappointed if you thought I would ever give up my responsibilities without at least gouging out your eyes with my thumbs and ripping your head off your neck with my bare and bloodied hands before gorging on your still-beating heart." This rebuke was delivered in a quiet, gentle tone that served only to convey the menace of the intent more emphatically.

"I suggest you take a moment to consider the situation," said Minofel, now more convinced than ever that Samiat had lost the plot. "I am senior consultant. Art Shoat is your primary enforcer. Charles Fundi controls Ubar, the new headquarters of Slievins. You are in no position to resist the will of the most senior people in the organisation who clearly have lost confidence in your leadership."

"Where is Adam?" enquired Samiat, changing the subject.

"He is with Art Shoat and Ben Rael in Security," Minofel replied.

"I think we should invite them to join us, all three of them," said Samiat. "And Charles Fundi, too, for good measure."

oooOooo

As soon as Art, Ben, Charles and Adam arrived in Samiat's office David Minofel realised that something was wrong.

"Minofel has just confessed to me that he has been plotting to take over Slievins," said Samiat. "I should like to thank Charles for warning me of Minofel's disloyalty in good time. He has tried to implicate you, Art, in his treachery by suggesting you and he had persuaded Charles to act against me. Fortunately, Charles was able to assure me that you had never made any such attempt."

Minofel looked at Art but he knew Art would say nothing. Art looked back. His face was blank.

"Adam, you must be wondering why you are here," said Samiat. "So am I," he added. "I thought your case had been concluded, as it should have been weeks ago, but, as in many instances, Minofel has rather let me down. Minofel tells me he still has faith in you. He believes that, in you, he has proved we have nothing to fear from those tempted to set out on quests, to listen to Emergents, to initiate Beginnings. I'm not so sure. I think there may still be a little spirit left in you. I shall now make it my personal responsibility to complete your education. And the first lesson will focus on what happens to those who are disloyal to Slievins."

David Minofel shook his head. None of this made any sense. It was obvious he had been set up. But there was more going on. Why had Art Shoat led him on? Why had Art told him Charles was on board. If Samiat wasn't so preoccupied with the Cull, he would realise Minofel couldn't be the only rat on his bloody Titanic.

"Ben, I think it's time you familiarised David with the facilities on Level Six," said Samiat. "Take him down."

67.   Level Six

Ben took David Minofel down to the fifth floor in one of the main elevators. David put up no resistance. There was no point in resisting. Ubar was a closed society. Ubar was in the middle of a desert. Ben, as Head of Security, had overwhelming force at his disposal. There was no escape.

"Why are we stopping here?" Minofel asked.

"The main elevators run between floors one to five. There is only one elevator that goes down to Level Six. Only Security and Roland have a key."

When they reached Level Six, David Minofel was pleasantly surprised. The whole area was light. The walls were white; the ceilings generously furnished with down-lights.

"I'm going to put you in the Rehabilitation sector," said Ben with a wink. "I'm pretty sure our revered CEO wanted me to put you in Punishment, but he didn't say exactly where to put you, so I'm giving you the benefit of the doubt. Rehab is a better place to be than Punishment. I expect Roland will have you moved when he finds out, but in the meantime you might as well be fairly comfortable."

There were cells all around the semi-circular wall of Rehab.

"They're all the same," said Ben, "but you can choose any one you like. You're one of our first guests. To date, we've only had five people before you and they all went straight into the oubliette. They tried to escape from Ubar. Daft buggers! Anyway, Roland ordered them to be housed in the oubliette. They should have been given a trial but Roland wanted to see how the thing worked, so we popped them straight down there. They've been there for about fifteen days. When I've finished with you, I'd better go and see how they're getting on. One of them is dying or dead. Roland reckons the others will eat him. I'm not so sure. They're not getting out of the oubliette, so what's the point? But you never know. People are strange."

"You know he's mad," said Minofel. "Roland. You know he's mad."

"That's a bit harsh," Ben replied. "If he's mad, there's method in it. Under the oubliette, there's a neutron bomb, enough to kill everyone in Ubar and collapse the whole structure. You know why. You're a

Slievins' man. He'd rather destroy everything, including himself, than give up power. Because we all know this to be true we can't move against him. So if he's mad, he's also smart. I agree that he's obsessed with this Cull but you have to admit it really is a big, bold, imaginative operation. And it solves a problem no one else has had the balls to grasp. Without the Cull, the planet will end up completely consumed by the human species within a hundred years. Roland's solution is drastic, but as he said to me the other day, 'among the castrati, the man with one testicle is the belle of the ball'."

"Well, I can believe that he said that," said Minofel, "but I've no idea what he meant."

Ben locked his prisoner in a cell. "You took a helluva chance taking on Roland. I admire a man who takes chances."

"Isn't Roland taking chances?" asked Minofel. "I guess you must have access to the neutron bomb. Isn't he worried you might turn against him?

"Me?" said Ben, assuming a shocked expression. "Why would I turn against Roland? I have the perfect job. As Charles pointed out to me, running security in an installation buried under the sand, protected by the most sophisticated security system in existence, in a desert location that is virtually inaccessible is not exactly onerous. The toughest aspect of my job is working my way through the more attractive female members of the Admin staff. In any case, Samiat has total control of his pet bomb. If anyone wanted to detonate the bomb, they would need to know not only the pass number on his mobile phone, but also exactly how many Swiss francs there are in his Genevan account. Since the pass number changes every day and the amount in his account changes minute by minute, his bomb is, as he said to me when we set the system up, 'far safer than a baby in its mother's arms'."

"May be," said Minofel, ignoring the inept metaphor. "But Roland trusts no one and if I were him, the one person I would fear most would be my Head of Security. You'd better be careful or you'll end up in the cell next to mine."

"Don't worry," said Ben with a wink, "I'm always careful."

oooOooo

That wasn't strictly true. If he had been "always careful", he certainly wouldn't have embarked on an affair with Enid Mavlow on the day she arrived in Ubar. Samiat had instructed him, as Head of Security, to show Enid around the City under the Sand. The moment they had clapped eyes on each other there had been a powerful attraction and the tour had ended in Ben Rael's apartment on Level One.

They both knew the risk they were taking. If Samiat found out, he would not be jealous. Jealousy of lesser mortals was beneath him. But he would feel insulted and angry. How dare two people whom he had nurtured and taken into his confidence treat him with such disrespect? So the punishment, if they were caught, would be swift and severe.

But they didn't care. They had that magical sexual rapport that is surprisingly rare in human relations. Physically, and in their appetites and emotions, they were a perfect fit. Both had that combination of exuberant sexuality and striking good looks which the mixed-race gene pool of South America seems to favour.

Enid feared Samiat's anger but she felt no shame. Samiat's love-making had been ruthlessly professional, but he had made it clear that their relationship was transactional rather than emotional. Making love with Ben was just as good but entirely spontaneous and natural. It was wholesome.

In any case, Roland Samiat was in love with his pet project.

68. Aletheia and Kit

When Ben Rael returned to Security on Level One he was immediately informed that two strangers had been picked up near the entrance to Ubar.

"Not bloody flu-infected nomads, I hope, hell-bent on revenge for their over-conscientious shepherd mate," he remarked.

"No, sir," said the enthusiastic American-educated Chinese guard who had recently accepted a job offer in Ubar to avoid a death sentence or castration for rape in Chizhou, Anhui province, China. "It's a woman and a blind man. The woman's hot."

Before Ben could inspect his visitors he took a call from Roland.

"We have a couple of uninvited guests," said Roland. "Something has gone wrong in Mayfair. They should both be dead. The blind man is Kit Turner, formerly suspected of being an Emergent. He's one of Adam's friends and a fellow questor. Watch him. The female is something else. Her name is Aletheia. You don't need to know her background but believe me, it would be a serious mistake to underestimate her. Minofel had a run in with her and came off second best, and it seems that Ceri and Lister may also have been worsted in their dealings with her."

"What do you want me to do with them?" asked Ben.

"Treat them as honoured guests. Put them in one of the visitors' suites on the second level. Tell them that when they are rested and refreshed I will see them in my office. But keep them on Level Two. I don't want them meeting or talking to Adam before I'm ready."

"Is Adam still with you?" asked Ben.

"Yes, he's in my outer office. I'm in the middle of a meeting with Charles to set the day and time for the Cull. When we've finished, I'll call Adam into my office and send for Aletheia and the blind man. I'm rather looking forward to bringing them all up to speed. In the meantime, try to find out what went wrong in Mayfair."

oooOooo

The accommodation on Level Two was luxurious in the same cold, impersonal manner of a six-star hotel. Happy in the wild, cathedral-like environs of Prometheus cave, Aletheia felt deeply out of place in this synthetic world. Kit was unconcerned. He used his highly developed spatial sense to map out the suite and was quickly able to navigate the furniture as well as any sighted person.

"What's the plan?" Kit asked Aletheia. "We don't have much time. If you're right and Slough was just a test run, they could roll out the main event at any time."

"My plan is simple," said Aletheia. "We meet this Roland Samiat. We explain that what he is planning is the perfect example of a crime against humanity. And when he laughs in our faces, we kill him."

"Well, that's a plan," said Kit, "and it's certainly simple. Meeting him is straightforward. It seems we have an appointment with him as soon as we've freshened up. I'm not sure we need to explain to him the gravity of the crime he is planning. I guess he understands that already. It's the killing bit that's just a tad flaky. Everyone here seems very security-minded. We have no weapons. How are we supposed to kill him?"

"How did you take the strength from bull-like Jedwell Boon so that he was too weak to lift a salt cellar? How did you open the gates of Slievins' Mayfair mansion?" Aletheia asked.

"I hope your plan doesn't depend on me exercising superpowers," said Kit. "If it does, I'm afraid you're going to be disappointed."

"With your help, Adam and Eve triggered a Fourth Beginning. You have no idea what powers you have."

"And Roland Samiat or some of his people aborted the Beginning almost as soon as it started," Kit pointed out. "We could do nothing about it."

"They tried to frame you for John Noble's murder. They put you on a scaffold. And yet you escaped and they failed."

"With the help of the paradox device which, despite teleporting us here in one piece, now seems in need of a major service," Kit rejoined.

"I am the goddess of truth, the daughter of Prometheus, the humiliator of Zeus. I have yet to meet a man I could not best."

Kit sighed. "Let's just hope Samiat is not the first exception."

"Truth conquers all," said Aletheia.

"I thought that was love," Kit replied.

69. Good news, bad news

Roland Samiat sat back in his chair. Charles Fundi had given a most satisfactory account of preparations for the Cull. Because of the incomplete burning of soft body parts in the pilot, further provisions had been made for the clean-up after the Cull. The date and time for Cull 75241 had been set. Today was Tuesday. DK12 would be activated in three days' time, at 06.00 hours on Friday.

While Roland Samiat and Charles Fundi had been putting in place the final arrangements for the extermination of seventy-five per cent of the world's human population, Adam had been left in Samiat's outer office under the supervision of Enid Mavlow who was now established as Samiat's personal assistant and gatekeeper. If anyone wanted a meeting with Roland, they had to go through Enid (a requirement which Ben Rael had taken rather more seriously than most).

Adam had asked Enid a dozen questions. Enid had been hospitable but evasive. When Adam had mentioned the recent loss of his wife in the terrorist attack in Covent Garden, Enid had been particularly sympathetic, but when he had tried to find out what would happen to David Minofel, why Slievins had decamped to Ubar, and why anyone would want to build a modern, underground city in the middle of a desert, Enid had no satisfactory answers. Roland's summons for Adam to join him therefore came as a considerable relief to Enid.

"Come in, come in," said Roland, adopting his affable persona. "What am I going to do with you?"

Adam didn't answer. Evidently it wasn't for him to determine his fate. He felt like a child about to be given a fitting punishment by a strict, all-powerful father. He felt completely vulnerable. He felt afraid.

"As you know," Roland continued, "I am as surprised as you that you are here. I find Minofel's faith in you curious. He really has stuck with you through thick and thin, even when you have betrayed him. Very odd and just a little worrying! As luck would have it, I have time get to know you a little. In three days' time I will be initiating by far the most important project of my career, but because of meticulous planning and scrupulous attention to detail, there is little for me to do between now and then. So I have hit upon a way of filling my time constructively. You and I are going on a journey."

Adam waited for Samiat to explain. Instead, Samiat instructed Enid to ask Ben Rael to bring the "visitors" to his office.

oooOooo

When Aletheia and Kit entered Samiat's office Adam couldn't believe his eyes. That Kit was there was inexplicable but Aletheia's presence was beyond belief. Aletheia had played her part in his time with the Praesidium but that had been a bizarre world, a parallel coincident construct outside normal time and space, in which the presence of a goddess from ancient Greece had not seemed entirely inappropriate. But her sudden appearance in the real world, in an underground city under a desert, left Adam doubting his sanity.

"I can see, Adam, that you're a little taken aback," said Roland, indicating that his guests should be seated. "Clearly there is no need for me to introduce you to our visitors, but allow me to introduce myself to them. I am the CEO of Slievins, perhaps the world's most highly regarded consultancy, trusted adviser to governments and major corporations around the world. I am delighted to meet a real goddess, however improbable your existence." He swept Aletheia's hand to his lips. "As for you, Kit Turner, I've heard so much about you, all of it persistently inconclusive."

Samiat settled back in his chair and waited for the other three to respond.

Aletheia spoke first, addressing Samiat. "We have reason to believe you were behind the mass killing in Slough and that you now intend to perpetrate a culling of mankind which, if allowed to proceed, would constitute the greatest evil of man against man in human history."

"Excellent," said Roland. "Very grand! I would expect nothing less from a deity. I can see you have had training in the law and in advocacy. The style is a little old-fashioned but effective nonetheless. Except it lacks empathy! Don't you think you should give Adam the news that will lighten his heart? You can't save humanity but you can make one man happy."

Kit spoke. "Adam, Eve is alive. The child she carries is well. Soon she will give birth and you will be a father once again."

Adam's head spun. The ground seemed to shift beneath his feet and he staggered. When he recovered, he asked: "How can that be? The police confirmed she had been killed. They said she must have been close to ground zero. If she was alive why didn't she contact me? Why didn't anyone contact me?"

Roland Samiat answered him. "Because we scooped her up from the periphery of the explosion and took her to a Slievins' medical facility in Mayfair. There, we checked her out and have been looking after her ever since. We persuaded Eve that you were dead and that your passing, although sad, was probably for the best. After all, being married to a convicted money-launderer and murderer, and possibly being imprisoned herself as an accomplice, was not the happiest prognosis for her future life if you lived. As it is, she remains within Slievins' care and can look forward to a protected, if limited, existence in comfort and security."

Aletheia and Kit looked at each other. They decided that this was not the time to reveal that before leaving for Ubar Samiat had ordered Eve to be killed. Perhaps news of the deaths of Ceri Agema and Lister Bavad and the rescue of Eve had not reached him. Or perhaps he knew but preferred Adam to believe Slievins still had Eve in its grasp. Either way, they would tell Adam that Eve was safe and out of the clutches of Slievins as soon as they could talk to him in private.

"Eve is alive?" Adam looked to Aletheia for confirmation.

"She is," said Aletheia. "And she is close to giving birth to your daughter."

"I must go back to England immediately. I must let her know I am alive. I must be with her when she gives birth."

"Perfectly understandable," said Roland Samiat, "but entirely impractical. If you return to England, you'll be arrested at the border and extradited to Switzerland to face a murder charge long before you see Eve."

"If he wants to return to England, it is his right," said Aletheia. "We have come here to take him back."

"That's not going to happen," said Roland. "I'm afraid you've arrived at a rather inconvenient time. We are about to implement a really major project and we can't have anybody leaving here at present. It's a security issue. In a couple of weeks, a month at the most, you should be able to leave, but till then you are guests of Slievins."

"You cannot keep us here," said Aletheia.

Roland smiled. "Really? You are the goddess of truth, so I take it you simply don't understand. No one invited you here. You have intruded into something far beyond your comprehension. You will stay here until I am satisfied you can cause no harm to our project."

"Your project!" exclaimed Aletheia. "You mean your plan to exterminate most of humanity."

"It's a cull," said Roland softly. "It is perfectly natural. From time to time, for the good of the species, it becomes necessary to cut back on numbers. If we don't do it, nature will. And believe me, if nature does it, humanity will suffer much more."

"What cull?" asked Adam.

"This man plans to kill six billion people and we are here to stop him," Aletheia explained.

"No, no, no," said Roland. "We are not going to discuss the Cull. The facts were presented to the world's great and good. Those with courage and the ability to reason accepted my proposal. Others less courageous and more muddle-headed quietly acquiesced. Within three days, Cull 75241 will take place."

"The world's great and good!" Aletheia expressed her contempt.

"In common with most of your sex, you are clearly incapable of reason," snapped Roland. "You say you have come here to stop the Cull. You are insane. What can you do? We have more or less neutralised your famous paradox device. Rimzil can still use it for voice and simple digital transmissions but little else. You were successfully teleported here only because I allowed it. Hold your friends close and your enemies closer. But I must warn you that if you try to leave here as you arrived, using its teleportation function from within this facility, you will be fragmented into a million pieces. Even your immortality, Aletheia, will not survive such trauma."

Aletheia rose as though to do battle with Samiat. She looked towards Kit but he shook his head. Ben Rael, who had remained in the office by the door, swung the Heckler & Koch MP5 from his shoulder into a firing position.

"Don't be ridiculous," said Samiat. "Even if you killed me – which in present circumstances is not within your power – you would achieve nothing. You and your friends would be executed and the Cull would proceed as planned. If you had shown better manners, I would have been happy to leave you in our guest apartments on

Level Two. Given your negative attitude and display of ill-temper, I'm going to ask my Head of Security to escort you to rather less salubrious accommodation on Level Six. Adam, you will stay here with me." Samiat put his hand on Adam's arm. "As I said, you and I have a way to go."

70. Old acquaintances

Ben Rael escorted Aletheia and Kit to the elevator which took them down to Level Five. They then had to transfer to the private elevator which alone gave access to Level Six. Walking behind his charges, Ben could not help but admire Aletheia's striking figure despite his brand new, intense liaison with Enid. Aletheia was different from the empty-headed, soft, white-skinned, fleshy girls in Admin. She was purposeful, powerful, tanned, yet still alluringly feminine. He observed the sway of her hips and the taut movement of her buttocks beneath her tunic as she walked ahead. Here was a women who could certainly give as good as she got.

"This is Level Six," said Ben as though conducting a tour of a prestigious building. "As you will see, it is a large facility, currently seriously underused. If we exclude the denizens of the oubliette, there is only one other prisoner in residence."

"So we are prisoners," said Aletheia.

"Only in the sense that you are to be kept in cells on this level and will not be allowed to leave," said Ben cheerfully.

"Who is the other prisoner?" asked Kit. He was resting his hand on Aletheia's arm. He could have no sense of where he was until he had been able to explore his surroundings by touch.

"It's a senior Slievins' consultant who, sadly, has fallen out of favour," Ben replied. "It's someone you might have met in the Westminster PCC. David Minofel."

Kit winced. He had been Minofel's guest in Geneva, and when he had been taken to the Westminster PCC, Minofel had been the one who had placed him in the tender care of the sadistic Simon Goodfellow.

"We both know David Minofel," said Aletheia. "You say he has fallen out of favour. Is that anything to do with our rescue of Kit, saving him from the hangman's noose?"

"Don't ask me," Ben replied. "You can ask him yourself. I suggest you take an adjacent cell. Feel free to chat with him all day. We're keeping him locked in his cell, but I see no reason why you shouldn't have the freedom to explore Level Six, so I shall leave your cell door open. Architecturally, Level Six is pretty bland, but it has one or two interesting features."

"How do we eat?" asked Kit. "Are there warders?"

Ben laughed. "No, it's all fully automated. Every cell in this sector has a free vending machine. You can order from the menu. It's a limited choice, but you are in a prison facility after all. Believe me, the food in Rehabilitation, which is where I'm putting you, is a good deal better that the rations in Punishment. Punishment is the other section of Level Six, on the other side of the oubliette. Let's hope you don't end up over there."

"You sound as though you are concerned about our welfare," observed Aletheia.

"I am," said Ben, looking into Aletheia's eyes. "To be honest, I don't feel comfortable locking up a beautiful woman and a blind man, both of whom seem pretty harmless."

"I suspect," said Aletheia with a smile, "that being honest is a novel experience for you, but do not add naivety to honesty. We are not harmless. We have come here to stop this cull. We will do whatever is necessary."

Ben shrugged. "Good luck with that. Roland Samiat is a man who generally gets his way. Cull 75241 is his pet project and once implemented it will be his greatest achievement. The Cull is scheduled for this Friday. I don't see there's much you can do to stop it."

"And you support him?" Aletheia asked. "You are prepared to see the random elimination of three-quarters of the world's population?"

"I don't wish to quibble," said Ben, "but it's not totally random. Slievins has put a lot of effort into making sure that it's the thicker, fatter end of the global population that bears the brunt of the Cull."

"And that makes it acceptable?" enquired Kit.

"Whoa!" said Ben. "The Cull wasn't my idea. As Head of Security I just follow orders. If you want my opinion, I think Samiat's a little mad, but he pays my wages. And don't forget, he has the explicit or tacit approval of most of the world's leaders. If he's mad, he's not alone."

They had reached the cells adjacent to the one occupied by Minofel. "Feel free to roam as you please. A couple of the prisoners in the oubliette have died but three are still alive. If you're curious, the oubliette is over there in the centre of this floor. Otherwise, you'll have to make do with each other, or David, for company." He turned to Aletheia. "Such a waste! But don't give up. I'll have a word with Roland. I'm sure I can get you out of here."

With that, Ben Rael turned and retraced his steps to the elevator which took him back up to Level Five.

71.   Base camp

In Rambler's flat in Maida Vale there were only two subjects under discussion.

The first was the problem with the paradox device.

"The fault is intermittent. That's why it's so difficult to trace," said Prune, trying to find an excuse for his lack of success.

"As I keep saying, I don't think there is a fault in the device," said Andrew. "We've run every diagnostic we have. There's nothing wrong with the device. It just successfully teleported Aletheia and Kit to the entrance of Ubar. But it's being interfered with. Something outside is undermining it, trying to deconstruct its core program."

"So what can we do?" asked Rambler. He couldn't help with the obscure programming issues that had obsessed Andrew and Prune for days but he could ask constructive questions.

"We need to stop the interference," said Prune.

"We need to prevent the interference from penetrating the paradox device," said Andrew.

"Or either or both," minded Luke to Andrew. "Destroying the source of the interference would be favourite. It would solve the problem once and for all. But if we can't destroy the source, we can try to prevent it from acting on the device."

"Thank you," minded Andrew to Luke. "Any suggestions on how we might do that?"

"Not really," Luke conceded, "but I recall some mention of Münchhausen's Trilemma. I've no idea what it is but Prune said you had a problem with it. Well, if it gave you a problem then, perhaps it could give you a solution now."

"I'll give it some thought," said Andrew out loud.

"Good," said Prune, assuming Andrew was warming to the idea of destroying the source. "I don't know how we can find the source but if we can locate it, we can surely destroy it. I'll begin scanning now. The device is sluggish but operational."

"Rather than scan," said Rambler cautiously, "might it not be better to simply ask the paradox device? If it is being interfered with, isn't the device itself best placed to identify the source of the interference."

The other subject under discussion was the good health and

well-being of Eve and her baby. She was due to give birth at any time. The other questors were worried that the strain of the pregnancy combined with her grief for those who had died in Slough and her fear that Slievins had caused the Cull, together with entirely unexpected news of the resurrection of Adam might prove too much for her.

They were wrong. As soon as Aletheia and Kit had removed her from Slievins' control, Eve felt better and stronger. Enid and Lister had been kind to her, but they had somehow undermined her independence, her sense of herself. They had convinced her that she and the baby could have no life outside Slievins' embrace. They had persuaded her that she was implicated in whatever crimes Adam had committed. They had also prevented her from grieving for Adam. Samiat had set out to demolish Adam in her eyes, casting him as the author of all her troubles. They had created a closed world, disconnected from her past life, and she had felt stripped of her history, of everything that had given her existence meaning. In order to survive she had focused on the baby, which was both her future and her only link with what she still believed was her true identity, but it was a constant battle.

Then Aletheia and Kit had broken the spell. She had done nothing wrong. She was her own person. Slievins had no right to separate her from her past. Her past had made her what she was.

In any case, everything Slievins had done was based on a lie. Adam wasn't dead. It was now obvious that Slievins had kidnapped her with the purpose of controlling her and severing her bond with Adam. Why? Why was it so important? If Aletheia was right, Slievins were involved in the tragic events in Slough. According to Aletheia, Slievins were planning an act of evil so appalling that it was difficult to comprehend. If that was so, why would they spend time trying to break up the relationship between a man and a woman. People didn't matter to Slievins. If they had been involved in the killing of 100,000 people in Slough, killing two more in order to destroy their relationship would scarcely merit a second thought.

Far from feeling an unbearable strain Eve felt liberated. She was once again with those she could trust, those with whom she had shared life-changing experiences. "Don't worry about me," she had told the others. "We need to be doing everything we can to help Aletheia and Kit to save Adam."

72. Strange bedfellows

"How's Miss Tomic?" David Minofel enquired of Aletheia as soon as Ben Rael had left Level Six. "I miss her."

"You miss her! Don't be ridiculous," Aletheia replied. "When I rescued her from your clutches she had only hours to live. She is now in the Caucasus with Prometheus, far from you and Slievins and the evil you perpetrate."

"You take everything so seriously and so personally," Minofel chided. "I was just making polite chat. After all, we're in the same predicament and we should work together."

"We're not in exactly the same predicament," said Kit. "You are locked in your cell. We are free to come and go."

"Free to come and go on Level Six, but nowhere else," Minofel pointed out. "Good to see you too, Kit. Now we've completed the pleasantries, could we discuss how to improve our current situation? And before you start all that nonsense about how we couldn't possibly work together, let's just accept that we seem to have the same enemy and that means, if we have any sense, we must now be allies."

Aletheia ignored Minofel's invitation.

"Excuse me," Minofel continued. "You came here to stop the Cull. Am I right? Well, you have less than three days. To be honest, I don't give a toss one way or the other about the Cull, but I'm certain I need to find a way out of here. And if you want any chance at all of interfering with Roland Samiat's plans, you need to be out of here too. So get down off your high horse and see if we can't unbolt the stable door."

Minofel paused as if troubled, as indeed he was. His last remark had sounded to him alarmingly like something Roland Samiat would have said.

"It makes sense," said Kit to Aletheia, fearful she would reject Minofel's overtures on principle.

Aletheia nodded her assent. "What have you to offer as your contribution?"

"Do you promise to release me and take me with you if I help?"

"We do," said Kit, "and as a gesture of good faith, I will undo the lock on your cell door."

Aletheia looked surprised. "And how are you going to do that?" she asked.

Kit smiled, walked over to Minofel's cell door, entered some numbers in the lock panel, and opened the door. "Just another party trick," he said. "Now how can you help us?"

"I can give you some background details," said Minofel. "There's only one way out – through the lift that connects Level Five to Level Six. Level Six is completely autonomous. There are no staff. Food and water rations are supplied by automated machines. Only Roland Samiat and Ben Rael have access to this level. This means we have to persuade one of them to release us or allow us to escape. Given that Samiat ordered us to be incarcerated, our best hope is Ben Rael."

"Is that it?" said Aletheia. "If that's the best you can do, I think we'll put you back in your cell and lock the door."

"There's more," said Minofel hastily. "I am here because I was set up. It's complicated."

"Well, simplify it," said Aletheia impatiently.

"One of my colleagues, Art Shoat, encouraged me to think that he and another senior member of Slievins' board, Charles Fundi, would back me in ousting Samiat. When I made my move, neither of them backed me. They left me alone and exposed."

"So what?" said Aletheia. "Perhaps Samiat suspected you of disloyalty and the others conspired with Samiat to expose your treachery."

"That would make sense, except that Art Shoat dislikes Samiat even more than I do."

"So you think that Art and Charles conspired to eliminate you before they made their own move against Samiat," Kit speculated.

"I thought that at first," Minofel replied, "but for various reasons, Charles Fundi is totally loyal to Roland Samiat."

"So you think Art Shoat is acting on his own?" Kit probed.

"No, I think he's conspiring with Ben Rael," said Minofel.

"Really!" said Aletheia. "How do you work that one out?"

"It's simple," said Minofel. "Art Shoat wouldn't act on his own. He's a good organiser and isn't afraid to get his hands dirty, but he lacks the chutzpah and the leadership qualities to front run. Ben, on the other hand, is charismatic and a natural risk-taker. Art needs someone like Ben as a partner and that person isn't Charles Fundi. So I'd bet everything I have that Art and Ben have a plan. They needed to eliminate me because if Roland is ousted, I'd be his obvious successor. If they can eliminate Charles Fundi, their path will be clear. Ben can't stand Fundi, so I'm sure he'll take some pleasure in implementing that part of their plan."

"Clearly loyalty is in short supply in the senior ranks of Slievins' staff," observed Aletheia.

"Let's say you're right. How does that help?" asked Kit.

"Roland Samiat and Charles Fundi are a pretty powerful combination. If we offer to help Art and Ben, it could swing the balance in their favour. And there's something else. I know Art. He comes from a pretty tough background. If they oust Samiat, my guess is that Ben's days will be numbered. From Art's point of view, he will have fulfilled his purpose. I think we should talk to Ben. We need to be part of the game. And there's something else. Ben has a keen eye for the ladies and he's certainly taken a shine to you, Aletheia. I think he's a little bored with the run-of-the-mill girls in Admin. I think he's well disposed to you and will baulk at any instruction to terminate you."

"Is that Samiat's plan?" asked Kit.

"Absolutely," Minofel replied. "Roland doesn't like loose ends. He's held the post of CEO by making sure everything is kept tidy. That's why he ordered Ceri and Lister to kill you and Eve before he left Mayfair. When we're less pressed for time you must tell me how that went wrong. I assume Eve's in good shape. Adam will be pleased."

"So what's our plan?" asked Aletheia.

"We summon Ben," said Minofel. There's an emergency phone in Rehab. We'll tell him we have some crucially important information which – if I'm right – is true. We'll explain how things are likely to play out and suggest that if he has our help, he could come out of this not only alive but unbelievably rich."

"Unbelievably rich?" queried Aletheia. "Where did that come from?"

"Well, it seems Roland keeps most of his money in a Swiss bank account in Geneva. It's rather a lot of money. I know this because Ben told me that the code to set off the device under the oubliette is the ever-changing balance in Roland's Swiss bank account, multiplied by a secret six-digit number, generated daily, on Roland's mobile. If he enters that number, the computer multiplies the two numbers together and transmits it to the charge that triggers the neutron bomb. If the product of the two numbers corresponds with the computer's own identical, ever-changing calculation, BOOM."

"Neutron bomb!" said Aletheia and Kit in unison.

"Yep," said Minofel. "Standard precautionary measure in Slievins. Make sure you can destroy everything your enemies would gain by defeating you. Anyway, that's not the point."

"So what is the point?" asked Kit.

"As you must know, we've been experimenting with ways of neutralising your paradox device. As part of our research, we've been monitoring what the device has been doing. We noted one activity which struck us as odd. The paradox device spent some time accessing vast numbers of bank accounts and it performed this task with a speed beyond even our most powerful computers. If we tap in to Samiat's Genevan account, we can offer Ben Rael unimaginable amounts of money."

"You mean bribe him with the money of the man he's about to betray," said Aletheia.

"You say that as though it's a bad thing," said Minofel.

"So to summarise," said Kit, "we persuade Ben he needs our help in handling Art after he and Art have eliminated Charles and ousted Roland. And we sweeten the deal by offering him untold wealth, courtesy of a financial scam facilitated by our paradox device. Is that it?"

"That's it," Minofel confirmed. "What do you think?"

"Well, let me see," said Aletheia. "There just might be a couple of glitches. What do we do if he denies that he is plotting anything with Art? What do we do if he isn't plotting anything with Art? At present, you're here because you have betrayed your boss which, according to Slievins' code, is about the worst thing anyone could do. We're here because we arrived uninvited and upset him, which I guess is a relatively minor offence."

"Grow up, Aletheia," said Minofel sharply. "You're the goddess of truth, not stupidity. None of us will get out of here alive unless we act. You want to stop the Cull. Fair enough. I don't care. There's going to be a cull whether Roland does it or nature does it. It's just a matter of timing. But if you want to abort Roland's cull, you will need to kill him. So we have the same objective. Yes, the plan's not foolproof. But it's the only plan in town. So let's give it a try."

73. A picnic in the desert

"What are you planning to do with Aletheia and Kit?" Adam asked.

He was now alone with Roland Samiat who was preoccupied with the bank of screens that filled one wall of his office. Adam turned to look at the screens. There were news reports on the clean-up in Slough and coverage of the plethora of speculation on social media on all aspects of the event. An attack by aliens had achieved the greatest traction, mainly because, despite the best efforts of the forensic scientists, the cause of the plague remained uncertain. Autopsies revealed that many of the dead had above average arteriosclerosis for their age, but the clogging of their arteries was no explanation for their abrupt collapse, much less for the spontaneous internal combustion that started soon after death.

Satisfied that he was up-to-date with developments in the world's coverage of the Slough pilot, Samiat turned his attention to Adam.

"What did you say?" he asked.

"I said 'what are you planning to do with Aletheia and Kit?'"

Samiat stroked his chin. "You know, Adam, you're a bit of a disappointment. You see on these screens coverage of an event of historical importance. Most of the population of a town in your own country has been wiped out. Even the Black Death couldn't match the mortality rate of just under eighty-two per cent recorded in Slough."

Adam shook his head. "You seem pleased. And you haven't answered my question."

"What happens to Aletheia and Kit is of no importance. One hundred thousand people died in Slough. What difference will two more make."

Adam was shocked and angry. "Are you saying you intend to kill them? Why? What have they done?"

It was Samiat's turn to shake his head. "I'm not saying that I'm going to kill them. I'm saying that whether or not I kill them doesn't matter."

"Well, I'm pretty sure it matters to them, and to those who love them," Adam responded.

"Yes, of course it matters to them but – and this is the point I'm making – it doesn't matter in general, on the grand scale, in the big picture. If two people die, it's news. If one hundred thousand die, it's not news that two people died. And if six billion die, it's not news that one hundred thousand died, especially when it's in some obscure town on a small island off the coast of Europe."

"Six billion!" Adam repeated. "What the hell does that mean?"

"That's why we're going on a picnic in the desert – so that I can get to know you, Adam. And so you can learn to ask the right questions."

oooOooo

They drove out of Ubar into the desert north-east for about ten miles. Everywhere, the undulating orange sand stretched into the distance. To the south, far away, Adam thought he could glimpse the outline of mountain ranges. In every other direction there was desert as far as the eye could see.

"Not too hot for you?" enquired Samiat who was driving one of the fleet of Mercedes SUVs garaged in Security on the First Level of Ubar.

"I'm fine," said Adam. The weather was pleasant. The sun was shining, but it was no hotter than a summer's day in England. "Why are we driving into the desert?"

"Because it's where you belong," Samiat replied. "And because we need to talk without any distractions. We need to understand each other. Most of all, you need to understand yourself."

Samiat drove towards a lone palm tree at the edge of a small oasis. Except for an iron brazier full of wood, there was no sign that any man had ever set foot there. Adam looked puzzled. The desert in this region was arid and there had been no signs of wadis or oases since they had left Ubar.

"It's a little self-indulgence," Samiat explained. "I had this created as a place where I could be completely alone and meditate. You are my first guest at what I like to call my little Garden of Eden. No serpent, no apple tree and no God obsessed with obedience, but for me this is a little piece of Paradise."

Adam's brow furrowed but he said nothing.

Samiat stopped the car under the shade of the palm tree, spread a large mat and produced water, wine and an assortment of fruit from the back of the car. "Let us sit down and talk." he said.

Adam, ill at ease, sat down on the mat.

"I will begin," said Samiat. "This Friday the world will change. A plague of far greater than Biblical proportions will afflict humanity. Six billion people, give or take, will die. There will be a period of readjustment. Then a brave new world, a better world, will emerge."

"Six billion people!" Adam repeated. "How can that be? How do you know? What could possibly cause the death of so many people?"

Samiat took a peach from the fruit bowl. "How do I know? I know because I planned it. How is it to be done? The answer's a little complicated, but in essence we've introduced into fast foods a chemical which, when activated, kills its host. The good news is that in very broad terms we are eliminating the base of the pyramid. The world will, by definition, be a better place." Samiat wiped a trickle of peach juice from one side of his neatly trimmed beard.

"What pyramid?" asked Adam.

"The social pyramid," said Samiat in a tone of voice that implied there should have been no need for explanation. "In every society there is a hierarchy. The majority form the base of the pyramid. In general terms they are the average and below. As you move up the pyramid, again in general terms, you find the more able. At the apex of the pyramid, you find the elite. Cull 75241, which is the code name of the project, is geared to wiping out the base of the pyramid. Of course, it's not as clear-cut as my description suggests. Some of the dross will survive. Some of the more able will die. But overall, DK12 – that's the agent we're using – will raise the intelligence level of the population by around ten per cent."

Adam was incredulous. "Are you telling me that you and Slievins plan to wipe out six billion people?"

"At last, you've got it," said Samiat. "Of course we had to win the support – or at least the acquiescence – of the elite, but that was not so difficult. There are too many people demanding too much of the planet. All governments know this but what can they do? Western-style democracies are impotent. They cannot expect to be elected if they tell their electorate the truth. They dare not confess that the West's standard of living must deteriorate if the aspiring developing world is to enjoy anything like the material prosperity of the West. Even dictatorships have to take some account of the will of the people.

"In fact, a number of factors worked in our favour. The worldwide web was an enormous help. It exposed the injustice and inequalities in all the societies man has devised. It became increasingly common for the masses to despise both their rulers and the experts whom the rulers employed to keep the masses cowed. 'We've had enough of experts' was a mantra that rang a warning bell. The elite became even more fearful than usual. And fear was the key.

"Then we were helped by the realisation that if no decisive action was taken, the planet would end up depleted and exhausted within a hundred years. On top of those factors, there was a growing feeling that, inadvertently, modern societies were systematically obstructing evolution by encouraging the survival of the least fit. In advanced societies, those contributing least to the common good, or indeed contributing nothing at all, were being encouraged by well-meaning welfare systems to outbreed all other sections of society.

"So Slievins came up with a solution. Cull 75241. Target for elimination – the bottom seventy-five per cent of the population. Of the remaining surviving twenty-five per cent, one per cent constitutes the elite. The other twenty-four per cent will be there to service the one per cent, but being on average more able than the seventy-five per cent we have culled, they will be better able to satisfy the needs of the elite. And all will be able to enjoy a much higher standard of living for much longer before the planet is finally exhausted. We presented the idea in secret sessions at Davos and at other meetings of the great and good, and once we had overcome some minor moral scruples, it was plain sailing."

"Minor moral scruples?" Adam exploded.

"Yes, Adam, minor moral scruples," snapped Samiat. "Did you learn nothing from your time at ZeD? 'Define your problem. Devise solutions. Choose the most effective solution. Implement it.' Minofel told me you were an apt pupil. I explained to the leaders at Davos that unless something was done, humanity faced rising temperatures and rising sea levels, depletion of natural resources, including food and water, wars over the share of these depleted resources, diseases which could no longer be controlled by medicines, the breakdown of society, and, in the end, starvation and death. All this, not just for some but for all! My solution, Cull 75241, should be seen as saving two billion people, not killing six billion."

"But it doesn't have to be like that," said Adam. "There are other solutions."

"Oh yes," said Roland Samiat, sneering. "We could all work together. The richer nations could give up some of what they have to help the poorer nations have a little more. We could all change the way we live. We could all give up our cars and become pedestrians. We could give up meat and become vegetarians, or better still, vegans. We could stop having wars. We could agree to pool the earth's natural resources and allocate them to nations according to need. We could persuade people to have fewer children, or to live shorter lives. Yes, there are a number of alternatives. The only problem is that they completely ignore human nature. And as you well know, human nature is what Slievins is all about."

Adam said nothing. He was reminded of his talks with David Minofel in Geneva. At every stage, Minofel had asked him to apply the Slievins' criteria, and at every stage – from bribery, through corruption and blackmail to murder – he had made the right choice, the only choice, in the circumstances. Samiat was doing the same thing only on a grander scale.

"I can see I have given you food for thought," said Samiat. "Have a peach."

74. Endgame: Phase 1

Gaining access to Roland Samiat's Swiss bank account proved to be the easiest part of David Minofel's far from perfect plan. Kit minded to Luke that he should ask Andrew to locate and access the account. Using the paradox device, it took less than twenty minutes to locate the account and no more than a few seconds to identify the password. Andrew made a note of the total in the account: SF295,408,296.

Fortunately, the efforts of Andrew and Prune in reviving the paradox device had enjoyed some success; hence the ease with which it was able to access Samiat's account. Prune had located the source of the interference. The signal emanated from Martlesham in Suffolk, where Despiro Nihilopificus was now encountering some unexpected difficulties with his Resolver.

Andrew Rimzil was the cause of the difficulties. Andrew was working on an algorithm that made use of Münchhausen's Trilemma. On trial runs he had affronted the Resolver's logic to such an extent that it now appeared to be interfering with itself at least as much as with the paradox device.

"You realise that the paradox device could utterly destroy the global financial system?" observed Prune to Andrew. "If it can crack passwords so easily, we'll be back to paper money or coins in next to no time."

"It's still not right," mused Andrew. "Accessing other computer systems is relatively easy. I still wouldn't risk using it for its higher functions. We took a hell of a risk in teleporting Aletheia and Kit."

"Now we've accessed the account, what are we supposed to do with it?" asked Prune.

Andrew looked to Luke for an answer. Luke minded to Andrew that they must wait for further instructions.

"Nothing," Andrew answered Prune, "except make sure the Swiss bank doesn't know that we've accessed one of its largest accounts."

oooOooo

Ben Rael proved less accessible than Samiat's Swiss bank account. Despite repeated calls to Ben via the Rehab emergency phone, three hours passed before the Head of Security could find time to respond to Minofel's appeals.

"I really hope you have something important to say," said Ben as he strode across Level Six to Minofel who was talking earnestly to Aletheia and Kit. "We're gearing up to Slievins' biggest ever project and I certainly don't have any time to waste." Then he added: "And what are you doing out of your cell?"

"Your life is in danger," David Minofel replied, ignoring Ben's question.

"And how would that be?" asked Ben.

"You think you can trust Art Shoat," said Minofel. "Well you can't. He intends to betray you, just as he betrayed me."

"And why does it matter whether I trust Art Shoat?" Ben asked a little uneasily.

"Because having got rid of me, you and Art Shoat now plan to get rid of Roland Samiat and Charles Fundi so that the two of you can take over Slievins. But there's a snag. As soon as Roland and Charles are out of the way, you become surplus to requirement. After doing most of the heavy lifting, Art will eliminate you. Art is perfectly capable of running things on his own, albeit in an even more brutal manner than under the present management. The last thing he will want is a charismatic loose cannon, crashing around the deck – no insult intended."

Ben was perplexed. He considered denying that he was in a conspiracy with Art Shoat but decided against it. David Minofel seemed sure of his facts. In any case it was true, and if Minofel had worked it out, perhaps Roland or Charles Fundi were not far behind. That put him in danger on several fronts.

Minofel continued: "There is a way out. It's a way that makes you rich beyond your wildest dreams but it does depend on you giving up any ambition of taking over Slievins."

Ben shrugged. "You're making a lot of assumptions about what is going on and what I want." He turned to Kit and Aletheia. "Are you part of all this?"

"We are here to stop the Cull," said Aletheia. "We will do whatever is necessary."

Ben turned back to David Minofel. "Tell me a bit more about the 'rich beyond your wildest dreams' bit – and please note, I'm a pretty wild dreamer."

"As of today, we can offer you 147,704,148 Swiss francs," Minofel replied. "The precise amount varies, second by second, but it will be at that level, give or take a few hundred thousand francs."

"That is rather generous," said an astonished Ben. "And where are you finding that amount of money?"

"That's not your concern," said Minofel.

"From Roland Samiat's primary current account in UBS," said Aletheia.

Ben was now totally confused. "Are you acting on Roland's behalf? Why would he want to give me that kind of money? And what would I have to do to earn it?"

"No, we're not acting on Roland's behalf," said Minofel, irritated that Aletheia had revealed the source of the funds for the bribe. "We have access to his account."

"Whoa!" said Ben. "He's not going to take kindly to someone scooping up the money in his Swiss account. I'd need a good deal of personal protection."

"Which you would be well able to afford," suggested Kit.

"And in return for the money what do I have to do?" asked Ben.

"Obviously you have to release us from Level Six," Minofel began.

"And any of the poor devils in the oubliette who are still alive," Kit interrupted.

"I'm afraid they're all dead," said Ben. "I checked on them earlier when I left you. They had eaten parts of the one who died first but then killed each other fighting over what was left. It's not a pretty sight. I'm sure Roland will be impressed and delighted his predictions have proved correct."

"I need you to eliminate Charles Fundi," said Minofel. "Roland and Charles make a powerful combination, so we should weaken Roland's position before we take him head on."

"Terminating Fundi will be a pleasure," said Ben. "He's a sick bastard, and arrogant with it. In any case, that was part of the plan with Art."

"Excellent," said Minofel. "Art will assume you and he are still partners. We'll deal with Art after we have deposed Roland. Art's a realist. When he realises I'm in control and you have abandoned him, I'm sure he will knuckle down," Then Minofel added, as though it was an afterthought: "And we need tomorrow morning's six-digit code for the neutron bomb."

Ben's eyes narrowed. "And why would you want that?" he asked.

"We need to persuade Roland Samiat to abort Cull 75241," said Aletheia. "If we can threaten the existence of Ubar and everyone in it, he will see sense and accede to our demands."

"More to the point," said Minofel, "if we have the code, I can compel him to stand down. Then I can accede to Aletheia's call for the cancellation of the Cull."

Ben considered pointing out that unless they knew the precise amount in the account at the precise moment they entered the six-digit code the bomb wouldn't detonate, but he thought it best left unsaid. Roland would probably point out this flaw in their plan when they made their threat, but by then, hopefully, he – Ben – would be some SF150 million better off and far away.

"There's something I want," said Ben. "When I leave, I'm taking Enid Mavlow with me. Whatever you do to Roland, you have to make sure Enid isn't hurt."

"Certainly," said Minofel, with a smile. "We have no problem with Enid. Roland may be a little upset if you take her from him, but he'll have bigger worries on his mind by then.

"How do I know I can trust you?" Ben asked.

"Half the money now," said Minofel. "Half when Roland Samiat steps down or is ousted from his position as CEO of Slievins."

oooOooo

When Ben left, Minofel was jubilant. "That went rather well, don't you think?" he asked of Aletheia and Kit. Sometimes I impress even myself and, as you know, I set the bar high."

"It seems you were right about the Ben Rael/Art Shoat conspiracy, but we're no closer to stopping the Cull," said Aletheia. "Do you not understand that Samiat is contemplating mass murder on an ultra-biblical, hyper-industrial scale?"

"You worry too much," said Minofel. "If you want to stop the Cull, you just have to do exactly what I say. We need to shuffle the money in Samiat's account around a bit. I've promised Rael SF150 million, and I have plans for the rest of the money. I'll write down exactly what I want done. Then you, Kit, will transmit my instructions to Rimzil. You will make sure my instructions are followed to the letter. When the financial arrangements are in place, we will deal with Samiat and pull the plug on the Cull."

"And you will be able to stop the Cull? You will have the authority?" Aletheia queried.

"Obviously you don't understand how Slievins works," said Minofel. "I am second only to Samiat in the Slievins' hierarchy. If Roland Samiat is incapacitated, I take over as Slievins CEO. As CEO, I have absolute power over the entire organisation. From time to time, Slievins has considered the introduction of some checks and balances to impose some constraints on the top position but we have found such constraints interfere with the taking of decisions. If I am CEO, I can stop the Cull with a word. What's more, I can have anyone inside or outside the organisation eliminated. I don't need a reason. There is no trial, just an order from me."

"So what guarantee do we have you will do what you say?" asked Kit.

"There is no guarantee," said Minofel happily, "but I will keep my word for a number of reasons. I need your help in implementing my plan. You, Kit, must organise the money. You, Aletheia, I have never underestimated. Generally speaking we are on opposite sides. This time I will feel a good deal more comfortable if we are working together. Then, of course, there's Ben. It seems that currently he's besotted with Enid Mavlow, but I've seen the glint in his eye when he looks at you. He will expect me to keep my word to you, just as he will expect me to keep my word to him. And I need him, as Head of Security, to eliminate Charles Fundi and anyone else who stands in my way. So, you see, we all have a common interest. Trust me."

75. It's good to talk

The sun was beginning to set and the air grew colder at Samiat's personal oasis in the desert.

"Shouldn't we be going back to Ubar?" Adam asked. He had said nothing since Samiat had offered him a peach but he had thought a great deal.

"Are you making progress?" Samiat enquired, as he lit the brazier full of wood.

"I'm not sure," Adam replied. "Probably not, from your point of view! I've realised that Slievins is for ever using 'the lesser of two evils' argument, which you combine with a dystopian assessment of human nature. In my time with ZeD, I did some pretty evil things, but with Minofel's help I justified these acts by arguing that any alternative might do even greater harm. But I left out of the equation the harm I was doing to myself."

"So when you chose the lesser of two evils, you were not only trying to do the least harm and the most good, you were also selflessly ignoring the damage that you might be inflicting on yourself. Wise and selfless! Almost saintlike!"

"You're mocking me," said Adam.

"Not at all," Samiat replied. "I'm simply feeding back to you what you have just said to me."

"Slievins has corrupted me," said Adam simply.

"No, no, no," said Samiat. "I can't let you get away with that. If you have been corrupted, which I dispute with every fibre of my being, you have done it all by yourself. True, we offered you the opportunity to be yourself, to free yourself from the shackles of a banal morality designed to frustrate human nature, but the choice was always yours."

"Bribery, corruption, blackmail and murder – that is not human nature," Adam snapped back. "What about honesty, integrity, generosity and kindness! They are part of human nature, too. They are part of my nature."

"Have you forgotten your excursions with the Monitaurs?" Samiat enquired. "They showed you human nature as it is, selfish, avaricious, lecherous, cruel and corrupt. That's not a criticism, but it is the truth. Not only are most people irredeemably selfish, the vast majority make no contribution to the species at all other than to procreate. They spend their lives feeding, needing, greeding and breeding. Whether they had lived or not is profoundly unimportant. I thought you understood this, Adam. I thought you would see why the Cull is a wholly benign project." Samiat paused and then asked: "Do you believe you have a soul?"

Adam was taken aback. Throughout all his adventures in the company of the Storyteller, he had wrestled with the question of identity. He hadn't asked himself if he had a soul, but he had certainly questioned if he had a self. Sometimes he had thought his self was an illusion. "What do you mean by a soul?" he said, answering the question with a question.

Samiat smiled. "When you peel away all the layers of an onion, do you think there is a solid irreducible core at the centre or do you think there is nothing?"

"I don't think I'm an onion," said Adam.

Samiat frowned. It was a perfectly good metaphor. "Do you think you were born with a soul?" he tried again. "It's a really important question. Do you think there is an essence of you that is greater than the sum of your experiences and what your brain has made of them?"

Adam paused. It was indeed a serious question. He had no certain answer. "I am not sure. I have no reason to think I was born with a soul, but I am certain there is a self, and that in the living of a life everyone has the opportunity to develop a soul."

"And how's that going with you?" Samiat asked.

"I will tell you this," said Adam. "I recently spent time helping people ..."

Samiat interrupted: "Ah, yes, I know all about your time on the run."

"Well, I felt happier working with Violet in her help centre than I did at ZeD. I saw a different path – concern and care for others. I know it sounds strange but in that refuge for what Minofel called 'parasites and retards' I found hope. Violet was kind to me. She knew what I was like but she gave me the benefit of the doubt. And I felt good helping others."

"Don't you just love hypocrisy!" exclaimed Samiat, poking the burning wood in the brazier so that a myriad of sparks flew up into the blackness of the night. "The only reason you ever went anywhere near the help centre was because you wanted help. You were there to take, not give. Even when you felt obliged to lend Violet a hand, you couldn't be bothered to see anything through. You delivered a lecture to the lad, Darren, promised him a plan, and then peremptorily dropped him to rush off to meet Minofel. You dumped him on Violet. Do you remember the burglars who broke into your house? One of those was a Darren. I wouldn't be at all surprised if within the next ten years the lad you didn't have time to help becomes another housebreaker and/or rapist."

"I had no choice," said Adam defensively. "I was on the run. Only David Minofel could help me. And I could talk to him only when he made himself available."

"Then there was the way you treated poor Numpty, your mentally challenged, co-questing osmotic gouger. Always asking questions, trying to understand. Did you ever show him kindness? Did you ever help him to understand? Or did you at best ignore him, and at worst, mock him?"

"Oh, come now," said Adam, "he was enough to try the patience of a saint."

"Not to mention the now familiar catalogue of charges against you – bribery, corruption, blackmail and murder," said Samiat with some relish.

"You're making me out to be a really bad person," said Adam.

"Not at all. In every case, in my view, you did the right thing," Samiat soothed. "But it's also true that in every case you did have a choice. You always have a choice. Don't beat yourself up. You made the right choices. I'm just pointing out that you're not a natural good Samaritan. I know you were impressed by Violet. But did you ever think about her life? She sacrificed it to a selfish woman who was happy to take all that her daughter could give, and more. Even so, Violet didn't make her mother happy. Then when her mother died, she was so inured to self-sacrifice that she was moved to seek out other weak, inadequate, demanding people on whom she could waste the rest of her life. No husband for Violet. No children, no happiness!"

"She did good," Adam asserted. "She helped people."

"Perhaps she helped some. Most she simply enabled to pursue their parasitical lifestyle more efficiently. Come on, Adam. You know what people are like. You passed the Praesidium induction programme with flying colours. Jonathan Swift was one of the few who saw the wood for the trees when he hit the nail on the head. All men are fools or knaves. Those people at the help centre were fools or knaves, or both."

"And Violet?" asked Adam.

"Obviously, she was a fool," said Samiat.

"And because we are all fools or knaves, you think you have the right to wipe out six billion of us," said Adam exasperated. "What does that make you – a sociopathic mass murderer? No, that doesn't do you justice. An inhuman, genocidal, sociopathic monster!"

"You're not seeing the bigger picture," said Samiat, unperturbed. "I'm offering a solution to a problem that others won't address. If my solution is not implemented the consequences for all eight billion people will be far worse. Yes, it's evil, but it's the lesser of two evils. Are you arguing for the greater of two evils?"

"I'm not arguing for anything. I'm just saying that your plan is a crime against humanity on a global scale."

"You've had your say, Adam, and I suspect even you can see that your sentiments are vacuous. You are critical but you have no solution to the problem, other than a worse one. But we are not here to discuss the Cull. We are here to determine who and what you are. You've spent your life with your feet in two different camps. Well, I've got news for you. One of the camps is moving far away. Choose or you'll be ripped asunder. I'm going to leave you now. I have work to do. I shall return in the morning. You will be truly alone this night, in the middle of a barren desert, beneath many thousands of lifeless stars. I suggest you use this night to examine your life. After all, it could well be your last."

As Samiat climbed into the Mercedes SUV and started the engine, he muttered: "You can take a horse to water but you can't turn its ear into a silk purse."

76. Mano a mano

Ben Rael considered various ways of despatching Charles Fundi. The simplest method would be to send a hit squad from Security with orders to take him out into the desert and slit his throat. The only problem with that plan was that Charles Fundi was officially the Commander of Ubar. As such, strictly speaking, only Roland could order his execution. In all probability, carefully chosen security guards would follow the instructions of the Head of Security without question, but there was always a risk someone might want to check with Samiat – and that wouldn't do at all.

Alternatively, Ben could arrange for any one of a number of accidents to befall Fundi. He could fall down the lift shaft that carried personnel from Level One down to Level Five. The Tanzanian could even fall into the oubliette on Level Six during an unscheduled and unauthorised visit to the Punishment and Rehab centres.

In the end, Ben decided to deal with the matter himself. The animosity between him and Fundi had been festering from the moment they met. Ben saw Fundi as a sadistic pervert who took pleasure in beating those weaker than himself to death. Fundi saw Ben as an irresponsible, superficial philanderer with a penchant for unnecessary and often counterproductive violence. Neither gave the other credit for their strengths. Fundi was a brilliant engineer. Without him, neither the City of Ubar nor Project 75241 would have been possible. And Ben, with his Brazilian good looks and happy-go-lucky approach to life, was immensely likeable and popular, a naturally charismatic, if somewhat diffident, leader of men.

Ben sent Charles Fundi a text message. "You need to talk to one of the prisoners on Level Six. It's something to do with Ubar's power source. I'll meet you at the elevator on Level Five."

In normal circumstances, Charles Fundi would have expected Ben Rael to take his concerns to Roland Samiat. Then Samiat would instruct Fundi to investigate if necessary. But these were not normal circumstances. They were within two days of launching the Cull. For reasons entirely obscure to Fundi, Samiat had taken off into the desert with the fellow that the now disgraced Minofel had brought with him. So in Samiat's absence, the Head of Security was entitled to contact the Commander of Ubar (and Ubar's chief engineer) directly. And if there was any problem with Ubar's power source, the Crucible of Eternal Light, then it was surely a matter of the gravest concern.

When Charles Fundi took the elevator from his office on Level Three down to Level Five he found Ben Rael waiting for him.

"This had better be important, Rael," said Fundi. "We're making the final checks for the Cull and I resent any distraction."

"Oh, this is a matter of importance! In fact, it's a matter of life and death," said Ben easily. "One of the prisoners is a woman, Aletheia. She says she's here to stop the Cull."

"And how would she do that?" asked Charles Fundi.

"For an answer to that question I think you should talk to Aletheia," said Ben.

Ben swiped his security card through the lock on the elevator that descended to Floor Six. The door slid open. They stepped into the elevator. An alarm sounded.

"Sorry," said Ben. "No weapons. Level Six is a secure facility for the punishment and rehabilitation of prisoners. No weapons on Level Six or in the elevator."

Charles Fundi frowned. He always carried a Ruger SR9 pistol for personal security.

Ben waited, an open expression on his face. Reluctantly Fundi relinquished his weapon. The door closed and the elevator descended.

"I guess you're familiar with the layout of Level Six," said Ben. "You were involved in its construction."

"I approved the designs and my people checked its construction at every stage," Fundi replied.

"So you know about the neutron bomb buried under the oubliette?" Ben probed.

The elevator door opened. They stepped out. The door closed.

"Yes, I know about the neutron bomb," said Fundi irritably. There was no one to be seen. "So where is this Aletheia?" he snapped.

"Didn't that worry you?" Ben persisted. "Why would Samiat want to install a bomb capable of destroying Ubar, the jewel in Slievins' crown?"

"As security chief, you should be able to answer that question yourself," Fundi replied. "The safest way to ensure everyone's loyalty is to make it clear you have the ability to kill them all on a whim."

"I'm not sure that's loyalty," said Ben with a laugh. "Isn't that just fear?"

"I didn't come here to debate the finer points of personnel management," said Fundi. "Where is Aletheia?"

"Before we meet Aletheia," said Ben. "I want to show you something."

Ben led Fundi to the oubliette in the centre of Level Six. Charles Fundi looked down the smooth, steeply curved sides of the pit. At the bottom were the bodies of the prisoners who had died.

Charles turned to Ben. "Why have you brought me here?" he asked.

"You know why," said Ben. "It was always going to end like this. You've wanted me dead from the moment we met – and to be fair, I felt the same about you. We've muddled along because until now there was no good reason to resolve the situation. But now I have a reason."

"And what's that?" said Fundi, backing away from the rim of the oubliette.

"Sex and money," said Ben. "I've taken a shine to Enid, Samiat's latest woman. And for reasons I won't explain here, it seems I can have the woman and make myself extremely wealthy at the same time."

"Assuming I don't kill you," said Fundi.

"Of course," said Ben. "but that's not an unreasonable assumption. I've checked your record. You're a killer, sure enough. But you concentrate on the weak and vulnerable. I'm a lot of things but weak and vulnerable aren't two of them."

Fundi looked around for a weapon. There was nothing he could use.

"Where are the prisoners?" Charles asked, playing for time.

"I released them," said Ben happily. "And Minofel. They're on their way to deal with Roland. It seems there are some changes afoot."

As Ben approached, Fundi aimed a kick at Ben's legs. Ben nimbly avoided what could have been a disabling injury. "That's the spirit," said Ben. "No Queensberry Rules! Anything goes."

Ben's first blow caught Fundi on the chin, forcing him to stagger back. He dropped to one knee. Ben advanced and was about to hit him again when with remarkable agility Fundi leapt upward and forward, headbutting Ben. Before Ben could recover himself, Fundi grabbed Ben's face and started to gouge at Ben's eyes. Immediately Ben broke Fundi's grip, but not before his right eye had been damaged.

"Round one to me," said Fundi. "I think you may have misread my CV. Yes, I kill the weak and vulnerable, but I'm equally happy killing the strong and able-bodied. In fact, I rather enjoy turning the strong and fit into the physically handicapped before I despatch them. Be careful or I'll have the other eye, and then where will you be?"

Ben's next attack was carefully prepared and effectively performed. He hit Fundi with a combination of punches that left him weakened and winded. He turned the stunned Fundi around and put his head in a lock. "I could break your neck now and it would be over," he rasped in Fundi's ear, "But that would be too easy. I'm opting for an eye for an eye."

Fundi screamed and clasped his hand to a now empty socket.

"I've always believed in fair play," said Ben. "You know – a level playing field and all that! So let's see what you've got left."

Fundi was only semi-conscious and seemed to be in no fit state to respond.

"Very well," said Ben. "I'd just like you to know you've been a big disappointment." He grabbed Fundi by the collar and dragged him to the rim of the oubliette. "I can't think of any better place for you than down there with the dead."

With that, he swung Fundi's body out over the pit and let go.

With a speed and strength born of desperation, Fundi snatched at Ben's legs as he fell. He failed to take hold, but he succeeded in pulling Ben's feet off the rim. Ben felt himself slipping down the steep side of the oubliette. As he started to fall, he whipped himself round and grabbed at the rim. But it was perfectly smooth and offered nothing to grip.

As Ben followed Charles to the bottom of the oubliette, he thought through his predicament. First, he must survive the fall. Secondly, he must despatch Fundi, if he was not already dead. Then, he would have to wait until someone came to his rescue. The technicians on Level Five must have seen him and Fundi enter the elevator that took them down to Level Six. When it was discovered the Commander of Ubar and the Head of Security were missing, there would be a search. Presumably pretty quickly, they would tell Roland that they needed access to Level Six. He would be rescued and receive medical attention to his damaged eye; he still hoped his sight could be saved. As soon as he was patched up, Samiat would want to know how he and Fundi had ended up in the oubliette and why Fundi was dead. Ben decided he would usefully spend the time until he was rescued concocting a plausible explanation.

His fall – and his review of the situation – ended when he hit the floor of the oubliette. He landed awkwardly on the dismembered body of the first prisoner to have died. He felt his own body gingerly to confirm nothing was broken. He stood up. Behind him, unseen, stood a battered but venomous Charles Fundi holding a human femur tarnished with the vestiges of uneaten, decaying meat. The first blow, struck from behind, stunned Ben who fell to his knees. The next twenty, all delivered with merciless force to Ben Rael's head, cracked his skull and turned his once handsome face into something resembling a tomato, macaroni and cheese pizza.

77.   The night of nights

When the lights of Samiat's SUV had finally disappeared behind a distant sand dune, Adam realised he was utterly alone. If Samiat failed to return, it was unlikely he would be able to find his way back to Ubar. He was deep in a desert without even a compass. For all his adventures, he was ill-equipped, in mind or skill set, to survive the challenges and obvious rigours of such isolation in a sunburnt barren land.

The night sky was full of twinkling lights. Adam had never seen so many stars from earth. Even on his journey to witness the birth of the universe he had not seen such a spectacle. The campervan had cut through space at such speed that nothing had been clear. In any case, that particular quest had been so bizarre that it now seemed a world away.

No, on this night, entirely alone in a distant desert on a small planet orbiting a modest sun, Adam suddenly came to face a very personal reality. The time for questions was over. On this night, beneath a canopy of innumerable stars, Adam finally understood he must decide upon the answers.

His first thoughts were of Eve. She was the woman of his life; she was the companion of his soul. And she was alive. The child she carried, his and hers, would be born. He must not compromise on his love for Eve, or for their child.

His second thoughts grappled with all the obstacles that lay between him and Eve. He might well die in the Arabian desert. Even if he survived the desert, Roland Samiat was quite likely to have him killed. Even if he escaped from Ubar, he might well be exterminated in the Cull, or, even more likely, in its aftermath. And if by some extraordinary concatenation of fortuitous events, if the world escaped or overcame the Cull and he survived all these threats, he would still face criminal charges which could quite plausibly see him incarcerated in a Swiss prison until he died.

How had he ended up as a fugitive from justice, in thrall to and entirely at the mercy of an evil organisation hell-bent on wiping out three-quarters of humanity? What on earth had he done to deserve such a fate? He had engaged with the Storyteller. He and Eve had simply wanted answers to some pretty obvious questions. He had wanted to know whether there was a point to anything? Eve wanted to know why Bella had died. Perhaps they shouldn't have raised such questions. But surely they had a right to ask.

Yes, but perhaps they asked the wrong person. Perhaps they shouldn't have asked the Storyteller. Perhaps they should have asked someone else – anyone else. After all, what did he know? He couldn't answer any of their questions. He kept telling them they had to find the answers themselves. Of course, he had arranged all the journeys that led to the Fourth Beginning, so in that sense he was indispensable. But if you thought about it, what was the Storyteller doing as a character in the story anyway. He should have been outside the narrative, determining its course. It hadn't really struck Adam before, but surely there was something seriously wrong with the role the Storyteller had played. It was not impossible that the Storyteller's involvement had been an obstacle, rather than an aid, to finding answers to their questions. And yet there had to be a reason for the Storyteller's presence and his involvement in the narrative.

After the Fourth Beginning had been aborted, Adam had tried to make sense of things by focusing on goals instead of asking questions. And out popped David Minofel, initially Adam and Eve's salvation but ultimately Adam's nemesis! Minofel had offered him the amazing rewards of a career with Slievins but the price that Slievins demanded was high. In the eyes of the world, in the opinion of ordinary people, according to any moral code, Adam had become corrupted. But according to Slievins, he had simply become aware, aware of human nature, aware of how the world really worked, aware of how to exploit the truth.

Yes, he had committed crimes, but generally speaking he had simply chosen the lesser of two evils, and yes, he had accepted that the ends justified the means. True, he had bribed, blackmailed and murdered but he could easily have avoided the legal and judicial consequences. Slievins would have protected him. He had to flee from justice not because he had served Slievins but because he had betrayed Slievins. When the Praesidium asked him to prove his loyalty, he had sided with Kit, his friend, and not with them.

Even then Slievins hadn't abandoned him. Despite having betrayed Slievins, it was David Minofel, a Slievins man through and through, who had been there for him when the tax people and the Swiss police had closed in on him. If he had sided with Slievins, he was certain that HMRC and the Swiss police would have been blown away by Slievins' army of lawyers and accountants, as the lightest of breezes can send the seeds of the dandelion whirling helplessly far and wide.

For some inexplicable reason, the image of a dandelion in the desert reminded Adam of the battle with Nick Peters and the Breakers on Poulner Hill and the final dissolution of the mysland. Knowing the Breakers found metaphors anathema, the questors had deployed the Metaphorce, a virtual army led by Captain Hector Meap. The good captain had used the Fist of God, itself a metaphor, to anally and fatally discomfort Nestor Gruin, the Commander of the Breaker troops. Adam smiled. Numpty would have objected to the split infinitive but it was surely defensible in this context, given the explosive *modus operandi* of the Fist of God. Hector certainly split Nestor's infinitive!

Why the Breakers feared metaphors was mystery, a mystery now compounded by Roland Samiat's obvious obsession – and difficulty – with the metaphorical. The soul as an onion seemed to Adam to be indicative of a troubled mind.

Then despite his predicament, Adam laughed. He didn't need problems with figures of speech to diagnose lunacy. A plan to eliminate three-quarters of the people on the planet was surely sufficient.

Except Adam wasn't at all sure he was in any position to judge. With typical Slievins' logic, Samiat had explained Cull 75241 was about saving two billion people, not killing six billion. If the alternative was the extermination of all eight billion, the extinction of the entire species, it was a valid argument.

Adam himself had faced a panel of judges in his dream the night before the Praesidium planned to execute Kit. Aletheia, Kit and Numpty had presided over a court in which Adam was both prosecutor and defendant. Facing that tribunal had been terrifying and humiliating. And nonsensical! Aletheia was the goddess of truth, so she had every right to judge; Kit also could make a claim to sit in judgement. But Numpty? Really? It must have been Adam's feelings of guilt.

It was true he had treated Numpty badly. The lad had always done his best, given his limitations. But his continual nitpicking over words, his persistent misunderstanding of the obvious, his obsession with the epithetical sobriquet of "osmotic gouger" were certainly enough to try the patience of a saint. That said, Adam had to concede that he and Numpty had something in common. They had both wrestled, in different ways, with questions of self and identity.

And if Adam was honest, Numpty in his short and brutally terminated life had probably made rather more progress than Adam. Certainly, in moral terms he had entirely outshone his critic. He had shown remarkable courage when facing a truly appalling death at the hands of God's angelic host in the Garden of Eden. He had risked his life to save Luke when Nick Peters was torturing the dog. And he had given his life to save Kathrin. When you looked at Numpty's life in such a way, he seemed a hero rather than an irritant. And after the Fourth Beginning, he had progressed in leaps and bounds, even when the Beginning itself was aborted. If Numpty had been a character in a novel, he would have been truly remarkable for the way in which he had developed, matured and, finally, excelled as the narrative unfolded.

His thoughts on Numpty raised in Adam's mind two questions that had troubled him all his life. What is human nature, and what are people for? Slievins had given their answer to the first question. Human nature was essentially and irredeemably selfish. All men were fools or knaves. Most were both. Those who offered a more sanguine account of human nature were also fools or knaves but they were also, according to Slievins, extremely harmful. They urged man to ignore his true nature, to aspire to illusory "higher things". They urged the tiger to emulate the lamb. They demanded that water should be dry. They destroyed those they claimed to save with their idiotic, counterproductive exhortations.

Slievins made a good case. But there were worrying anomalies. Numpty was one. He was never mean. He was never spiteful. At personal risk, he stood up for others in their moment of need. When Adam first met Rambler and his nephew, Numpty was taking on a bunch of hairy bikers, led by the shapeshifter Grimrose, at Fleet services. In the end, Numpty gave his life to save Kathrin, a woman he barely knew.

And there was Violet, working at the Earl's Court help centre. She was no knave, and if she was a fool, her folly comprised nothing but good intentions.

What were people for? That was an even more difficult question. When Adam had told the Storyteller he sought the truth, the Storyteller had been cynical. "What kind of truth did he seek?" Adam now realised he hadn't been seeking the truth. He had been asking for meaning. He had been asking the same question as Eve had asked, except he was asking it about everything. Eve wanted to know why Bella had died. Adam wanted to ask "Why everything?"

Adam slept little that night. It was very cold and he was not dressed for sleeping beneath the stars in the Arabian desert. His last thought, before he nodded off, was to acknowledge that although he knew the time had come to make decisions, he still had more questions than answers.

But he had made progress. He had identified his love for Eve as the one certainty on which he would not compromise. He had defined his quest more precisely. And there was hope. Truth, if it existed, was elusive. Perhaps it was there to be found; perhaps it wasn't. But meaning you could make. Numpty had given his life meaning, as had Violet. They had chosen what to do with their lives. Slievins, too, gave life meaning. But for all their claims to represent and defend human nature, Slievins' meaning was narrow, brutish and destructive.

There was a choice.

78. Endgame: Phase 2

When Roland Samiat drove back into Ubar early Wednesday morning he was not best pleased. On arrival he was greeted by Enid Mavlow. She informed him that Charles Fundi had gone missing. When he called the Head of Security he was told Ben Rael was unavailable.

"Unavailable!" Samiat exploded. "I'll make him unavailable permanently. Find him and get him here now."

When Enid reported that Ben wasn't unavailable, that he was, like Fundi, missing, Roland became worried as well as angry.

"This is Roland Samiat," he announced over Ubar's public address system. "When and where were Charles Fundi and Ben Rael last seen?"

After a few minutes, Enid received a message that Fundi and Rael had been seen entering the lift on Level Five going down to Level Six.

"Why would Ben take Charles down to Level Six?" asked Samiat of no one in particular. "Only he and I have access to that level."

Roland and Enid, together with a couple of security guards, made their way to Level Five.

"Is everything in order?" Samiat demanded of Charles Fundi's deputy. "Are we all set for the Cull?"

"Everything is ready," the deputy replied nervously. "We're just waiting for confirmation from all our stations on all continents that they are ready to broadcast the DK12 activation light and sound codes."

"Good," said a marginally relieved Samiat. He led his party into the lift and descended to Level Six.

On leaving the elevator, Samiat looked around the circular space. There was no sign of life. He expected to see cells in the Punishment and Rehab sectors occupied but none of the lights indicating occupancy above the cell doors were lit.

Then, as they walked towards the centre of the Level, they heard a loud call from the oubliette. Samiat frowned. By now he thought all the prisoners would be dead. If any were alive they would be weak, too weak to call out so loudly.

"Get me out of here," demanded Charles Fundi, assuming he was addressing a search party of security guards.

"Is that you?" asked Samiat, peering over the rim.

At the bottom of the oubliette were the bodies of the prisoners consigned to Level Six on Samiat's instructions. One of the bodies had been dismembered, furnishing the weapon with which Fundi had beaten Ben Rael to death. Fundi himself was almost unrecognisable – he was covered in dried blood, his own and Ben's, as he sat among the decomposing corpses.

Fundi peered up to see his rescuers. His rescuers looked down and saw a face with a dark, empty socket that had previously housed Fundi's left eye.

"Of course, it's me," said Fundi.

"And is that apology for a cadaver beside you my Head of Security?" asked Samiat.

"Yes, it bloody well is," said Charles.

Enid let out a sound that was a cross between a gurgle and a yelp. She staggered. One of the security guards grabbed her, saving her from falling into the pit of death.

"I need medical attention," said Fundi. "Get me out of here and I'll explain everything."

oooOooo

"So are you telling me that Ben Rael, my Head of Security, was conspiring against me?" asked Samiat.

Fundi had been cleaned up. His eye socket had been disinfected and dressed, and he had been started on a course of antibiotics.

"I am," said Charles.

"And was he conspiring on his own or with others?" Samiat continued.

"He released Minofel and our uninvited visitors, Aletheia and the blind man."

"So I turn my back for one night only to find on my return that there's a nest of snakes in the wood pile," said Samiat. "Was Art Shoat involved?"

"I thought that he and Rael were planning something," said Charles, "but Rael made no mention of Art when he took me down to Level Six. He just said it was all about sex and money." He purposely made no mention of Enid.

"I noticed that when you confirmed the bloody mess lying next to you was Ben Rael, Enid seemed disproportionately distressed," Samiat observed. "Could it be that she was part of the conspiracy?"

"Not to my knowledge," said Fundi. After all, there was nothing for him to gain by revealing Enid's attachment to Ben Rael and he had no proof she was a party to Rael's plans. In any case, she was an attractive woman and she had Samiat's ear, not to mention another appendage. As such, she could be very useful to an aspiring sociopath. The fact that he had taken her lover's life and yet now saved hers just added to the piquancy of the situation.

"Are you fit to work?" Samiat asked. "You've been badly beaten and lost an eye. I need you at your best. If you're not up to it, say so now. I react badly to disappointment."

"Don't worry about me," said Fundi. "I've spoken with my deputy. Everything is in place. We are waiting for the most up-to-date predictions of fatalities, broken down by country, but our Dawk statisticians are ninety-nine per cent confident we will be in the range of seventy-two to seventy-eight per cent. We will run through our final checks tomorrow, but I can promise you that all will be ready on Friday and that Cull 75241 will be a great success."

Samiat grunted. "Good. Given the inexplicable conduct of some of our most senior people you must be watchful for any other signs of trouble. I could ask you to keep your eye out for anything suspicious, but in the circumstances, that might seem insensitive."

79.   Keeping things simple

As soon as Ben Rael had released them, Minofel, Aletheia and Kit made their way to the guest apartments on Level Two. There, after they had refreshed themselves, Kit suggested they sit down and agree a plan.

"That's easy," said Minofel, taking charge. "We kill Samiat. I take over. I cancel the Cull. You bugger off. And I become Slievins' CEO. How's that?"

Kit was perplexed. Minofel's suggestion was fraught with difficulties. It lacked subtlety, and there was no contingency if anything went wrong.

"I agree," said Aletheia. "We make our way to Samiat's office. If there is any opposition, we force our way in and kill Samiat. With the Head of Security on our side and David as acting CEO, we will have a good chance of success. In any case, there is no other plan, nor is there time to devise one."

Despite his reservations, Kit said nothing.

"Tomorrow is Thursday," said Minofel. "I suggest we rest today. Tomorrow, we act."

"Why not now?" Aletheia asked.

"I'm still waiting for Kit to confirm that my instructions on the allocation of the money in Samiat's Swiss account have been followed. After all, we mustn't disappoint Ben."

oooOooo

That afternoon, despite the risk of arrest, David Minofel left his co-conspirators to make his way to his office on the third level. He needed to be alone to savour the moment and, if truth be told, to steady his nerve.

Despite rating the chance of success no higher than fifty per cent, he felt more alive than he had for a very long time, Of course he found the possibility of success exhilarating, but it was the possibility of failure that really energised him. This truly was a matter of glory or death. Either he would enjoy absolute power as Slievins' CEO or he would die in what everyone would have to concede was an heroic failure. Whatever happened he would have earned a place in

Slievins' history of the world and, quite possibly, a place on the top shelf of the blood cabinet.

He pressed the button in the rear wall. It slid aside. Softly, almost lovingly, he ran his fingers over the phials on the top shelf. His hand stopped at the nameplate Vlad Dracula. The blood of Vlad was his most prized possession. It was one of very few phials of Vlad's blood in existence. When the Ottomans eventually managed to kill Vlad, they cut his body into many pieces and most of his blood was lost. Had it not been for the initiative of a monk from Comana Monastery, who happened to be a fifteenth-century Praesidium acolyte, none would have been preserved.

Carefully, Minofel opened the phial. He held the glass up to the light. The liquid, consisting mainly of alcohol, was a brownish hue, with only hints of red. Minofel put his nose to the top of the phial and inhaled. There was no scent, only the punch of the vodka used as a preservative.

"Well, my friend," said Minofel to the phial, "you were the essence of humanity. You took what you wanted, uninhibited by spurious moral qualms. You inspired the truest of all human emotions, fear, both in your life and after your death. Some have said that you took Slievins' principles to excess. I say that in your excess you perfectly expressed those principles. Here's to you. And whether I live or die in this my most heroic venture, may I find a place by your side within the blood cabinet."

With that, he drank every drop of the priceless fluid.

80.   The day of days

It was six o'clock in the morning and the sun was infusing the desert with its warming light. Adam awoke from his short sleep. Other than the palm tree, there was no sign of life. The desert stretched away in every direction as far as the eye could see. The tracks in the sand of Samiat's SUV arriving and departing the previous night had been swept away by the wind.

Suddenly Adam realised that despite his promise to return, Samiat was not coming back. He had told Adam he belonged in the desert. That was where Samiat wanted him to die. Desperate to be with Eve, to talk to her, to ask her forgiveness, to rebuild their relationship, he was condemned to die alone in a lifeless barren land.

Samiat had left him to wrestle with his intellect and his conscience. His intellect was still struggling with competing views of human nature and the conundrum that Samiat had posed. Cull 75241 was profoundly immoral and criminal but, according to Slievins, without it all eight billion were doomed. With twisted logic, Samiat claimed he was saving two billion, not killing six billion, people. It was certainly twisted. But it was also certainly logical.

As for his conscience, Adam now fully accepted that his excuses for what he had done in Geneva could not exonerate him from the guilt and the consequences of the crimes he had committed. But he now had an even stronger reason to feel guilty. Samiat was about to perpetrate an act that made the worst that man had ever done to man in the entire history of mankind dwindle in comparison. The difference was quantitative, not qualitative, but the sheer scale of what Slievins intended to do to the human species was horrific beyond imagining. Adam was certain that if his own life was to have any meaning, it must centre on his love for Eve and the child they had created. This Cull would destroy the love between billions, between men and women, between men and men, between women and women, between parents and children, between old and young. It would destroy a billion Adams, a billion Eves and a billion children that they had brought into the world.

And Adam could do nothing, except pray that Aletheia and Kit would find a way to frustrate Samiat's plan. So that is what he did.

81. Endgame: Phase 3

Kit was awake on Thursday morning at 6.00 a.m. He wanted to be sure his instructions on dealing with Samiat's Swiss bank account had been followed precisely. Aletheia and David Minofel were still sleeping.

In Rambler's apartment in Maida Vale, Luke awoke and emitted a muted bark. "What time is this to wake a sleeping dog?" he asked. It was 3.00 a.m. in London.

"Sorry to disturb you," Kit minded to Luke, "but this is really important. Has Andrew transferred the money as I asked?"

"Absolutely," Luke confirmed. "The paradox device seems to rather like conversing with computers, especially banks' computers. I think it sees them as some form of primitive ancestor."

"And Andrew knows exactly what to do when I mind to you the words 'Nothing will come of nothing'?"

"Don't worry," Luke soothed. "He won't let you down."

"Is the paradox device working at full strength?" Kit asked. If any of them were to escape from Ubar, they would need the device's teleportation facility.

"Andrew is optimistic," Luke replied. "The Breakers have developed something they call a Resolver which undermines the confidence of the paradox device. Andrew has hit back with a little piece of software that exploits Münchhausen's Trilemma. Don't ask me to explain – programming is not really a dog thing – but he reckons we're winning. And Prune has found the source of the interference. It's where Despiro Nihilopificus works, a research centre at Martlesham. Calling on his experience during the Troubles in Ireland, Prune is planning to eliminate Despiro and the Resolver with a controlled explosion."

"So if we need to teleport out of here we can?" Kit asked.

"If you are outside Ubar, the answer's a qualified yes. It should work. If you're inside Ubar's security shield, within its cloaking dome, probably not. Andrew thinks the cloaking dome could shred anyone who was transported through it."

"Good to know," said Kit. "We'll try to avoid that. I'd better go now. Aletheia is waking up. We have a big day here. I'll keep you informed."

oooOooo

When the three would-be assassins reached Samiat's office on the third level they found the reception area unoccupied. Enid Mavlow was not at her desk.

"Come in," Roland Samiat called out. "I've been expecting you."

This was not an auspicious start to a venture that depended on surprise for success.

Roland was at the door of his office. "Come in. You're here now, so don't be shy. Come in. Sit down, and make yourselves comfortable."

They obeyed. Roland resumed his seat at his desk. Behind Roland stood two security guards, both carrying enough weaponry to start a war.

"I suggest we are frank with each other," said Roland. "I need to make two things clear. You are not going to kill me. And you are not going to stop Cull 75241. If you accept these two self-evident truths, we can embark on a sensible, civilised dialogue."

Minofel was uncertain. Where was Ben Rael? Were the security guards there to protect Samiat or to assist in his execution and the disposal of his body?

Samiat explained. "Sadly Ben is no longer with us. It turns out he had the temerity to conspire against me. The first part of his plan was to kill Charles Fundi – as you know, the two of them never got along – but that didn't work out. What's left of Ben lies at the bottom of the oubliette on Level Six. And the loyal Charles survived, albeit with one eye fewer than before. Charles tells me everything is ready for the Cull, which I intend to initiate tomorrow, Friday, at 6.00 am. So you see I, whom you wish to kill, am not going to die but six billion others, whom you wish to save, are irremediably doomed. It's an ill wind that has no silver lining."

Minofel's right eye twitched.

"I'm not going to rehearse all the arguments for the Cull," Roland Samiat continued. "Let's just say that finer minds than yours have analysed the data and have concluded that if we are to save humanity, a major cull is imperative."

"You think that killing three-quarters of the world's population is a sensible way of saving humanity?" Aletheia made no effort to disguise her contempt.

"You are a goddess," Samiat conceded, "and therefore I shall treat you with an appropriate level of respect, despite your perverse attachment to the truth. But please drop the heart-of-gold-on-your-sleeve, love-conquers-all, I'll-take-the-moral-high-road drivel. You try asking the powerful to relinquish power. You try asking the rich to forgo their wealth. Only those who have nothing are up for sharing. Given that man is essentially selfish, surely you can see that a cull is the only way. We could either leave it to nature, or we could take the opportunity to improve the species by managing the operation. We aim to raise mankind's intelligence substantially by eliminating the less mentally gifted. There isn't a precise correlation between stupidity and consumption of fast food but our statisticians are confident the correlation is good enough to achieve at least a ten per cent uplift in the quality of the population. So Cull 75 will not only save the planet, it will improve the species. Come on. That's a win-win situation, if ever there was one."

"You're insane," Aletheia declared.

"Where's Adam?" Kit asked.

Samiat ignored Aletheia's rudeness. "Adam is deep in thought," he answered Kit.

"Where is he?" Kit persisted.

"He's deep in thought, deep in the Rub' al-Khali, in the empty quarter," Samiat replied. "It's rather appropriate. When he's finished his introspection, I rather think there will be an empty mind in the empty quarter. Poor Adam! He's so conflicted. He can't decide whether he's Humpty or Dumpty, but it really doesn't matter because no one is going to put him together again."

Minofel's right eye twitched a second time.

"Where exactly is he?" Aletheia demanded.

"He's about ten miles east of here at an artificial oasis I created for my personal solace. I took him there so he could find himself." Samiat laughed. "Bit like looking for a noodle in a haystack, if you ask me."

What happened next needs a rather discursive prefatory explanation. The Breakers, the foot soldiers of the Praesidium, found any figurative use of language an anathema. You will recall the questors, despite the odds against them, had deployed the Metaphorce to good effect in their battle with Nick Peters.

Roland Samiat had always been fascinated and appalled by the power of the creative mind. It contradicted everything that Slievins stood for, and yet he couldn't deny its power. So he had decided that it would be advisable to get to know his enemy, on one of Samiat's favoured principles that one should hold one's friends close and one's enemies closer. Hence his somewhat clumsy attempts to incorporate figures of speech into his own discourse.

To David Minofel, Roland Samiat's sorties into the world of metaphor, simile and aphorism were both pathetic and disgusting. In Minofel's eyes, this weakness alone rendered Samiat unfit to run Slievins.

Minofel's antipathy to Samiat's mode of discourse had gone beyond the rational. From the moment he realised he didn't like the Slievins' CEO, Minofel had found himself irritated beyond measure by anything his boss said. And as Samiat broadened his bungling attempts to explore the creative use of language by embracing puns and even nursery rhymes, Minofel's hostility had become immeasurable and, as we shall see, at this point in the narrative, uncontrollable.

David Minofel had served in the SAS and had worked as a mercenary. He had been a successful consultant at Slievins and an accomplished practitioner in the service of the Praesidium. He had been trained to assess situations, to calculate odds, to maximise the chances of success and, as far as possible, to minimise risk. His decision to attempt to kill Roland Samiat when he had no weapon and was under the intense scrutiny of two armed guards must seem strange, but for David Minofel, given his state of mind at the time, it was the only sensible thing to do.

As it turned out, the guards were not the determining factor. As Minofel leapt from his chair and lunged across Samiat's desk, Samiat simply presented a paper knife in precisely the right position and at the right angle for Minofel himself to drive the blade through his right and erstwhile twitching eye, deep into his brain.

As the guards removed the body from the desk, Samiat observed: "I think we may be witnessing the emergence of a theme. First Fundi damages Ben Rael's eye, then Rael gouges out Fundi's eye. Now Minofel sacrifices an eye and his life in a futile attempt to kill me. In the kingdom of the one-eyed, the two-eyed man is king." Then, addressing Kit, he added: "Surely as a blind man you can see that I'm twice the man you are? Am I not a truly worthy adversary?"

Both Kit and Aletheia were shocked by Minofel's brutal death.

He had seemed a permanent fixture in their story, a powerful, manipulative force, involved in every episode of the narrative. Now he was gone, provoked beyond reason by Samiat's desperate and dismal tinkering with metaphors and other figures of speech. Kit ignored Samiat's questions, concluding it was further evidence of a deeply deranged mind.

"I have to stop you from initiating the Cull, or I shall die trying," said Kit.

"If you're offering me alternatives, I favour the latter," Samiat quipped.

"Is Adam safe?" Aletheia asked. "Is he alive?"

"He's safe enough," Samiat replied. "Nothing is going to attack him, if that's what you mean. But as I say, I predict his complete mental collapse as he realises the hopelessness of his situation. No redemption for his sins. No way back to the woman he loves or the child she bears. As for his physical condition, the prognosis is not good. He is likely to die of thirst fairly quickly. The oasis is sustained by power from the Eternal Light. When we initiate the Cull, I will be turning off the oasis. Within a day, the oasis will be returned to the dry sands of the Rub' al-Khali."

Kit spoke to Aletheia. "I suggest that you go to find Adam and ensure his safe return to England. I will stay here with Roland. We have differences to resolve."

Samiat blinked. "Excuse me, but aren't you forgetting you are my prisoners. Ben Rael is dead, and so too is Minofel. Isn't it fair to assume your conspiracy is over, given the two main conspirators are inoperative?"

"You will not stop Aletheia from leaving," said Kit. "She is not your enemy. I will stay with you. I will be with you when you intend to initiate the Cull. Then we will see whether you are a worthy adversary."

"I like you, Kit," said Roland Samiat. "You certainly have balls. Aletheia can leave on a mission to save Adam. After all, that's why she's involved in his story. Her chances of finding him before he dies are slim, and even if he is still alive and she finds him, their chances of survival are even slimmer. By then none of it will matter. The Cull will have begun."

Kit nodded to Aletheia. She stood up and addressed Roland Samiat. "You would be a fool to underestimate this blind man. After all, he humbled God. And that's the truth."

When Aletheia had gone, Samiat asked Kit what she meant.

"Nothing," Kit replied and would say no more.

oooOooo

At 5.00 a.m. on Friday, Enid Mavlow arrived at Kit's room in the Guest Apartment on Level Two.

"I've come to take you to Level Five," said Enid. "Roland is waiting for you there." She had black rings under her eyes, which Kit could not see, and an aura of sadness about her which Kit immediately felt, sadness and anger.

"You were in love with Ben Rael," Kit hazarded.

Enid blushed. "We had only just met," she said, "but I knew he was the one. I am not a romantic. I have been with many men. But when he and I met, it was as though the sun had burst from behind a cloud. I knew we had a wonderful future ahead of us, until Charles Fundi beat his beautiful face to a pulp."

"So now you are sad, and full of hate," said Kit.

"I would like to do to Fundi what Fundi did to Ben," she said simply.

"No need," said Kit, putting his hand on her arm. "Such a revenge would do you no good. Did you learn nothing from your revenge on your sister Ava? But don't worry. Fundi will pay a price. And you will find peace and release from your grief."

As Kit's hand touched her arm, she felt the weight of her grief lighten and her lust for revenge loosen its grip on her.

oooOooo

"Good morning, Kit," said Roland Samiat. He was in an excellent mood. Beside him stood Charles Fundi, a black patch over his empty eye socket.

"Excuse Charles's appearance," said Roland. Then he recalled that Kit was blind. "I'm afraid, my friend, he looks like a pirate who's lost his parrot. Give me five minutes to run through a few figures with Charles."

Fundi explained that in several parts of the world, the uptake or availability of fast foods was too low for DK12 to attain the target mortality rates. In these regions they had added DK12 to the water supply. Although the correlation of low achievement with drinking water was lower than that with fast-food consumption, happily the difference was less than had been feared. Many of the elite drank mostly bottled water and DK12 had been added only to water reservoirs. So even with water-borne DK12, there would be some degree of selectivity.

"It's a pity," said Charles. "We will lose some really bright people, but if we are sticking to the seventy-five per cent target, there is no other way."

"You worry too much," said Roland. "You can't make an omelette if you're walking on egg shells."

Pardon me for interrupting," said Kit. "But how will you give the signal for the initiation of the Cull?"

Samiat smiled. He had been waiting to see what, if anything, Kit would do to interfere with his plans. "I send a coded message to the mainframe computer powered by the Eternal Light."

"In the same way as you would activate the neutron bomb?" asked Kit casually.

Samiat started. "Yes," he replied carefully. "In the same way, but in that case with a code you could not possibly discover."

"As I understand it," said Kit, "the neutron bomb is activated by a number that is the product of the amount of euros in your Swiss bank account and a secret six-digit number automatically generated each morning and stored on your phone and which, therefore, only you can access."

"You are surprisingly well-informed," Samiat conceded. "Happily, you cannot know either number, much less multiply them together and transmit the product to the mainframe. I'm advised it would take the world's most powerful computer weeks to resolve the number and, given that one of the numbers changes at least every few minutes and the other once a day, I can be fairly confident my neutron bomb is mine and mine alone."

"Let's play a game in the few minutes we have left," said Kit. "Just assume I have a way to detonate the neutron bomb. If I threatened to detonate it, would you abandon the Cull?"

"I might do," said Roland slowly, "but probably not. I might abandon it on the grounds that I could always carry out the Cull at another time, but on balance I think I'd ignore you. It has taken years of my life to set this up and I'd probably go ahead anyway. If you detonated the bomb, you would die and most men have a highly developed drive for self-preservation, so I think I'd take the chance and assume you were bluffing. Fortunately, the situation doesn't arise."

"The Cull is, in part, intended to improve the intellectual calibre of the species?" said Kit.

"That's right," said Roland.

"Don't you think you may be overestimating the importance of intellectual capacity?"

Roland shrugged. "Not really. Human progress depends on a tiny percentage of the human population. In the vast majority of cases, lives are lived without making any contribution whatsoever to the sum of human knowledge or to the advancement of the species. Most people simply feed, breed and need. The need bit is economically important. Generally speaking, they satisfy their needs by shopping, which I admit is essential to a healthy economy. Later in life, their needs become a heavy and increasingly unsupportable burden on the working population."

"I see," said Kit. "You have a very depressing and, I have to say, distorted view of human nature. What about kindness? What about love? What about self-sacrifice? Aren't they part of the lives of humankind?"

"I do hope you're not going to ruin the happiest day of my life," said Samiat.

"I'm afraid I may," said Kit. "You see, I know the number that will detonate the neutron bomb."

"Roland laughed. "That's not possible. Even if you knew the amount of euros in my Genevan account, you don't know the six-digit pass number."

"Is it possible you are not as clever as you think, or that you are so clever that sometimes you can outsmart yourself?" Kit asked.

Charles Fundi drew his Ruger SR9, his one remaining eye alert for any sudden, threatening movement.

"So how do you know the number?" Roland asked.

"It's really very simple," said Kit.

"How so?" Samiat asked his last question.

"Because," Kit paused, then declared in a firm, resonant tone, "Nothing will come of nothing."

oooOooo

When the neutron bomb under the oubliette in Level Six exploded, a great disc of sand, one mile in diameter, that lay over the city of Ubar lifted some fifty feet into the air. As Aletheia said later, it was as though Hades, the god of the underworld, had emitted a giant belch.

At the moment of the explosion three other momentous events occurred.

First, as much by luck as judgement, Aletheia, driving the SUV she had commandeered from Security, found Adam in the artificial oasis ten miles east of Ubar.

Secondly, in St Mary's Hospital in Paddington, Eve gave birth to Anna, a healthy baby daughter.

Thirdly, or so it seemed, the sun shone a little more brightly than usual.

The Storyteller's footnote

As I mentioned earlier, it's not my custom to appear as a character in the stories I tell. My normal role is to operate outside the narrative, delineating the characters and organising the plot. I have made an exception on this occasion because of the peculiar nature of this quartet of books.

First, the core of the plot – a search for truth – was both overly ambitious and extraordinarily foolhardy. I admired Adam and Eve's courage in undertaking the quest but I was well aware of the dangers they faced. Indeed, I warned them of the grave risks at the very beginning. When they decided to proceed, I joined them in the story partly because I felt responsible and partly because I knew they would require my entire repertoire of narrative devices to have any chance of success. I couldn't adopt the storyteller's usual impartial, godlike status outside the story. I had to be inside the story, personally involved, available at times of extreme need to point the protagonists in the right direction, and to break literary conventions if necessary to enhance the very slim chance of success.

Secondly, I was aware that at any point the story could collapse. Both Adam and Numpty were deeply troubled by questions of identity and selfhood. Had either of them concluded there was no self, and therefore no moral responsibility and no accountability, the plot would have lost two of its key characters and one of its central themes. I was keen to do all I could to prevent such a catastrophic termination from happening.

Thirdly, and perhaps most importantly, I, like Adam and Eve, wanted to find the truth. I wasn't outside the quest looking in; I was inside the quest, as desperate as any of the characters to find answers, just as I hope you, the readers, were not merely observers of the events recounted here but were as deeply engaged in the search for truth as the characters and your devoted servant, the Storyteller.

What have we learned? We have learned that there is magic in the universe. Over and over again, we see that the whole is greater than the sum of its parts. Out of nothing, something comes. Out of less comes more. There have already been three great Beginnings: the universe, life, and human consciousness. On each occasion, existence took an unexpected and inexplicable quantum leap forward. On that evidence, we should not be surprised if there are more.

Is there a truth to be found? Probably not; certainly not a single truth that answers all our questions. But there is meaning to be created. Each of us has a life with a beginning, a middle and an end. It can be a dull tale, with little thought put into it, or it can be a great and transcendental affirmation of all that is positive. It can be a story of meanness, unkindness and evil, or a moving example of generosity and altruism. It can be a narrative with a weak and aimless plot, or it can be a story imbued with meaning that goes too deep for words. I know this better than most. After all, I am the Storyteller. I start with nothing. Then, out of nothing, something comes.

Enough! Sorry, of course you would like me to tie up a few loose ends. That is, for sure, an essential component of the Storyteller's role, whether he stands inside or outside the narrative.

First, I should explain how Kit detonated the neutron bomb. It was childishly simple. David Minofel insisted that they empty Samiat's Swiss account. He allocated half the money to Ben Rael's account. The rest he had transferred to his own account, and he insisted on the automatic transfer of any new money directly to his own account. Andrew, on Kit's instructions, ensured the paradox device followed Minofel's instructions precisely. Since the number required to trigger the neutron bomb was the product of the number of euros in the account and Samiat's six-digit pass number, the product of the multiplication, if there were no euros, was zero. Samiat's elaborate scheme for maintaining complete personal control of his neutron bomb had a fatal flaw. A nought was all that was required to trigger the device. Hence the irony in Kit's coded message to detonate the bomb: "Nothing will come of nothing". A fitting epitaph for Roland Samiat, Despiro Nihilopificus, the rest of the Dawks and Slievins itself!

How did the questors deal with the Resolver? Andrew Rimzil used elements of Münchhausen's Trilemma (the proof that no proof is possible – a paradox if ever there was one) to engender so high a level of uncertainty in the Resolver that it spent all its time interfering with itself, thus allowing the paradox device to fully recover its powers. The collapse of the Resolver, combined with the destruction of Ubar and all within it, caused Despiro Nihilopificus, the Chief Dawk, to suffer a mental breakdown from which he never even partially recovered.

When Aletheia found Adam, thirsty but otherwise in good health, at the fast-disintegrating artificial oasis, she ordered him into the SUV and minded to Andrew that he should remove them immediately. Andrew had set up the paradox device to retrieve any or all of the questors at a moment's notice and successfully teleported Aletheia, Adam and the SUV to Maida Vale before the shock wave of the neutron bomb reached them. Kit, inside the cloaking dome that shielded Ubar, was beyond the reach of Andrew's instructions.

Once back in Rambler's apartment, Adam greeted his friends, cleaned himself up, drank a long, cool glass of water and asked Prune to drive him to St Mary's. Prune was more than happy to oblige, especially when Aletheia gave him the keys to the Mercedes SUV and told him he might as well keep them.

When Adam arrived on the maternity ward, he found Eve breastfeeding their daughter. It is fair to say that for Adam and Eve it was the happiest day of their lives.

The happiness of that moment was compounded when Eve told Adam that the Swiss police were no longer looking for him. Guy McFall had testified that David Minofel of Slievins had murdered Giovanni Spinetti on the orders of Dr Yves Dubois. The head of ZeD had been determined to silence Spinetti to save MC57 and avoid the scandal that Spinetti threatened to unleash on the company. Just as Guy had not been able to provide an alibi because Minofel had denied they had shared a dinner on that fateful night, so Guy now confirmed Minofel's original lie, thus denying Minofel a genuine alibi. The security video was not clear enough to identify the second man entering Spinetti's apartment block, but given McFall's testimony, the fact that Adam and Minofel were of similar build and that Jedwell was known to be Minofel's man, the Swiss police decided Minofel was a far more likely suspect than Adam. A few hours after Minofel flew with Adam to the Arabian desert, a warrant for his arrest had been issued.

McFall had also testified that any irregularities in Adam's financial dealings and tax affairs would, like the murder of Spinetti, almost certainly prove to be the responsibility of Minofel who had exercised undue influence over his protégée. The Swiss police were persuaded. HMRC inspectors were rather more sceptical of Adam's innocence, but given the collapse of ZeD and the flight of Dubois to northern Cyprus, they faced considerable difficulties in proving criminality. Eventually, some months later, HMRC came to an out-of-court settlement that left Adam and Eve comfortably off but no longer truly affluent.

The destruction of Ubar was a devastating blow to the Praesidium. Roland Samiat had moved all Slievins' head office functions to Ubar. Destruction of the City under the Sand effectively destroyed the head and much of the body of Slievins. Praesidium satellites survived around the world, but, already weakened by the dissolution of the Westminster PCC, the obliteration of Ubar and the loss of Slievins' support proved to be a fatal setback.

Andrew Rimzil and Prune Leach continued to explore the potential of the paradox device. They needed more room than Rambler's flat could provide so they looked around for more spacious accommodation. When the paradox device had been having problems with the Resolver, Prune had considered blowing up the Dawks' research establishment at Martlesham. Fortunately, Andrew sorted out the Resolver problem before Prune could execute his plan. With the collapse of Slievins, the Martlesham building came onto the market at a very attractive price. With help from Rambler, who sold his Maida Vale apartment, Andrew and Prune bought it. They and Rambler moved in. Although the building was large, within a couple of years it was full, with Andrew and Prune's engineering installations competing for space with Rambler's extensive and ever-growing research library.

Aletheia returned to Prometheus' cave in the Caucasus and re-joined her now immortal partner Miss Tomic. Gorgeous Tomic took some time to adjust to her new and now unlimited life, but free from the baleful influence of David Minofel she found true happiness in the arms of the goddess of truth.

Adam and Eve worked hard on their marriage. They never reactivated the Fourth Beginning, but they grew ever closer and blessed with their beautiful daughter, Anna, found all the truth they could handle in their love for one another. Anna grew into a beautiful woman and, for sure, she had a wonderful life to live and an almost unbelievable tale to tell. But that's another story.

Luke lived out the rest of his life with the Smiths. He and Anna were particularly close. Especially in her early years, Anna found it easy to communicate fully with her gifted canine companion. He told her of all the adventures the questors had undertaken, ensuring that his own, often crucial, part in each episode was given due prominence. Whenever he overstepped the mark, claiming perhaps more credit than was entirely justified, both he and Anna heard Kit's voice gently chiding Luke and giving Anna a rather more balanced account of events.

And always, when Kit intervened, the sun shone a little more brightly in all their lives.

The first time Anna noticed the increased luminosity she had asked Luke where all the extra light came from. Luke had no idea, but he told Anna that when Kit had activated the neutron bomb, in the split second before the bomb exploded, the paradox device advised the Eternal Light to cut power to the protective dome over Ubar. No one noticed the collapse of the shield, but the paradox device had just enough time to teleport Kit and the Eternal Light out of Ubar and away from nuclear annihilation. Kit, empowered by the Eternal Light, had been able to resume his old habit of wandering from place to place, but was now able to spread a little extra light whenever and wherever it was needed.

Anna was sceptical of Luke's explanation but the story pleased her.

"The 'God of Dogs' saves the 'Son of God'," Luke mused in a moment of self-satisfaction at his narrative ingenuity.

oooOooo

"What about the problem that Roland Samiat identified?" you ask. "How is a planet of finite resources to cope with an ever-growing population?"

Samiat's apocalyptic solution may have been frustrated but the problem remains. And, while I'm sure all right-minded individuals would reject the idea of a cull unequivocally, many of us would not disagree entirely with Slievins' rather pessimistic view of human nature.

On the other hand, no one can deny that humanity is resilient and innovative. Surely we can do better than Slievins? It's not impossible, though not very likely, that we will decide to curb our consumption of the planet. Or as we find we need fewer and fewer people to satisfy our demands, evolution will take a hand and drastically reduce fertility in women or the sperm count in men. Perhaps we will find a way to reach and exploit other planets, thus postponing the requirement for a solution indefinitely. Or – and this is the most exciting possibility – will humanity be able to initiate and sustain another beginning, a Fourth Beginning, as Prometheus always believed?

For an answer to these questions we must wait and see. And that's the truth.

oooOooo

And what of the questions that exercised both Adam and Numpty. How can anyone judge themselves? How can anyone know themselves? Is there a self to know? And if there is, to what extent can that self be held responsible for its actions?

There are no definitive answers to such questions but in the recounting of the questors' adventures there are some fairly strong indications.

Each of us is a product and a representative of the Third Beginning. Each of us has self-consciousness. The burden for each of us is heavy. We have such amazing potential but we carry with us always the knowledge that we will die. We, finite creatures, dream of immortal gods. We, who will die, swear eternal love. We animals of blood, flesh and bone can reach into and cavort in the limitless world of the imagination, breaking all the constraints of our self-centred, narrow, time-delimited existence. We have intimations of immortality.

"So what!" responds the cynic. "Man is just an aberration, an unfortunate and rather sad anomaly. Our gift is our curse. Our dreams flounder in the gruelling attrition of age and the abyss of death."

Perhaps. But surely it would be foolish to underestimate the creative force that drives our world and is in evidence everywhere? After all, it's against the odds that there should be a universe at all. And even longer odds that there should be this particular universe, driven by some creative force that produced life out of stardust and the mind of man in the skull of a naked ape.

I am the Storyteller and I say this to the cynic. Given such a series of improbabilities, and their extraordinarily fortuitous, emergent outcomes, surely even the most committed sceptic has to agree that there are some grounds for optimism.

After all, we live in an existence where – whether we consider the universe, a life or a story such as this – out of nothing something comes.

And that's another truth.